an obstinate, headstrong girl

for Paul and Jary,

love always Abigail

an obstinate, headstrong girl

by a lady

ABOOKS
Alive Book Publishing

"Fern Song," by Hildegarde Flanner, from *The Hearkening Eye* (Ahsahta
Press, 1979). Used by permission.

"The Next Story," "Rolling Naked in the Morning Dew," and "Berry
Renaissance," section 5, "Gospel and the Circle of Redemption," by
Pattiann Rogers, from *Song of the World Becoming, New and Collected
Poems* (Milkweed Editions, 2001). Used by permission.

"The common living dirt" from *Stone, Paper, Knife* by Marge Piercy,
copyright © 1983 by Middlemarsh, Inc. Used by permission of Alfred
A. Knopf, an imprint of the Knopf Doubleday Publishing Group, a
division of Random House LLC. All rights reserved.

Special thanks to Virginia Sanchez.

Additional copies may be ordered from the publisher for educational,
business, promotional or premium use. For information, contact ALIVE
Book Publishing at: alivebookpublishing.com, or call (925) 837-7303.

Book Design by Eli Sedaghatinia

ISBN 13
978-1-63132-005-7
ISBN 10
163132005X

Library of Congress Control Number: 2014941069
Library of Congress Cataloging-in-Publication Data is available upon request.

First Edition

Published in the United States of America by ALIVE Book Publishing
and ALIVE Publishing Group, imprints of Advanced Publishing LLC
3200 A Danville Blvd., Suite 204, Alamo, California 94507
alivebookpublishing.com

PRINTED IN THE UNITED STATES OF AMERICA

10 9 8 7 6 5 4 3 2 1

A Deprecatory Note from the Author

I do not pretend to understand how I came to find myself in America, or in the twentieth century. Nothing of the kind has occurred to me before, nor to any other person in the whole of my acquaintance. At one moment I was in our dear cottage at Chawton, opening a closet to search for my pelisse, and at the next I found myself deposited in an alien realm of bewildering speed and noise.

Fortunately, I soon encountered a kindly person—Miss H. Abigail Bok, the author of "A Dictionary of Jane Austen's Life and Works"—who professed sympathy for my bewilderment and undertook to be my guide and protector in this foreign circumstance. She encouraged me to continue in my writing, assuring me that even in this future world my efforts would find an appreciative readership. She it was who arranged on my behalf the publication of the work before you.

It is my hope that one day I will return to Chawton and my beloved sister, Cassandra. In the meantime, I am determined not to repine, but to continue deriving pleasure from observation of the peculiarities of character that are to be discovered in any neighborhood.

Chapter One

It is a truth universally acknowledged that a young man in possession of a wife must be in want of a fortune. However little known the feelings or wishes of a neighborhood might be, on the man's first entering it, this truth is so well fixed in his mind that any assets he finds he considers as his rightful property.

Every family must have some connection on whom they rest their hopes of betterment. An uncle, a distant cousin, a son bright with promise—to the ordinary run of family members this individual figures, by common if tacit consent, as the savior who will one day offer the rest a miraculous escape from the tedium and humiliations of their everyday lives. That the paragon might have other aspirations rarely occurs to the dreamers; and that he might not have it in his power to rescue all is a possibility never to be contemplated, for to do so would be to invite the death of hope.

For the Bennet family, this repository of idle dreams was Aunt Evelyn.

"Mr. B, great news! Your sister has provided for us at last!"

"Indeed, my dear? Why do you think so?"

"A fat envelope has arrived from Lambtown, California, from an attorney's office. What else can it mean? What a great thing it'll be for Lydon!"

Mr. Bennet halted his progress toward his sanctum, the office he had carved out of a corner of the garage. He could think of several things such a missive might portend, and none of them as pleasing as his sister deciding to turn over her fortune to the family of a brother she hadn't laid eyes on in twenty years. All he said, however, was, "Why Lydon in particular? I hadn't understood that Evelyn had a particular affection for our youngest son."

"Well, maybe not; but Lydon's need is the greatest, of course, for here he is married, and at such a young age, with a wife to support and no doubt children of his own before long."

Mr. Bennet blanched at this prospect and his frown deepened. "You'd better hand it over, then." He took the envelope and, deaf to his wife's protestations, retired with it to the garage.

He was there a long time, and when he rejoined the family circle, just as dinner was ready, he could be seen to be troubled.

As was the common way in the Bennet household, the table this evening was not graced by the attendance of the entire family; they were too many, and their pursuits too various, for togetherness to be either likely or desirable in such a small and shabby room. Young Lydon and his even younger wife, Jenny, were missing, doubtless enjoying the easy hospitality of some of Jenny's friends from the air force base. Mary was present in body but her mind was elsewhere occupied; from the studiousness of her expression, some recondite theological justification must have been puzzling her, though she knew better than to offer it to the table for debate. Kitty, always a little deflated when Lydon was not present, was indulging her allergies in a good sniff. John was at work, leaving Lizzy to ensure that dinner got on the table despite the state of her mother's nerves, overset by the miseries of suspense.

Once they were assembled, her curiosity could no longer be suppressed. "You take pleasure in teasing me!" Mrs. Bennet cried. "You have no sympathy for my nerves. What did it say? I've been waiting for hours!"

"What did *what* say, Mama?" asked Kitty, enlivened by the prospect of distraction.

"The letter, my sweet! A letter from a lawyer's office in Lambtown!"

"Oh, a lawyer. What is there in *that* to get excited about?"

"What is there to get excited about? Don't you remember? It was your aunt Evelyn who inherited everything from your second cousin, old Adolphus Bennet. She must be as rich as Croesus, and never a penny of it has she shared. I don't count her inviting Lizzy to visit in the summers; that's nothing. But you can count on it, she's decided to do right by us at last! We've waited so long for this day, and suffered with the greatest patience while she enjoyed every luxury in California. Why she took this long, and ignored our needs all these years, I'll never know; and your father never lifted a finger to get Adolphus's will overturned, though anyone could see the money was not rightfully hers. But if she's ready to take care of us now, no word of complaint will pass my lips! In fact, I—"

"What's the matter, Papa?" Elizabeth interrupted her mother's raptures without ceremony. "You look angry. Is Aunt Evelyn still crossing swords with you?"

"No, she has laid all the old conflicts to rest," said Mr. Bennet.

"I knew it! She has provided for us!" Mrs. Bennet crowed.

Mr. Bennet frowned at her. "In fact, she has herself been laid to rest. Messrs. Baldwin and Perry have written to tell me that my sister is dead."

A short silence ensued. But Mrs. Bennet was made of sterner stuff than to be derailed by unavoidable tragedy. "Well, of course I'm sorry to hear it, but there's no use crying over spilt milk, I always say. What does the letter say of the will, Mr. B? What does it say of the will?"

Lizzy knew she ought to intervene, but for the moment was

unable to do so. Of all the family, she had known Aunt Evelyn the best. Evelyn Bennet, asked to serve in the role of godmother, had taken a strong fancy to the merry infant Elizabeth at her christening, the last time she had visited the Bennets before the quarrel that had caused an irreparable breach between brother and sister. She had remained estranged from Mr. Bennet and the rest of the family for two decades, but when Lizzy was eight years old, Evelyn had petitioned through family intermediaries to be allowed a visit from her eldest niece. Not wishing to close the door entirely on his nearest relation (and seconded by his wife, who already treasured expectations regarding Adolphus's fortune), Mr. Bennet had agreed to send Lizzy to California for a summer fortnight.

The visit had been a success, and thereafter Lizzy was permitted to spend a part of every summer with her aunt until she was sixteen, when she commenced working during the summers to earn her spending money and save for college. Once she had assured her mother several times that Aunt Evelyn lived in a very modest style, nobody had taken much interest in these visits except her elder brother, John, who had elicited over the years the intelligence that Aunt Evelyn possessed a great many books and had read them all; that Lambtown was a picturesque small town, almost a village, in the Santa Ynez Valley (wherever that might be), a place where the local people for generations had mostly farmed and ranched; and that Lizzy had derived from Aunt Evelyn the love of gardening that eventually became her career.

Not even John knew the strength of Lizzy's attachment to her aunt. Evelyn Bennet had challenged and expanded her mind, offered her the companionship of intelligent conversation and feminine confidences, and inspired her through the example she embodied of a busy life engaged with the neighborhood she inhabited.

Those summer visits had allowed young Elizabeth to understand that one's life could be conducted on terms very different from her parents'. It had also afforded her a vision of wealth that bore little relation to the picture of indulgence her mother was now delineating. "Oh! My dears, you can't imagine how long I've dreamed about this moment! No more worrying about where we'll find the money for the heat! And the clothes we can afford! Only think, Kitty—no more of Lizzy's castoffs and hand-me-downs for you! Your own gown for the spring dance on the base! And—"

Mary broke in on these effusions. "It would be more to the point to buy Kitty a new Bible, Mother."

"What would I want with that?" protested Kitty. "At least clothes you can put to some practical use. But Mama, can't I buy a car?"

Mr. Bennet had listened to them all in gathering wrath. "I must beg all of you not to be spending any fortunes just yet," said he. He rose from the table. "I'm going back to my office. Lizzy, when you have finished your dinner, please see me there."

Chapter Two

L izzy did not delay after the rest of the family had eaten. Consigning the dishes to her younger sisters' care, she hastened to the garage and knocked on the door of her father's retreat.

She found him staring at a corner of this comfortless chamber—little more than a closet, with unfinished walls perilously holding up rack upon rack of bookcases, and a space heater under the battered desk fighting a losing battle against the damp. As the family had grown, Mr. Bennet had been pushed out of the main house along with his precious book collection, which in Mrs. Bennet's view contributed to Kitty's allergies. But, refusing to yield entirely to the demands of his wife and offspring, he had carved out this space in the garage and declared it his own. Rarely did anyone else enter his office, and it was never cleaned.

Here he pursued a series of business ventures—photography, consulting, a mail-order enterprise doomed from the start by the absence of capital to purchase any goods in advance of orders received—that never seemed to succeed in producing full-time employment or providing for his large family. The well-timed demise of more provident parents had supplied him with a large house and a sufficient income for necessities, but had not stretched to giving his children access to the same quality of education or opportunities for gentility that he had enjoyed. So he diverted himself with the newspaper, the political debates of the day, and (when he could afford them) books on philosophy and current affairs, until he added a well-stocked mind to the tally of his discontents.

Lizzy had always felt that to see her father in his office was to see him for what he was, and she eschewed the experience whenever possible. But she was his favorite child, so inevitably she saw more of him, and more of his retreat, than the others. He had an affection for his eldest, John, but Lizzy was the dearest and the one in whom he most saw himself. Whether Lizzy saw her father in *herself*, she preferred not to contemplate too closely.

Now she approached him without a word, kissing him on the forehead and moving books off a chair before settling down to await what he had to say.

"I didn't mention this at dinner because I didn't want your mother to get the wind up. The letter to me wasn't the only thing that came in the packet from Lambtown. Most of it was for you." He sighed and silently handed over some papers: an unfolded missive on the letterhead of Messrs. Baldwin and Perry, attorneys at law, and a sealed envelope.

A quick glance at the envelope showed it to be addressed to herself in the shaky hand of her aunt's last years, and she pocketed it without comment. The letter from the attorneys she read.

January 5, 1999
Dear Ms. Bennet [it said]:

It is our sad duty to inform you of the decease of your aunt, Evelyn Elizabeth Bennet, on December 26, 1998. In accordance with her wishes, she has been cremated and her ashes interred at the Cemetery of All Saints' Episcopalian Church here in Lambtown. A local social organization of which she was a member for many years, the Live Poets Reading Society, plans to hold a memorial reading in her honor in February; we hope you and your family will be able to attend.

She had entrusted to us her legal and financial affairs for several decades, and it is by her wish that we write to you today.

First, she asked that we arrange for a member of her family to visit Lambtown and make arrangements for the disposal of her personal effects. While she did not stipulate that the family member be yourself, on several occasions she expressed the hope that it would be.

Secondly, she has named you the principal executor of her estate, with the request that you employ the services of our firm to assist you in the performance of these duties. If it is not convenient for you to spend much time in Lambtown, we can conduct the necessary business long distance; but under the circumstances, it would facilitate the execution of the Will and the realization of her wishes if you were able to stay here for a period of some months. The enclosed letter in Evelyn Bennet's hand provides details about what she wants you to do.

A copy of her Last Will and Testament is also enclosed, along with the papers you will need to sign if you accept the responsibilities your aunt has asked you to take on. Execution of these documents will allow us to open probate and take some initial steps in furtherance of her wishes. Please note that certain of the enclosed documents require notarization.

My partner and I look forward to meeting you in person and working with you to realize your aunt's vision. She was beloved and respected by all of us in the community of Lambtown.

Sincerely,
Melvin G. Perry, Esq.
Messrs. Baldwin and Perry, Attorneys-at-Law

Lizzy laid down the letter and looked up at her father. Gesturing at the other papers before him he said, "The will leaves you a small stipend, my dear: not enough to live on, but enough to smooth out bumps in the road. The bulk of her money is going to form the principal assets of a charitable foundation she has created and wishes you to administer. Her house and land also become the property of the foundation. Do you know what purpose she wants this foundation to serve?"

Lizzy was all amazement. "No, she never spoke of it to me. I can only assume her instructions are in the letter she has sent. There is nothing for the rest of the family?"

"Nothing, which is about as much as we all deserve."

"Still, Mama will not be happy. How are we to tell her?"

"She will have to be told, I suppose," said Mr. Bennet vaguely. "Do you think you will want to do as your aunt asks? It's a lot of responsibility for someone your age—and I don't like to think of you going off across the country and living on your own."

Lizzy struggled to conceal how eager she was to do that very thing, and to undertake whatever project her aunt had set for her. She knew how much her father relied on her for rational companionship, and dreaded the jealousy Kitty and Lydon, not to mention her mother, would not hesitate to express upon learning that she was being singled out for preferment. And she would hate to leave her beloved brother John, even for a few months. If she accepted this challenge, she did not doubt, the immediate future would be rife with vexation and distress. She replied cautiously, "Let me take a little time to read what she asks of me, and to consider the consequences. I'm leaning toward honoring her wishes—I don't know who will do so if I don't—but I promise to study all aspects of the question before making up my mind."

With this, her father had to be satisfied, and he let her go off to bed.

She gained the privacy of her bedchamber without being waylaid by inquisitive family members and curled up in a sagging armchair to read her aunt's letter. The opening words immediately transported her back to those summers of her childhood, and when it was borne in on her that one of the closest companions of her mind was truly gone forever, she had to stop reading and cry for a time. Her aunt wrote of that closeness in terms that mirrored and sharpened her own memories, and

Lizzy momentarily resented her parents' self-imposed poverty, which had kept her in recent years from spending time with such a beloved friend. But Lizzy was not by nature bitter, and she quickly resolved to recognize no obstacle that would keep her from remaining close to Aunt Evelyn in spirit.

The letter addressed various practical matters of personal belongings and small gifts to friends, and then embarked on a description of her charitable foundation, which she named the Live Poets Foundation of Lambtown, and its aims. As she read on, Lizzy became increasingly mystified and not a little dismayed. The task before her seemed straightforward enough—quite pleasant, in fact—so she could not understand why Aunt Evelyn was insistent that all of her work be conducted in the strictest secrecy. She was not to tell family or friends what she was doing; she was not to confide any part of the project to residents of Lambtown until it was complete. Thinking back on the town as she had known it in her childhood, she could imagine no reason why secrecy should be called for. But her aunt was clear and emphatic: no one in the area must be told, no local people aside from the attorneys could be consulted for advice or assistance.

This requirement certainly posed some dilemmas for Lizzy. She knew her family well enough to realize that some of them at least would be certain that she was keeping the money to herself, money that she could share with them if she chose. She would have to endure their recriminations and resentment without justifying herself. Though she had grown up in a city, she understood enough about small-town life to realize that the residents of Lambtown would be just as curious about the project as her relatives, and perhaps even less scrupulous in trying to uncover the mystery. Although the mission of the foundation was plain enough, bringing it to fruition would require expertise that she did not possess; she would need advice that she could not seek openly. It all seemed more difficult than it had to be. Lizzy wondered whether it would be appropriate to pursue her aunt's goals without honoring her stipulations: it seemed so unnecessary to put this strain on her relationships with family and neighbors. She read her aunt's last paragraph several times, trying to puzzle it out:

> *My reasons may be unclear to you now, my dear, but I am persuaded that as you spend some time in Lambtown, you will see what I have seen: that the town has fallen ill in spirit. With my body equally ill, I have neither the time nor the energy to try to heal it; the only thing that makes me feel better is to think of you the way I knew you as a child—your joyousness, your wit untinged by cruelty, your quick mind and generous heart. I believe you are the cure for what ails my beloved community, and I hope that in healing it you will find the joy you deserve. Perhaps it is selfish: I like to think of you here, and I like to think of you furthering my heart's desire when I am gone. But what is youth for, if not the pursuit of quixotic goals? I hope you will trust me and be inspired by the vision I see—at least enough to give a few months or years to it, my dearest niece.*

Lizzy sat up late mulling over the letter and her memories, now and then smiling or rubbing the mist out of her eyes, or rereading a passage of the long letter. It must have required a tremendous effort for her aunt to write it out by hand; the script was shaky and trailed away unevenly in places, and Lizzy realized that most of her recent letters had been typed, with only the signature in this spidery hand. Such extraordinary exertion bespoke great seriousness on Aunt Evelyn's part: this must have been among the most important undertakings of her final weeks of life, what she chose to do when she knew she had little time or strength left for anything. It behooved Lizzy therefore not to take it lightly—to do so would be to take her aunt lightly, to dismiss as insignificant a life well lived and a treasured relationship. It could not be done.

A soft tap on the door interrupted her reflections, and looking up she realized that it was already eleven-thirty and John must be home from Starbucks. He came in hard on the heels of his knock and hurried over to kiss her cheek and give her a quick squeeze about the shoulders. "Mama said that Aunt Evelyn has died!" he cried. "Oh, honey, I'm so sorry. You loved her so much. Tell me." He curled up at her feet, resting his chin and arm on her knees.

Lizzy smiled at the "Tell me" which had been the opening for so many comfortable exchanges with her favorite sibling. He always knew when she needed him to be the big brother. She stroked his hair, still cold from the bus ride home. "I'm so glad you're here, John. We got a letter from a lawyer saying that she died just after Christmas. They enclosed a letter she wrote for me, too."

She paused, realizing that for the first time in her life, she could not tell even John about her dilemma. To do as her aunt asked would mean leaving her dearest remaining friend in the dark. But while she was making up her mind, she could still talk to John about things that mattered. "The moment I knew she was gone I saw how much I've missed her. I guess she was always in my mind, and it had become such a habit for me to hold mental conversations with her that I didn't fully realize how long it's been since I really saw her, or had an *actual* conversation with her. I could see from the signatures on her letters that she was getting shaky, but it never really occurred to me that she could be seriously ill! She never said anything!"

"I suppose she didn't want you to worry about her when you couldn't do anything to help. She probably realized that no normal girl in her twenties would leap to the conclusion that someone was going to die—you just wouldn't think that way."

"And now I'll never see her again!"

John smiled. "You can still have those mental conversations."

"But somehow it's different—they would seem less real."

"That you'll have to work on," John agreed.

"It's just—I learned so much from her—not so much facts as ways to understand the world—ways to be in the world. She lived with a kind of grace that I always wanted to imitate. And she had a gift for being friends, real friends, with people. I wish you'd known her too."

"Oh, I think I knew her a little bit—at least through the ways you changed each time you came back from visiting her. She always brought out the best in you, you know."

After a bit Lizzy said, "She wants me to go to Lambtown. She wants me to do some work for her there. It would take months, maybe a year or more."

John thought about that for a moment. "No doubt she had her reasons. If you want my advice, I think you should do as she says. She was *good* for you, Lizzy, and there's no reason she shouldn't continue to be. And getting away couldn't do you any harm. I know you've got your business going here, but you could garden for people in California, too—and all year round, not just seasonally! Do you really see yourself staying in Columbus all your life? In this house all your life? You could do so much more."

"But I'd be away from you! And Dad, and all the family, of course."

"Well, and what of it?" John said cheerfully. "This isn't the nineteenth century—we've got phones, and e-mail, and I've even heard of these devices called airplanes! We wouldn't forget about you. And you'd let me come visit you out there on the western frontier, I hope."

"Try to keep me from sending you a ticket!"

"In fact, Mama may be so curious about Aunt Evelyn's life that she might insist on us *all* going out there."

Lizzy grimaced. "You mean, she's so curious about Aunt Evelyn's supposed fortune. Oh, goodness, you don't think so, do you?"

But as usual, John was right.

Chapter Three

"Created a *nonprofit foundation*? What was she *thinking*? What about her family? She can't have been in her right mind. Nobody in their right mind would give their money to some charity—and not even a real charity, one she made up herself!—while ignoring their own family. It can't be legal, we *must* have a claim. It's clear what must be done, Mr. B: we'll all go to California and challenge the will. Those lawyers will understand when they see how many children we have, and how needy we are. What about Lydon? Married, with a wife to support, and who knows when a baby will be on the way! What will become of all of us? We must do something! We have to go there and see this lawyer, and stay till we get justice!" Mrs. Bennet, in full cry over the breakfast table.

Mr. Bennet, hiding behind the newspaper, made no reply. John and Lizzy endeavored to explain to their mother that Aunt Evelyn had every right to do as she pleased with her own money, that she had been perfectly clear-headed and knew her own wishes.

"But it *wasn't* her own money," protested Mrs. Bennet, "it was Uncle Adolphus's money! If you had only contested his will years ago, Mr. B, we wouldn't find ourselves in this fix now! I hold you responsible for this. How she could have been happy all these years with money that wasn't rightfully hers I will never understand, and now we have to go to all this trouble to get it back."

Accustomed to his wife's outbursts, Mr. Bennet continued to read. But the idea of going to California was fast becoming fixed in her mind, and soon she was to receive support from an unexpected source.

Her younger son and favorite child, Lydon, had recently been persuaded to marry the eighteen-year-old daughter of a brigadier general in charge of a hush-hush space project at the nearby Rickenbacker Air Force Base, after the general had found Lydon drunk and in bed with his equally inebriated daughter. Brigadier General Cromwell Hughes was not the sort of man to brook such an insult to his daughter's virtue, no matter how frequently it might be offered nor with what complaisance it might have been received. His first idea was to beat the young man to a pulp and arrange for him to be shanghaied to some hot and dusty foreign land, but inquiries into Lydon's family and background had induced him to think again. The Bennets might not be well off and they appeared to be a cohort of civilian slackers, but the family name was old, and they did own a beautiful Victorian house near Short North. General Hughes was a practical man, and he was aware of the limits of what could reasonably be expected from his daughter Jenny. A marriage took place.

When Jenny and Lydon brought him the news about Aunt Evelyn and her will, they found the general in his study, examining a map. This being nothing unusual, they launched into their tale without preliminaries. The general only half attended to them until they reached the point of explaining that Aunt Evelyn had lived in Lambtown, California, and that Mrs. Bennet hoped to pursue her fortune there.

"Stop—did you say *Lambtown, California?*"

Lydon and Jenny were startled by this sudden interest in their narrative, for they were accustomed to talking in the general's presence only for the pleasure of hearing themselves speak. But they dutifully repeated the location and then, as the general appeared to have nothing more to add, continued with their tale. They did not realize—because the general did not feel obliged to share his concerns with two such useless people—that they were offering him the solution to a dilemma. General Hughes had recently been informed by Space Command that he was being transferred to Vandenberg Air Force Base in central California to oversee the testing phase of the rocket project. He liked to keep Jenny and, of necessity, Lydon under his eye, having no confidence in the Bennets' ability to guide them into productive lives. And according to the map he had been consulting, this Lambtown they were speaking of was situated no more than half an hour's drive from the base, separated only by a line of hills from the community in which he would be quartered. So he listened with greater tolerance than was his custom to the young couple's gossip, and at his first opportunity dropped in on the Bennets.

Years of overcompensation for the prevalent military view of air force officers as effete hedonists had transformed Brigadier General Hughes into the kind of figure certain to terrify the likes of Mrs. Bennet. She was greatly in awe of Lydon's father-in-law, and being largely ignorant of the distinctions of military rank, was certain that "brigadier general" sounded very impressive and must be more important than titles like "lieutenant general" or mere "general." The scorn he made little effort to conceal did him no harm in her eyes; it merely further convinced her that this was a personage to be reckoned with. So she was effusively polite when he appeared on her doorstep, fluttering about him with offers of wine, whiskey, and the most comfortable seat in the living room.

Lowering himself instead into the hardest chair available to him, General Hughes got right to the point. "That scrub Lydon tells me you're thinking of moving to California."

Mrs. Bennet, overlooking the slight to her baby, launched into a voluble explanation of the circumstances, which was ruthlessly cut short.

"Do it. I'm taking a post at Vandenberg, just over the hill from Lambtown, and I mean to keep Jenny under my eye. She can keep living with you, but I'll see she gets a civilian job on base."

"Well," said Mrs. Bennet smugly, "I'm not sure a job will be necessary. We'd be going to secure a family inheritance—"

"All the more reason to see young people properly employed. You should put that Lydon to work, since he's too lazy to get an education and doesn't have the backbone to serve his country."

"Oh, I couldn't bear to see my darling boy in harm's way! My nerves wouldn't stand it! I don't know how the mothers of soldiers survive."

"They survive *because* their children put themselves in harm's way," snapped the general. "But I'm not here for blamestorming. I don't care whether he was born a useless puppy or taught to be one. I intend to keep the blowback from ruining Jenny's life, and that means keeping them nearby. You can piggyback on my moving van and get your furniture redeployed for free, but you have to be ready to break camp in three weeks."

It was not to be supposed that Mr. Bennet would readily accede to such a scheme, based as it was on thoroughly misguided assumptions and involving so much inconvenience to himself. Yet he found most of his family arrayed against him. Lizzy had to go; John would prefer to be where Lizzy was; Kitty was wild to meet a whole new set of flyboys; and Mrs. Bennet could not be persuaded that where she lived had nothing to do with the final disposition of Aunt Evelyn's estate.

Of the whole family, only Mary raised any objection: California to her meant Hollywood, a cesspit of godless liberals who were all very much better looking than she ever would be. She paid as little heed to the representations of her elder siblings, that the Santa Ynez Valley was hundreds of miles from this Babylon and worlds away in lifestyle and worldview, as they paid to her sermonizing on the subject. Lydon and Jenny thought California had to be an improvement over Columbus in January, and they might as well be there as not, especially if it meant skirting the wrath of General Hughes. It rapidly became a matter not of *whether* the move was to be made, but of how it was to be accomplished in time.

Mrs. Bennet was principally concerned with which items of furniture would make the best impression in California; Mary, outnumbered, retired into her tracts for fortification against the inevitable onslaught of vice. To Kitty, Lydon, and Jenny, imminent departure meant that every drop of pleasure must be squeezed from their friends at the base, so they were not often to be found at home. Thus it fell to John and Elizabeth to corner their father and overcome his resistance to engagement with economic realities. He was reluctant to look beyond the tender packing of his precious library, but their united tact and persistence prevailed, and he was convinced at last that the most prudent course would be to lease the family home for a year under the supervision of a property management company and to rent a house in Lambtown for a similar period.

John gave notice at Starbucks and Lizzy notified all her landscape business clients, and they were left only, in the brief moments each night before exhaustion claimed them from their labors of the day, to reflect with a degree of chagrin on the shallowness of the roots that bound them to their hometown. Family members were cajoled and coerced into packing all but the last-minute necessities, and Lizzy's gardening crew was pressed into off-season duty painting and sprucing up the shabby rooms.

In the end, Mrs. Bennet was pleasantly surprised by the ease with which the management company found a professional couple eager to pay a premium rent for an address with such cachet, and she felt confident that she was well on her way to becoming the toast of Lambtown society.

In vain did John, after some painstaking research on the Web, caution his mother that California's real estate market was not the same as Ohio's. "Oh, don't be silly!" cried Mrs. Bennet;

"Lambtown is no more than a village compared to Columbus! You can't ask big-city prices in the middle of nowhere."

"Perhaps not," said John, "but by the same token, there are many fewer places available for rent, so the prices are not held in check by competition. And houses in general there seem to be not as large as in this neighborhood. We should consider ourselves lucky if we're able to find anything big enough for all of us."

"There's no chance I'll share a bedroom with Kitty, if that's what you're hinting at," said Mary. "I won't have her crashing around at all hours of the night, and playing that dirty music all day!"

Kitty jumped up to demonstrate her mastery of the latest moves to grace the hip-hop chart toppers on MTV, while Lydon and Jenny laughed uproariously at the outrage on Mary's face.

John smiled, but pointed out that country-western dance styles might fit in better in Lambtown, where ranchers had been the leaders of society for a hundred years. "Perhaps we shouldn't set our sights on becoming the toast of the town, Mother," he suggested, "but instead settle for showing ourselves pleased with the company we find ourselves in."

Mrs. Bennet bristled at his implication. "I'm sure my children are good enough for any company! If you and Lizzy weren't so high and mighty, you'd have as many friends as Lydon and Kitty do. Young people who know how to have a good time will be welcome anywhere."

"I expect so," said John amiably, and continued packing the china.

Chapter Four

In the end, the Bennets kept the brigadier general's moving
vans waiting no more than half a day before they were ready
to set off, on a frozen but sunny afternoon in the last week
of January. Lizzy had sold her battered work van, so the family
squeezed into two cars for the journey—Mrs. Bennet's more
eye-catching than practical Chrysler and the Rabbit General
Hughes had bestowed on his daughter in honor of her sixteenth
birthday.

As Lizzy and John did most of the driving, they saw little of
each other during the four-day trek, beyond adjudicating the
family quarrels that inevitably erupted at shared diner meals
each evening, or seizing a few moments before breakfast to consult on which route would be most likely to steer them away
from severe winter weather. Eventually they detoured south to
Arizona to avoid the treacherous passes of the Rockies and the
Sierra Nevada. Keeping well south of the fleshpots of Las Vegas,
they hurried across the Southern California deserts and navi-
gated the traffic of Los Angeles to reach the Pacific Ocean at Ven-
tura on the second day of February.

Here Lydon took the wheel of his wife's car, so Lizzy joined
her parents, John, and Mary for the final leg of the journey. A
hazy sunshine warmed the coastline, and only the contrails of
high-flying jets disturbed the azure of the sky. It was so warm
that they were able to open the windows to enjoy the soft ocean
breezes in their shirtsleeves. Mrs. Bennet was voluble in her
praise of all she saw: the beachside mansions, the green hillsides,
the red tile roofs of Santa Barbara, the flowers blooming on the

freeway medians, all spoke to her of the new life of wealth and ease that lay within her grasp.

Lizzy took delight in pointing out to John the drama of the scenery that unfolded once they turned off the main highway. The wild peaks of Los Padres National Forest looming over Lake Cachuma were as impressive as they had seemed in her childhood, and lovelier even than her memory of them, seen now for the first time in the lush green of the rainy season, the easternmost peaks capped with snow. As they drifted down into the heart of the Santa Ynez Valley her heart became too full for speech. She was seeing it all through her aunt's eyes and thinking of what she had gained and lost from Evelyn Bennet's life and passing.

When they left the road at the Lambtown exit, Mrs. Bennet looked askance at the rows of dilapidated mobile homes squatting under bare-branched cottonwoods by the offramp. But she scarcely had time to exclaim, "This can't possibly be Lambtown! Evelyn would never live in a place like this!" before the road had swept around a bend and they found themselves in a spruce village of Queen Anne structures and commodious ranch houses. The center of town, swiftly attained, consisted of cheerfully painted century-old buildings whose signs proclaimed them to be wine tasting rooms, art galleries, cafés, and boutiques.

As much as Mrs. Bennet was relieved, Lizzy was dismayed: such tourist-friendly trappings must be the development of the past few years, for they formed no part of her memory of the place. From her youthful visits she recalled a sleepy town with old-fashioned, practical shops catering mostly to ranching families, and while Aunt Evelyn had mentioned changes, she had touched on them only lightly and with her customary mix of philosophy and humor. Still, it was Lambtown, and Lizzy was happy to be back.

They found a motel on the dusty edge of town, overlooking a wide pasture, and gratified the manager by booking nearly half the rooms for an indefinite period of time. John and Lizzy left Lydon and Jenny exploring the HBO channels and Mary the Gideon Bible while they sallied forth to stretch their legs in a walk through the town before dinner.

The winter dusk was falling and the air was rapidly turning pleasantly chilly as they peered into the windows of the closing shops. A sizable cluster of people, gathered on the corners of a cross street up ahead, caught their attention, so they strolled over to see what was afoot. On closer inspection, the crowd proved to be groups of families lining the sidewalks, most dressed in the day's work clothes but some in Sunday finery, even a few women wearing long, layered skirts and lacy blouses of the kind traditional in parts of Mexico. Fathers had hoisted small children on their shoulders and older siblings watched over youngsters, while everywhere the rhythmic syllables of Spanish fell upon the ear, along with some words in another language unfamiliar to Lizzy and John. The sound of guitars, drums, and trumpets, a trifle discordant from the distance, could be heard a few blocks away.

"It's a parade!" cried John. At the sound of words spoken in English, some of the nearest adults turned and acknowledged his presence with a wary courtesy. They stepped aside to make room for John and Lizzy to cross the street, but after a little hesitation moved back into their positions when it became clear that the two were stopping to watch.

Lizzy looked about her with the liveliest interest, enjoying the challenge of figuring out family relationships and the drift of conversations without understanding most of the words used. She had learned some Spanish at Ohio State and spoke a casual hybrid Spanglish with a few of her landscape workers, but the swift, idiomatic exchanges going on around her were beyond her skill. John spoke no Spanish at all, but his open, happy face and silly pantomimes soon secured the trust of the children in his vicinity. Before long he had several little ones swinging off his arms with squeals of delight while others clamored to show him their own imitations of barnyard animals.

Lizzy, observing this scene with smiling indulgence, did not fail however to notice that John's friendly overtures were regarded with some uncertainty by the parents, and with surprise and disapproval by the occasional Anglo passerby. Indeed, the mostly white shopkeepers and salespeople were hurrying to depart the commercial district, brushing past the loitering families to reach their cars. A few drivers even made some show of honking at those in the crowd who had stepped into the roadway to watch for the parade's approach, chasing them back onto the sidewalk before roaring off.

She was curious about this display of impatience with what seemed to be a festive occasion. But her attention was soon diverted by a small group of people loitering on the opposite corner who had the well-groomed look of the wealthy, and at least one of whom seemed to be charmed by John's games with the children. She had just drawn her brother's attention to his admirer when the procession came into view. Young girls in white dresses appeared first, solemnly guarding the flames of candles in glass holders, followed closely by women holding up elaborately dressed dolls and men bearing wide bowls full of what appeared to be grain.

"I wonder what the story is with the dolls," John murmured.

An older man who had been standing nearby answered him. "You're interested in our traditions? The figures they are carrying are called Niños Dioses. They're images of the young Jesus being brought to the temple. You can see that many of the figures are crowned to show that this is the Holy Son. They're also dressed with sandals, *huarachitos*, which represent Jesus in his human incarnation."

Lizzy turned to the gentleman eagerly. "Would you explain the rest to us? We're new here, and we don't even know what holiday is being celebrated."

"It's Día de la Candelaria, or Candlemas in English," he said. "It's a day of purification and blessings. The girls' candles stand for the sun beginning to return as winter fades—that symbolism goes back to before Christianity, of course. The men are carrying seeds to be blessed by the priest before they're planted, although in this climate some of the planting has already been done—"

At this point he was interrupted by the blare of music as a series of small bands, each not more than three to six people strong, strode by. Each band was playing a different tune, in fine disregard of its rivals; and each group wore a different outfit, some as simple as white pants and shirt with a colored sash, others very elaborate costumes with frogged and embroidered jackets, hats with tassels, and decorated boots.

"Those are different social clubs," the gentleman raised his voice over the hubbub. "Each one has its own uniform, its own regalia and passwords and traditions. Some of the groups are of Mexican descent, and others are from Peru. Many of the sheepherders who work in this area are Peruvian, so we have a variety of traditions coming together in this parade."

"Oh, there's the Virgin of Guadalupe," cried Lizzy, as a bier went by carried by six young men, carefully balancing a large statue on top. It was a tall, dark-skinned female figure in a rose-colored robe covered with a mantle spangled with stars, perched atop a sickle moon held aloft by an angel; gold waves radiated outward from all around her.

The older man looked pleased. "So you recognize *la virgen*. Our church in town is Our Lady of Guadalupe, so she is our patron saint here as well as for the Mexican immigrant workers."

After a few more enthusiastic, discordant bands tramped by, the end of the procession was marked by a small cluster of shiny new pickup trucks, driven at a crawl by waving, exuberantly honking young men.

"Pickups are sacred to the Virgin as well?" remarked Lizzy, the twinkle in her eye robbing her words of any offense.

The gentleman chuckled. "Another Candelaria tradition from Peru, but one that our local boys have been eager to adopt. New vehicles are also brought to the church for blessing today."

"That big blue Ram is very impressive—not to mention the driver," said Lizzy, as she met the eye of the handsome youth behind the wheel. He gave a flourishing bow in their direction as he crept by, and could be seen to glance several times in the rear-view mirror as he proceeded down the street.

The older gentleman looked proudly after the departing truck. "So you have an eye for my son, George," he said with a smile. "I'll let him know that he's earned the notice of the prettiest newcomer to arrive in Lambtown in many years! May I tell him the name of the young lady gracious enough to look kindly on him?"

Lizzy blushed, but John stepped in. "Sir, it's very nice to make your acquaintance. My name is John Bennet, and this is my sister Elizabeth. Our whole family is here for a while, on family business."

The gentleman exclaimed, "Are you Evelyn Bennet's family, then? She was well known here, and is greatly missed. It's doubly my pleasure to meet you in that case. My name is Frank Carrillo, and I hope we can get better acquainted. Will you be attending the Red and White Ball?"

Lizzy responded with alacrity that she had never heard of it, but any event with *ball* in the name was certain to be popular with her family.

By this time the bystanders were moving into the streets to follow the procession to evening Mass. Mr. Carrillo, with apologies, said he needed to be going with them; the Bennets, in turn, made their excuses as they needed to return to their family before they were missed.

As they were turning to go, Lizzy observed that the young man across the way in the group of rich-looking Anglos was still eyeing John. "I think you should wave at him," she said mischievously. "Clearly you've provided more entertainment for him this evening than the parade did!"

John laughed and begged her to be serious; but as they made their way back to the motel, he could not help commenting on the young man's seeming goodwill, his evident good manners, his appearance in general.

"I give you permission to like him, John; such a paragon of every imagined virtue indeed cries out for admiration. And it's important to take care that we admire those who admire us already: it makes for a pleasing symmetry in our social relations."

"Perhaps you'll be so kind as to let us ride in the flatbed when you go cruising with your Latin George in his Ram pickup," retorted John. "If you're as successful in making a conquest of the son as you were with the father, I expect it won't be long before we're all riding out together."

In the exchange of such nonsense they made their way back to the motel and shepherded their family off to dinner. Their tardiness was readily excused, at least on the part of their mother and Kitty, by the news they brought of a ball in the offing. Both elder siblings were happy enough that the ensuing speculation about what that event might entail led the conversation away from any mention of interesting young men.

Chapter Five

The morning brought Lizzy's appointment with Melvin Perry, her aunt's attorney, and she was dismayed to learn that most of her family was bent on accompanying her. Lydon and Jenny weren't awake yet, but Kitty was eager to discover what entertainments the town had to offer, Mary needed to locate the nearest evangelical church before Sunday, her father wanted advice on locating rental properties, and her mother cherished hopes of persuading the attorney to overturn Evelyn Bennet's will forthwith. Lizzy was aware that in agreeing to see her immediately on her arrival Mr. Perry was putting himself out, and she cringed at the first impression of her that would be conveyed by a mass descent of the Bennet clan upon his offices. But not being one to dwell overmuch on circumstances she lacked the power to alter, she accepted the entourage with good grace. John, sizing up the situation, came along to help without being asked.

Mr. Perry was plainly surprised by the crowd that filled his small waiting room, but, as his secretary was not just then present to manage for him, took control as best he might by pretending that it was simply a brief social encounter, an opportunity for everyone to be introduced before his true business with Lizzy began. He did his best to absorb all the names and field all the questions that soon were being thrown his way: the evangelical church was on the highway, about five miles distant, the Episcopalian one a block away from the center of town. There were no movie theaters or shopping malls in the neighborhood, nor would any local buses take Kitty to them; both involved a drive to Lompoc, near Vandenberg Air Force Base, or to Santa Barbara. The local real estate agents did not do much rental business, though they could inquire at the office of Morris Collins, a Realtor who had recently been appointed the mayor of Lambtown. But there was another possibility: he himself had a client who owned a newly built house she was not yet ready to occupy, and he would ask whether she might be willing to rent it out for a time.

For Mrs. Bennet, such subjects were interesting enough, but insufficient to distract her from her chief preoccupation. She interrupted with "It's a sad business about this will. How did Evelyn come to make such a peculiar arrangement? And what are you doing to fix it?"

Even Mr. Perry's suavity was no proof against this sudden attack, and he turned to Elizabeth in some perplexity.

"Mama, you know that Aunt Evelyn had every right to arrange her estate as she thought best," Lizzy said in minatory tones.

"*You* would think so, of course, since it's all to your benefit! But I have other children to look out for, and I can't allow one to run off with what belongs by right to everyone."

Lizzy cast an agonized glance at her father, but he was enjoying himself too much to heed her appeal.

"Ma'am, I can assure you that every provision in your sister-in-law's Will is legitimate," said Mr. Perry. "Her assets were free of any encumbrance and her mind was clear, so she was at liberty to dispose of her estate how she wished."

Mrs. Bennet was inclined to dispute this view, but John stepped in with the suggestion that the purpose of today's meeting was simply for Lizzy to discover what her responsibilities were, and perhaps Mama would like to see something more of Lambtown now? If they found a local newspaper, they might learn more about the ball they'd heard about.

Mr. Perry seized on this new idea with evident relief. "You

mean the Red and White Ball? It's one of the biggest social events of the year in the valley! It's put on by the Hispanic Heritage Club to benefit their charitable programs. My secretary is one of the organizers, and I'm sure she'd want me to give you invitations." He rummaged in her desk and came out with the cards, then led Mrs. Bennet to the exit by the expedient of holding them out in her direction while retreating to the door. "It was a pleasure to meet all of you, and I hope to see you again at the ball." John herded his parents and younger sisters out, and Mr. Perry closed the door on them at last.

Once they were settled in his sanctum, Lizzy repressed the impulse to apologize for her family, and turned directly to the business at hand. She assured him that she was fully prepared to execute her aunt's wishes as they had been described to her, though many aspects of the task were unfamiliar, and some mysterious. "I don't really understand the requirement of complete secrecy," she said. "From what I recall of my visits with my aunt, she had many friends who enjoyed reading and books; why would it be necessary to conceal her plan to turn her home into a public library for Lambtown?"

"When you have been here for a while, her concerns may become clearer to you, along with the scope of her ambition and the challenge you face. A key factor to remember is that she envisioned a library that would serve the *entire* community, not just the community of her immediate friends. How to achieve this is something you'll have to figure out on your own. You will also need to be alert to the pockets of resistance that exist here toward any project that would offer equal access to all elements of the community. I urge you to remain discreet and keep your plans as private as possible. Do your family members know what you are doing?"

"No, I haven't confided in them. They know that she created a charitable foundation and that she made me a personal bequest, but that's all."

Mr. Perry appeared relieved. "I'm sorry if her requirements put you in an awkward position with regard to your family, but—"

"I understand," Lizzy hastened to insist. "Those of my relations I would be tempted to confide in will give me the benefit of the doubt, and the others will believe what they wish regardless of anything I might say. I'm more concerned about the expectations of my aunt's friends and acquaintances here. I imagine they will have questions and, as permanent residents of Lambtown, a greater legitimate interest in the outcome."

"Perhaps I can smooth your way a little bit there," said Mr. Perry. "I'm a member of the Live Poets reading group that included most of her closest friends, and I can explain your presence among us in a way that may deflect much of the curiosity. The natural assumption will be that you and your family, as her closest relatives, are all her heirs, and I can allow that assumption to stand without refuting it until you are prepared to unveil the library."

"What about zoning? Isn't Aunt Evelyn's house in a residential district? Could there be legal concerns on that head?"

"She obtained a variance some years ago, when the idea first came to her, so it can't be stopped in court. But I would caution you to bear in mind that it's crucial to win the hearts of the community in this case, not just avoid legal challenges. And there may be some hurdles from the Planning Department."

"My aunt specified some particular gifts and bequests for various friends in her letter to me, but I was wondering about her housekeeper, and the nurse who cared for her at the end. Did she provide anything for them, or should I be doing so?"

Mr. Perry nodded approvingly. "There are monetary bequests for both of them in a codicil to her will, and those will be paid in due course, after probate. I also have a set of keys to her house for you." He went on to outline the financial details of the will and the charitable foundation with Elizabeth, offering some helpful advice on developing a work plan and a budget. They parted with on each side a favorable impression of the other.

Lizzy's first aim was to visit Evelyn's house, and as it was an object with her to make this first visit alone, she set off immediately, while the rest of her family was elsewhere. Even John's company would not have been completely welcome as she faced the empty rooms and gardens that her aunt had inhabited: he did not share the memories and emotions that such scenes would evoke, nor did she feel equal to describing them.

On turning the corner and approaching the house, Lizzy was surprised to find that the garden was in tolerable order. To her expert eye it was clear that someone had continued to care for it during Aunt Evelyn's illness, perhaps even after her death. Changes had occurred in the years since her last summer visit to Lambtown; she recalled an English-style garden of lawn, roses, and mixed perennials, but now few traces of such a charming but unsuitable design remained. In its place were hardy natives and Mediterranean-climate plants, most of them unfamiliar to an Ohio girl, and she realized that here was another wall of learning for her to scale. She knew from reading that the seasonal cycles of rain and drought prevailing in California required unfamiliar adaptations from plant and gardener alike, and wondered where the nearest nursery might be. If she were to revive her landscaping business here, she would need to master at least the basics without loss of time.

For now she paused briefly to admire the skill with which Aunt Evelyn had laid out the garden—most drought-tolerant landscapes she had seen in photographs were casual sprawls of ill-assorted plants, but here the loose forms were arranged with discipline and respect for fundamental principles of design, and the counterpoise of tradition with an unfamiliar plant palette was pleasing and intriguing to her eye. This early in February, little was blooming save for narcissi tucked into the corners, but everything had been tidied after the last growing season, and already fresh shoots were starting to appear.

But she was here for a purpose, not to loiter about admiring a garden. Giving herself a little shake, Lizzy turned to enter the house. She had always loved the building's wide-armed Craftsman style, but its simplicity and heavy grace were inextricably bound up with her aunt's presence there. Now it was impossible not to fear that some of the grace might be lost—would it be just a house like any other?

It was not. Indoors as well as out, all was well-kept, though a thin film of dust coated the surfaces inside and the air felt a little stuffy; but on every side were objects her aunt had treasured, which spoke of her interests, her passions, her personality, her sense of humor. The rooms were not cluttered, but well-stocked with the signifiers of a lively mind and an active life. Reminders of places she had been, beliefs she had held, and friends she had held dear were everywhere—and the books especially told tales of the person she was. Lizzy wandered, and touched, and smiled or speculated on the meaning of all she saw.

The kitchen was the room that really brought home to her the finality of her aunt's absence. There were no odors of food, no dishes in the drying rack, no fruits in the bowl on the counter, only a dish towel folded neatly and hanging on a hook. She had never seen anything so empty. After that, she could not quite bring herself to go into her aunt's bedroom—not just yet.

Instead, Lizzy sat down in the dining room and unfolded the letter from her aunt. She made a list of all the things Evelyn had wanted friends to have, and then passed the next half-hour locating what she could of these items and laying them out on the table. She found her aunt's address book and labeled each gift with the name and phone number of the recipient. The activity focused her memories on the associations inspired by this or that in the house, and it was painful to think of sending these mementos off to live elsewhere. But she was a young woman, and her mind would not look backwards for long. Soon her imagination turned to picturing how the house was to be turned into a library that would become a gathering place for all of Lambtown, and she was going from room to room, picturing a children's story circle here, computers over there, and rows of chairs for readings and book signings in the parlor in front of the fireplace.

While she was thus occupied, she was startled by a knock at the front door. A lady of about her father's age, who seemed vaguely familiar, was on the doorstep, eyeing her with a little suspicion. Lizzy introduced herself and added, "I think we may have met some years ago? You were a friend of my aunt's?"

Much relieved, the lady cried, "Oh, you're Elizabeth! I'm so glad you've arrived. Yes, Evelyn and I were very close, especially the last few years, and I remember meeting you when you were a child. I'm Mary Gardiner; I live across the street, and have been keeping an eye on the house since it's been unoccupied."

Lizzy invited her in and did the honors of the house as best she might, with nothing in the fridge or pantry save a bottle of sparkling water and an old packet of cookies. Nibbling at the cookies in the living room, Lizzy and her guest both laughed and agreed that their heyday was past. Lizzy, recalling that among the items on her aunt's list were a few for Mrs. Gardiner, jumped up and went to collect them from the dining table. She shyly offered to her guest a first edition of *Elizabeth and Her German Garden* and a delicate antique Chinese perfume bottle.

"My aunt left me some instructions for gifts she wanted to offer to various friends," she explained. "These are what I have located so far for you."

"Your aunt and I became friends over this book!" Mrs. Gardiner exclaimed. "I was trying to decide whether to leave my first marriage, agonizing over a choice between the troubles of a life I knew and the perils of the unknown. She lent me this book, and the story echoed my dilemma and clarified my choice for me. Evelyn had a gift for guiding people in the right direction without ever uttering a word of advice."

"I think she's doing that for me right now," said Lizzy, with a little smile.

"Yes, I believe she is. I don't want to say too much, but I did witness her will and am the one person in town, aside from the attorneys, who knows a little about what your project is. You may rely on my discretion, and any help I can offer you—though in your aunt's spirit, I should try to avoid *advising!*"

"Perhaps you'll be able to help me with insights into Lambtown and the issues that prompted her to secrecy."

"Perhaps I can," said Mrs. Gardiner. "In the meantime, are you here on your own? Do you plan to live in the house?"

"No, my entire family has come. We're looking for a house to rent. I told them this house wouldn't be big enough for everyone—and in any case I figured some construction work would be necessary here, and it would be very inconvenient to have a crowd of people in residence."

"How many are you?"

"There are eight of us—my parents, four brothers and sisters, and my younger brother's wife."

"Eight of you! Good heavens. This is a small town, and there aren't a lot of opportunities here. How will you ever find things to do?"

"Well, my mother works in the home—as in fact does my father, he's self-employed. My elder brother, John, worked at Starbucks in Columbus, and will probably look for something similar in this area. Mary is still getting her education; Lydon's wife, Jenny, is the daughter of an air force officer who has just been transferred to Vandenberg, and I expect he will find her a job on base. Lydon will probably look for work there, too, or somewhere nearby; and Kitty may follow his lead. I was a landscape contractor in Columbus; I'll need to learn more about the local plants and seasons before I can do any design work, but I may be able to get some garden maintenance jobs in the meantime."

"Well, that's something I *can* help you with," said Mrs. Gardiner. "My husband Edward owns the nursery here—Gardiner's, out on the Old Coach Road. He can teach you what you need to know and put you in touch with possible clients. But will you have time to work, on top of all your responsibility with the foundation project?"

"I like to be busy," said Lizzy cheerfully. "I won't try for full-time employment, but a couple days a week of gardening will be good for me. I like working outside, and doing physical labor. I noticed that somebody has been tending the garden here—and very beautifully, I must say."

"Yes, that's my husband. He really admired Evelyn's eye for plant selection and design, and it's been his pleasure to maintain it according to her standards. I only wish he took as much care over our own garden! I grow herbs and flowers to make essential oils and perfumes, and he tends to leave the maintenance to me."

"Oh, I remember my aunt having some wonderful noncommercial perfumes; I loved to sneak into her room and try them out. Were those yours?"

"Yes, indeed. I hope you'll use the ones she had left over, and enjoy them—it would be sad to think of them just being thrown away."

Lizzy confessed that she had not yet been able to go into her aunt's room, but would be sure to rescue the perfumes when she did.

Mrs. Gardiner nodded sympathetically. "You'll be able to face it in due time. Meanwhile, I hope you'll all come to the memorial for Evelyn being held by our reading society, the Live Poets, and read something in her honor. I've taken over for her as the organizer of the group, and it'll be at my house, on the twenty-third at seven o'clock."

"I'm sure we'll all want to attend," said Lizzy, hoping silently that she could make it so. "What can I bring?"

"Our gatherings are potluck, so any side dish or dessert, or even something to drink, would be welcome. I'm taking care of the main course options. Normally our group is only ten people, but we've opened up this meeting to anyone in the community who wants to honor your aunt. I expect a lot of people will want to attend."

Chapter Six

On returning to the motel to find the rest of the family, Lizzy was greeted with enthusiasm by her father. "You were sorely missed this afternoon," he said. "I went to find that real estate agent the lawyer mentioned, Morris Collins. What a character! And I had nobody to share the joke with. But you'll meet him: he's coming by here to talk further with us after he closes his office for the day."

"You weren't able to determine when you met him whether he had any rental listings we could look at?"

"Not in so short a time as half an hour, as you'll understand when he arrives."

"I would've thought that five minutes would've sufficed for such a simple question."

"Five minutes didn't suffice for mutual introductions," said Mr. Bennet, his eyes alive with laughter. "Wait and see."

Considerably intrigued, Lizzy sought out John for enlightenment, but he said their father had been no more forthcoming with him. They had not long to wait, however, before Mr. Collins put in his appearance, in a well-polished sedan that from behind could almost be mistaken for a Lexus. Family members were duly gathered in the motel lounge, where they discovered a man of about thirty, tending slightly to corpulence, who bobbed bows to each one in turn.

"Welcome, my dear Bennet family, welcome!" he cried. "As the mayor of Lambtown—for just last month I took that title, having been selected for the office from among the ranks of the Town Council, to which I had the honor of being elected in November, though I had no expectation of being singled out from among my peers in my first term—though perhaps it was due to my position in life, and in the town—my work as a Realtor allowing me to mingle with all my constituents, but especially my membership in the Enclave providing connections to our most exalted ranching families—"

"What is the Enclave?" demanded Mrs. Bennet, the phrase "exalted ranching families" having captured her attention.

Mr. Collins looked shocked. "Surely you've heard of the Enclave, ma'am! Though, of course, you arrived only yesterday, but I would have thought that even in Ohio, word of—but perhaps you don't move in circles where—well, in any case, in sum, the Enclave is the premier social organization of the Santa Ynez Valley. It was founded by the earliest families to settle here, the Fremonts (now, unhappily, all died out), along with the de Bourghs and Darcys. The Enclave owns the polo grounds out on Old Coach Road, a beautiful facility, with meeting rooms and a dining hall and stabling for over a hundred horses!"

"So it is, in fact, a physical enclave, not just a state of mind?" inquired Mr. Bennet.

"Of course! It's a country club. Membership is by invitation only, but anyone who wishes to be a person of prominence must belong. It's much more than just the polo team and tournaments: they host charitable events and social occasions, and support many good works in the community. I have the honor of the patronage of the greatest lady hereabouts, Catherine de Bourgh—owner of considerable property just outside town—she is much interested in land use issues, and I've been able to be of service to her in such matters with the Realtors' association, so she put me up for membership in the Enclave with the idea that I could fill the post of recording secretary. And it was she who advised me to run for the Town Council, where I could assist her further in promoting the kinds of policies that will most benefit the first citizens, and, by extension of course, all the lesser inhabitants of the valley. As I said, the council voted me, among all their number, to conduct their meetings and serve as first among equals, as the mayor! So it is in that capacity, as well as in my professional position as a Realtor, that I have the honor of welcoming you to Lambtown."

John and Lizzy were struck dumb by all this eloquence, while the younger members of the family had already wandered away. But Mr. Bennet's greater preparation for this speech, or more tenacious mind, had allowed him to follow all the twists and turns, and now he judged it time to turn the conversation into a more fruitful channel. "I congratulate you, Mr. Collins, on achieving so fortunate a position in life, and at such a young age. We're pleased to be settling for a time in Lambtown, where my sister Evelyn Bennet lived for many years, and are looking for a suitable house to rent. My daughter Lizzy tells me that my sister's house would not be large enough for our whole family—"

"Ah, yes, the Evelyn Bennet residence," interrupted Mr. Collins. "Four bedrooms, but only two baths, alas, as is frequently the case in older houses. Such a pity; the absence of modern amenities takes so much value out of our older homes. In a newly built house of that size, of course, you would see at least three full baths, plus a half-bath downstairs and maybe another in the service quarters. Should you wish to put it on the market, however, I'll do the best I can for you. There are those who find the Craftsman style charming, and will put up with the inconvenience for the sake of curb appeal."

Finding her voice, Lizzy thanked him politely but said her aunt's house was not at present for sale. Mr. Collins seemed inclined to dispute the wisdom of this, but Mr. Bennet cut him off.

"It's our present need for housing that concerns us," he said. "We don't expect to live here permanently, so our interest is in rentals, not houses to buy; and we hope to find something of five or six bedrooms."

"Allow me to persuade you to reconsider, " protested Mr.

Collins. "Even if your stay is not permanent—though who would not wish to remain in such a beautiful place as the Santa Ynez Valley, which, I flatter myself, has no equal anywhere in the country—as a business decision it is always to your benefit to own, not rent. Whatever norms may apply in Ohio, in California the advantages of home ownership are unequaled. The market here is almost continuously appreciating, and in this area, a small ranch on land that can be subdivided is an excellent investment, even over the short term. I could show you—"

"Thank you, Mr. Collins, but we are not equipped to take on the responsibilities of a ranch: we are city folk, and know nothing about farming or animal husbandry. And as I still own my house in Columbus, buying a second property would have tax disadvantages. We want to keep things simple, and are looking to rent, not buy."

Mr. Collins tried to argue the point from a variety of directions, but was at last compelled to divulge that he knew of no rental houses in the area of the size desired by the Bennets, though he would let them know if anything turned up. Mrs. Bennet, who had been favorably impressed by the young mayor's account of his social connections, now tried to redeem her family's standing in his eyes by asking casually if they would be seeing him at the Red and White Ball.

Unfortunately, this sally backfired. "The Red and White Ball? Oh, no, Mrs. Bennet, by no means. I don't know what you've heard, but allow me to give you a hint, as one who understands the local society best. It can do you no credit among those who really matter to be seen at that event. I'm sure it is all for a very good cause, and many of our Latino residents are respectable members of the community. As mayor, I naturally stay on good terms with everyone—but that doesn't mean I would rub shoulders with them at a public event! You won't wish to confine your acquaintance to row-crop farmers and the managers of convenience stores. To be sure, some of the best families will buy tickets, as a courtesy to their employees. Still, you should choose wisely where you go while you're making your first impression here. I assure you, people will be watching, and if you aspire to be noticed by the leaders, you'll be careful what company you keep."

Fortunately for the Bennets, since Mr. Collins proved to be of no use whatever in locating accommodations for them, the client Melvin Perry had mentioned expressed her willingness to lease her house to them for a year. It was a brand-new construction in a planned community on the outskirts of town, intended eventually to face a new golf course. The golf course itself was still under construction, however, and the owner preferred not to move in until after all the sod was laid and the tractors and odors of fertilizer had dispersed.

To Mr. Bennet the noise was odious, the concatenation of architectural styles in the faux-grand mansionette even more so; but Mrs. Bennet was delighted. The pillared portico, Sub-Zero refrigerator, master shower with jets squirting from all directions, and golf course all expressed the person she wished to appear to be as she made her debut in Lambtown. By the beginning of the next week, their furniture had been delivered and they were settling in.

The Red and White Ball now became the focus of discussion in the family circle. Inquiries had uncovered the intelligence that it was so named for its dress code—red gowns for the ladies, white tie for the gentlemen—and for its Valentine's Day theme. On hearing this, Mr. Bennet declared that no force on earth could get him tricked out in a rented monkey suit and demanded to hear no more on the subject—a command that received as much deference as his commands generally did. Mrs. Bennet was torn between concern that their attendance would give the wrong impression and fear that there was no other immediate way to make her debut in the neighborhood. The younger generation, unencumbered by worries about social standing, simply felt it would be fun to dress up and dance. Even Mary thought there was no great harm in a little amusement in the name of charity, once she heard it spoken of at church as a popular annual event. So Mr. Bennet was persuaded to buy tickets for the rest of the family, so long as they agreed not to pester him about his determination to remain at home.

After a shopping expedition to Santa Barbara to buy their dresses and rent evening clothes for John and Lydon, Lizzy set to work in good earnest on her aunt's house, clearing out furnishings and possessions that could not be used for the library or by the family—the necessary precursor to giving the contractor recommended by Mr. Perry free rein to destroy and to build what would be required to transform the house into a library.

She had found a serviceable used pickup truck at a lot in Santa Barbara; once all the excess linens, beds, lamps, and so forth were inventoried, she was ready to deliver them wherever they might be needed. On her rounds of meeting Aunt Evelyn's friends to deliver their bequests, she had inquired about local charities that would take such goods, but nobody seemed to know of any—Salvation Army, Disabled Veterans, and the like were all too far off to be helpful. It was impossible to drive around the valley, however, without realizing that the poor were everywhere—living in the mobile home village by the highway, working in the fields, cleaning the motel rooms the Bennets had stayed in when they arrived. She decided to call on the priest at the Catholic church, since he had a large farmworker congregation, to seek advice.

Our Lady of Guadalupe proved to be housed in a repurposed Grange hall at the less desirable end of town, a simple clapboard structure with a corrugated tin roof. The parish offices were around the back, and Lizzy explored the premises until she located Father George Austen, an elderly, fragile, and ill-tempered-looking person. She introduced herself and explained her dilemma.

Father Austen glared at her for a moment, and then invited her to sit down. "You have some household items for the needy," he repeated in a cracked voice.

"Um, yes," said Lizzy, wondering why he seemed confused about such a simple matter. "Roughly half the contents of my late aunt's house, in fact. Here, I have a list."

Father Austen looked it over, and read it again. "Do you mean you wish to sell these goods?" he barked.

"No, selling them seems like unnecessary trouble, and from what I've seen around here, there are plenty of people who might find them welcome."

"That's not what most people see when they come to the Santa Ynez Valley," said Father Austen drily. "They see vineyards and tourist shops and beautiful scenery."

"Well, naturally! But surely the locals know better!"

"The locals are mostly ranchers. As a group they tend to value hard work, frugality, and self-reliance; and they expect those who work for them to share those values."

"Self-reliance and frugality mean one thing to a landowner and something very different to an immigrant farmworker, I imagine," replied Lizzy.

"Many people don't believe in providing assistance to illegal immigrants—and it can be hard to tell who is legal and who isn't."

"I'm sure it is," said Lizzy, "but it hardly makes sense for the community as a whole to deny people basic necessities for fear that their papers are not in order."

Father Austen's grim frown bored into her. "You are a peculiar young woman," he said.

Lizzy, undeceived, grinned at him brazenly. "I most certainly hope so."

"Humph." He picked up the phone and pressed the intercom button. "Rose, come in," he said, and hung up again.

A nervous-looking middle-aged woman entered from another room. "Yes, Father?"

"This Miss Bennet has some things to donate. Work it out between you," he snapped, dismissing them both.

Once out of the priest's presence, Rose proved to be as effusive as he was laconic. She exclaimed again and again over Lizzy's list, waving her hands and running off onto tangents about this family of parishioners and that until Lizzy was completely bewildered. "Oh, mercy me, look at all these things—*five* beds? And the chairs and desks—and a convertible sofa! There will certainly be competition for *that* item, since it takes up so little space during the daytime. I was just with the Ortiz family the other day, and their uncle Hector has arrived; his wife is already here, of course, and two of their children, we had to establish their residency so they could go to school, though they always miss the first few weeks during the grape harvest—oh, this is too much, are you *sure*? I'm sorry, dear, I don't mean to cry, but—really, a *computer*? And eight sets of towels, six in good condition—oh, bless you, you can't imagine!"

Finally Lizzy pieced together the intelligence that Rose managed a storeroom of donated goods at the church, and needy people could take what they needed from it on Sundays after Mass.

"That will be perfect for the linens and clothing and small items. But do you have any ideas about how to distribute the furniture?"

Indeed Rose did, though it required all Lizzy's attention and ingenuity to understand what they consisted of, buried as they were in a rush of detail about families Rose had visited, children for whom she was seeking to obtain asthma inhalers, fathers injured in the fields, housing issues, food prices, transportation problems, and more. Eventually it was agreed that Rose would telephone Lizzy as she sorted out the particular needs of individual families, and Lizzy would load up the appropriate items in her truck for them to make deliveries together.

Lizzy was not overly confident of Rose's ability to pursue

such an organized plan of action, but it turned out that her scattered style was confined to her habits of speech; in short order they were coordinating almost daily deliveries of furnishings to households all around the valley.

For Lizzy, accustomed as she was to seeing urban poverty, it was an eye-opening experience. She had not known that anyone in the United States lived the way migrant workers did. Extended families, those lucky enough to have shelter, crowded a dozen men, women, and children into a tumbledown two-room trailer with no functional heat or plumbing; children slept on the floor; clothes or empty sacks of rice or cornmeal were used to cover holes in the windows. Women worked in the fields with the men except for a designated caregiver for several families' children; this courageous soul tried to keep her charges from coming to serious harm while cooking, washing, hauling water, tending the sick, and nursing the youngest. Lizzy saw water supplies kept in old pesticide drums, perishable food lying unrefrigerated on open shelves, untreated gashes and sores on children playing in muddy yards. *How do these people stay alive?* she wondered, and the possessions she had to offer seemed pitifully inadequate.

Expecting her Spanish to be stretched to its limits, Lizzy found that many of the families didn't even understand it: natives of remote villages in Mexico and Central America, they spoke Quechua and a variety of other ancient tongues dating back to before the Spanish conquest. It was difficult to imagine how people facing such a struggle to supply their most basic needs were able to function in modern American society.

The children seemed often more adapted to their surroundings than their parents, picking up a little English and Spanish with their secondhand clothing and toys. The bolder ones would designate themselves intermediaries between the adults in their household and the two Anglo visitors, explaining such matters as they deemed sufficiently important to transmit across the gulf.

Rose was evidently a trusted confidante to those able to communicate, and Lizzy overheard a great deal about men who provided or who drank away their earnings, women's and babies'
health problems, older children who were good and helped out
and went to school, or who ran wild and brought greater burdens on their families. The church worker took in all this information and did everything she could to provide advice,
encouragement, and relief in crises.

Back at the parish office, Rose was organized and tenacious
in her pursuit of elusive items such as schoolbooks, medicine,
and food. Those potential donors who resisted all her persuasions were ruthlessly turned over to Father Austen, who in a few
pithy words could shame or terrify merchants into generosity.
Lizzy came to enjoy her visits to the simple little church, whose
almost sole adornment was the striking Virgin of Guadalupe
statue she had seen in the Candlemas parade. The passion of its
two inhabitants lent a fierce joy to their nonstop battle to keep
their poorest parishioners off the edge of the precipice.

Lizzy didn't say much to her family about these activities:
her father would have worried about her safety, her mother
would have been all amazement at her wishing to mingle with
Catholics and in such sordid surroundings. Mary's religiosity
took an emotional, not a practical, turn, and the younger ones
were off every day in Jenny's car seeking diversion in places
more lively than Lambtown. John was trying hard to find work,
with no success so far, and she didn't want to add to his
anxieties. His tender heart she feared might break if he witnessed the scenes of extremity that were revealed to her, so she
referred to her expeditions only in the most general of terms,
and allowed his imagination to fill in the details according to his
own gentle fancy.

Chapter Seven

With so much to do, Valentine's Day weekend and the Red and White Ball were soon upon them. When all her children appeared, arrayed in their finery, before her, Mrs. Bennet could not but be certain that their conquest of Lambtown was assured of success, for "I can't imagine that a handsomer family will be seen anywhere! Nobody ever had better-looking children than ours."

Mr. Bennet looked up from his book. "And you are as handsome as any of them," he said. "Perhaps I should be going to this affair, to ensure that no manly rancher rides off with you across his saddle-bow."

"You flatter me, my dear. I may have had my share of beauty in my time, but with five grown-up children I should give up thinking of such things."

"In such a case, a woman rarely has much beauty to be thinking of."

Mrs. Bennet bridled, and blushed, and herded the family out to their cars.

The ball was being held in the high school gymnasium, daringly transformed *à la* casbah with yards of pink tenting, filigreed lanterns, and small café tables for intimate conversation. The Bennets were among the early, but not the first, arrivals, as the orchestra was playing a mix of sentimental and jazzy standards from the forties.

They were politely greeted by the president and board of the Hispanic Heritage Club, and then left to their own devices. Fortunately, Frank Carrillo was already present and, recognizing his young acquaintances from the Candlemas parade, came over with his wife to meet the rest of the family.

"I'm sorry to say that my son George hasn't yet arrived," said he, with a teasing glance at Lizzy; "but he'll be here soon, I'm sure, to give himself the pleasure of meeting you properly. I hope you'll save a dance for him."

Lupe Carrillo made an instant hit with Mrs. Bennet by exclaiming over her good-looking family, and they were soon deep in conversation about the joys and trials of motherhood. Mrs. Carrillo, having only one child, was safely inferior to Mrs. Bennet in this regard, so the latter's happiness with her new friend was complete.

John inquired of Mr. Carrillo about the Hispanic Heritage Club.

"Our group was formed in the 1880s, not so long after the first American families settled here, which happened in the 1870s when the stagecoach road went through, followed soon by a railway. Those arteries brought some trade to the area, and the Americans started sheep ranching—hence the name of Lambtown. Before then, all the land had been in the hands of a few Mexican families, who had held the property rights going back to when California was part of Mexico. Our rights to the land were confirmed by the U.S. government when California became a state, but in the 1870s some of the Mexican families started to sell or lose land to the Anglos."

"Was your family here at the time?"

"My Carrillo ancestors held the largest cattle rancho, covering this entire section of the Santa Ynez Valley and up into the canyons to the east—the land that is now owned by the Darcy and de Bourgh families, who were among the first Americanos to arrive. My farmland west of town is all that remains of our original land grant."

"So the club was founded in reaction to the changes taking place?" asked Lizzy.

"The original Spanish-speaking families saw the area becoming Americanized, and waves of immigrants from European countries were also settling here—Italian farmers, Basque sheepherders, later on the Danes at Solvang—and we wanted to band together to preserve some aspects of our traditions and way of life. Over time, the Hispanic Heritage Club became involved in preservation of the Spanish missions in the Santa Ynez, and other philanthropic work. We host the Rodeo Days over Fourth of July weekend, where we have a *charreada*, a display of traditional Mexican riding techniques. It's kind of a relic now, so many of the ranches here have turned to raising thoroughbreds—the ones that haven't converted to vineyard—that it's hard to find local riders who know the old *charreada* style. We have to bring in riders from Mexico for the shows. My son, George, is one of the few local boys who rides in the Rodeo Days. I don't know why more young men don't learn *charreada* skills: it certainly makes George popular with the young ladies!"

"This area seems to have a lot of special events—balls, parades, rodeos," said John. "I didn't realize we'd moved to such a party town!"

"It's not *my* idea of a party town," said Lydon, "with no nightclubs, no bars, not even a cineplex! Have you checked out Mattei's Tavern, over in Los Olivos? Not exactly a happening crowd."

"I'm not sure why *you* are checking out taverns, Lydon, since you're not old enough to drink," said John. Lydon hunched his shoulder.

Mr. Carrillo smiled politely. "Lydon is very right, of course. For younger people's entertainments, you need to go to Lompoc or UC Santa Barbara. Perhaps that's why we have so many special events throughout the year—because everyday life here is so dull."

"Oh, come on, Lydon, I want to dance," said Jenny, and dragged her husband off. Kitty trailed along in their wake, hoping to win a partner from among the scattering of military men present.

"Miss Elizabeth, I understand you have met Father Austen," said Mr. Carrillo.

"Yes, I think he's a dear."

Mr. Carrillo chuckled. "He would hate to hear you say so."

As they talked, Lizzy was taking great pleasure in looking about her at the variety of people and dresses, from dowdy to daring. It mattered little to her that none of the young men present had yet approached her for an introduction or a dance. Nevertheless, it was clear that the Bennet family was attracting a good deal of attention and curiosity; she saw various clusters of people glancing their way as they chatted, and amused herself with imagining the drift of their speculations.

But soon enough the interesting subject of the newcomers gave way to a greater stir of excitement. There was a bustle at the door and everyone turned to gape as a resplendent group of young men and women made their appearance.

"It's those people we saw at the parade, Lizzy," whispered John. Lizzy saw that he was right: the man who had admired John was there, in company with the same group of friends.

"Well, who would ever have thought," cried Mrs. Carrillo, "that Fitzwilliam Darcy himself would grace our ball with his presence!"

"Who is he?" Mrs. Bennet wanted to know.

"See, over there—the tall one," said Mrs. Carrillo, pointing to one of the men in the cluster around John's admirer. "He's our most eligible bachelor, owns half the land in the area, but he doesn't mix much with the locals. Every year he buys tickets to the ball, but he's never attended before. When his parents were alive, it was different. They could be counted on to show up for community events. But young Mr. Darcy is always going around with his prep school and college friends."

"And who are the people with him?" asked John.

"I don't know all of them, but the handsome blond man is Charles Bingley, and the woman in the flapper dress is his sister, Caroline. Bingley is Darcy's best friend from school, and he recently settled here and is opening a business in town. He seems to have quite a lot of money, too, though not as much as Darcy—I hear his father ran a chain of department stores in Oregon or someplace—but he's a lot friendlier than Darcy. Oh, look! They're coming over!"

Mrs. Bennet scarce had time to wreathe her face in smiles for such exalted company before the group was greeting the Carrillos. Charles Bingley, the one who had appeared to take an interest in John, was seen to have an easygoing, open courtesy while the others stood back, prepared to be bored with their surroundings. On Mr. Carrillo's presenting the Bennets, Bingley exclaimed, "Oh, good! New arrivals! I'm glad to be replaced as the new face in town; let the world be inquisitive about someone else for a change. I'm a city boy, and not used to being such a center of attention." Smiling on John, Lizzy, and Mary, he added, "Now that my sister and I are old-timers in Lambtown, maybe we can show you around the way Darcy did for us when we first got here—what do you say, Caroline?"

Caroline gave a faint smile and concurred without noticeable enthusiasm. Undeterred, he turned to Lizzy and suggested, "Why don't we get started by finding our way around the dance floor?"

With a resigned shrug for John, Lizzy assented. Bingley proved to be an excellent dancer and charming companion, with a cheerful line of banter that was amusing without being too personal. Lizzy enjoyed dancing with him, but didn't take his compliments seriously; and he asked enough questions about her brother that she was happy to lead him back to John at the end of their dance. She left them chatting and strolled around to keep an eye on her younger siblings.

Kitty, Lydon, and Jenny had found a congenial group of

young airmen and neighborhood youths, and were having some noisy but apparently harmless fun. The music was shifting into higher gear with *banda* and *norteño* numbers, and Kitty was laughing immoderately at her own attempts to master an unfamiliar dance style under the tutelage of a heavily tattooed young man. At that moment another ripple of excitement moved through the assemblage—or at least the more youthful and female portion of it—as all eyes turned once more to gaze upon a new arrival.

Spurning the *de rigueur* white tie uniform for the evening, Frank Carrillo's son, George, was posed in the doorway, clad in the formal dress of a Mexican cowboy, tight black pants and short jacket adorned with silver, above fancy decorated cowboy boots. A sigh of female ecstasy gusted around the room, and much as she was amused by his skill at drawing attention to himself, Lizzy was not proof against the allure of the picture he presented. He was easily the handsomest man present, even better looking than John, and carried himself with an air of confident athleticism that was not lost on any of the women present. He savored for a moment the happiness of being the man on whom every female eye was trained, and then Lizzy had the happiness of being the woman on whom his attention finally came to rest. He walked straight from the door to her side.

"It is a sin for such a beautiful woman to be standing by the wall while others are dancing," he said.

"I'm loath to shock the neighborhood by sinning in a public place," she replied, smiling.

"Allow me to rescue you from degradation, then. My name is Jorge Carrillo, and I am at your service, Jezebel."

"If you're certain I won't drag you into my depravity…" said Lizzy, as he led her onto the dance floor. Not wishing to carry the line too far, she added, "But I have met your parents, and your father said your name was George?"

He smiled. "So you have been asking about me? My father

has taken on American ways, it's true, but I'm more traditional."

"Jorge it is, then," she agreed, and turned her attention to keeping up with his steps in the *cumbia*. Unlike many of the other youthful dancers, he moved with grace but did not cross the line of propriety; she liked his demeanor, and suddenly found herself enjoying the evening more than she had anticipated.

The dance ended and was succeeded by a slower number, but Jorge exhibited no inclination to lead her to the sidelines. He struck up an easy conversation on neutral subjects, and in speaking of the climate of California versus that of Ohio, the differences between big cities and small towns, and the like proved that the most commonplace topics may be rendered interesting by the skill of the speaker. He was charming and lightly flattering, always turning the conversation to humor before it became too personal.

While attending to her own pleasure, Lizzy still had an eye for her brother's, and she observed that although Charles Bingley danced with a variety of ladies in the room he favored none with special attention, and between each round of dancing he could be seen chatting with John. She asked Jorge about him.

"Charley Bingley? I don't really know him, but everybody seems to like him—even though he hangs out with Darcy."

"Darcy is less popular? I have to admit he looks conceited to me, but I would think his position in the neighborhood would have rescued him from disapproval." They looked across to the refreshments table, where Fitzwilliam Darcy and Caroline Bingley were standing in an uncompanionable silence of shared ennui.

"Oh, the Anglo ranching families think they're superior to everybody—especially their brown neighbors. Some of the cattle and sheep ranchers aren't so bad; they're at least marginally in touch with the real world. But the thoroughbred breeders are totally snooty—they think pursuing the sport of kings makes them royalty. And the Darcys and their cousins the de Bourghs are the worst! I'm amazed Darcy even showed up here; Bingley must have dragged him. Bingley is the social type, and likes mingling. For Darcy an event like this must be torture—how will he ever wash off the stain of rubbing shoulders with dirt like us!"

"But I thought your family was among the original settlers in the neighborhood," said Lizzy, considerably surprised. "Wouldn't that count for something with a snob like Darcy?"

Jorge laughed. "Hardly. The old Anglo families act like history began when they settled here. They've convinced themselves that my father is nothing but an immigrant row-crop farmer."

"But why?"

"Because it's dangerous for them to acknowledge the truth: that they seized half our land illegally. They're nothing more than robber barons, no matter how much they pretend to be the local aristocrats."

Lizzy was shocked. "How could they get away with that?"

"It's not as if California was a civilized place back in the 1870s. It hadn't been a state for long, and American lawmen were few and far between, while the Mexican governors had been chased out. Basically, land ownership was determined by who commanded the most gunfighters."

"Much the way the Spanish and Mexican settlers took land from the Indians, I expect," observed Lizzy.

"Not exactly. The Hispanic settlers here lived side by side with the local tribe, the Chumash: they shared skills and technologies, and farmed and hunted together. That's why most of the remaining Chumash descendants have Spanish surnames—they intermarried and blended into one people. My mother is of Chumash descent; so you could say that we're more of an original family on her side than on my father's."

"But if your land was taken illegally, can't you get it back? Like Jewish families recovering works of art that were stolen from them by the Germans in World War II."

Jorge smiled ruefully. "You know the expression, 'To the victors go the spoils'? The Darcys have all the old land grant papers and other legal documents in their archives, and they don't let anyone have access. That's why Darcy hates me, of course. He thinks everyone should bow down and adore him—and he hangs out only with the people who do! But I call a spade a spade, and he can't stand it."

"What about the de Bourgh family? Are they here tonight?"

Jorge laughed. "You've got to be kidding! Darcy's bad enough, but Catherine de Bourgh is the worst. She's his aunt, you know, and luckily the last of the de Bourgh line. She's old-school—she'd rather hunt varmints like us than dance and drink punch with us. She thinks she's the queen of the valley, and everyone calls her Catherine the Great behind her back."

"I hope she's not as fond of her horses as her namesake," remarked Lizzy.

"Who knows what goes on in that huge, fancy barn of hers? Actually, though, we're lucky she thinks herself too high-and-mighty to mingle with us. The people she *does* see, she likes to boss around and direct their lives. She's always getting in everyone's business."

They were interrupted in this interesting conversation by Mrs. Carrillo, who, thinking her son had paid enough attention to one girl, called him over to dance attendance on the daughter of a friend. Lizzy, intrigued by all she had heard, moved toward the refreshments table to observe Fitzwilliam Darcy more closely.

He proved an unrewarding subject, as he scarcely opened his lips for ten minutes at a stretch. He was a good-looking man, tall and well-built and looking remarkably fine in white tie and tails, but nothing to Jorge Carrillo in her estimation. Lizzy's head was full of Jorge; his gallant manners, the flattering distinction of his singling her out, when it was apparent that he could easily claim the notice of any young lady in the room. As she was thus pleasantly engaged, she observed Charles Bingley accosting Darcy, and made no scruple about listening to their conversation.

"Darcy, why are you standing around like a statue? It's called a dance for a reason: you're supposed to *dance*."

"Do you really expect me to make a spectacle of myself gyrating to this stuff, Charley? It sounds like a polka, for heaven's sake. Besides, who would I dance with? Your sister already has a partner, and there is not another woman in the room who could tempt me out on the floor."

"Oh, come on, Darcy, there are lots of promising girls here. What about one of those Bennets? They're new in town, and very pretty. The elder one, Elizabeth, seems nice, too. She's right over there; let me introduce you."

"Who?" Darcy turned around and met Lizzy's eye before she could turn away. He studied her for a moment and then turned back to Bingley. "You call that 'very pretty'? Besides, I saw her earlier dancing with George Carrillo; if that's the kind of company she prefers, she's welcome to it. You'd better get back to it, Charley; you're wasting your time with me."

Lizzy was left to enjoy the just reward of eavesdropping, but told herself that the source of the slight robbed it of much of its sting. The exchange had confirmed her observations of the man, as well as Jorge's description; and she moved away with no very cordial feelings about him. She told the story with great wit to her mother and John, however, and recovered her good humor in the enjoyment of the ridiculous.

Chapter Eight

The dance provided rich fodder for discussion in the Bennet household the next day, when all their new acquaintances and all they had heard and learned were thoroughly canvassed at lunch after church. The Bingleys and their friends were naturally the focus of Mrs. Bennet's attentions, and more attention was paid to Charles Bingley and speculation over his presumed inclinations than was entirely comfortable for Mary, who held Old Testament views on the subject. Once she had left the room, however, the rest of the family was free to suppose whatever they wished.

"He did dance with a lot of girls," allowed Mrs. Bennet, "but he always came back to stand by John."

John, blushing a little, said he had found Bingley good-humored and able to talk sensibly about a variety of subjects.

Impatient with this evasion, Mrs. Bennet tried another tack. "What do you think, Lizzy? You danced with him: did you get the impression he was gay?"

Mr. Bennet rolled his eyes and said to his elder son, "You'll live to be sorry you took your mother to those meetings—what was that group's name?"

"PFLAG—Parents and Friends of Lesbians and Gays," Lizzy answered for him. "Mama, we're all glad you're now so supportive of your son's sexual orientation, but John can take care of himself in the romance department! And think how embarrassing it would be if you assumed Charles Bingley was gay and he turned out not to be. He didn't give out any hints one way or the other when we were dancing."

"Maybe he isn't sure himself," suggested John. "Sometimes people aren't, you know, especially if they haven't had the opportunity to be around a lot of other gay people. I imagine it might not be too comfortable to be out in a community like this. What do you say we just enjoy making friends with him?"

This was too much to ask of Mrs. Bennet, who had little interest in anyone on whom she could not pin romantic expectations. So she turned her attention to Lizzy, describing to her husband in immoderate terms Darcy's rudeness. "What a proud, unpleasant man! Why did he even attend if all he was going to do was walk here, and walk there, thinking he was better than everybody and too good to dance with Lizzy? I don't care if he *is* the richest bachelor in the neighborhood, I detest him. But at least she was admired by the Carrillo boy—and very handsome he is, too, and a lot nicer! It won't be long before he's calling here, I'm sure."

As if to support her parental authority, the phone rang; but it proved to be Morris Collins. "I was concerned that since you're new in town," he told Lizzy, "you might have no one to wish you a happy Valentine's Day."

"That would be a great pity, wouldn't it?" she replied, mindful that her family was listening.

"The honor of Lambtown must be upheld, and, as mayor, it is my honor to uphold it. It's important that we pay heed to the demands of society and not neglect such occasions as this to pay the kinds of compliments as may be appealing to ladies."

Lizzy made a noncommittal reply, reflecting inwardly that his explanation robbed the compliment of much of its value.

"Of course," persisted Mr. Collins, "when the ladies in question are as charming as you—and all the females of your family, I need not add—one's duty and one's pleasure coincide. So—"

Alarmed at the direction in which his remarks seemed to be tending, Lizzy cut in. "I'm certain all of my family will be grateful to you for your kind thought, Mr. Collins," she said. "I'll be sure to pass your good wishes along to them. Good-bye now."

Jorge waited the standard three days before calling, but call he did, and met with a warmer reception. His happy notion was that Lizzy, as a gardener, might like to see more of the native plants in the area, so he proposed a drive up into Los Padres National Forest the following Saturday. To this she agreed, reflecting that after a long week closeted with the carpenter, laying plans for the transformation of Aunt Evelyn's house, a day spent out of doors would be exactly what she needed.

It proved to be one of those perfect winter days for which California is justly famous: the sun shone through just a hint of chill in a sky of deepest blue, against which the mountains to the east of the valley were sharply etched. It was too early in the year for most wildflowers and the oaks in the cattle pastures were still leafless, but the effects of the rainy season could be seen in a green haze spread over the rounded foothills. They drove through vineyards, bare at this time of year, and climbed gradually into more rugged, mountainous terrain. Perched high above the road in the cab of Jorge's pickup, Lizzy felt that life held few greater pleasures.

As they reached the elevation where pines began to mingle with the oaks, the shrubbery was covered with clusters of white flowers like veils cast over the heads of the slopes, their scent heavy on the air. Jorge called this buckthorn and said there were blue varieties that came out later, when the California poppies were in bloom. When Lizzy remarked on the brilliant green stone formations along the way, Jorge beguiled her ear with tales of nineteenth-century plunderers of serpentine and cinnabar.

The road topped a high ridge and descended steeply into a canyon, where they stopped at a picnic table shaded by sycamores to eat lunch. As they ate, grosbeaks and warblers sang out melodious territorial admonitions around them, and a cold running stream gurgled past their feet. Lizzy was entranced by all the unfamiliar plants and birds, and no less so by her companion, who spoke knowledgeably about the natural and human history of the area, from the geology to the medicinal uses the local Chumash Indians had found for the plants they encountered, and how she could avoid hazards like poison oak. She felt all the envy that a descendant of immigrants might be expected to feel for someone whose roots were planted far deeper in their homeland, who seemed to her more authentically American than she could ever aspire to be. He had a true history with the place he inhabited, and she liked him for taking pride in his heritage.

They descended the mountains by another road into a beautiful little valley of well-tended cattle and horse pastures. Lizzy admired the tidy white fences, the sprawling meadows beside cottonwood-lined streambeds, and entertained romantic visions of a life lived in harmony with surroundings such as these.

They stopped to watch some heavily pregnant mares that were cropping eagerly at the lush grass. Jorge's mood turned melancholy. "This canyon is one of my favorite places on earth," he said. "Every time I come here I wonder how my ancestors could have forfeited this land to the Darcys and de Bourghs."

"Oh! Is this their land?"

"Yes, this is part of Pemberley Ranch. Darcy owns most of the canyon, and the hills on both sides, and the watershed. His ancestors managed to secure both appropriative and pueblo water rights over the stream, and nobody around gets water for their fields without his permission. His life might have been mine, as it was my ancestors'. It's very painful to see this land, which was the heart of my family's life going back centuries, millennia even, in someone else's hands—especially in the hands of that jerk Darcy."

"He seems to take good care of it."

"Oh, I think he does, in his way. His pride would demand that he follow good stewardship practices, so his neighbors would have nothing to despise him for. But it doesn't come from his heart. It isn't part of who he is, the way it is for me. For him it's a matter of his reputation, and of good business. I've heard he's thinking of switching from ranching to planting vineyards, because he could make more money."

Remembering the vineyards they had driven through—artificially sculpted hillsides stripped of all trees, with trellis poles marching up the slopes in precisely spaced rows—Lizzy was distressed. "I know the vineyards are supposed to be beautiful, and I like wine as much as the next person, but it would ruin this canyon if they did that!"

Jorge agreed. "The vineyards always look to me like military graveyards; they're so depressing. And to cultivate the grapes you have to keep out the birds, the raccoons—none of the wildlife can thrive in a controlled monoculture environment like that. Ranching has always found a way to coexist with the chaparral, but winegrowing is more lucrative, so what do the landowners care? As long as they make their buck."

"It would be terrible to destroy this beautiful place just to extract more profit from it!"

"I feel exactly as you do, and I don't come here very often because I dread what I might see," said Jorge. "I used to work here in the summers when I was a teenager and old Mr. Darcy was alive; he was okay. But now I'm not welcome, and I haven't set foot on the land for several years."

"What was it like, having to be just an employee on land that should have been your own?"

"Oh, in those days I didn't care, I just wanted to earn a little money, and have the chance to be here. The stories my mother told me when I was little, the traditional tales of her people— you can recognize some of the landmarks described in them out here. For instance, there's one story that talks about an ancient manzanita that has arched over itself and formed a tunnel; one day, while I was hunting for a lost calf, I found it, just up and over that ridge there. Those old tales—where they took place is like a character in the story, you know? And so when I wandered on this land, it was like the stories were coming back to life, like no time had passed, and everything the Anglos have done could just disappear. Like my people were still here, and free."

"It doesn't seem fair that people who want land only to extract monetary value from it should have property rights that supersede those of people whose souls are all intertwined with it. In a just world, the opposite would be true. But why aren't you welcome here anymore?"

"Old Mr. Darcy never treated me like an inferior. He was the salt of the earth, not a snooty preppy like his son. Old Mr. Darcy would pick up a shovel and work right alongside you. He liked me, which his son couldn't stand. So after he died, his son found an excuse to fire me."

"Darcy has lost both his parents, hasn't he? Were they older people?" asked Lizzy.

"No, they both died in a car crash. They were hit by a drunk driver on San Marcos Pass one night, when they were coming home from a concert in Ojai. Practically the whole valley came to the funeral; everybody liked them. But Darcy wouldn't speak at the memorial, and didn't talk to any of his neighbors. He just sat there like nothing had happened."

Their date gave Lizzy much to ponder, about her adopted community and about how different two young men from the same place could be. She ended the day even more pleased with Jorge Carrillo than before. She had never met anyone like him. It seemed to her that he combined a lively charm with very proper feelings on things that mattered. They agreed on everything. And the injustice he and his family had suffered at the hands of the Darcys made him particularly interesting to her affectionate heart. Her passion for justice was aroused, and she longed to find a way to recoup what he had lost and bring the current Darcy low.

Chapter Nine

The memorial for Aunt Evelyn was now upon them, and Lizzy, hoping to persuade all her family to attend, spent hours locating appropriate readings for each one. In this effort she was not entirely successful, as her relations had their own ideas of taste. Lydon, who had just seen *Splendor in the Grass* for the first time and was enamored of Natalie Wood, was determined to read Wordsworth's lines from which the title was drawn, shrugging off John's objection that the poem was about the death of a child. Mary pored mightily over her Bible and in the end settled, to Lizzy's disappointment if not surprise, on the Ninetieth Psalm ("You have set our iniquities before You, our secret sins in the light of Your countenance. For all our days have passed away in Your wrath; we finish our years like a sigh"). Kitty and Jenny refused to read anything at all, and Lizzy was inclined to think that the less her younger siblings were heard from at the event, the better.

On arriving at the Gardiners' house, the Bennets discovered quite a motley crowd assembled. Lizzy recognized some of the faces from the ball, and turned sharply to avoid meeting Morris Collins's eye, colliding with Charley Bingley as she did so. He promptly led her and John off to make further introductions among the younger set. His friends all had a sleek, well-fed look that led Lizzy to guess that these were members of the Enclave families Mr. Collins had made so much of. The appraising way some of them sized up her clothes confirmed her surmise, and she found herself every bit as ready to dismiss them from her mind as they were eager to abandon her and cluster around Fitzwilliam Darcy when he appeared in the doorway. But her satirical grimace in John's direction was intercepted by one young woman, less glossy than the rest, who smiled at her with shrewd comprehension.

"Charlotte Lucas," she reminded Lizzy, extending her hand as John strolled off with Charley, chattering animatedly. "They *are* a little transparent, aren't they?"

"I can't quarrel with their taste in slighting me," said Lizzy, "but I'm not sure fawning over Fitzwilliam Darcy is much of a compliment to their understanding. And I'm certain it isn't good for him to be so lionized: he seems by nature very proud, and such attentions can only make him smug."

"Is it any wonder that such a fine young man, with family background, money, everything else in his favor, should think highly of himself?"

"I would think more highly of him if he didn't think of himself at all."

"But who among us has the nobility of spirit to do that?"

"Very true," agreed Lizzy with a laugh.

Caroline Bingley drifted up to them, looking and smelling expensive. "Ah, Charlotte, Elizabeth Bennet," she said, doing them the honor of remembering their names. "What a mob this is. I certainly hope not everyone plans to read, or we'll be here all night! And what do you suppose *they* are doing here?" she demanded, indicating a pair of Mexican men, standing apart in a corner looking stiffly awkward. "Are we going to have Spanish poetry as well as English?"

"Neruda has some beautiful poems about love and loss," Lizzy couldn't resist saying.

"I heard that they worked for Evelyn Bennet in her garden," said Charlotte.

"In that case, I should go speak with them," said Lizzy promptly, seizing her chance to escape Caroline Bingley.

She was rescued at length from her laborious attempts in halting Spanish to make the men feel welcome by Mrs. Gardiner's calling the group to order. "Thank you all for coming this evening to honor our dear friend Evelyn Bennet. As most of you know, many years ago she created a forum for her friends and neighbors to enjoy the companionship of the mind—the group of readers we have known as the Live Poets Reading Society. We've gathered each month ever since and read aloud to one another from works serious and frivolous, in poetry and prose, anything that inspired us, intrigued us, entertained or enlightened us. Our group has no assignments, no deadlines or rules to follow—we simply get together to enjoy the fellowship of the written word.

"It is difficult to imagine our circle of friends without her in it, but equally difficult to imagine a better way of honoring her than by meeting to read in her memory. We hope these readings will bring her among us once again.

"But we know our meetings will never be quite the same, so those of us who have participated in the Live Poets for years spoke over the weekend and decided that we can be Live Poets no longer. We will go on meeting and reading together, but henceforth we will be known as simply the Poets—for the heart of the Live Poets is gone."

She paused to collect herself, and continued: "Before her voice was silenced but when she knew she had little time left, she asked me to read something to you after she was gone. So here are the last words of Evelyn Bennet, as composed by Christina Rossetti." And she recited Rossetti's "Remember":

Remember me when I am gone away
Gone far away into the silent land . . .

The readings ranged over a wide variety of styles and reflected many tastes. Some evoked personal details of Evelyn Bennet's life, while others were more universal expressions of death and loss. For Fitzwilliam Darcy, who had known her only slightly, the evening began with feelings of discomfort and regret that he should have yielded to Caroline Bingley's insistence that they attend. He felt himself to be intruding on others' grief, and was wary of the danger that the occasion might revive his feelings about the loss of his parents, which he had struggled always to keep under regulation. And it was as he feared: the language of the readings worked a transformation on him as he listened, opening his heart to the commonality of bereavement and requiring the utmost self-control to maintain his outward composure.

Having observed enough of the Bennet family at the Red and White Ball to anticipate their contributions with little enthusiasm, he was pleasantly surprised by Mr. Bennet. He liked the dry reserve with which he read some lines of Swinburne's:

From too much love of living,
From hope and fear set free,
We thank with brief thanksgiving
Whatever gods may be
That no life lives forever;
That dead men rise up never;
That even the weariest river
Winds somewhere safe to sea.

Darcy wondered if the man realized how many different ways those words could be taken, and thought with wry amusement that he did.

But the simple lines of William Penn's "Union of Friends," read by Edward Gardiner, effected his undoing: "Death cannot kill, what never dies . . . Death is but Crossing the World, as Friends do the Seas; they live in one another still."

Darcy was thus experiencing an unfamiliar state of emotional vulnerability when one of the Bennet girls arose to speak. He recognized her vaguely as the one who had danced with George Carrillo, and prepared himself for inanity. She named the author of her selection, a poetess he had never heard of, and the name— Pattiann Rogers—did not inspire him with optimism.

Lizzy stood before the group of strangers a little breathless, concerned to do proper honor to her aunt and her own feelings, and unsure how her reading would be received. But there was nothing for it but to forge ahead.

All morning long
they kept coming back, the jays,
five of them, blue-grey, purple-banded,
strident, disruptive. They screamed
with their whole bodies from the branches
of the pine, tipped forward, heads
toward earth, and swept across the lawn
into the oleanders, dipping low
as they flew over the half-skull
and beak, the blood-end of one wing
lying intact, over the fluff
of feathers scattered and drifting
occasionally, easily as a dandelion—
all that the cat had left.

Darcy lost the thread of the poem for a moment in his astonishment. What could this girl be about? What had this folderol about a dead bird to do with anything? But even as he told himself of his outrage, he could not take his eyes off her, the way her whole body vibrated as she plunged through the words. He dragged his mind back to attention.

Mothers, fathers, our kind, tell me again
that death doesn't matter. Tell me
it's just a limitation of vision, a fold

of landscape, a deep flax-and-poppy-filled
gully hidden on a hill, a pleat
in our perception . . .

Darcy felt the turn in the poem, and unconsciously leaned
forward to meet what was coming.

But this time, whatever is said,
when it's said, will have to be more
reverent and more rude, more absolute,
more convincing than these five jays
who have become the five wheeling spokes
and stays of perfect lament, who, without knowing
anything, have accurately matched the black
beaks and spread shoulders of their bodies
to all the shrill, bird-shaped histories
of grief; will have to be demanding enough,
subtle enough, shocking enough, sovereign
enough, right enough to rouse me, to move me
from this window where I have pressed
my forehead against the unyielding pane,
unyielding all morning long.

After this extraordinary recitation the girl sat down again
without ceremony. To Darcy it was as if she had stripped naked
and run through the room—and he was mortified to find himself
dwelling on this analogy rather longer than was necessary—but
he could not entirely convince himself that he was outraged. No
sooner had he gotten it clear in his mind that she was outré, a
philistine, than his thoughts returned to dwell on the recollection
of her intensity, hypnotized by the little breaths she took between lines, the concentration in her dark eyes. And he could
not ignore the inconvenient truth that after the first major loss
of his own life—that of his parents—he had felt the same in-

tractable pain, the same stubborn tenacity of grief that echoed through her words. The readings went on, but not even Shelley's "Adonais," Whitman's "Last Invocation," or the stray Psalm could fix his attention.

At last the final reading was complete, and Darcy found Caroline Bingley at his elbow. "I can guess what you're thinking," she said.

"I certainly hope not."

"You're congratulating yourself on your good fortune in never having been so foolish as to join the Live Poets. Can you imagine spending many evenings in this fashion? The insipidity and yet the noise; the nothingness and yet the self-importance of these people! I must hear your thoughts on the subject."

"You're doomed to disappointment, I'm afraid. I considered it a very appropriate way to honor a friend's memory; and my thoughts were running on more agreeable lines. I was meditating on how the honest expression of authentic emotion can enhance a woman's beauty."

Caroline immediately demanded to know who had inspired these reflections.

Still in the grip of poetry's enchantment, Darcy replied, "Elizabeth Bennet."

"Elizabeth Bennet! The passionate little birdwatcher! You astonish me. Maybe you're smelling the roses because your inamorata is a gardener. Did you know that Lizzy Bennet is a gardener? She's working for some friends of mine. When you're married, she can re-landscape Pemberley Ranch—tear out all your mother's beautiful flowerbeds."

"A woman's imagination is very rapid; it jumps from admiration to love, and from love to marriage, in a moment."

"Oh, I think it was *your* imagination that did that," said Caroline. But seeing him retire behind his habitual wall of indifference, her fears were allayed, and she continued to indulge her wit at the expense of the Bennets and the neighborhood at large.

Chapter Ten

A t breakfast the next morning John had some news to impart. "I'm starting a job today. Charley Bingley—" he colored slightly as every eye at the table turned his way—"is opening a chocolate shop in a few weeks, and he wants me to work there. He thinks I'll be good with the kids. He says there are too many places in town that cater only to adult tourists—the wine-tasting rooms, galleries, and stuff—and Lambtown needs more family-friendly businesses. I'm going over there this morning to help with decorating ideas and taste the varieties of hot chocolate that are going to be served."

The entire Bennet family dived enthusiastically into speculation and suggestion. Were pastries going to be sold? Lunches? Was it more gourmet shop or teddy-bear tea room? But Kitty, everyone agreed, came up with the best idea. "I remember once eating in a restaurant that had children's advice painted on the walls. Things like 'Never trust a dog to watch your food.' Maybe you could collect chocolate sayings and use them for decoration, or print them on the table mats or something. They would be good conversation starters, and would put people in the chocolate mood."

Not even Mary could find any harm in this, and everyone immediately began to throw out suggestions.

"It's never a bad time for chocolate."

"The future is uncertain: eat the chocolate first."

"If you have melted chocolate on your hands, you're eating too slowly."

"Forget love—I'd rather fall in chocolate!" cried Lizzy, getting up to find a pad and pencil so she could record their ideas.

"Save the Earth—it's the only planet with chocolate," said Mr. Bennet, emerging momentarily from behind the paper.

"Some things in life are better rich: coffee, chocolate, men," said Mrs. Bennet.

Mary, blushing at her own audacity, proposed, "If God had intended us to be thin, he would not have created chocolate."

"Why should I have only one piece of chocolate when I have two hands?"

Soon they were waving off the eldest-born for his first day of work armed with two pages of sayings. Lizzy accompanied John on his walk because she needed to buy a hoe in town. Before they reached the town center, they were joined by Bingley and Darcy, also making for the chocolate shop. As John regaled Charley with the list of epigrams, Lizzy was left to walk behind with Darcy. He appeared disinclined to speak, so she didn't trouble herself to propose a topic of conversation, until they came to the middle of a block, where she noticed a broad dirt track running through a gap between two buildings. She stopped and peered down its length, observing that it continued for a considerable distance in either direction, interrupted only by the paved streets.

"This was originally the route of the narrow-gauge railway that ran through the Santa Ynez Valley in the 1870s," explained Darcy. "When the tracks were torn out, the right-of-way became a bridle path."

To Lizzy's horticultural mind, any stretch of bare dirt was a wasted opportunity. She asked, "Do people still ride on it?"

"Not to my knowledge. None of the shops have hitching posts any longer, so there would be no convenient place to tie up in town."

"So it's derelict space."

"Long-term residents would probably prefer to regard it as a historical landmark," he said quellingly.

Indifferent to Darcy's reproof, Lizzy parted from the group and made her way to the tool store, her mind alive with conjecture. She was remembering her aunt's fondness for working the soil, her desire to bring together the parallel but segregated lives of the people here. She thought about the farmworkers' families who couldn't afford to buy the fresh fruits and vegetables they tended in the fields; whose lives were invisible to the property-owning residents of Lambtown; who slipped in and out of the town center like shadows, trying not to be seen. The old bridle path would provide an ideal space for community garden plots! Shouldering her new hoe, she set off to find Father Austen.

He was unencouraging. "Who owns the right-of-way?" he demanded. "City? County? Have you ever tried bringing up an idea before the Planning Commission in these parts? It's like the First World War without the bunkers."

"I was thinking in more informal terms," Lizzy confessed. "Just give anyone who was interested a twenty-five-foot section and get a bunch of volunteers out on a weekend to dig and plant. Maybe nurseries would donate tools and seeds? Wouldn't the local garden club be interested in taking on a project like this?"

"The garden club is Enclave."

"Well, then, they could afford to support it, couldn't they?"

"Don't be stupider than you have to be, girl! If they didn't want the bridle path to be a bridle path, it would be something else. They think it lends tone—reminds them of the days when the landowners were all-powerful. The wasted space shows that we're a community that can afford to waste space."

"Maybe the shopkeepers would support it as a civic beautification project."

"They might if you were planting flowers, though many of them probably use the space for making deliveries to the back of their shops. And even if the shopkeepers were on board, the Enclave would think flowers were too bourgeois. Vegetables for immigrant laborers? You're dreaming." He paused, champing his jaw. "Talk to Rose. She's just such a dreamer as yourself."

Lizzy was undaunted, and she was certain she knew where to turn for help. Rose being out for the day, she went to see the Carrillos.

Mrs. Carrillo welcomed her into the retrofitted adobe that was their farmhouse and said she was just fixing lunch; her husband would be in from the fields shortly. "Put me to work," said Lizzy promptly; "I'm from a family of eight, and can cook anything."

As they worked side by side, Lizzy resisted the impulse to speak either about her community garden idea or about Mrs. Carrillo's son, but instead engaged her in small talk about the neighborhood, the valley, and the herbs flavoring the chicken soup on the stove. Like Jorge, Lupe Carrillo was well versed in the traditions of her Chumash ancestors, and soon she was offering Lizzy a bite of miner's lettuce she had collected from a damp spot on the property, giving her a comparative taste of oregano and *epazote,* and holding forth knowledgeably about the leaching step essential to making acorn flour. "Not that I ever use acorn flour," she added. "It's one thing to respect tradition, but another to be a slave to it. When the supermarket is ten minutes away, it's a stupid Indian who would spend days soaking and drying and grinding flour."

"Still, it's nice to know that some people preserve old skills. One day a massive earthquake on the San Andreas Fault may demolish the tribal casino, and somebody will have to know how to put dinner on the table."

Mrs. Carrillo gave a snort. "Most of the folks around here who call themselves Indians would be pretty well lost if *that* ever happened! Me, I like to live the way I have always lived, casino or no."

The kitchen door opened and Frank Carrillo appeared, pulling off his muddy work boots on the mat. He greeted Lizzy affably and added, "Is George home for lunch, then?"

As Lizzy blushed Mrs. Carrillo replied, with a minatory glare at her husband, "I don't expect him. Elizabeth stopped in to visit you, and she's been such a help."

Once they were settled at the table, Lizzy broached her idea. "I want to create a community garden in my aunt's memory. It would be open to anyone who wanted to cultivate a plot, but the main priority would be to offer space for the farmworkers' families to grow some fresh food for themselves. It would help their children get better nutrition. And their place in valley life seems so tenuous—I thought it might integrate them more into the community if they were seen to be doing something productive, permanent. *You* know many of them, both as an employer and as a fellow parishioner: what do you think?"

"Are you asking if I would give over some of my land for a co-op farming scheme?"

"Not at all; I've found some unused space in Lambtown that would be great for it. I'm asking if you think people would like the idea—if they would participate."

"Well, farmworkers put in long hours of hard labor already," said Mr. Carrillo dubiously. "I'm not sure they'd want to spend their time off doing more of the same."

"Maybe the women and children would do most of the work? And the fathers might like to teach them, to pass on their expertise to the younger generation? It could be good for strengthening family ties."

"Maybe," said Mr. Carrillo, "though many of the women also work in the fields, and many of the men like to drink in their time off." Lizzy blinked but said nothing. "And of course, many—possibly most—of them are illegal; they try not to be too visible, for fear of *la migra*—the INS. With my own workers I tend to follow a 'Don't ask, don't tell' policy. My foreman hires them through a contractor, who checks their papers, so it's not my responsibility to know their status. As long as they do the work, I pay them cheerfully and don't pry. They're allowed to keep any produce from my fields that isn't marketworthy, and most of the farmers hereabouts do the same."

"That's very generous," said Lizzy tactfully. "But do you think it might be a source of pride to grow their own food? To have a bit of soil they could call their own? Even if they didn't *own* it per se, they would have control over it."

Mrs. Carrillo smiled. "The way you describe it, it sounds wonderful. Just maybe don't get your hopes too high that everyone will see it the way you do."

"Many of the workers are migrants," added Mr. Carrillo. "They go up and down the state, and even into Oregon and Washington, as different crops need tending or harvesting. They might not be here to reap what they sowed in the garden. The people who would be the most in need of supplementing their diets are the least likely to be in a position to take advantage of the opportunity."

Lizzy was appalled. "And their whole families travel with them? How do the children ever get any education?"

"Often they don't," said Mrs. Carrillo. "Extended families with a good support network can sometimes afford to keep a home base in one area, especially if one member of the family has managed to get a permanent job. But their lives depend a lot on luck — all the working members of the family staying healthy, work being available in the right place at the right time, nobody having an accident or getting deported. It's hard to get a secure foothold in this country, especially for the rural indigenous people of Mexico and Central America who don't even speak Spanish, much less English. Planting a garden, watering and tending it over a whole season, harvesting — that might be a bridge too far for many of them."

"Where is this unused space you've found?" Mr. Carrillo wanted to know.

"It goes right through the middle of town. I was told it used to be a bridle path, but now nobody rides into downtown

Lambtown anymore and it's just sitting there, not being used."

"*The bridle path?*" Mr. Carrillo burst out laughing. "That precious artifact of Anglo history, where the railroad went through? To hear the Enclave families talk about it, you'd think it was the cradle of civilization. It'd sure tweak their noses to co-opt it for the natives' use."

He sat with his thoughts for a moment, a look of mischief betraying their tendency. "You should tell George about this," he said suddenly. "He would love the idea of taking back the land, even just symbolically. And he's a great gardener, you know."

"Frank!" cried Mrs. Carrillo in a scandalized tone.

A look passed between husband and wife. "Well, it would be something constructive," said Mr. Carrillo defensively.

"But would it be legal?" asked Mrs. Carrillo.

"What's the worst that could happen?" replied her spouse. Then, remembering their guest, he added decisively, "I'll tell George about your idea. I'll bet he'd be happy to help you. I can donate mulch and seeds if you get it off the ground."

Well satisfied, Lizzy headed off to Mr. Gardiner's nursery to solicit a donation of hoses, shovels, and work gloves.

Chapter Eleven

In the days that followed, a variety of Lambtown residents proved unable to resist the appeal of Lizzy's enthusiasm, even the practical Rose finding herself drawn into a supporting role. As predicted, Jorge was delighted with the scheme, and if he was rarely available to provide material assistance he was always willing to offer moral support and an attentive ear to tales of the project's ups and downs. Taking seriously the warnings she had been given, Lizzy tried to be discreet, but it was impossible that the plan should fail to become known beyond her immediate confidants. She learned that the secret was out after church a few weeks later, when Morris Collins came striding through the chattering congregants so purposefully that there was no time to conceal herself. Taking her arm in a proprietary manner that she found odious, he drew her a little apart from her family.

"Miss Elizabeth," he said, "I'm glad of the opportunity to speak with you. You're a very elusive young lady, always flitting here, and flitting there, and never at home when I call. I would think you were avoiding me—" he chuckled indulgently—"had I not been hearing from all sides about your many and varied activities. If it isn't helping to decorate Mr. Bingley's Chocolate Bar, it's doing renovations on your aunt's house—though if you would allow me to offer some advice on that score, as a person who has lived here all my life, and owing to my position as the mayor may be thought to have my finger on the pulse of the community, so to speak—it would be wiser to hire a local carpenter instead of bringing one in from Lompoc. It gives a secretive impression, which I'm sure you didn't intend, but people will place their own construction on your actions, however innocently you meant them."

Lizzy had nothing to say on this subject, of course, as she could scarcely reveal that the out-of-town carpenter was engaged to build bookcases for the secret library; but mercifully, Morris was moving on to his next grievance. "And I even hear that you're doing good works among the poor, with the staff of Our Lady of Guadalupe—though of course here at All Saints' there are opportunities to satisfy the charitable impulse, so it might not be thought necessary to stray among the Catholics. But I'm glad to have this opportunity to venture a humble suggestion to you, if I may be so bold as to give you some guidance, about some of your activities in the, shall we say, *horticultural* arena? The leadership of the Enclave is very interested in your family, your aunt having been a respected member of the community, and your brother John being so popular with Charles Bingley and his friends, and, I might add, I myself having made a point of mentioning you to Catherine de Bourgh! I think I'm not saying too much if I just mention that they're considering extending to the Bennet family a most flattering invitation. But if I might just drop you a little hint, nothing could be more harmful to your chances of joining the Enclave than working in other people's gardens, especially for such city types as the Winiarskis—well enough in their way, I'm sure, but not true Lambtonians—"

"But Mr. Collins, I'm a gardener," interjected Lizzy as he drew breath. "I must have something to live on just like everyone else, and how am I to do so if I don't pursue my profession?"

"Yes, yes, of course, it's important to be an active person, and gardening—such as your aunt pursued, growing flowers on her own property—is a very genteel activity. But these stories I'm hearing, of plans for a public garden, for illegals to grow vegetables somewhere right in town—! That would be a disaster! Trust me, the Enclave families won't tolerate any such goings-on. For you to entangle yourself with an undertaking of that kind would ruin everything for you here. I must beg you to think about what you're doing. You'd be shunned; nobody will speak to you!"

"Might I interrupt?" asked Charlotte Lucas, approaching with a look of demure amusement that said she had overheard at least some portion of this speech. "I'm sure you'll forgive me, Morris, but I need to speak with Lizzy." Mr. Collins had no choice but to bow himself away, disgruntled.

"Thank you," said Lizzy.

Charlotte laughed. "Did I hear him right, was he warning you about your community garden plan?"

"Does the whole town know about it?"

"Pretty much. I don't know when I've enjoyed myself so thoroughly, watching all the gossip and hand-wringing. You and your family certainly are livening things up around here. Personally, I think it's a great idea: helping people to help themselves. Why not? Folks would love the plan if they had thought of it on their own; all the old rancher families hate welfare, and worship hard work and self-sufficiency. You don't strike me as being particularly the social butterfly type, but if you ever want to meet some of the so-called leading families, I'd be happy to take you along to one of their shindigs. They're just nervous because they don't know you." Without waiting for any polite expressions of gratitude, she continued, "And you could do me a favor. I'm dying to be the first to get a peek inside The Chocolate Bar, and I hear your brother is close to Charles Bingley. Any chance—?"

"John is going to be working there," said Lizzy. "We were just heading over to do some last-minute work before the opening tomorrow. Why don't you come along?"

They stopped on the way to pick up sandwiches for the work crew, and upon arrival discovered the place to be abuzz with activity. The odor of fresh paint (with a few drops of vanilla added to cut the chemical fumes) vied with enticing scents emanating from the kitchen, where baking was under way for the opening day's pastry display. Couches and armchairs grouped around the walls were swathed in drop cloths so that John and Charley, on ladders at opposite ends of the room, could finish stenciling the chocolate sayings above the windows. Other baristas-in-waiting were washing glasses, stacking mugs and napkins, and arranging stools around the high oval tables in the middle of the shop. To Lizzy's amazement, even Fitzwilliam Darcy had turned up after church, shedding his tweed jacket to carry a tray piled high with small plates from the back room out to the counter.

The arrival of the sandwiches led to an alteration in the scene; the drop cloths were whisked away and everyone settled down in groups to eat. Lizzy had the satisfaction of observing that Charley and John gravitated toward a pair of armchairs set a little apart; her pleasure remained undiminished even though this arrangement meant that she and Charlotte were left tête-à-tête with Darcy. He seemed ready enough to sit with them, though once settled with his plate and glass of iced tea he had little to offer to the conversation.

Charlotte inquired politely whether he was expecting a good foaling season and he replied that he was, but when he failed to elaborate on the subject she made no effort to pursue it. She commented approvingly on various arrangements in the shop—the color scheme, the stylish martini glasses for the Aztec chocolate drinks, the bookshelf and modem hookups that aimed to encourage people to linger, the puzzles and games stacked in baskets to amuse younger visitors. Lizzy regaled her with some of the chocolate epigrams that her family had been coining for days, which had grown increasingly outrageous and unsuitable for a family establishment, until Darcy finally shot to his feet and fled to the storeroom, chased by their laughter.

"PMS jokes work every time!" said Lizzy. "I knew I could scare him off. Why did he have to sit here, if all he was going to do was stare down his nose and never open his mouth?"

"Has it occurred to you that maybe he likes you?"

"I certainly hope not! I can't for the life of me understand why Charley likes *him*. Charley's so friendly and easygoing; he gets along with everyone, while Darcy gives offense wherever he goes."

"You won't find too many people around here who dare to be offended by Darcy's manner," cautioned Charlotte. "He's not talkative, and because he was sent away to school he doesn't have a lot of friends of his own age among the locals. But the Darcys have been important in the valley throughout its history—there probably wouldn't even be a Lambtown without them. His parents were very involved in the community, and they quietly helped a lot of people through hard times. They established the area as a major center for thoroughbred breeding, using their Kentucky connections. Darcy's first name comes from his cousins the Fitzwilliams, you know: they've won more Derbies than any other breeders. And the Darcys have always been very fair about water distribution. He may not be hail-fellow-well-met, but he's a good land steward and a good neighbor."

"So people are nice to him because he's rich and they can't afford to offend him. I prefer a Charley Bingley—people are nice to him because they actually like him."

"Charley certainly is good-natured, and he has a way of disarming even those who might be prejudiced against him—this is a pretty conservative area, you know."

"How could anyone be nasty to someone as sweet-tempered as Charley?" cried Lizzy.

"Some people may tolerate him only because they see that he's under Darcy's wing; Darcy's a protective friend, and won't let anyone be rude to him."

"Well, if Darcy can keep people from hurting Charley's feelings, I suppose he has his uses. You *would* try to make me do justice to a man I am determined to hate! Don't wish me such an evil."

Charlotte smiled but said no more.

The opening of The Chocolate Bar was soon upon them, but Charley Bingley's sunny aspirations for his enterprise were unsupported by the day, which dawned rainy and cold. Indeed, as John remarked ruefully, the sky was so gloomy that the day could scarcely be said to have dawned at all. Monday was a slow time in Lambtown anyway, as most of the winery tourists were weekend visitors; and John greatly feared that the inclement weather would keep all the townspeople at home. A ribbon-cutting ceremony had been planned, with the town council in attendance and Bingley and Morris Collins doing the honors, but even this would have to take place indoors. Would the opening be entirely ignored by the community? Would Charley and John sit all day waiting for customers who never materialized?

Mrs. Bennet was happy enough to think of the pair walled up for hours in solitude, face to face over a tray of *pain au chocolat*, but Lizzy saw her duty clear and did not hesitate. "I have no Monday clients, and even if I did I couldn't work the soil on a wet day like this," she said. "I have to stop in briefly at Aunt Evelyn's house to speak with the carpenter, but then I'll be free to spend the whole day at the shop. I can sit right by the window so the place will look busy."

John protested against such a sacrifice.

"No sacrifice involved, I assure you! I'll visit with you when things are slow, and read or work on garden designs while you're busy; and you can ply me with treats till I'm too fat to fit through the door. Maybe I should bring a few changes of clothing—or a disguise—so it will appear that different customers are sitting there at different times of the day."

John had to smile at her nonsense, but could not give over worrying altogether. He paced here, and paced there, and changed his sweater several times before the hour arrived.

John and Lizzy found Charley little calmer. He was fussing over the arrangement of pastries in the case, and moving the silverware from one spot to another and back again. He greeted them absentmindedly and then exclaimed without warning, "Dusty Springfield has died!"

Lizzy murmured sympathetically, and said she had a Dusty Springfield tape in her truck; would Charley like to play it over the P.A. system as a tribute?

Darcy, arriving at that moment and shaking out his umbrella on the doorstep, remarked that Stanley Kubrick had also died over the weekend: "Perhaps you could add to the gloom by projecting *A Clockwork Orange* on the walls," he said.

Lizzy glared at his lack of sympathy for his friend's feelings, but Bingley just rolled his eyes and laughed reluctantly. "Darcy can be a nasty piece of work when the weather puts him out of sorts. A day like today, when he can't be riding the range, brings out the worst in his nature. But I won't be afraid of him, with his great height and his cutting tongue. I'll simply refuse him service and he'll go away soon." He accepted the offer of the Dusty Springfield tape, and Lizzy, with an arch look of triumph in Darcy's direction, seized his umbrella and scurried out to find it.

When she returned, the dignitaries were arriving. Morris Collins hastened to her side with expressions of solicitude. "You're soaked through, Miss Lizzy! You'll catch your death if you aren't more careful!" He would not hear her stout denials and assurances that an Ohio native was not easily harmed by such winter weather as central California offered; and he could scarcely be drawn away from fussing over her until the scissors were pushed into his hand for the ribbon-cutting. Lizzy was then finally allowed to retire with John behind the counter while the opening solemnities were conducted. Charley offered toasts of cocoa all around, Dusty Springfield was switched on, and The Chocolate Bar was in business.

They need not have worried: the local residents' curiosity demanded that nearly every citizen appear at one time or another during the course of the day. The first round was van-driving mothers, fresh from dropping off their children at school and intent on loading up with calories before proceeding to the gym to shed them again. They sampled the various cocoas, from traditional American sweet hot chocolate with marshmallows to the dark, bitter ancient Aztec recipe (a trifle sophisticated for the early hour), and devoured chocolate-covered doughnuts. Before long a luncheon contingent of shopgirls arrived, to nibble at salads and gooey chocolate chip cookies warm from the oven.

Midafternoon saw a little lull, when a few cold, wet ranchers came in for something hot to drink. Lizzy listened in on their desultory talk of calves being born, wild pigs trampling fences, high water in the canyon fords, and the like, and then school was out and she had to jump up to help John and the other barista field the avalanche of questions and demands. The noise level rose to an unbearable pitch for an hour or so, and then the kids vanished as quickly as they had come.

"Like an infestation of locusts," said Lizzy, returning to the window seat with a sigh.

John laughed at her and said he had found them invigorating, though perhaps they wouldn't *all* come every day. There was another small run later, of professionals stopping in to pick up desserts to take home for their families, and even Lydon, Jenny, and Kitty made it back from their jobs in Lompoc before it was time to close. They pronounced the place to be fat but not phat, but this disparagement didn't stop them from gorging themselves on the remaining cookies. Charley was exhilarated and exhausted in equal measure, and they all left the shop to the baker and made for home.

After the rush of opening day, business slowed down to a more normal rhythm. A period of wet weather drove Lizzy to spend a good many hours in her favorite window seat, whenever she could be spared from overseeing the construction work inside the library-to-be, and she saw much of Bingley's friends, who were faithful visitors though they partook sparingly of the high-calorie fare. Caroline Bingley often came in to toy with a salad and the reputations of her friends, abetted by the other ladies of her set. She rarely failed to plant a few barbs in Lizzy, asking her honeyed questions about how she managed to keep her nails so clean or wondering what it must be like driving a pickup truck when the back roads were so muddy.

These sallies often were delivered side by side with remarks to John so archly caressing that Lizzy was scarcely able to keep her countenance. That he was male must be the sole justification for his higher value in Miss Bingley's eyes, and Lizzy could only be amused that Caroline Bingley, in her attempts both to please and to wound, should fail so signally in achieving her object.

On a slow day at The Chocolate Bar, when John had the day off and Lizzy had left to work at her aunt's house, Caroline Bingley relaxed with a sigh into the armchair Lizzy habitually occupied. Darcy had stopped in for a quick coffee, and Bingley settled down with them both.

"How delightful it is to have the place to ourselves!" exclaimed Caroline. "I was starting to think that Lizzy Bennet was taking up permanent residence here. I almost expected to find a sleeping bag rolled up behind this chair."

"She certainly has been a faithful customer," said Charley.

"She hardly lends cachet to the ambiance, though. Completely devoid of style! And she comes in at all hours looking almost like a savage—in ragged jeans, windblown, and I swear caked in mud."

"She dresses casually, but so do all the ranchers," replied Charley. "I haven't seen her looking dirty. I think she comes so she can spend time with her brother; they seem like a very close-knit family. I like to see siblings who have so much affection for each other."

"Oh, John is okay, but the rest of the Bennets! They're all conceited, and so grasping—why would the entire family move halfway across the country, just to secure what little fortune Evelyn Bennet had to leave? The mother is definitely on the make;

she's out for money however she can get it, by inheritance or by marrying her kids to it. And then there are the younger ones: they think about nothing but partying! Elizabeth's only marginally more subtle than her mother; she clearly has ambitions to crawl out of the mud. It's all I can do not to laugh when I see her pathetic attempts to pass herself off as an intellectual. *You* were a history major at Cornell, but you don't carry around volumes of Gibbon. Did you see her just now? Sitting there reading Alexander Pope, with the book held up high so everyone could see the cover! I despise that kind of artifice."

"There is a pettiness in *all* the arts that women employ to capture the attention of the opposite sex," said Darcy.

"She doesn't seem at all calculating to me," protested Charley. "I think she's just one of those people who enjoys everything life has to offer. Every time she comes in I feel energized."

Making a quick recover, Caroline retorted, "Oh, she has a rude kind of high-spiritedness, like an untrained puppy. But a puppy at least has the merit of being genuine—and you will never convince me that Lizzy Bennet is genuine."

Chapter Twelve

Though Lizzy was not privileged to hear the terms used to describe her, she cherished no illusions about Caroline Bingley's regard for her or her family. John was inclined to take a more lenient view, describing Caroline as warm and thoughtful; and it was in vain that Lizzy warned him not to presume too much on the friendship. She was convinced, moreover, that Fitzwilliam Darcy shared Caroline's views, and her conviction gained strength from his demeanor whenever she encountered him at the shop. He spoke little to her but seemed to watch her all the time — "As if I were the most objectionable creature he has ever met," she said to John, who only laughed at her. "But forget about him; that's not why I came in. I want to read you this wonderful poem I just found — it's perfect for the season. There's time before the lunch rush, isn't there?"

John loved her enthusiasm for poetry almost as much as she loved poems, so how could he demur? "So long as it isn't an epic."

"Well, it *is* a little long, but you have five minutes, don't you? It's by Marge Piercy, and it's called 'The Common Living Dirt.'"

And she launched eagerly into Piercy's ode to the earth,

delicious now, rich in the hand
as chocolate cake: the fragrant busy
soil the worm passes through her gut
and the beetle swims in like a lake.

Oblivious to her surroundings, Lizzy declaimed the passionate lines demanding respect for the soil as if they were her own manifesto, never looking up until she achieved the final stanza:

> *Because you can die of overwork, because*
> *you can die of the fire that melts*
> *rock, because you can die of the poison*
> *that kills the beetle and the slug,*
> *we must come again to worship you*
> *on our knees, the common living dirt.*

Lizzy suddenly became aware that John was urgently signaling something with his eyes, and glanced over her shoulder to find herself once again under Darcy's scrutiny. He had come in for an early lunch with his foreman, Reynolds, and they were standing patiently behind her waiting to order sandwiches. Behind them was Caroline Bingley, derision writ large upon her countenance.

Blushing furiously and furious with herself for blushing, Lizzy stammered an apology and retired to her habitual window seat. But she recovered her equanimity quickly, since she cared little for Caroline's or Darcy's disapprobation except as it tempted her to enjoy herself at their expense. For his part, Darcy made no comment about her flight into verse, and while Caroline was exchanging a few words with her brother at the counter he settled into a far corner with Reynolds to resume their interrupted discussion of pasture management.

"The forecasters are saying that we're going into an extended cycle of drought years," said Reynolds. "If they're right, perennial pasturage would be crucial to the cattle program—especially if we decided to produce grass-finished stock, which might be a good idea since the price per pound is so much higher for grass-finished beef. We could seed-gun eastern grama grass into all but the hottest pastures."

"Going perennial would require us to irrigate the whole ranch, not just the horse pastures," objected Darcy. "Where would we get the additional water? I'm not prepared to reduce allotments to downstream neighbors. Even by moving the cattle to higher pastures in the late spring, we can't give them enough forage for the entire season. I doubt the expense would be offset by the return, anyway, though you're welcome to work up some numbers if you want. I'd also be concerned about sowing anything like clover or alfalfa too close to the National Forest lands: we don't want to be accused of promoting the invasion of non-native species."

"But most of the grasses that grow on the hills today aren't really native anyway—they were introduced by the Spaniards."

"Perhaps, but we don't want to contribute to the problem on federally preserved land. Some ranchers are even initiating programs that encourage restoration of native species, and I'd like to look into that. Regardless, the core problem remains our water supply. I'm afraid we'll have to leave grass-finishing to those who have the climate for it."

"Oh, Darcy, I hope you won't change anything at Pemberley Ranch," exclaimed Caroline, fluttering over to their table.

The two men looked up, startled.

"Your land is too beautiful ever to be altered!" she cried. "Whenever I see it, I'm reminded of what Gary Snyder wrote about 'hills that look like warm sexy animal bodies.' It would be a tragedy to have those big irrigation pipes marching up over them. And to lose the seasonal cycles, to have the hills green all the time and never turning that wonderful golden color—promise me you won't do it!"

"I've said that I'd be reluctant to do so."

"I think Pemberley Ranch is one of the most beautiful spots on earth!"

Darcy bowed slightly, and turned back to Reynolds. "I've heard that a three-year study is under way at the University of California reserve on high intensity–short duration grazing. I'd like you to keep tabs on the findings—does it increase the desirable forage? Does it affect the spread of nonnative species? Are there any impacts on the cattle?"

Caroline tried again. "If you would please me, you'd never do anything to Pemberley at all, but leave it in its natural state."

"If I did that, I'd be a very irresponsible landlord. Its natural state, as you call it, has been carefully managed for generations."

"I'm sure your parents would be very proud of the care you take with it."

Darcy was silent.

"Charley, when you buy your ranch, I hope it will be just like Pemberley."

"It would be, if Darcy would sell me Pemberley," said Charley, coming out from behind the counter to refill the foreman's iced tea.

"Sell Pemberley Ranch! I can't imagine anyone but a Darcy living there—that's how it has always been."

"Well, if you define the word *always* as lasting only a century or so," Lizzy couldn't resist saying.

"But before that time, it wasn't a ranch," Caroline pointed out triumphantly.

"Ranch or raw land, I wouldn't have the first idea what to do with it," said Bingley, laughing. "Darcy's birthright is safe from me."

"You're a man, then, who knows his limitations," said Lizzy, smiling at him. "That's an admirable quality."

"If you can call it admirable to be too lazy to learn new skills, then by all means consider him admirable," said Darcy.

"Charley is your friend!" Lizzy protested.

"It's useless to leap to my defense—though I'm grateful for such a display of courage on my behalf," said Bingley. "There's no point in being shocked by Darcy: he will always say whatever he believes, regardless of the consequences."

"So long as the burden of the consequences is borne by others?"

"Be careful, Darcy," Charley warned, "you may have met your match for ruthless candor in Elizabeth Bennet!"

"I don't fear her," said Darcy.

"Now, *that* I have to regard as a challenge," said Lizzy, "and I can never resist a challenge. I'll have to study how to make you fear me."

"I wish I could be such a feminist as you," said Caroline. "You drive a truck, and work the soil, and don't hesitate to intimidate any man! I am too much the woman, I fear, to follow your example."

"I've always felt that intimidation existed only in the eye of the beholder," replied Lizzy. "A person who is comfortable in his own skin neither feels intimidated nor feels the need to intimidate others. We can all be different without those differences implying superiority or inferiority."

"And yet you want to make Darcy fear you!"

"It's purely a defensive strategy: I'd like to avoid being treated with the brand of friendliness he displays toward your brother. I take delight in cheating a person of their premeditated contempt."

Darcy tossed some bills on the table and rose with Reynolds. "If it will satisfy either of you, I'll admit freely to a fear of becoming the battleground on which two such redoubtable opponents wage war. Bingley, I leave it to you to broker a treaty." And so saying, he quit the field.

Lizzy would have hazarded the opinion that Darcy, evidently not a stupid person, would thenceforth have given The Chocolate Bar a wide berth. But no, the provoking man was back at lunchtime the very next day, apparently with no other object than to be provoked in his turn. She could not say why he thus sought company, for once there he sat in the corner and buried his nose in the latest issue of *The Stockman Grass Farmer*. But Caroline Bingley being again present, he was not long permitted to mind his own business.

Caroline sat down in his line of sight, but he did not look up; so she moved to the counter and made an elaborate show of considering this pastry and that, without ultimately ordering anything. At last she hit upon a desperate measure, and went to sit at Lizzy's table.

"Have you tried the iced mocha latte, Lizzy? It's very refreshing—clears the palate after too many of the sweets. I'd be happy to treat you to one."

Lizzy was surprised, but accepted the offer. Caroline succeeded no less in the real object of her civility: Darcy, equally surprised, looked up. Caroline immediately invited him to join them, and included him in her offer. He declined, observing that he could think of only two reasons why they would share a latte, and his joining them would defeat either purpose.

"What can he mean?" Caroline asked Lizzy conspiratorially. "Can you imagine what he might be thinking?"

"Not at all," said Lizzy, "but I'm sure that whatever he intends, it is to our detriment, and the surest way of frustrating his purposes is to ask him nothing about it."

"But I have to know!"

"I'm happy to explain it to you," said he. "Either you want to have a good gossip about mutual friends, or you realize what a charming picture the two of you make, sitting there framed by the window. If the first, I would be in the way; and if the second, I can admire you much better from across the room."

"Outrageous!" exclaimed Caroline. "How can we punish him for such unchivalrous words?"

"Nothing could be easier," said Lizzy. "We must make fun of him in our turn. You know him so well, you must know where his vulnerabilities lie."

"But I swear I don't. I've never seen in him the faults of temper or vanity that so many men fall prey to. If we tried to make fun of him, we'd just make ourselves ridiculous. He needn't worry."

"Darcy is not to be laughed at? That is an uncommon advantage—and uncommon I hope it will continue, for it would be a great loss to me to know many such people. I love to laugh."

"Caroline gives me too much credit, of course," said Darcy. "The wisest and best of men can be made to look ridiculous by someone who's determined to mock them at any cost."

"Certainly there are such people," replied Lizzy, "but I hope I'm not one of them. Without resorting to cutting down the blameless, I see enough follies and weaknesses everywhere for me to find plenty of amusement. But follies and weaknesses, I'm told, are precisely what you lack."

"Perhaps that isn't possible for anyone. But I certainly make every effort to avoid those weaknesses that would expose me to ridicule."

"Such as vanity and pride."

"Vanity is a weakness, of course. But pride—there are things a person can justifiably be proud of. I wouldn't necessarily consider it a character flaw."

"Have you finished your analysis of Darcy?" inquired Caroline. "And what is your conclusion?"

"I'm satisfied that he has no defects: he admits as much without hesitation. I am curious about one thing, though, Mr. Darcy: do you seek to avoid character flaws to make yourself more perfect, or merely to escape ridicule?"

"I make no claim to perfection. I have plenty of faults, but they are not, I hope, of understanding. I may be, perhaps, too unyielding—certainly too much for the comfort of those around me. I find it hard to overlook the faults of other people, or forgive them when they've offended me or done me harm. I don't easily compromise, or change my mind once it's made up. Some would say I have a resentful nature; when a person forfeits my good opinion, it's lost forever."

"I can't argue with you: refusal to forgive is a flaw indeed! But you have chosen your fault well—I can't laugh at it. You've made yourself safe from me." Lizzy prepared to return to her reading.

"There is, I believe, in every character a tendency toward some defect or another, which not even the best efforts can overcome."

"And yours is a tendency to hate everybody."

"And yours," he returned, "is willfully to misunderstand them."

"And here are the lattes!" exclaimed Caroline.

Her brother Charley, coming out from behind the counter with the drinks, seconded her. "And let us hope *their* good qualities are something we can all agree on."

"I see why you opened The Chocolate Bar, Charley," said Darcy, making an effort to smile. "You want to sweeten all our dispositions. You dislike debates, I know, and hope to silence this one."

"Perhaps I do. Debates are too much like quarrels to suit me. If you and Elizabeth will postpone yours until some other time and place, I'd be very grateful."

"That is no sacrifice on my part," said Lizzy cheerfully. "I have work to do, and no doubt Mr. Darcy would much rather continue his reading."

To all appearance he obeyed this suggestion, though it is hard to say whether *The Stockman Grass Farmer* or his fair adversary occupied the larger share of his thoughts.

Chapter Thirteen

All things considered, Lizzy was not sorry to see the weather clear up and find herself obliged to return to work. The early and extended California spring gave her great joy, and she was eager to be out in it. Because of the days missed during the storms, she had to put in extra time with her garden maintenance clients; and the physical work helped her rearrange her thoughts, which she found to be unusually tangled. Nobody in her family had any serious trouble in their life, and the growing attachment she observed between John and Charley Bingley was a source of great satisfaction; yet she felt herself not at peace. The upheaval of moving, and the challenges she had set herself, might be enough to account for any vexation of spirits, but as she examined each possibility in turn, it did not seem to be sufficient excuse for her ill-humor. There was little she could do to advance the library project until the carpenter had completed his tasks, so she was happy enough to spend most of her time out of doors. Digging into the soil with spade and trowel, setting out new life to take its chances in the world, helped bring a serenity that was welcome.

As she was thus agreeably engaged in the front garden of a client's house, she heard the clop of horses' hooves approaching in the roadway. She was still enough of a city girl to enjoy the sight of horses, so she sat back on her heels to watch them approach—until she recognized the riders as Caroline Bingley, Caroline's friend Claudia, and Fitzwilliam Darcy. She immediately bent forward again and busied herself with the salvias she was bedding out.

". . . he's correct enough, but was slow to develop," Darcy's voice wafted over to her. "As a two-year-old, he was still gangly and immature. But now the trainer assures me all that is behind us, and he's ready to run in the Derby."

"That's so exciting! Imagine what it would be like if a horse you bred won the Triple Crown!"

"This one won't," said Darcy. "He's a sprinter—lacks the stamina for the Belmont. I don't even plan to enter him there."

"Your cousins the Fitzwilliams have a Triple Crown winner to stud, don't they?"

"He's retired, but two fillies by him are popular brood mares nowadays."

"Well, look who's here!" cried Caroline, reining in as she came abreast of the driveway. "Lizzy Bennet! Is this one of the places you work?"

"As you see," said Lizzy, continuing to ply her trowel.

"Oh, the gardener," said Claudia. "Are you thinking of hiring her? Isn't Eusebio doing a good job for you?" She and Caroline giggled together.

Darcy, his forbidding expression at variance with his words, said, "It's a very fine day to be out-of-doors—worshipping the common living dirt, as your poem said. I remember my mother taking great pleasure in working her garden on a spring day like this."

Lizzy was no more impressed by this stab at courtesy than she was by the disdain of his friends; nor was she moved by the way he sat his horse, or the chiseled profile under his hat. She returned an indifferent reply and got up to fetch a flat of verbena. Once it became clear to the riders that she was not going to rise to any bait, they rode on.

Darcy's chivalrous impulse had not been lost on Caroline, however little it had pleased its intended object. She had in fact deliberately chosen the direction of their ride to present Lizzy to him in the guise of a common laborer, thinking to give him a disgust of her; and as they rode, she couldn't refrain from picking up the thread.

"I love your mother's gardens! I'll never forget the time back in college when we all came to Pemberley Ranch on spring break and the weather was so warm and clear, and she was hosting the Vernal Equinox garden party that year. The flowers were at their peak bloom, and all the Enclave families were there, dressed to the nines. I remember saying to Charley, 'This is the most beautiful place in the world; we should come to live here as soon as we graduate.' Your mother was the perfect hostess; she made us all feel like part of the family."

"The Vernal Equinox party won't be up to Pemberley standards this year," Claudia complained. "The Lucases are hosting it, so we'll have to listen to Mrs. Lucas dropping names of Garden Club people nobody's ever heard of, and Mr. Lucas finding ways to mention his Grammy award."

"But I'm sure the Bennets will be very impressed with them both, and Mrs. Bennet will try to convince everyone who'll listen that she comes from one of the first families of Columbus, Ohio!" Caroline said.

"Do you think they'll be invited?"

"I'm afraid so: Charlotte seems to like Lizzy Bennet for some reason. Maybe she feels sorry for her. It's bad enough her brother has to work as a waiter, but gardening for perfect strangers? You have to wonder why that family has such an affinity for menial occupations."

"Will she be able to get the dirt out of her hair in time?" Claudia asked. Both friends laughed uproariously. "Maybe Charlotte's hoping she can give some professional advice to the Lucases on their landscaping, and earn her supper."

"I wouldn't have a problem with the Bennets if they knew their place. But they're thrusters, everywhere I go I find them trying to push their way in. They're so provincial they don't even recognize the gulf that separates them from the world they're trying to inhabit. I wish somebody would drop them a hint."

"I heard Morris Collins is pursuing her. If they hook up, she'll be inescapable," said Claudia gloomily.

"But she seems to favor George Carrillo—I heard she even went to their house for dinner the other day. Meeting the family! Sounds serious. So maybe she'll find her niche in the end."

"What is it about Earth Girl, anyway? What's so irresistible about her?"

"Ask Darcy. You aren't entirely immune to her charms, are you? Though how you see them through the dirt, I couldn't say."

"Why are we even riding?" demanded Darcy. "If all you wanted to do was dissect your acquaintance, you could've met for coffee. Are we going to have a gallop or not?"

Lizzy, meanwhile, had derived no more satisfaction from the encounter. As she slapped place mats and napkins on the dining table at home, she described in vivid terms what had passed. "I'll bet Caroline Bingley rode that direction just so she could mock me at work. The people around here are insufferable! They're so class-conscious and self-satisfied, as if just being rich made them important!"

"From a worldly perspective, being rich *does* make them important," said Mary. "But if you refuse to share their values, you immunize yourself against their snubs. They can't hurt you if you don't care what they think."

"Nonsense!" cried Mrs. Bennet. "Of course they can hurt us, because if they take a dislike to us we won't be received. I expect you were sharp with them, Lizzy; you tend to be a little sharp, and it puts people's backs up."

"Heaven forfend a daughter of yours should be sharp," said Mr. Bennet. "By all means, Lizzy, you must study your mother's example, and learn to be duller."

Lizzy was not to be diverted. "Caroline Bingley is bad enough, with all her snide insinuations about dirty fingernails.

But I think Fitzwilliam Darcy is the worst of all. He wears his family background like a suit of chain mail, and stares down at you from his high perch of superiority as if you were a serf! You should have seen him on that horse, like the lord of the manor surveying his fiefdom. His idea of finding common ground is to talk about how much his mother liked to garden? I'm sure what she called 'gardening' was standing around pointing and telling the undergardener, 'Plant it there.'"

"Well, Lizzy, if you *will* grub around in other people's yards, you have to expect people to treat you like the help," said Mrs. Bennet practically.

"I've heard this Darcy fellow is the worst of villains," said Mr. Bennet. "Didn't your friend Jorge tell you a hair-raising tale of fraud and piracy? Isn't Darcy the wicked thief of the grand Carrillo heritage? What can you expect from such a person?"

"Avarice, I believe, is an emotion that bears little relation to one's actual state of need," said Mary. "From all I've heard, rich people can be just as greedy and jealous as poor ones. A man doesn't have to be hungry or desperate to covet what his neighbor has."

"Well, there you are!" said Mr. Bennet, quizzing Lizzy. "No doubt Darcy covets what Jorge Carrillo has."

Lizzy blushed and thought better of pursuing the subject, though her feelings of offense had not abated. Her thoughts were turned in a happier direction, however, by the arrival of John from The Chocolate Bar, more full than ever of "Charley says" and "Charley thinks," till he became in his turn the focus of the family's wit and wisdom. He had borne home, moreover, a fancy engraved card of invitation that Charlotte Lucas had dropped off at the shop—no less than the entrée to the Enclave's Vernal Equinox garden party, eight days hence.

Mrs. Bennet was ecstatic. Inquisition of various informants had elicited the information that this annual party was one of the few Enclave events during the year to which nonmembers were invited, and for some time she had been scheming for ways and means to secure an invitation. To owe her admission to Lizzy's popularity was a blow, but a sustainable one considering the outcome.

"You sly thing," she said, "all the times I have mentioned the Vernal Equinox party, you never said a word about knowing the hostess's daughter!"

"Charlotte said something to me once about meeting some Enclave people, but I didn't think anything of it at the time," Lizzy confessed.

"Vernal Equinox, is it?" said Mr. Bennet. "It sounds very pagan to me. I warn you, I won't attend if I am expected to strip naked and jump the bonfire."

"I think that's May Eve," said Lizzy.

"I will find better company with a book than at a frivolous society event, whatever the rest of you decide to do," said Mary.

"I'm sure your hostess would prefer not to see your long face, if that's your attitude," snapped Mrs. Bennet.

Lizzy considered following Mary's example, but eventually decided that since the invitation was probably intended as a compliment to herself, it would be churlish to decline—as well as high-handed to send other members of her family where she didn't go. Although the event held little attraction for her beyond the usual pleasure of getting dressed up for a party, she resigned herself to making the best of it. In this assessment of what was called for she was encouraged by John, who was by this time sufficiently in love to want to go anywhere Charley was likely to be found; and by her father, who wanted the company of one who could laugh with him at the frailties of the pretentious.

The Lucases' property proved to be a modern ranchette on the outskirts of Los Olivos, set among the one-acre-vineyard and miniature-donkey-breeding enterprises of semiretired attorneys and businessmen who had retreated to the bucolic life from the Los Angeles megalopolis over the past decade. The well-tended landscape was very pretty in an Iceberg rose and lavender kind of way, but Lizzy found more of taste, and considerably more of originality, in her aunt's modest garden. The day was fine enough that only the elderly needed to retreat into the house, so the ladies were able to parade the lawns in flowered dresses and hats, ruing their decision to wear high-heeled sandals, which sank into the turf at every step. Lavish spreads of tea sandwiches and savory finger foods were arrayed on the terrace, and a string quartet vied manfully with the chatter of guests on the deck around the pool.

Much of the Enclave conversation seemed to revolve around horses, their breeding, training, and riding, which left the Bennets a little at a loss. Mrs. Bennet, after a few stabs at guiding people into more congenial subjects, found herself largely ignored and had to draw what consolation she could from ogling the jewelry on display. Mr. Bennet got further by feigning sufficient interest to lure his interlocutors into speaking in the code of their cultus, and could be seen listening with enjoyment to detailed accounts of which stallions were throwing the best crops of foals, that could run long or short; of which ranches produced the best horses for cutting or reining; of how many times this horse or that stood to stud in his first season; of children's victories in the egg-and-spoon event of English gymkhana; of a disastrous chukka on the polo ground in which three riders suffered broken limbs. John was drawn up into the crowd around the Bingleys, leaving Lizzy at the mercy of Morris Collins, resplendent if inappropriate in a velvet smoking jacket.

He was seen to be in a state of excitement, which rendered him even more voluble than usual but less easily understood. After listening attentively for several minutes, in which the words "honor" and "graciousness" and "privilege" were often repeated, Lizzy eventually gathered that she was to be granted the felicity of becoming acquainted with Catherine the Great. She was unmoved by the prospect of meeting the august lady, beyond a faint curiosity to judge for herself a person of whom she had heard so much, but there seemed no excuse not to go along with him.

Morris was in ecstasy at being the one to introduce her into such exalted circles, and he had much advice to impart on the occasion. She was adjured to speak up but to observe the silence of respect; to give honest answers when questioned but to show proper deference; to stand until invited to sit but not to hover over her; and more in the same vein until she would have been thoroughly bewildered had she paid him any heed.

Though Lizzy had never seen the lady before, she knew instantly when she was in the Presence by the alteration in Morris's demeanor. Suddenly letting go of her arm, he turned aside to execute a series of small bows. She followed the direction of his obeisances to behold a tall, stocky woman with a strong-featured, sun-weathered visage. Catherine de Bourgh, seated in a wing chair in the living room, was not a woman rendered formidable by silence. She had been holding forth to some other guests when Morris appeared, but she dismissed them and barked, "Did you bring me the girl?"

"Yes, ma'am, if I may have the honor of presenting to you Miss Elizabeth Bennet, of Columbus, Ohio, the niece of Evelyn Bennet. Miss Lizzy, Miss Catherine de Bourgh." He led Lizzy forward; she put out her hand, but found it ignored.

"Go away, Morris," said the great lady, and "Sit here," to Lizzy. Lizzy sat, and submitted with a calm expression to the close scrutiny of her face and person. Evidently Catherine found nothing in her appearance to comment on, for after a minute she continued: "Your aunt was a respectable member of the community, though occasionally she indulged a regrettable sense of whimsy. Do you think she would approve of your carryings-on?"

"I'm here at her request, to carry out her final wishes," replied Lizzy.

"Do you really expect me to believe that she asked you to create some communistic garden for the field hands?"

Lizzy had to acknowledge that the community garden was not her aunt's idea. "But I think she would've liked it," she added.

"Nonsense! The scheme must be abandoned at once. We pay our workers for their labor, and educate their children in our schools for free. They should be grateful for the opportunity and make their own way. So it has been for immigrants to this country for centuries. To give special privileges to the Mexicans just encourages them to be lazy and expect handouts."

"I'm not sure being offered the chance to work a small plot of land can really be seen as an incitement to laziness. If they don't work at it, they won't see any harvest. And I was hoping that people from all walks of life might want to participate in the community garden, and get to know one another better in the process."

"The people around here know one another as well as they want to, and considerably better than *you* know any of them. Upon my word, you give your opinions very decidedly for a newcomer! And how do you think the farmstand operators will appreciate your scheme to undermine their business? Had you thought of that?"

"I hadn't, but I'd imagine that the farmstand operators derive most of their business from tourists."

"You know nothing of the matter! But it makes little difference, because your communal garden won't be allowed. You'll have to find some other way to pass the time. Do you ride?"

"No."

"Everybody rides here; you'll have to learn. If you go to the Westerly Stables and mention my name, they'll take good care of you."

"You are too kind."

"Are you here on your own? I don't hold with girls traipsing around the country on their own."

"With two of my younger siblings old enough to vote, I think I can say that I'm past my girlhood. But as it happens, all my family is here, at least for a year."

"Do you have many brothers and sisters?"

"I have two of each, and one of my brothers is married."

"That's a very large family. In this day and age, having more than two children must be considered irresponsible. Where did you prep?"

"We attended public school in Columbus."

"*Public school!* Are your parents *liberals?*"

Lizzy made no reply.

"With an education like that, I expect none of you attended college."

"My brother John and I are college graduates, and my sister Mary is applying next year."

"Hm. And your parents came west as well? How can your father afford to leave his work behind?"

"My father is self-employed, so his work may be said to go wherever he does."

"'Self-employed' covers a multitude of sins. What exactly does he do?"

"Aunt Catherine, are you grilling Ms. Bennet?" Fitzwilliam Darcy had come up behind them.

"Oh, you've met my nephew, have you?"

"Yes, ma'am."

"Darcy, your cousin Anne is here; I invited her for the foaling season. You should go find her."

"I'll certainly do so, if I may first borrow Elizabeth. Charlotte Lucas mentioned that she was looking for her," he answered, and drew Lizzy away.

"My aunt can be a little overpowering," he said once they were out of earshot.

"I am unbloodied and unbowed," Lizzy replied, though secretly she was grateful for the timely interruption.

"I've seen enough of you to believe that."

"I expect you were rescuing *her* from *me*, and not the other way around," said Lizzy.

He smiled. "I won't say you're mistaken, because you couldn't possibly imagine that I meant any such thing. And I've known you long enough to realize that you sometimes take pleasure in expressing views that aren't in fact your own. My aunt has been in a position of command for much of her life, and at times it can be difficult for her to set those habits aside in social situations."

"I'm glad we don't live in a feudal society, or I might be in the position of having to follow her orders. I can't say I fancy a life of vassalage."

"Any rural area perhaps retains certain feudal aspects to its social structures," Darcy replied seriously. "Those who own most of the land will always have greater rights than others, as well as greater responsibilities."

Lizzy was shocked. "I don't think the privileged should ever be allowed greater rights in America, nor should ordinary people permit them to assume such rights."

"Perhaps I should have said 'greater liberties.'"

"It should be the work of everyone in a society to minimize the disadvantages of low economic status. Leveling the playing field benefits everyone."

"That may be easier to achieve in an urban setting, with its broader economic base. The opportunities for advancement in a rural economy are fairly limited."

"Not if a little imagination is used, and if there's a will to make a difference," said Lizzy with spirit.

Darcy made no reply, but handed her over to Charlotte and made off across the terrace, where he could be seen talking to a slight, mousy girl with a huge shawl wrapped tightly around her.

"Oh dear, have you and Darcy been arguing again?" asked Charlotte. "What was it this time?"

"Rank and its privileges."

"I should've sent someone else, but I thought he was the one who could best extricate you from Catherine the Great. He seemed happy enough to undertake the errand."

"Mr. Darcy is all politeness. But I think I've had enough of the Darcy–de Bourgh officiousness for one day. Who is that girl he's talking to now?"

Charlotte peered across the way. "Oh, that's his cousin Anne. I heard that Catherine had summoned her—she has ambitions in that direction."

"Ambitions?"

"Catherine is a fan of dynastic matchmaking. She hopes that Darcy and Anne will get married."

"Somebody told me that Catherine de Bourgh had no immediate family. Did I get that wrong? Is Anne her daughter?"

"No, she's the daughter of Earl Fitzwilliam, the brother of both Catherine and Darcy's mother. The Fitzwilliams are from Kentucky, and have one of the big thoroughbred farms there."

"So she wants her niece and nephew to unite the family stud. I thought that was bad breeding practice." Lizzy laughed. "Perhaps it's one of the feudal responsibilities he was referring to. Well, if that's what passes for love in his world, he's welcome to it. I'm glad to be a lowly peon if it means I don't have to marry as an economic strategy."

"So you would marry only for love? I would've said that *most* marriages have at least some element of economic strategy to them."

"I'd rather not marry at all; but if I were to do so, I'd want it to be a partnership of mind and spirit, not simply a mercenary arrangement."

"That's a very high standard to achieve and sustain," said Charlotte. "And how can you really know someone well enough to be sure they'll become that type of partner? I believe it's best to have as little true love as possible for the man one is to marry. Men are nothing but pleasure seekers; they see nothing beyond gratifying themselves in the moment. Women are left exposed by their feelings: society teaches us to seek dependency, and we're trained to rely most on those who are the least dependable. We're maneuvered on all sides into becoming vulnerable to the careless usage of unscrupulous men."

"Unscrupulous, or merely heedless? I can't believe that all men are evil and deliberately wish us harm."

"Perhaps. But they're given every encouragement to be selfish beings, to flatter their vanity and inflated sense of worth at our expense. I believe they know instinctively that in our weakness lies their best opportunity for strength. So the only remedy for us is not to be weak—to get from them what we need without endangering our hearts. There is a kind of honor in giving a man what he needs so as to ensure that we have what we need."

"You can't truly believe that such a dreary existence is the best to be hoped for!" Lizzy protested. "Surely, if one can develop a relationship based on mutual respect, a true companionship is possible. And what would you do with the heart you've protected so zealously?"

"Save it for my children."

Lizzy smiled and nodded, but remained unconvinced. Looking over toward John and Charley, heads together, talking earnestly, she said, "I can't have a brother like John and think so poorly of men in general. I've never known a human being with such goodness and sweetness of character. And Charley Bingley seems much the same. Seeing them both gives me hope for humanity; and seeing them find each other fills my heart with joy."

Charlotte eyed them with skepticism. "They make a perfect couple, to be sure. Everybody knows gay men are a superior evolutionary form. And if there was any chance that either one of them might look my way, I'd snap him up in a minute. I was speaking of men who might be *available*. And even with all their good character and appealing qualities, I'd be surprised if John and Charley found their path to happiness a smooth one."

"I assume you mean that prejudiced people will disapprove of their relationship. But they must have sources of happiness in each other's company that will allow them to ignore other people's ill-will. I hope they'll have children, too: John loves kids, and he'd be a wonderful parent."

At this moment the couple in question approached where they stood. "This beautiful party of your parents' has inspired my sister Caroline," said Bingley with a smile for Charlotte. "She wants to throw a bash for the younger crowd the night before Easter. I hope you'll both be able to come."

"We certainly chose the right time of year to move to Lambtown," Lizzy said. "Back home everyone would be barely out of hibernation, but around here it's nonstop events. If we'd known, we'd have moved here years ago. All you have to say to a Bennet is 'party,' and we're there."

Charley moved on to extend more invitations, leaving John behind to be teased good-naturedly by his sister and Charlotte. Seeing his favorite children together, Mr. Bennet came over to share with them the results of his researches into the sociology of the Enclave. "Have you heard about the Rancheros Visitadores?" he wanted to know.

Smiling at his evident pleasure, Lizzy shook her head.

"It's an annual gathering of the rich and famous from all around the country, right here in the Santa Ynez Valley. Movers and shakers—politicians, businessmen, entertainers—get together to ride horses and camp out for a week all around the valley. Ronald Reagan was a Ranchero. They make deals and connections and have outrageous parties: showgirls, hookers, the whole thing—like an equine Bohemian Grove! The Enclave has its own subgroup of the Rancheros, and what do you think they call it? Los Orgullosos!"

"My grandfather was one of Los Chingadores, I'm told," said Charlotte. "But don't tell my parents I know about it! Even though my dad was in the music business, the Rancheros are a little wild for his tastes these days."

Mr. Bennet was delighted. "Do you know the names of any of the other groups?"

"Oh, certainly; most of them are highly derogatory. There are Los Flojos, Los Borrachos, Los Tontos, and other names a young lady of the Santa Ynez is not supposed to recognize. In fact, a young lady of the Santa Ynez is looked on askance if she admits to any knowledge whatsoever of the Rancheros and their exploits. It's one of those lock-up-your-daughters times of year."

"When does it happen?" asked Lizzy.

"In May."

"I want to know if Darcy is an Orgulloso or a Tonto. I can't quite picture him as a Borracho or a Chingador."

"I'm sorry to have to disappoint you, but I don't think Darcy rides with the Rancheros, though he may let them use a campground on his land. That time of year, he's usually back east with one of his horses for the Triple Crown races."

Mr. Bennet wanted to hear more, but Mrs. Bennet, having endured a surfeit of snubs for the afternoon, was plucking at his sleeve and declaring her eagerness to depart, so he was obliged to make do with the fruits thus far harvested.

Chapter Fourteen

B y the end of March, the carpenter had very nearly completed his work in Aunt Evelyn's house, and it was time for Lizzy to start thinking about the next phase of her project. Tempting as it might be to linger in her aunt's burgeoning garden or to wander the local mountains discovering the new wildflowers that unfurled daily, after spending a pleasant morning weeding with Mr. and Mrs. Gardiner she knew she had to bring her attention to bear on choosing the right books to stock the shelves.

For this effort the Internet proved invaluable. Soon Lizzy was maintaining a lively correspondence with librarians across the West who had large Spanish-speaking constituencies; they were happy to tell her of the challenges they faced reaching out to their would-be customers and to share their book lists and other resources. Through them she learned that most of the nations to the south do not have free public libraries like those in the United States, so newcomers would need to have the concept of borrowing and returning books explained to them. Some immigrants must be reassured that a library had no connection to the Immigration Service, and that they would not have to pay a *mordita,* a bribe, to get a card. Bilingual computer programs were available, and children's and adult book collections in Spanish needed to represent a spectrum of regional and national root cultures. Bilingual storytellers were useful for attracting young children, and some libraries partnered with social service organizations to provide cultural literacy services for entire families. A video game room would draw in tweens. Older children and adults would be interested in histories and classic works by Hispanic authors in both English and Spanish. The card catalog should have subject entries in both languages.

Lizzy also found historical societies helpful in identifying books of local interest, both fiction and nonfiction, and she combed the Web sites of publishers and used-book sellers for titles. Her wish lists became so long that she feared she would need a branch library before the first ever opened, or before she stocked a reasonable collection for her English-speaking clientele. It quickly became clear, too, that her budget bore little relation to her ideas, and many titles would have to wait for future years to be acquired. Encyclopedias were particularly expensive, and procuring a basic reference collection put a large hole in her funds.

Immediately a further dilemma arose: if book deliveries started arriving at her aunt's house on a daily basis, the curiosity of the neighborhood would be aroused. Mr. Perry offered a solution: Lizzy could lease a small storage space in a warehouse area of Lompoc, where the rents were cheap, and have the books and other materials delivered there. To Lompoc, therefore, she went.

Lompoc, situated near the coast at the gateway to Vandenberg Air Force Base, proved to be a study in contrasts. A small, charming historic core was surrounded by several miles of strip malls and cheap housing for military personnel and workers in the service industries that grow up around military bases. Past these dreary suburbs, one quickly found oneself amid the vast, bright acres of industrial flower-growers and, scattered among them, the vineyards of a few lucky winemakers who had discovered in the area the perfect climate for Pinot Noir and other cool-weather grapes. It was a pleasure for Lizzy to drive through the flower fields, though they resembled Victorian carpet bedding laid out for Titans, and if the warehouse district was ugly, she found good company among a number of winemakers who fermented and stored their wines in the buildings around her own small rented space. One of them was willing to keep a spare key to her storage unit, and to take in packages for her so she wouldn't have to be on hand to accept deliveries.

Busily engaged one afternoon cataloguing a recently arrived set of New American Library classics, she was surprised by a greeting from a familiar voice and looked up to see Jorge Carrillo. He too seemed startled to encounter her there, but gratified her by the rapidity with which his expression of surprise gave way to one of pleasure. To his inquiry she replied evasively that she was doing a little work for a friend, and as he seemed no more eager than she to discuss what had brought him to such an out-of-the-way spot, the conversation soon turned to the neighboring enterprises. He was well acquainted with one of the nearby winemakers whom Lizzy had not met, and offered to escort her on a tour of the facilities. Lizzy accepted with alacrity, and locked up.

Jorge's friend Denny was an aging hippie who had gone back to the land around 1970. After a few decades he dismissed airily as his "lost years," he had started organic farming and eventually turned to growing grapes. For once his timing had been good, and he found himself in the vanguard of a lucrative new trend. His own taste buds were in a sorry state, but he had been fortunate enough to find a younger partner with an unimpaired palate who had become his winemaker, and Weed Patch Winery was born.

Denny greeted Jorge cheerfully and was glad to make Lizzy's acquaintance, though it was a few minutes before they were able to clear up some confusion about her profession. On hearing that she was a gardener, he asked a variety of incomprehensible questions about parsley, divine cactus, and belladonna, until Jorge clarified "landscaper," and the focus shifted to a tour of the winery. Here Lizzy found Denny only slightly more intelligible, as a flood of revelations about malo, native enzymes, and racking ensued. Eventually she pieced together the information that his 1998 vintage was fermented and in the barrels, and taste testing was under way for the final blends.

"I produce a few vineyard-designated wines for the snobs— they'll pay crazy prices for anything they think is exclusive—but here at Weed Patch, the action is all in the blends, from grapes I buy in from all over the state. Those are the really deep wines, the ones with nuance and character: my Viper Viognier, California Sunshine Chardonnay, the Rainbow Riesling. Today we're blending the María Pastora: it's Pinot, with Petite Sirah and a trace of Cab; come and help!" He settled them down in a windowless room, lit by a bare light bulb, at a small card table surrounded by perilously stacked barrels—"all Sirugue medium toast, second-year castoffs from Sanford, a bargain!"—and began siphoning off wine samples from all around them, scrambling up and down a ladder with fresh wineglasses for each one.

His shy and poker-faced partner, introduced as Carter, identified the qualities of each sample and noted the details and the barrel number in a marble-covered composition book. "Nose of violets and blueberries," he would say, "resin and tar aromas," "cola and black pepper on the palate," "leathery finish," or "creamy texture." The glasses, passed in turn to Denny, Jorge, and Lizzy, were all duly sipped; but Lizzy was unable to discern any of the traits that seemed so evident to Carter. It all tasted like plonk to her, slightly harsh, rough-edged red wine. She confided as much in a whisper to Jorge, who explained that this was young wine, and needed a year or two of barrel- and bottle-aging before it would be ready for table. Carter looked pained but Denny agreed happily, and said that he just enjoyed sitting around drinking the samples till the world went fuzzy. Lizzy, unprepared to spend an afternoon in quest of this state of mind, especially with no designated driver on hand, looked at her watch, exclaimed that she had an appointment, and extricated herself gracefully.

This stratagem almost came to naught when Jorge decided

to accompany her, but she hit on the happy notion of intercepting Lydon and Kitty as they got off work and inviting them to dinner and a movie. With this plan Jorge was happy to fall in. They found Kitty, already released from her salesgirl duties, idling at the counter in the coffee shop where Lydon was finishing his shift and waiting for Jenny to arrive from her clerking job at the base. Kitty's look of boredom vanished at the sight of Jorge, and with him as an added inducement she was all too delighted to take Lizzy up on her offer. Kitty plainly thought Lizzy a fool for sharing her swain when she could have him all to herself, and felt no scruples about trying to separate him from her older sister. She launched a campaign of flirtation that made up in vigor what it lacked in subtlety. Lizzy knew a moment's chagrin when she observed how readily Jorge played along; but when he included Lydon in the conversation with equal readiness, and both seemed equally pleased with his company, Lizzy concluded he was simply trying to be agreeable.

Indeed, they were a lively party after Jenny arrived and they made off for the mall and cineplex. Jenny and Kitty needed to be restrained from rushing into stores and trying on a variety of skimpy dresses to model for the gentlemen; over dinner they all argued happily about the threat of the Y2K crisis, and joined in mockery of Ricky Martin's claims to talent. Lizzy had been hoping to see the comedy with Robert De Niro playing a conflicted mobster and Jenny voted for the Sandra Bullock romantic comedy, but Lydon was wild for *The Matrix*, just opened, and received support from Jorge. So the ladies of the party yielded, knowing full well that a bored male is an unresponsive one, and sought consolation in the belief that regardless of the movie selected, their own interest would be focused more on the company than on the screen.

If Lizzy had been required to share Jorge's attention with the rest of her family that evening, she eagerly anticipated monopolizing it at Caroline Bingley's party on Saturday. She had heard that the hotter-than-hot L.A. dance-club band Ozomatli was booked to perform. Their blend of Latin and hip-hop styles was perfectly suited to showcase Jorge's talents, and as she dressed with extra care she indulged her imagination with scenes of their dance-floor triumphs. John, too, seemed to carry high expectations of what pleasures might be derived from the evening, for he came into her room several times to ask her opinion about different outfits. She thought him so handsome in his happiness that it mattered little what he wore, but solemnly gave her opinion on each in turn.

It was perhaps inevitable that Lizzy would find that an event to which she had looked forward with such impatient desire did not, in taking place, bring all the satisfaction she had promised herself. Until she arrived at the party and looked in vain for Jorge, no doubt of his being present had occurred to her. But that he was neither present nor expected could not, after anxious inquiry, be denied, and she was suddenly assailed by the suspicion that Fitzwilliam Darcy must be the cause. She was certain that Caroline Bingley would do nothing that might vex him, and in recollecting all Jorge had told her of his past dealings with the Darcy family, she became pretty well convinced that Darcy must be responsible for his exclusion.

The sharp disappointment consequent on this reversal of her hopes was hardly alleviated by the approach of Morris Collins. This gentleman had by no means abandoned the exercise of his benevolence on behalf of the Bennets; rather, his ambitions had merely narrowed to the benefiting of one member in particular. He was consequently on the watch for Lizzy. He had come prepared to enter fully into the spirit of jollification, and after some minutes spent praising the dimensions and appearance of the Bingley house, stupefied her with the intelligence that the word *Ozomatli* was derived from the Nahuatl name for the monkey god of music, and that he was prepared to teach her the steps of a traditional Aztec ceremonial dance in the god's honor once the band opened its set. Unable to think swiftly enough of a suitable excuse, she was obliged to accede to this scheme for her undoing. She wanted to flee to John's soothing company but, seeing him deep in conversation with Charley, lacked the heart to interrupt them.

All too soon the dreaded moment arrived. Morris Collins took his mentoring duties very seriously, and demonstrated the steps of the dance with a fine disregard for both the stares of the partygoers and the rhythms of the band; but he did not find an apt pupil in Lizzy. She tried swaying slightly while watching the band perform, but repeated tugs on her sleeve compelled her to turn to her partner; she tried dancing in normal fashion in the hope of bringing him to reason; he was not to be deterred. She prayed with deep concentration that some gentleman in the assemblage would recall the time-honored practice of cutting in, or, failing such a rescue, that the ground would open up and swallow her whole—better still, swallow Morris Collins whole! But it was not to be, and she was obliged to endure the snickers of the Enclave girls and the familiarities of her partner with what dignity she could muster.

Even humiliation must eventually end, however, and by confessing to Morris that their exertions had made her thirsty, she was able at last to remove him from the dance floor. The moment he turned away toward the bar she was off, hoping to disappear into the press of people before he returned. She found Charlotte Lucas but had time to exchange only a few words with her before she found herself accosted again, this time by Fitzwilliam Darcy, who, to her blank amazement, asked her to dance. Once again caught unprepared, she could think of no immediate excuse and allowed herself to be led away.

The band was taking a break and a ballad was playing on the sound system. He put his hand to her waist and led off with every appearance of confidence. Lizzy was uncomfortably aware that his choice of partner was occasioning a good deal of comment around the room, but while she shared the general astonishment her displeasure was even greater. It seemed to her a crowning insult that the man who had deprived her of all anticipated pleasure in the evening should seek to take pleasure in her company, and for Jorge's sake she was determined to make Darcy's path a rocky one. She danced, accordingly, in silence for some time, until she decided that not speaking suited Darcy's own inclination, and she could better destroy his comfort by obliging him to converse.

"I've been enjoying Ozomatli's music," she said, glossing over her previous scenes of public shame. Darcy looked skeptical. "I didn't realize their lyrics were so political, and it surprises me that Caroline Bingley would make such a choice for her party's entertainment."

"I imagine she booked them more for their popularity than for their politics," said Darcy.

Another silence ensued, and Lizzy's displeasure increased. "It's *your* turn to say something now," she said eventually.

He smiled, and assured her that whatever she wished him to say would be said.

"Very well," she replied, "that will do for the present. Perhaps in a while I may observe that it's better to hear a band at a private party like this than at a club full of smoke and strangers. But for now we may be silent."

"Do you follow set rules, then, for conversation while dancing?"

"Sometimes it's best. It would be very odd to go through an entire dance without speaking at all; and yet in some situations it's advantageous to arrange things so that as little can be said as possible."

"Are you consulting your own feelings in this, or do you imagine that you're gratifying mine?"

"Both," said Lizzy. "I see a great similarity in our dispositions. We're both antisocial, unwilling to speak unless we expect to say something that will astound the world with our cleverness."

"That's no very accurate portrait of you, I believe," said he.

"How well it may suit *me*, I can't pretend to say. You think it apt, undoubtedly."

"You must be a better judge of your motives than I could be."

He made no answer, and silence reigned again for a time. At last he roused himself to make an inquiry after the progress of her plans for a community garden.

"I'm optimistic that we'll be able to break ground in May," she replied. Then, unable to resist offered temptation, she added, with less truth than malice, "Jorge Carrillo has been a great help with the project. I couldn't do it without him."

The effect was immediate. Darcy missed a step and would have stumbled had Lizzy not compensated for the error. This time the pause was long enough for her to begin to regret her impulse, before he finally said, "George Carrillo is blessed with social skills that ensure his making friends easily. Whether he's equally capable of *retaining* them is less certain."

"He's been so unfortunate as to lose your friendship—or is it that his family were so unfortunate as to have impeded the Darcys' interests?—to his lasting detriment!"

Darcy frowned but said nothing. Only further infuriated by his arrogant unwillingness to defend himself, Lizzy persisted. "I've heard you say that once you make up your mind about somebody, you never change it; I've heard you pass judgment on even so close a friend as Charley Bingley. You are very cautious, I hope, in forming those judgments before you declare them?"

"I am."

"And you never allow yourself to be blinded by prejudice?"

He stared down at her. "I hope not."

"It's particularly incumbent on those who never change their opinions to be sure of judging properly in the first place."

"Naturally," said he. "May I ask you the purpose of these questions?"

His tone made Lizzy quake a little, and she tried to pass it off lightly. "I'm a student of character, and am trying to make out yours."

"And what is your success?"

"Very little. I hear such different accounts of you that I'm thoroughly puzzled."

"That doesn't surprise me," he said. "And I might suggest that if you so disapprove of judging others, you refrain from passing judgment on me at this time, as there's reason to fear that the exercise would not reflect well on either of us."

In the face of this, even Lizzy could say no more. In silence they ended the dance, and in silence he surrendered her to Morris Collins, hovering at her elbow with her drink.

If Lizzy had any thought of offending Morris by going off to dance with another man, this hope was speedily extinguished. Morris was elated to see her finding favor with the likes of Darcy, for it validated his own estimation of her. Taking her arm, he steered her over to a quieter corner and seated her on a couch.

"How lucky that I was able to introduce you to Miss Catherine de Bourgh at the Lucases' party," he said. "I suppose she asked her nephew to learn more about you."

"If she did, he gave no indication of it."

"Of course he wouldn't. I have the highest opinion of your excellent judgment in all matters within the scope of your experience, but you couldn't possibly know the ways of the Enclave families. It's clear that you impressed her favorably, and she wants to get her nephew's opinion before she decides on your family's eligibility. He wouldn't say you were under scrutiny, because that might make your behavior less natural. But I'm sure you passed the test with flying colors."

Reflecting on what had passed between herself and Darcy, Lizzy said, "I would be very surprised if he formed a good opinion of me."

"I admire your modesty in saying so, but I'm sure he did, and

I congratulate myself on making the introduction that set your feet on the right path. In a small community like this, it's so important to make a good impression with the right people. I think you can count on being invited to join the Enclave now."

"Unfortunately, I believe the Enclave is not for the likes of my family. None of us is a rider, much less a polo player, and since my parents at least don't expect to live here permanently, I don't imagine they would want to pay for membership in a private club."

"But you seem to be putting down roots in this community, Miss Lizzy! Don't you think you'd like to make a life here? If you do, surely your parents would want to give you the best opportunities possible. And what about all my efforts to open the way for you?"

Before Lizzy could think of a way to discourage him without giving further offense, she became aware of a stir in the crowd, and observed Caroline Bingley hurrying to Darcy's side. Caroline whispered urgently in his ear; he turned, a startled look on his face that slowly gave way to a very grave expression. Lizzy followed the direction of his gaze and saw John and Charley out on the floor, dancing together. All over the room people were starting to nudge each other and point, and an ominous buzz was rippling out through the crowd. She could muster no more than a hasty apology to Morris before springing to her feet. Quickly she sought out Lydon and Jenny and told them what was happening; in a moment all three had joined the pair on the floor and turned it into a group dance. Kitty caught sight of them from across the room and dived in, moving smoothly from executing a swing step with Lizzy to shimmying down Lydon's side. They had done the same previously for John when trouble brewed, and he quickly caught on and started them on a line dance they all knew. Soon others on the dance floor, assuming this to be part of the entertainment, joined in, until most of the dancers were moving in unison.

The moment of tension died down and the crowd's focus shifted back to Ozomatli, but Lizzy was uncomfortably aware that the eyes of Darcy and Caroline remained fixed on John and Charley. The few quick glances she hazarded in their direction showed that Caroline continued to whisper and Darcy's visage retained its still, guarded expression.

After the band finished its set John and Charley did not dance anymore, but they remained together throughout the evening, Charley making little attempt to perform the duties of a host and John glowing with a joy that could not be disguised. Lizzy was happy for them but concerned about the attention they continued to attract. Lydon, Kitty, and Jenny, exhilarated by the dancing and the punch, became increasingly raucous and drew no small amount of notice with their own antics. To Lizzy it appeared that had her family made a pact to expose themselves as much as they could during the evening, it would have been impossible for them to play their parts with more spirit, or finer success; and to crown her misery, Morris Collins sought her out yet again and refused to stir from her side.

"I understand why you left so abruptly earlier," he said with a magnanimity that made her want to hit him. "Your brother's impulsiveness could have resulted in disaster for you all. We are traditional-values folk around here, and while a girl may occasionally dance with a sister or even a friend, men don't commonly do so. You were quite right, and your actions showed a fine sibling loyalty, to cover up his—well, let us be Christian and call it a faux pas. I hope you'll caution him that in future such displays will not be tolerated, for he could bring ruin on your entire family. I'll remain with you for the rest of the evening, so people will see that you are not to be ostracized."

"Are you sure your good credit will survive association with the likes of me?" inquired Lizzy.

"Your scruples and concern for my well-being touch my heart," said he, drawing closer to her. "I believe my reputation in Lambtown is solid enough to sustain greater blows than this, and can only enhance your own—not that there is anything that can be said to *your* discredit, though if you would give over your gardening it would be easier—it's only that people don't know you, and first impressions are very important. Few people, once they've made up their minds, can be persuaded to change them." He patted her hand, and she was very close to losing her temper until Charlotte came by and good-naturedly engaged Morris in conversation about local business.

The only consolation for Lizzy was that Darcy, though often standing nearby, did not approach or speak to her again for the rest of the evening. She felt sure this was a consequence of her defense of Jorge Carrillo, and was glad of it. The evening could not end soon enough for her, but her younger siblings were having too much fun, and her elder brother was too engrossed by Charley, for them to leave betimes. But at last even Lydon could no longer ignore the absence of other company or his hostess's yawns and glances toward the door, and had to acknowledge that the party was over.

Chapter Fifteen

The ramifications of this dreadful evening did not delay in making themselves felt in the Bennet household. Lizzy may only have imagined that several people avoided meeting her family's eyes in church, but after they exited with their lilies even Mrs. Bennet could not fail to observe that various acquaintances moved away just as she approached with her brood. Turning on the least favored of her offspring, she demanded that Lizzy tell her what she had done to cause trouble at the party the night before.

With an agonized glance to see whether John had overheard, Lizzy begged her mother to keep her voice down. John probably didn't notice because he was scanning the crowd for Charley, but the Bingleys were nowhere to be seen.

"If I hear that you offended somebody with your argumentative ways, it won't be good for you," said Mrs. Bennet.

Lizzy thought guiltily of her set-to with Fitzwilliam Darcy, but could not imagine that her words might have done more damage than Lydon and Kitty's behavior or John's dance with Charley. Darcy didn't seem like the type of person to tell tales, and in any case, what had she said that he didn't deserve?

Her mother, observing Lizzy's defiant head toss, said, "I knew it! You *did* do something rash! You'll be the death of me. I try so hard to help all of you, without any thought for myself, and you thwart me at every opportunity. If you knew how I wear myself away worrying about all my children, and how hard it is on my nerves to see you throwing away your chances. And this is all the thanks I get for my efforts—oh, but here is Mr.

Collins coming over! At least we are not abandoned by *all* our friends."

If Lizzy cherished hopes that she had dimmed Morris Collins's ardor the night before, they were speedily dashed. Displaying no trace of diffidence and speaking with greater economy and determination than was his wont, he explained that he was on his way over to Solvang to tour the open houses in that area, and would like to take Lizzy along for lunch and the tour— "For even if my duties as mayor of Lambtown may be considered the more significant of my responsibilities, I by no means intend to neglect my career, and possessing an intimate familiarity with the region's available homes is central to my success as a Realtor."

Lizzy opened her mouth to decline this treat, but her mother forestalled her. "Certainly, Lizzy will be happy to have lunch with you. You'll enjoy seeing some of the Danish houses, Lizzy— go and have a good time, you aren't needed at home."

Lizzy, having walked to church in order to see the neighborhood children hunting Easter eggs, could not even follow him in her own vehicle so as to be free to escape at will; she was obliged to submit to his plan with whatever civility she could muster.

Morris whiled away the drive by relating details, with most of which she was already familiar, of Solvang's history. The hamlet (she would have said tourist trap) was founded in 1911 by Danish immigrants who transformed a treeless, windswept plain into a thriving community that resembled a Scandinavian village as seen through the eyes of Walt Disney, all half-timbered walls, artfully crooked rooflines, and one-third-scale replicas of Copenhagen landmarks. Adding to the cultural indeterminacy engendered by its appearance, Solvang also provided a home for a replica of Shakespeare's Globe Theatre, and the town's windmills sometimes attracted visitors who imagined they were in for a Dutch cultural experience. Inevitably, in recent years local wineries had seized on the opportunity to ensnare the bewildered, and had opened a number of tasting rooms along the main thoroughfare.

Morris Collins was more attracted to what might be called the traditional Solvang, and directed their steps to one of the Danish bakeries for a lunch of *æbleskiver* and *medistepolse*. They spent the meal flagging in the newspaper's real estate section the Solvang-area open houses, a scene of domesticity that would have diverted Lizzy had any other female been called to take part in it. Morris meticulously numbered the listings by price, and they set out to explore.

At each stop Morris spent considerable time in colloquy with the agent sitting on the house, which left Lizzy free to poke about and design landscapes for the property in her head. She was beginning to feel that she might escape the afternoon without significant discomfiture when, at a residence so ugly that no other house hunters would visit it, Morris cornered her in an upstairs bedroom that the dispirited agent had allowed them to explore unaccompanied.

"Miss Lizzy—" he began, but she was in no humor for his nonsense and interrupted him.

"You know, I prefer Ms.," she said firmly.

"Well, perhaps we know each other well enough by now that I may call you simply Lizzy; but in an attempt to convey my respect and esteem for you I have developed the habit of addressing you more formally. And it's about my respect and esteem that I wish to speak."

"Honestly, I wish you wouldn't."

"Believe me, your reluctance does you no harm in my eyes. I've detected in you on occasion a modesty and reserve that are very appealing to me, especially when they temper your liveliness and energy. The contradictions in your character are, I admit, fascinating to me, and I believe that fascination would be durable and would make a relationship with you rewarding. But personal chemistry is not all that a man in my position needs to consider: you have been brought up to understand good manners, and I've seen you speak charmingly to your elders and betters. You'd be an asset to me on social occasions, and my standing in the community would offer you advantages that wouldn't otherwise be extended to you. My business and personal dealings with Catherine de Bourgh are bound to open doors that you, too, could walk through, if you were walking by my side. Obviously, it would be premature for us to speak of marriage, but by visiting these houses today I wished to convey to you the assurance that in selecting you as my girlfriend, I'm declaring intentions that are only respectful and serious."

"You don't *select* someone to be your girlfriend," said Lizzy. "You spend time with someone, and maybe a relationship develops and maybe it doesn't. Before you go any further, Morris, I have to tell you that I have spent enough time with you to be quite certain that in this case, it *doesn't*. I'm sure you will make some girl very happy, but I'm equally sure that I am not that girl."

"My praise for your modesty may be leading you to take that virtue to extremes," said he. "You must allow me to be the better judge of what would make me happy, and assure you that this offer is not the impulse of the moment. Almost from our first meeting I singled you out—"

"Please pay me the compliment of believing what I say! I hope you'll be very successful in all your endeavors, and I'm convinced that in declining your offer, I'm doing all I can to ensure that outcome."

"I find it hard to believe," said Morris, "that on the eve of the twenty-first century, a girl—even one as well brought up as yourself—would take offense at the suggestion that a couple date for a while before thinking of matrimony; for I can think of no other reason why you would react this way. I have an important position in Lambtown and connections with the best families all over the valley; I have a good career and, as you've seen today, work hard to continue and extend my success. Perhaps in your pique you aren't seeing your own situation clearly! Your family are newcomers here, with no land or roots in the community. Despite your charms, it's by no means certain that anyone else will notice you. I expect you're just toying with me, in the hope of enticing me with suspense."

"Any suspense you're suffering is entirely your own doing, and would be over if you would only believe what I say."

"But how can I take you seriously, when you're saying things you can't possibly mean?"

"You must find a way. And while you're working on that, I'm going to go wait in the car until you're ready to take me home." Thither she repaired forthwith, Morris trailing after her alternately pleading and resentful. But she remained obdurate in the face of his every importunity, and in the end he was obliged to comply.

After such a weekend Lizzy might be excused for feeling beset, and she was well aware that no sooner would the story of her contretemps with Morris become known at home than her situation would only become worse. So when she returned to find a message from the Gardiners inviting her out to a last-minute dinner, she seized the opportunity for a respite.

Mary Gardiner had recalled that today was Evelyn Bennet's birthday, and it was her notion that a convivial evening at Mattei's Tavern would bring Evelyn's spirit close to those who had loved her. Mattei's Tavern was a nineteenth-century stagecoach stop in Los Olivos that had been serving travelers and the community for more than a hundred years; Lizzy loved its offbeat charm, the blithe mismatch of spartan Old West architecture and gaudy chandeliers, the plush, dark Victorian bar and the simple calm of the dining room situated in an enclosed porch.

They were happily settled with their bread and a bottle of

locally grown Chardonnay, and Edward Gardiner was discussing some details of the community garden planting, now only a few weeks away, when there was a stir in the room and Catherine de Bourgh arrived, trailed by her nephew and niece, Fitzwilliam Darcy and Anne Fitzwilliam, as well as a man of about thirty whom Lizzy had never seen before. This party took the best table in the room, a large, round one intended for eight. Lizzy turned slightly in her seat to avoid looking at them, determined to enjoy her present friends without distraction; so she was unprepared when Mr. Gardiner stopped speaking and looked past her in inquiry.

"Good evening, Mr. Gardiner, Mrs. Gardiner," said Darcy from behind her. Lizzy acknowledged him fleetingly and then prepared to ignore him, but he stood his ground. "There is extra space at our table," he continued, "and my aunt wondered if you might care to join us for Easter dinner, since your food hasn't yet been served."

Mary Gardiner, whose acquaintance with the de Bourghs and Darcys was of the slightest, appeared astonished, and Lizzy shook her head fractionally, but Edward Gardiner was of a gregarious disposition and agreed to the change without pausing to consider the feelings of the ladies. So Lizzy found herself yet again prisoner to undesirable company; as she smiled mechanically and allowed herself to be escorted to the center of the room, she formed a mental resolve to spend the next month camped in a tent on a mountaintop if that's what was required to escape such trials.

The demands of precedence at least spared her the misery of sitting near her new hostess or Darcy; she was placed quite on the opposite side of the table from them, between Anne Fitzwilliam and the unknown gentleman, who was introduced as Anne's brother Calvin.

"Cal was looking over a promising colt at Santa Anita," boomed Catherine to the table—and room—at large, "and kindly joined us here in order to escort Anne and me back to Kentucky next week. Our families have adjoining boxes at Churchill Downs, and of course I'll be attending the races in a year when both my nephew *and* my brother have a horse in the Derby."

Since his aunt's pronouncements rarely called for a response, Cal turned to his fair neighbor to open civilities. "Are you a horsewoman?"

"Not at all, though in such company I expect I should blush to admit it."

"By no means! I'm delighted to hear it, because if you were an enthusiast we'd be condemned to an evening of points and gaits and gory details of breeding that would make our wine blush."

Lizzy laughed. "Yes, I've been privy to a few of those discussions since I moved here. I love seeing horses but know absolutely nothing about them, and have never even been to see a horse race."

"Bravo! We must discover what you *do* know something about, and speak of that. I hear I missed quite a shindig on Saturday night. What was the name of the band?"

"Ozomatli. Very big on the L.A. scene right now. They were good—this wild blend of Latin and hip-hop that kept threatening to spin into chaos but somehow managed to keep it together. A great party band; I expect my father would describe them as 'dionysian.'"

"I'm sorry I missed that. It's been a long time since I enjoyed a good bacchanal. I see you've unwreathed the ivy from your hair."

"What are you talking about over there?" demanded his aunt across the table. Lizzy and Cal looked up to find all the company, silenced, turned in their direction.

"Of music, Aunt Catherine," said Cal composedly.

"Oh! Well, if you're speaking of music, let us all have our

share of the conversation. There are few people who enjoy music more than I do, or have a finer ear. Did you attend the Philharmonic when you were in Los Angeles?"

"No, I didn't. We were talking about a very different kind of music—the band at the Bingleys' party last night."

"That sort of noise may not be considered music at all. A wholly different term must be invented for it. Is that the sort of thing you enjoy, Miss Bennet?"

"I enjoy many different kinds of music, ma'am. What's appropriate for a concert hall would be less satisfactory if played in a parade; music intended for dancing would forfeit much of its pleasure if one had to sit still in rows listening to it. Each has its place."

"Are you fond of dancing, then?" asked Cal. "In that case, I'm even more sorry I didn't arrive a day earlier. Anne, I assume you and Darcy were there?"

"Anne's health wouldn't allow her to be out so late at night," said her aunt. Lizzy peeped over at the girl next to her, but she had nothing to add in support or refutation of this claim.

"And you, Darcy?" Cal persisted. "I know the Bingleys are your close friends. I hope you weren't a party pooper."

"I was there."

"You may have been there, but that doesn't answer my question. I've seen you stand in the corner nursing a single drink for an entire evening. Lizzy, I appeal to you as an impartial judge: was my cousin the life of the party, or its wet blanket?"

"Perhaps she was too busy to notice," said Darcy.

Lizzy laughed heartily at this. "Your cousin will give you the impression that I'm nothing but a wild party girl, the Britney Spears of the Santa Ynez. Next thing you know, everyone will be calling me Busy Lizzy. He should be careful, though, because he might tempt me to retaliate. I have indeed seen him behave exactly as you describe—and at a ball on Valentine's Day, no less, an occasion when everyone should make an effort to get into the social spirit. But in this case I'm in an awkward position, and it would be rude of me to make fun of him, since he danced with me last night."

"Oho, now it gets interesting!" Cal directed a sly smile toward his cousin, who stared at him coldly.

"On the contrary, Cal, I can't think of a stupider subject," said Catherine. "If you haven't anything to say that would interest the entire company, you can keep your mouth shut." And she turned to Edward Gardiner to ask his view of the new county zoning proposal. "Of course it's ridiculous to put restrictions on how the large landowners can develop their property," she continued without awaiting his reply. "These eco fanatics can't expect ranchers to give up the value of their land simply for the viewing pleasure of tourists. If I can make more money converting my property to vineyard, or even to tract homes, who has the right to stop me?"

"Those who hold large parcels of open land have responsibilities as well as rights," said Darcy. "Stewardship is an obligation to one's heritage, past and future."

"Bah! You're too sentimental. You're just like your father: I told him twenty-five years ago he should've signed leases with the oil companies to drill on Pemberley Ranch, but he was as foolish as you are. Leaving a good-size trust fund to one's descendants is heritage enough, and more likely to be appreciated by them. The land has always been exploited, and always will be. The trick is to change the means of exploitation as times change."

"Some forms of exploitation leave scope for future generations, while others end up destroying the asset. I prefer to use my land in such a way as to preserve value for my heirs."

"What nonsense! I warn you, Darcy, if you continue to be stubborn on this subject, I may put the management of my acreage in someone else's hands."

Her nephew remained silent.

"It seemed as if we got a decent amount of rain this year,"

said Mary Gardiner brightly. "Mr. Darcy, what is the state of the creeks?"

As the conversation fragmented into smaller groups, Lizzy tried to draw out Anne Fitzwilliam, but she could not be induced to utter more than the occasional monosyllable, so Lizzy turned back to her livelier brother.

To her relief he did not revert to the subject of the Bingleys' party, but asked about her family. "And did you grow up in the Santa Ynez?"

"No, we moved here only a few months ago, from Ohio. I spent summers here with an aunt when I was a child, but I haven't been back for many years."

"How do you like it?"

"I think it's one of the most beautiful places I've ever seen," said Lizzy. "Every day it gets lovelier. When we arrived, I couldn't get used to how green everything was, especially after January in Columbus. By the time the leaves pop there, summer is almost upon you. But here the spring seems to go on forever. Every week I see a new round of flowers coming out, and now all the valley oaks are leafing. I thought they were magnificent when they were bare, but now they're even more so. The ranches around here are an urban American's fantasy of what an English nobleman's estate must be like."

"Except without the crumbling castle."

"But who needs a crumbling castle, when you can have a snug ranch house, or a stone cabin? And I could do without an English estate's impoverished tenant holdovers from the medieval era, too."

"So this seems like a utopian paradise to you?"

"Not at all; I'm not blind to the suffering of the immigrant labor force, or the shortage of middle-class jobs. I was speaking only of the landscape."

"My cousin Darcy shares your affection for those oaks. I've seen him going over his pastures with a fine-toothed comb and instructing his hands to build wire cages around every spindly seedling he finds, so that the cattle won't eat them."

"Your cousin appears to have a very highly developed sense of noblesse oblige—from the lowly oak seedling to all of Lambtown and beyond, he seems to feel himself charged with the obligation of management."

"That makes it sound as if he went around interfering in everyone's lives, which is probably a truer portrait of my aunt's character. You should make allowances: he was brought up with the idea that he would assume a great deal of responsibility when his time came, and unfortunately his time came all too soon, when he was barely out of college. I give him credit for taking on his father's duties without resentment—I'm not sure I would have forfeited my youth so graciously."

"It's probably the fault of my upbringing," said Lizzy, smiling, "that I'm a little shocked by what seems like a feudal structure to the society here. I'm accustomed to seeing less separation of classes, and more social mobility. Around here, language, culture, *everything* separates rich and poor. And yet in some cases at least, the poor have a more authentic, and certainly longer, connection to the land."

"Like the old Chicano slogan, 'We didn't cross the border, the border crossed us'?"

"I hadn't heard that before, but yes, that's it exactly! Sometimes I feel embarrassed to be Anglo around here. Before I came west, I never questioned whether I was authentically American, or what that meant. Now I sometimes feel like an imperialist, or at least a marauder."

"Your scruples do you credit, but we can't undo history, and at some point descendants must be forgiven the sins of their ancestors."

"What are you going on about now, Cal?" demanded his aunt. "You can't monopolize him for the entire evening, Miss Bennet!"

"I beg your pardon, ma'am," said Lizzy. "Your nephew is a very tolerant conversationalist, and indulged me when I got carried away. I'll release him now to the table."

Cal looked less than entirely delighted at being thus given his liberty, but he—and indeed, the rest of the gathering, willy-nilly—obligingly listened to what his aunt had to say for the remainder of the meal. As nothing was beneath her attention that could furnish her with an occasion for dictating to others, this consisted chiefly of criticism of others' dessert choices, instructions regarding the weather they were to have on the morrow, and strictures on the service provided by the waiters, none of which required more than assent or endurance from her guests, though it added materially to the relief felt by all when the meal came to a close.

Back in the car, Mary Gardiner was profuse in her apologies to Lizzy and frank in her rebukes to her husband. "What were you thinking, putting us at the mercy of that harridan when we could have had such a pleasant evening together?"

"I thought perhaps Lizzy might prefer a dinner with people her own age. And she seemed to like Cal Fitzwilliam well enough."

"He was a very pleasant man," said Lizzy, "but I would have enjoyed your company just as well."

"Still, it was a shame, when we planned to have a quiet dinner in your aunt's honor," said Mary Gardiner.

"I'm not sure a quiet dinner would have been possible, even at our own table, once Catherine the Great had entered the room! I hope we can have our dinner on some other occasion."

And Lizzy was still able to derive some amusement from the evening, for she found her father waiting up for her return, so she was able to regale him with all the details of the great lady's manners. This shared pleasure, if it failed to erase from her thoughts the vexations of the weekend, at least almost sufficed to induce in Lizzy a spirit of philosophy. If she could laugh away her trials, she went a fair way toward forgetting them and recovering her naturally optimistic frame of mind. There are, after all, few consolations so restorative to one's own self-esteem as the opportunity to ridicule one's neighbors, even if the cost is to be laughed at in one's turn.

Chapter Sixteen

Those vexations could only recur in the morning, however, when her mother demanded to know the details of her afternoon with Morris Collins.

It was not to be expected that Mrs. Bennet would be any more ready than Morris had been to accept his *congé*. Her eldest daughter was not so dear to her that she might not be sacrificed on the altar of ambition, and Mrs. Bennet was quite prepared to do battle on Morris's behalf, so long as his interests tallied with her own. She displayed an alarming readiness to go seek him out so that Lizzy could apologize and beg humbly to be restored to his good opinion—but this Lizzy steadfastly refused to do. Faced with such resolute disobedience, Mrs. Bennet sought higher authority, in the form of her husband. She discovered him along with Mary in the study, reading quietly, and as her raised voice shattered his peace he demanded to know what was amiss.

"It's your obstinate daughter," cried she. "Here was Morris Collins, all eager to go steady with her—"

"Morris wanted to hook up?" demanded Kitty, drawn to the tumult. Mary shuddered.

"—and expressing himself very properly, mentioning his serious intentions and his willingness to smooth her path into the best circles, and what must she do but turn him down! I'm sure you were rude to him, too," she said, rounding on Lizzy.

"I may have been a little sarcastic," Lizzy admitted.

"And I've ordered her to apologize and try to make amends—if that's even possible, if she hasn't offended him too deeply—but she refuses! And now I'm afraid he'll shun us all, just because of her arrogance and obstinacy."

"It seems a hopeless business. What am I to do on the occasion?"

"You must act like her father, of course! Speak to her yourself. Tell her that you insist on her making it up to him."

"Step forward, child," said Mr. Bennet. Lizzy complied. "This is a serious matter. I am to understand that Morris Collins wishes to 'hook up' with you. Is this true?"

"I wouldn't use that term—but okay, more or less."

"And this proposal—or should I say, *proposition*—you have refused?"

"Yes."

"Now we come to the point. Your mother insists on your accepting him, for the sake of the family's social advancement. Isn't that so?"

"Yes, or I will never speak to her again."

"An unhappy situation confronts you, Lizzy. From this day you must be a stranger to one of your parents. Your mother will never speak to you again if you don't accept his offer, and I will never speak to you again if you do."

Mrs. Bennet swelled with outrage, but despite this setback was by no means discouraged. "Don't think I'll give way on this just because you won't support me! I'm accustomed to being the only person who looks out for this family's welfare. Nobody knows what I suffer, the sacrifices I make, in trying to secure the best for my children. And they are all ungrateful and undutiful."

"*I* am not undutiful," protested Mary.

"Who was talking about you?"

"If Morris Collins wanted to date me, I wouldn't say no," Mary persisted.

"Eww!" cried Kitty.

"Neither of you has anything to do with the question," said Mrs. Bennet. "If I were speaking to you, Lizzy, I would say that you're selfish and stubborn, and don't care what happens to the rest of us so long as you get your own way."

Since she was *not* being spoken to, Lizzy felt no obligation to reply; resignation to inevitable evils is the duty of us all, and is all the more easily achieved when the inevitable evil is found to be pleasanter than its alternative. But for the sake of her father and siblings she remained in the room while her mother continued to animadvert on her sufferings.

"I gave up my whole life and all my friends in Columbus to come here, and what is my reward? No friends, no money from Evelyn, nothing but disobedience and disrespect. Poor Lydon has to wear his life away working in that coffee shop, and Lizzy won't lift a finger to make things easier for him."

"*I* work hard, too, and nobody's doing anything for me," said Kitty.

Mrs. Bennet was not to be distracted from her woes. "Morris Collins was our best hope for establishment in this community, but does Lizzy care? Not a bit! She'd rather tear every joy away from me."

"Morris Collins's conversation was indeed a joy to us all, and I for one shall miss it," remarked Mr. Bennet. "Greatly though I valued his discourse, however, I can't go so far as to say that we are bereft of any joy when deprived of it. After all, there remain all the pleasures of your company, my dear."

Mrs. Bennet paid him no heed. "John is my only remaining hope," she declared. "He is the only comfort of my old age. When he and Bingley are together we won't need Morris Collins to make our way. If it weren't for John, there would be nothing left for us here."

Poor Mrs. Bennet! Even this last ray of hope was soon to be denied her. That very evening John and the other employees of The Chocolate Bar received an e-mail from its owner:

By the time you get this I will be in Kentucky. My friend Fitzwilliam Darcy has offered me a great opportunity: to accompany him on his annual trip to his uncle's stud farm and attend the Triple Crown races. I have always wanted to see the world of horse racing from the inside, and this offer is too good to pass up. You have all worked hard to get The Chocolate Bar on its feet, and I wouldn't have been able to do it without you. I am sending in a seasoned manager, Richard Hurst, from one of my other restaurants, to take over for me, and he will start on Wednesday. I know you will all welcome him and show him the ropes, and his experience will help grow the business. I have complete confidence in him, and can leave The Chocolate Bar and all of you in his hands without worry.

Thanks for making our first couple of months so much fun!
Charles Bingley

Lizzy was aghast. "How long has this been in the works? I had no idea he was thinking of going away."

"I knew nothing of it either," confessed John.

"But this is the official staff e-mail. What did he say about it to you directly?"

"This is the only message I received."

"He can't have just gone off without a word to you. And why would he bring in a manager from outside? He should have promoted you."

"I expect he thought I wasn't qualified."

"That's nonsense! You've done everything for that business from day one, right by his side." John said nothing. "And he can't mean he's going away for all the Triple Crown races—he'd be gone for two months!"

"There's nothing in this message to indicate that he means to come back at all," said John.

"Well, that's just crazy—of course he means to come back! I'm sure he'll call you as soon as they get to Kentucky. Nobody who's seen you together can have any doubt that he cares for you."

"I don't think you should encourage me to believe that."

"I think you should *know* it, not believe it. Whenever the two of you are together, he can't look at or talk to anyone else. Just the night before last he was dancing with you!"

"But I asked him, he didn't ask me," said John unhappily. "And when I did, I saw he paused for a moment before agreeing. I think he must have been just drifting along, enjoying a new friendship without thinking about it. You know, even people who wouldn't normally have anything to do with each other can get very close when they work long hours side by side under pressure. Maybe he simply didn't question it until I asked him to dance, and at that moment he suddenly realized where *I* thought our relationship was going. If that's true, then he's acting very responsibly, even kindly."

"If letting you down was his intention, I can see no kindness in doing it via a group e-mail."

"Oh, yes! He could have humiliated me publicly. He could have gone around calling me a faggot to all his friends."

"Whatever else he may be, I don't believe Charley Bingley is that kind of boor."

"No, he's the sweetest and kindest of men," said John with a sad smile. "Don't you see? He realized that I was thinking of him in romantic terms, when he had no such feelings about me. He thought it would be best just to go away for a while, in order to make it clear to me that no relationship was possible. I must be grateful that he's shown so much tact and forbearance."

"I see no such thing! I read it completely differently. I think he realized how deep his feelings for you had become, and panicked a little. Charlotte has told me that this is not the kind of community where gay people live openly, and maybe in this setting he's been able to ignore his sexual orientation—until you came along, and he fell in love and couldn't ignore it any longer!

So he needs a little time to think. He'll soon realize that the charms of a bunch of thoroughbreds can't measure up to yours, and come right back."

"I don't know. His friends and family probably don't want him to be gay, and if they think he's in danger they'll encourage him to stay away."

"And what if they do? He's his own man, and if he's gay they can't change it just by wishing it away. Though I can easily believe that his sister and Darcy would be arrogant enough to try."

"You mustn't call it arrogance—they care about him, and simply want him to be happy. And if he's ostracized where he lives, how happy would he be—someone like Charley, who's friendly to everybody, and enjoys company as much as he does?"

"If on mature deliberation you find that the misery of disappointing his sister and his friend is greater than the happiness of being with him, then I advise you by all means to think no more about him."

John laughed reluctantly. "Don't be silly. If I thought he cared about me, I wouldn't hesitate. If we were together and he was made unhappy here because of it, I'd suggest that we move to the city—to San Francisco, or maybe L.A."

"That's the spirit! I can well imagine Darcy and Caroline finding it inconvenient to their plans for him to be in love with you, but you have only to ignore them both, and all will be well. You have to trust in Charley to sort things out in his head; and I will *not* feel sorry for you."

"If he doesn't come back, the issue won't arise. A thousand things could keep him away."

"I can't imagine what those thousand things might be, but I can imagine one thing that would bring him back, and it's worth more than a thousand nothings."

Lizzy continued to work hard at reassuring her brother, encouraging him to keep faith in Charley's attachment, and believed she achieved a measure of success. She even refrained from urging him to quit his job in protest, though she clearly foresaw how uncomfortable it was going to be for him there, when people learned he had been passed over for an outside manager. They agreed to say as little as possible to their mother about Charley's departure, but even that little was enough to provoke a fresh round of bewailing and recrimination; and John quickly learned that his home was destined to be no more comfortable for him than his workplace.

Chapter Seventeen

I t was too much to hope that Kitty would keep to herself such thrilling events in the lives of her elder siblings, and despite spending her days at work in Lompoc, she was speedily able to ensure that all of Lambtown learned of their miseries.

Charlotte Lucas, seeing Lizzy at work in her aunt's garden as she drove by, stopped to express cautious sympathy that things hadn't worked out with Morris Collins.

"I would've said that congratulations, rather than sympathy, were the order of the day," retorted Lizzy. "It's a great relief to me. You know that hideous awkwardness when you are aware that someone is interested in you, but they haven't said anything so you can't warn them off? At least I was able to make my feelings clear—assuming he continues to accept my word for it, and doesn't slip back into thinking I was just being coy, or miffed, or shy!"

"Are you sure you *weren't* being coy, or miffed, or shy?"

"How can you ask me that? Even if there weren't other, more interesting men in town, do you believe I would strike such a mercenary bargain? My body, for access to the Enclave?"

Charlotte turned the conversation toward John. "How is he doing? I hope he isn't heartbroken at losing Charles."

"He isn't heartbroken, because he hasn't lost Charley! Charley's friends and family may wish that his feelings were otherwise, but they can't actually do anything to change them. He'll be back in no time."

Charlotte soon went on her way, just as certain as Lizzy that she knew the truth of these matters, and perhaps even better pleased, having heard enough to see her own road opening before her. For Charlotte's amiable intention was nothing less than to secure her friend from further harassment on the part of Morris Collins, by turning his attentions toward herself.

This she found surprisingly easy to achieve, despite how recently he had been bewitched by the charms of another. She did not doubt that a man who had so emphatically been rejected must be in want of a sympathetic ear, and this she was generous enough to offer. From wallowing in bitter feelings about the cruelty and deceitfulness of some females, Morris found mercifully short the path he must travel to be soothed by the balm of a very different kind of woman. Bathed in Charlotte's ready sympathy and the flattering deference she paid to his interests and concerns, he rapidly came to recognize in her the very partner he had been seeking, and was left only to wonder at his previous failure to perceive that he and Charlotte were made for each other. For her part, Charlotte did not find the charm of his courtship so compelling as to incline her to prolong it; accordingly, she took care that little time should be allowed to pass before he might be sure of her.

This turn of events not unnaturally left Morris elated: from the jaws of defeat he had snatched victory, and his prosperous love would spare him any extended period of humiliation. The Lucases, though not of the first rank in Lambtown, were well enough regarded to be members of the Enclave, and Catherine de Bourgh was certain to approve of his choice. He lost no time in making the news public.

Charlotte accepted the congratulations of her friends with composure. Lacking any ambition to test her mettle against the wider world, she had long wished to secure her position in her familiar sphere, but was aware that she could not forever rely on her parents' standing to determine her own. Morris might be an irksome companion and his attachment to her illusory, but he had a successful business and would always take care to do nothing that might jeopardize his access, or hers, to the circles of the rich and well-regarded. Without thinking highly of men she had always assumed them to be necessary to her comfortable establishment in life, and was satisfied to have secured one with so little inconvenience. Having scant respect for her partner must make it easier to pursue her own goals without regard for his, even should those goals diverge significantly in the future. On the whole, she had every reason to be content.

This tale of prosperous romance was carried to Lizzy by Jorge Carrillo, who sought her out at the Lompoc warehouse. She was shocked and disappointed that so promising a friend as Charlotte should be throwing herself away on one of the stupidest men she had ever met, and did not scruple to say as much to Jorge.

His face, which had been troubled while he was telling her the tale, brightened. "I'd heard that you were spending a lot of time with him, and was worried that you might be unhappy about the news."

"I wasn't spending time with him by choice! He kept attaching himself to me, and nothing would shake him off. On my own account I couldn't be more relieved; if I am sorry, it's about Charlotte."

"That's good to hear," said Jorge. "People had said you spent the whole evening with him at Caroline Bingley's party, and I thought—"

"If *you* had been there, I might have been able to escape him," said Lizzy.

He appeared gratified. "I wouldn't admit this to most people, but to you I can say that as the time drew near I realized it would be better for me not to be in the same room with Darcy, at a party given by his special friends. If he made a scene, it'd be unpleasant for others, not just myself. I didn't want to ruin the party for everyone else."

She admired his thoughtfulness, but it further excited her

anger against Fitzwilliam Darcy. "He has a lot to answer for! You shouldn't have to avoid him, he should be staying away from public places for the common good. Not content with spoiling the party for all your friends who missed you, now he's taken Charley Bingley off to Kentucky."

Jorge did not pretend to misunderstand her. "Is John missing him a lot?"

"I'm afraid his heart will break if Charley doesn't come back—and all because the arrogant Mr. Darcy thinks he can arrange everyone else's life to suit his purposes!"

"At least there's one bright side to all this: we won't be seeing Darcy again before June, unless his horse breaks a leg."

"Let's hope for the horse's sake that Darcy won't decide that a broken leg would suit his purposes," snapped Lizzy.

"Not something to joke about. I'm a great horse lover myself, and in fact I've been spending a lot of my time lately, since the weather has dried out, training for the *charreada* at the Rodeo Days this summer. But all work and no play makes Jorge a dull boy; so I was hoping you might take pity and go out with me on Friday. No Darcy, none of your siblings this time, not even my horse—just the two of us."

Lizzy was only too happy to fall in with this plan and be charmed out of her resentment; for a time her own enjoyment promised to supersede all family cares. But they could not be escaped when she got home and discovered that word of Charlotte and Morris had reached her mother. It was too much to hope that Mrs. Bennet's spirits would be equal to such a setback, and Lizzy had to face a fresh round of recrimination. Nor was Mrs. Bennet appeased by the prospect of Lizzy's date with Jorge: "He may be as handsome as he pleases, but what use is *that* if he has no money or connections? You're already starting to see the consequences of your stubbornness—and don't come crying to me when you find yourself completely cast out of Lambtown society!"

"If this is my punishment for saying no to the likes of Morris

Collins, I should do it more often. I really don't think a life of lonely spinsterhood is just around the corner for me. Dare I mention that I've also been invited to the meeting of the Poets this week? At least Mrs. Gardiner doesn't seem to feel I've put myself beyond the pale."

"Well, if that's what you consider good society—a bunch of people reading to each other—I wash my hands of you."

Mrs. Bennet's ill-humor was not the only reason for the gloom now pervading the household. Kitty was resentful because Lizzy wouldn't take her along on her date with Jorge ("It's just like you to keep everything good to yourself!"); Mary was sulking over the death of her hopes for Morris Collins; Mr. Bennet was practicing invisibility; and John, though he strove to appear as cheerful as ever, was finding it difficult to sustain his spirits as each day passed without a word from Charley.

Hoping her supportive presence would do John some good, Lizzy returned to her prior habit of spending what time she could at The Chocolate Bar. The new manager, Richard Hurst, seemed to be an idle fellow, a man of few words who was more ready to eat the wares than to sell them. He left the front room almost entirely in John's hands but showed little appreciation for his employee's hard work and steady disposition. John was increasingly obliged to come in to supervise on his days off, and forgo all work breaks during the day. It was not in his nature to complain, but the only time his countenance brightened was when the customers were children.

The new manager was not the only humiliation he had to face: it was not long before Caroline Bingley appeared in the shop. At first, with other customers present, she tried to ignore John; but as the tables emptied she could not avoid acknowledging him.

Having eaten half her salad, she pushed it away with an irritable exclamation.

"Is something wrong?" John asked.

"Oh, there's far too much dressing on this! I don't know how anyone could eat it."

"I'm so sorry. Let me get you a new one, with the dressing on the side."

"No, it's too late now, and that would just be wasting resources. I'm sure with Charley gone none of the employees are giving any thought to issues like that, but I'm not going to encourage you to ignore the bottom line."

"It's company policy to replace any meal that a customer isn't satisfied with," said John mildly.

"Oh, just forget it. I told Charley this place would fall apart as soon as his back was turned. But he was so excited to be leaving town—what was there for him here, after all? He's used to a more sophisticated way of life, and it was a great opportunity to see thoroughbred racing close up."

"I'm surprised you didn't go with them," said Lizzy; "surely Darcy invited you, too?"

Caroline refused to rise to this bait. "Oh, Charley and Darcy have so many friends in common—who knows where they'll be off to next? I wouldn't be surprised if they went on to Epsom after the Preakness, or to their college reunion, or headed off to Martha's Vineyard. If they do, I'll certainly join them. But I can't think of anything that would bring them back here anytime soon."

Lizzy was fully prepared to do battle on John's behalf, but intercepting the anguished look he cast her way, she bit back her retort and allowed Caroline to savor her triumph.

Supporting John's spirits was all that mattered to Lizzy; but this she found difficult to achieve without sacrificing the candor habitual to their relationship. It was impossible that her esteem for Charley should not suffer a diminution: much as she had always liked him, she could not think without anger, hardly without contempt, of the compliant, irresolute character that allowed him to be so easily swayed by the influence of his friends. Had his own happiness been the only sacrifice, he might have sported with it in whatever manner he chose; but when his behavior harmed John, complaisance was impossible. Encouraging her brother to hope, therefore, was becoming at once less tenable and less desirable—but how else was she to alleviate his misery? That his misery was acute she did not doubt, for all that he spoke little of it and made every effort to appear as cheerful as ever.

Such emotion as John was laboring under could not entirely be repressed, however, and when they were alone that night he confided some part of what he felt. "I'll always remember him as the kindest, finest man I've ever known. It's my fault for having felt too much, and assumed too much, so I have the comfort of knowing that no harm was done to anyone but myself. I know he would never deliberately cause anyone pain; it was my vanity that deceived me into imagining that he intended more than he did."

"I wish I could take so benign a view."

"You can't say you think he was deliberately leading me on! It's a dangerous road to start thinking of oneself as intentionally injured."

"Oh, I acquit Charley of malice. But thoughtless he may be, and certainly malleable. The more I see of people, the fewer I love, and the fewer still I respect."

"You mustn't give way to feelings like that! How will you ever find happiness without faith in the basic goodness of others? And if you lose respect for people whenever they make a mistake, you would have to stop respecting me for having been so mistaken in this case. I don't think I could bear the misery I'd feel if you did."

"How could I ever lose respect for you, the best and sweetest person I know?"

"Then please try to see Charley through my eyes, and spare me the pain of despising him."

Lizzy could scarcely oppose this wish, and thenceforth little was said of Charley Bingley by either of them.

Chapter Eighteen

Edward and Mary Gardiner were fast becoming favorites with Lizzy. In Mrs. Gardiner especially she found the ideal sort of companion: a friend who knew enough of her secrets for candor to be possible, but one whose own interests diverged sufficiently that she had little interest in spreading those secrets abroad. She well understood why her aunt would have grown so close to the Gardiners, and developed the habit of consulting with them in the manner that, under other circumstances, she might have consulted with her parents. It was, therefore, a pleasant respite to go to their house for an evening of readings and good food.

She went early to help Mrs. Gardiner with the cooking and other arrangements. While Mr. Gardiner was in the basement selecting wines, Mrs. Gardiner asked after John.

"His temperament is so mild that people often don't see how deep his feelings are," said Lizzy. "I'm afraid he's taking this disappointment quite hard. He was becoming very attached to Charley; and why not? Charley seemed to feel the same way."

"I didn't see them together much. What led you to think that Charles shared John's feelings?"

"Well, whenever they were in the same room—as they were for most of every day, working at The Chocolate Bar—they spoke almost exclusively to each other, and even when they weren't speaking, they would communicate through glances and gestures. I always felt like a third wheel around them, even though they're both very polite people. Isn't that kind of exclusive obsession a fair sign of love?"

"Or of a momentary infatuation, forgotten as soon as the object happens not to be around."

"But there was no 'happens' about it! I'm convinced that his sister and his friend, Fitzwilliam Darcy, deliberately cooked up a scheme to get Charley out of town. You should've seen them hissing together at the Bingleys' party when Charley danced with John. And right after that, Darcy bears Charley away for an unspecified period of time—an invitation nobody had heard of before they were gone? The whole thing stinks."

"Poor John! He doesn't seem like the kind of person who'll get over it easily. It should've happened to you, Lizzy; you would've laughed yourself out of it in no time."

"Are you saying I'm shallow?" asked Lizzy, smiling.

Mrs. Gardiner patted her cheek, apologized for getting flour all over her, and handed her a dish towel. "You know I'm not, I only mean that you have the saving grace of humor, and don't dwell on things as much. And when you choose to exercise the gift, you can be very perceptive."

"Uh-oh—when I choose to exercise it? Here I am, priding myself on my perspicacity—have you caught me being dense about some situation or person?"

"On the contrary, I'm so certain of your commonsense that I'm sure I'm only echoing the voice in your own head when I caution you about George Carrillo."

"Jorge!"

"So it pleases him to call himself, but George he was born, and he's every bit as American as you or I, for all his Latin-lover airs. He seems well enough behaved nowadays, but there's been trouble in the past, or so I've heard."

"What sort of trouble?"

"I don't know any details, but there was something that involved the Darcys somehow, and I know Frank and Lupe were very worried about him at the time."

"Oh, I know all about the thing with the Darcys! They took

their land from the Carrillo ancestors illegally, but the Darcys have all the documents in their possession, so the Carrillos can't prove anything. Darcy's father liked Jorge, and maybe he felt guilty about that history, because he gave Jorge a job; but Darcy got rid of Jorge as soon as his father died."

"Well, perhaps that was it. But do you know what George does for a living, or how he can afford that fancy truck, and his horse, and all his *charreada* trappings?"

"I don't think the subject of his job has ever come up," Lizzy acknowledged. "But I think he works in Lompoc, since I've met him there a few times. And as for money, I guess I assumed that his parents help him out. Doesn't his mother get a share of the profits from the Chumash casino?"

"Maybe so. In any case, I hope you'll think twice before falling in love with him."

"So that's your concern! Well, if I were to fall in love with him, concerns about his finances might have more of a place. But I assure you, it's not my intention to fall in love with anybody at this stage of my life; I have so many other things to do. Even so, I can't promise to be wiser than anyone else my age, and thinking once, much less twice, before falling in love is a lot to expect of a young woman. I admit that I like Jorge very much; we think alike on many subjects, I like his values, and you have to agree that he's extremely handsome! Perhaps it would be best if he could be persuaded not to fall in love with *me*, for how could I resist him if he did? It seems an unreasonable burden to place on my self-control."

Mrs. Gardiner, though she laughed, had a stubborn look and seemed poised to pursue the matter further, so it may have been fortunate that at this moment the doorbell rang and the Poets started to arrive. She put the roast in the oven instead and sent Lizzy off to answer the door. In passing hors d'oeuvres and trying to remember everyone's name, Lizzy promptly forgot all about the conversation.

The evening's theme, "burgeoning time," was productive of a wide range of enticing poetry, from the more predictable e. e. cummings and Rumi ("Again, the violet bows to the lily. Again, the rose is tearing off her gown") and Shakespearean sonnets to the surprising (a reading from the *Rig Veda*) and challenging (Wallace Stevens's "Credences of Summer"). Mrs. Gardiner read a piece by a western poet Lizzy had never heard of, Hildegarde Flanner's "Fern Song":

> *Had I the use of thought equivalent*
> *To the moist hallucination of a flute*
> *I could be saying how*
> *A certain music in my woods has driven*
> *A certain female fern to tear*
> *In panic from her good black root.*

> *But no transparency of clear intent*
> *Assisting me,*
> *I only guessed at what the singer meant*
> *That hour I heard his intervals prolong*
> *Beyond security of common song*
> *Into a raving sweetness coming closer*
> *While the lyric animal himself*
> *Was still remote,*
> *Since thrush may have a mile of music*
> *In one inch of throat.*

Mr. Gardiner intoned a good-size chunk of Whitman's "Leaves of Grass," which Lizzy had never admired; but she discovered that when read aloud it was hypnotic and moving ("The moth and the fish-eggs are in their place; The suns I see, and the suns I cannot see, are in their place; The palpable is in its place, and the impalpable is in its place").

Lizzy had been tempted to read again from her favorite Pattiann Rogers, the wild Hopkinsesque tumble of "Rolling Naked in the Morning Dew" —

> . . . *some people*
> *Believe in the rejuvenating powers of this act—naked*
> *As a toad in the forest, belly and hips, thighs*
> *And ankles drenched in the dew-filled gulches*
> *Of oak leaves . . .*

But she judged her audience to be a trifle too sedate for such aphrodisiac delights. Lambtown was growing on her, and she began to feel it might become a permanent home; with these feelings came an awareness that her behavior might sometimes be judged on terms not dictated by her own notions of propriety. It was one thing to measure her greater actions against the dictates of her own conscience: this she must always do. But in matters more transitory, and among people who commanded her respect, the exercise of discretion was not only practical but beneficial.

With such considerations in mind, she elected instead to offer the unexceptionable, an elegant selection from the fourth of Virgil's *Georgics*, on the subject of providing a salubrious location for beehives:

> . . . *Let there be clear springs nearby, and pools green with moss,*
> *and let a palm tree or an olive shade the entrance,*
> *so that when new queens command the early swarms*
> *in springtime, and the young bees are freed from the combs,*
> *a neighboring stream bank may entice them to escape the heat,*
> *and a tree in their path hold them in its sheltering leaves. . . .*

Certain of the particulars prompted a good deal of debate among the more literal-minded in the audience, as well as among those with firsthand experience of apiculture—was it really wise to smear mud over the surface of the hive, or did it need to breathe? And as the debate flourished around her, and Lizzy was asked to reread certain passages for clarification, she felt all the warmth of acceptance into a circle of her choosing.

Lizzy made her way home through the balmy spring night with a head full of words and wine and convinced that life held no higher satisfactions. Young men, be their attentions welcome or unwelcome, must perforce yield their position in her thoughts to the greater intoxications of verse. Certainly the satisfactions offered by the former were neither so enduring nor so unalloyed by vexation. Lizzy resolved to think of them no further.

Chapter Nineteen

Having by this time passed nearly three months in Lambtown, Lizzy was beginning to feel that she understood the community at large and how to work within its culture. The uneasy attention her community garden project was attracting had taught her a valuable lesson about the hazards of paying no heed to the status quo, and she could now fully appreciate her aunt's desire that she maintain secrecy about the library. Not that she was in any way discouraged on either score; on the contrary, the opposition she had encountered convinced her more firmly than ever that Lambtown would benefit from the disruptions her plans might entail. No, the lesson she had learned was simply that she was better off not talking to many people about what she was up to. Accordingly, after securing the necessary donations of tools and seeds from Edward Gardiner's nursery and Frank Carrillo's farm, she had said no more about it to anyone except Rose, who was organizing participation among the farmworkers' families. It seemed that scarcely any Anglos would participate, but Lizzy was not excessively disappointed by this, for the people whose need was greatest would be served, and the garden's location in the center of town would render it impossible to ignore.

The planting date was set for May first, International Workers' Day, and when she recalled Catherine de Bourgh's words on the subject, this Marxist touch amused Lizzy. If she was going to tweak the noses of the powers that be, she might as well tweak them well and truly. The date had an additional advantage, she discovered: it was the start of the Rancheros Visitadores week, and most of the townsfolk would be off at Mission Santa Inés to catch a glimpse of the celebrities and moguls as they embarked on their ride.

Lizzy was astir before dawn on the day, a fat moon still riding high, to transport shovels and hoes, trowels and hoses, stakes and string to the site. Lupe Carrillo arrived early with some large urns of coffee and lemonade and two cases of bottled water, and then scurried away before anyone could see her being supportive of the event. John sneaked over a large tray of pastries from The Chocolate Bar, informing Lizzy that the baker had made extra for her and wished her luck. Jorge and some of his friends came through with the promised truckloads of soil amendment, and Lizzy started digging it in.

Gradually some families began to arrive. The men, perceiving Lizzy hard at work, immediately picked up shovels and joined in; a few tried to persuade her to desist, but she merely smiled and kept at it. Rose soon appeared with some Anglo parishioners from the church and a handful of social workers from around the valley; they helped tend the children, chatted with the mothers, and set to work demarcating each family's planting plot. A clutch of service-minded sorority girls from UC Santa Barbara in short shorts had fun with the hoses, watering one another more than the soil they were supposed to be conditioning.

At eleven, Father Austen came over from the church, accompanied by four stalwarts carrying the statue of the Virgin on a bier. As they toted her from plot to plot, Father Austen read blessings and aspersed the earth with holy water. Men followed, sprinkling a light top coat of soil to protect the seeds, and muddied in a fruit tree here and there. The solemnities concluded, a boombox was turned on; Jorge, who had been absent for some time, returned with sandwiches and burritos for all, and a festival atmosphere reigned. Some of the politically minded men urged their children to poke tiny Mexican flags into their plots, and the air was filled with excited chatter.

Lizzy touched Jorge on the back as he was handing out the last of the meals. "That was such a generous thing to do," she said, smiling on him. "Thank you for thinking of it."

"It was nothing. Come with me, I want to show you my garden plot. It's not the usual stuff—we have enough vegetables at my dad's place already."

Jorge had selected an area away from the center of town, near the end of the bridle path where it petered out into an open field. Instead of the neat rows of edible crops, he had created what at first appeared to be an ill-organized ornamental garden; but on examining it more closely, Lizzy began to recognize some of the plants as native to the local mountains.

"It's a medicinal garden, made up of plants used by my ancestors," Jorge explained. "See, here, this big shrub with the crinkly white flowers? That's Matilija poppy: you crush the leaves and smaller stems to make a treatment for rashes and other skin irritations. This one is hummingbird sage—it makes a tasty tea that works as a decongestant."

"And isn't this one white sage?"

"Yes. Aside from its traditional use as an incense for purification in rituals, it has antibiotic qualities. Yerba santa here is another decongestant, and can stop asthma attacks. The funny purple flowers here? That's woolly blue curls, used with lemon mint as a stomach settler. Coffeeberry there in the corner is a laxative; amole lily, also known as soap plant, makes shampoo and is an antifungal. Buckwheat is an eyewash, anti-irritant; and it was used ritually to bathe newborn babies."

"This is the wild artemisia, isn't it?"

"Yes. That can break a fever. It's also good if you're dieting—it reduces your craving for fatty foods. *Epazote* here is used to season foods, and it helps with cramps. Some people say it can cause spontaneous abortions, but I don't believe it—certainly not in the quantities used in cooking. The seeds have been used to get rid of intestinal parasites, but that's getting a little bit dangerous for me. This one with the white budlike flowers is everlasting—that reduces swelling and bruises."

"Are the California poppies just for looks, or do they have some purpose?"

"The whole plant is crushed and made into a tincture for anxiety; it's a great sedative. Athletes and employees of large corporations have to stay away from it, though: the compounds in the plant are chemically similar to opiates, and can give you a false positive on a drug test."

"I think I'll stick to walking and appreciating the beauty of California poppies in the wild when I need relaxation," said Lizzy. "What's the wonderful plant with the white trumpet flowers?"

"It's jimsonweed; we call it *toloache.*"

"Jimsonweed! Isn't that a hallucinogen? You hear about kids dying after experimenting with it."

"Well, any medicinal plant can be harmful if you don't prepare it correctly, or use the wrong dose—just like any over-the-counter or prescription drug. When taken correctly, it's a wonderful pain reliever."

"Where did you learn all this?"

"My mother makes some remedies from local plants, as well as brewing herbal teas from the chaparral. But most of our traditions are no longer living—you have to read about them in books. Some of the old hippies I know are surprisingly good sources: they apprenticed themselves to Indian shamans and medicine men when they were young, and learned a lot of stuff that otherwise would have been lost when their teachers died. A few of the old cowboys and sheepherders were smart enough to study the ways of the Indians, too, in order to learn better how to survive on the land."

"It's sad that you have to learn so much of your own heritage from outsiders," said Lizzy.

"For me, it's more like the best revenge, " said Jorge. "It's my peaceful way of taking back my birthright. I'm more of a spiritual warrior than a fighter, anyway—just like I never understood those Indians who want to get back at Anglos by gouging money out of them in casinos. To me, that's just modern cattle rustling."

As they walked back toward the group, Lizzy reflected once again that Jorge was more to be envied than pitied. He knew who he was, in ways that most Americans, separated by thousands of miles from their ancestral homelands and traditions, never could. Even though his heritage was to a degree reconstructed, it was real, and rooted in the place he lived. So many American traditions, from Valentine's Day to Halloween, were the products of American commerce, concocted to profit from the emotional void of uprooted populations—and most Americans didn't even realize it or know what was missing in their lives! She found herself jealous of a life that seemed more authentic than her own.

At least, she thought, gazing about her at the transformation of the bridle path, she could have the satisfaction of doing something positive for the community. She was helping people in dire need, and bringing the invisible out of the shadows. The community garden might not look like much right now, with its wisps of string outlining a crazy patchwork of nearly bare plots, but it represented, in her mind, the start of transformation for Lambtown.

Her complacency was rudely disturbed by a shout. A couple of local shopkeepers, returning from the sendoff of the Rancheros Visitadores, had come upon the scene of festivity. "What are you doing here?" one of them yelled. "Don't you have your own trailers to party in? We don't need you coming into town and trashing the place. Clean up all this litter and get out!"

As Lizzy rushed forward, the music was switched off and a hush fell over the community gardeners. "It's not litter!" she cried. "These are gardens! Just give it a few months, and the whole area will be green and productive. What was it before? A dusty, empty path. And you can't order these people to leave. They have just as much right to public space as you do—and greater need of it as well, because they have less private space than you."

She could hear Rose behind her, translating rapidly into Spanish to the families who were hovering uncertainly, poised to flee. One of the shopkeepers looked thoughtful, but the other bristled at her.

"Nobody wants that stupid music disturbing the peace in town. They're acting like they own the place! Most of them are probably illegals, so don't talk to *me* about their right to public space. They have no rights! Maybe I should just drop a dime on the INS. *La migra*," he added, for the benefit of his audience.

"Whether they're documented or undocumented, the fact remains that they live here, just like you. Can't you see that it's in everybody's interest to integrate them into the community? If their kids have an education, they're less likely to become delinquents. If they have enough to eat, they're less likely to covet your stuff. If they get proper medical treatment, they won't infect your family with diseases. This is what America is—the place where everyone has a chance for a better life, regardless of their country of origin. We're making a stand here, in the middle of Lambtown, for the American way!"

A few cheers went up behind Lizzy as this was translated, some of the bolder young men entering into the spirit of the occasion, while their elders hushed them and a few groups started to steal away. The more aggressive shopkeeper appeared ready to dispute Lizzy's version of the American way, but his friend restrained him.

"We can't do anything over the weekend," he said, "but we'll call the Town Council, the Chamber of Commerce, and the zoning office on Monday. There's no point in confronting people now. It's not like they're spray-painting graffiti or burning anything down."

"What are the tourists going to think? They come here for the pretty scenery and fine wines, not for dirty farmworkers."

"You mean the tired, the poor, the huddled masses yearning to breathe free?" cried Lizzy, entering fully into the spirit of the occasion. "Maybe the tourists should go visit Monaco instead, or Gstaad."

"Don't waste your time with her," counseled the calmer shopkeeper, dragging his friend away. "We can deal with it on Monday."

Lizzy was left in possession of the field, but feeling curiously deflated and dogged by forebodings. She turned back to the community gardeners, only to find the party breaking up. Father Austen was still there, standing grim and fierce beside the Virgin; he acknowledged his parishioners one by one as they began to depart, seeing that each family got at least one of the donated tools to take home. Jorge was joking with some of the younger men, trading pleasantries laced with bravado.

Rose's enthusiasm was undiluted by doubts. "You were magnificent, routing the enemy! Only imagine having Emma Lazarus at the tip of your tongue. One hears it everywhere, but nobody really remembers the quote, or gets the words right. Is it 'huddled masses' or 'teeming masses'? *I* never know. I wished I'd had a torch to hand to you, so you could hold it aloft like the Statue of Liberty."

"I hardly think a torch would have improved matters," said Father Austen.

"Well, no, perhaps not; but what a day this has been! Everyone so happy to take part, so many good workers! And the children enjoyed poking in the seeds. Little Marisela Ornelas cried when her parents made her leave! I'm sure the mothers will come and bring their children for the watering, aren't you? And when things start to grow, the business owners will come to appreciate it, don't you think? You will be a local hero, Lizzy, surely you will!"

Father Austen snorted, but he patted Lizzy's hand kindly and said, "Pay no mind to what people say," before departing for his church, the Virgin of Guadalupe swaying on her bier in his wake.

Lizzy, cleaning up the last empty seed packets and sandwich wrappers at the site and loading Mrs. Carrillo's urns into her truck, reflected on Rose's words. She was not so sure that routing the enemy had been the most prudent choice, and wished uneasily that the term *enemy* would be found to be mere hyperbole. Once the immediate cause of her righteous indignation was removed she had to laugh at herself a little, even as a small corner of her mind questioned the wisdom of planting her statement in quite so public a spot. It was done, however, and on the whole she felt considerable satisfaction about the day's enterprise.

Chapter Twenty

Her confidence lasted more or less until Monday, when Lizzy sustained so early a visit from an agitated Morris Collins that she had not yet finished loading her truck for the day's gardening jobs. If she harbored any concern that the nature of their last encounter might throw a constraint on this meeting, she need not have worried: for Morris, the equanimity of Lambtown was seriously disturbed, and no personal considerations could be given commensurate weight.

"It won't do!" he said without preamble. "I warned you particularly, weeks ago, that a public garden wouldn't be tolerated. Even Catherine de Bourgh condescended to speak to you on the subject. I remember clearly her words, as she reported them to me: 'Miss Bennet's communist ideas may do very well wherever she came from, but she can't be allowed to disseminate them here. I told her that I forbade her to proceed with this garden scheme.' Do you deny it?"

"Catherine de Bourgh can say anything she wishes to, but she has no authority over me. Nor does she have any authority over the bridle path—it isn't her private property, is it?"

"Words fail me!" cried Morris mendaciously. "How can you be so cavalier? You know Miss de Bourgh to be the first citizen of Lambtown—indeed, perhaps of the entire Santa Inez Valley, or Santa Barbara County—"

Lizzy couldn't resist. "Really? Wouldn't that come as a surprise to Brooks Firestone? Julia Child? Michael Jackson? Fess Parker? Oprah Winfrey?"

"Jumped-up celebrities don't compare to an elder member of a distinguished original family. She is the embodiment of our traditions, our way of life here, and we must all defer to her judgment, especially since she has nothing but the well-being of the community in mind. Who knows better than she what is best for us? So gracious, so generous—"

"How does an empty former bridle path serve the community's well-being better than feeding its poor?"

Morris drew himself up to stand upon the dignity of his office. "There's no point in speaking to you when you're in this mood. You have at times a boldness about you that is very unbecoming. When I think of what might have been, I wonder if Providence didn't take a hand to arrange everything for the best—but perhaps the less said, the better on that subject. I came to tell you that at the request of the Chamber of Commerce, the vandalism of the bridle path has been made the subject of a special Town Council meeting tomorrow night. If you believe your actions have a justification, you may defend yourself at that time."

This was not a speech calculated to chasten Lizzy Bennet. For the greater part of the morning, the beauties of a seventy-two-degree spring day and the pleasures of working in good earth were lost on her, as she muttered her defiance and rehearsed her defenses. "*My boldness makes me unattractive?* People around here take their medieval views way too far! Obey Catherine the Great because she's from one of the original families? Frank and Lupe Carrillo would be surprised to hear that! What do traditions matter when weighed against human suffering? If I'm so unattractive, why were you all but proposing to me a few weeks ago?"

But Lizzy was not formed for ill-humor, and it was not in her nature to increase her vexations by dwelling on them. Before long she allowed the peace of sun and soil and hard labor to creep back into her spirits. She laughed at her own inconsistencies, but was not amused by the challenge facing her. She could not help but feel that a lot of people who had very little to call their own, and few options for defending themselves, were dependent on her ability to win the citizens of Lambtown around to her views. Because of language and education barriers, perhaps in some cases because of legal status, the farmworkers were not in a position to be their own advocates. She had raised their expectations, and she could not allow them to be dashed.

So it was with considerable inward trepidation that she entered the council chambers the next evening and filled out her speaker card. Looking about her, she saw all too many of the local shopkeepers and too few of her friends. At the last moment, however, she was encouraged to espy Rose slipping in, accompanied by one of the farmworker's wives Lizzy knew, Graciela Albariño.

It was one of the innovations Morris Collins had introduced with his ascension to the mayoralty that all of the town council members should wait until everyone was assembled before entering the room in a body. In the past, they had wandered in whenever they arrived, and the half-hour before the meeting was called to order had afforded an excellent opportunity for informal business to be conducted under the table by those citizens who had the ear of one or another councillor. Morris had no objection to such arrangements, but he was concerned that the average citizen be suitably impressed by the dignity of office. He had toyed with the notion of introducing a dress code for the councillors, but the ranchers who had held office for a generation quashed this scheme with little more than the expression on their faces. Morris had, however, convinced the undersheriff—who shared his views about the respect due to government functionaries—to order the room to stand and be silent while the council members filed in and seated themselves.

This little ritual completed, the meeting was called to order and the mundanities of agendas and minutes settled with dispatch, everyone in the room being intent on getting to the drama as soon as might be. Lizzy, having never in her life attended a public meeting of this kind, forgot her nervousness momentarily in observing the show. She was interested to notice that her attorney, Melvin Perry, was among the council members; but as he never looked in her direction, she could not begin to guess his thoughts about the controversy at hand.

Just as the treasurer was announcing that she had not prepared a report because this was not a regularly scheduled council meeting, John slipped in and settled next to Lizzy, taking her hand with an encouraging smile. He had not expected to attend, but at the last minute decided to risk his supervisor's wrath by leaving The Chocolate Bar before evening cleanup was complete. He was just in time; Morris was rising to introduce the main order of business.

"As you all know, over the weekend a group of people entered Lambtown and dug up a large portion of our historic bridle path. This so-called community garden project was undertaken without authorization, and no permit was requested or obtained for the assembly. The Council has agreed to hold this special meeting to consider how the town should respond to this unlawful act, and explore what remedies are possible. There will be a period of public comment in which each person who has filled out a card will be allowed to speak for three minutes, and then the Council will deliberate on the matter. Names will be called in the order that the cards were submitted; when your name is called, please step up to the microphone, identify yourself, and begin to speak immediately. The audience is to remain silent during this period, and any ad hoc comments from the room will not become part of the public record."

The initial remarks came from shopkeepers and presented the expected arguments—what would the tourists think; the garden would bring riffraff into the town; access would be blocked to the rear entrances of shops—for which Lizzy had already prepared rebuttals. The president of the Historical Society entered a plea for respecting the history of the thoroughfare (Lizzy's planned reply: why hadn't they laid down railroad tracks then, since it was originally a narrow-gauge railway right-of-way?); the president of the Garden Club thought a community garden might be a good idea, but perhaps better located near the farms on the western edge of town, so its beneficiaries would not have so far to walk. The reasonableness of this notion gave even Lizzy pause, and threw into relief the intransigence of the next speaker, Saturday's irate shopkeeper who wanted to bring down the INS on anyone who set foot in their garden plot.

Lizzy's turn came, and after speaking of the extreme poverty she had seen among the farmworkers and the poor nutrition of their children, she said, "I'm hearing a common theme among the comments so far: people want the poor among us to be invisible. They're dirty, their lives are messy: let's hide them away where the tourists can't see them, where we don't have to see them and be reminded of their suffering. But isn't that a lie? Lambtown's prosperity is built on their backs—it exists because of them, not in spite of them. Shouldn't we be proud of *all* that we are, not just the happy, shiny version of ourselves? All of us had ancestors who were hardworking immigrants; can't we relate to the current crop of newcomers? We speak of the people working in the community garden as 'they,' 'them'; but aren't they actually part of *us*? What could be more American than embracing those who are new to our land? *That's* what I want the tourists to see when they come to Lambtown! That's why the community garden needs to be in the center of town, not off somewhere hidden away like a shameful secret."

The speakers came and went, most opposed to the garden or at least its location, though preponderantly they framed their objections in practical terms: Who owned the property? Who would pay for the water? What about stealing?

At last Rose got up and approached the microphone with Graciela. "I have nothing to say myself on this subject," she began, "but I will translate the remarks of my friend Graciela Albariño." Graciela began to speak in a low-voiced monotone. "I've lived in the United States for thirteen years. My children were all born in this country. I can't read or write, so it's hard for me to get a job. My husband knows how to write in Spanish, but we don't know English. He travels with the crops most of the year, but makes little money—enough for the rent and some rice. If he's sick, we don't eat. If there is a heat wave or a storm and the crops spoil, we don't eat. He has been beaten and robbed for a day's wages. He has been cheated by bosses who take his labor and then say his papers are not in order, they will not pay him. My oldest son is nine, he wants to quit school and work to pay for food for the little ones. I tell him to stay in school; if you work in the fields you will die in the fields, die with nothing like an animal. If I can grow my vegetables, I hope my son will stay in school. Thank you."

There was a short silence, and then Morris Collins rapped his gavel on the table. "That last testimony will be stricken from the record of the meeting. The person who signed up to speak, Rose O'Connor, admitted she had nothing to say; the subsequent remarks were made by a person who did not fill out a speaker card, so they are out of order. The period of public comment is now over, so the Council will take this matter under advisement."

The council members shifted in their seats as they weighed their interests; nobody seemed eager to speak up. At last Melvin Perry cleared his throat, shuffled the papers before him, and requested the floor.

"In the few days that have ensued since the events of Saturday morning I have attempted to research some of the legal issues posed by the planting of the erstwhile bridle path. My findings are preliminary and inconclusive, but perhaps nevertheless germane to the discussion.

"First, there is the matter of the property's ownership. The narrow-gauge railway owned the right-of-way at the time the company went out of business in the nineteenth century. Lambtown does not have a statute providing for derelict properties to revert to the town's ownership, and in any case when the right-of-way was established, there was no town. So to determine who owns the land would require us to identify who were the railroad's shareholders and contact their descendants. *All* their descendants," said Mr. Perry dryly, looking over his glasses at Morris Collins. "I imagine this would be the work of years, and the fees would bankrupt the town.

"So. If we stipulate that the ownership of the bridle path area is for practical purposes unknowable, what other options lie open to us? Our distinguished mayor mentioned the absence of authorization to dig and plant on the property. Again, our laws contain no requirement that authorization be obtained from the town to cultivate the soil. I imagine our landowners might have a thing or two to say if such a law were to be proposed. Property owners have an undeniable right to authorize such an undertaking—which returns us to the central dilemma of establishing ownership. If said owners were located, they might be persuaded to lodge a complaint of trespassing or vandalism.

"Finally, our mayor referred to the possibility that the gathering constituted an unlawful assembly. Typically, for this charge to be lodged, the Sheriff's Department must be on the scene at the time the group is assembled and must detain the perpetrators in the act. Charges after the fact must meet a stringent evidentiary standard and, failing that standard, are generally thrown out of court."

Mr. Perry paused and scanned the silent room. "I fear," said he, "that the situation before us does not lend itself readily to official response. Perhaps it is less a matter for the government to resolve and more one to be addressed through community cooperation. Perhaps we might wait and see, if you will, how the garden grows before we judge the harvest to be reaped from it."

It was not to be expected that such a course would be fully satisfactory to anyone, but on the whole Lizzy felt it was the best outcome she could have hoped for. She could only reflect on the wisdom of her aunt's choice of legal adviser, and hope that no truculent citizens would take the outcome into their own hands.

Morris Collins was not entirely prepared to let the conflict rest in this manner; but as his ingenuity could not suggest other possibilities and his fellow councillors, being considerably in awe of Melvin Perry's erudition and withering logic, were disinclined to oppose his conclusions, little more could be said.

Chapter Twenty-one

Cinco de Mayo and the end of the Rancheros Visitadores ride came and went, leaving most of the male half of the populace in a state of satiety and exhaustion, and more than a few cherishing secret feelings of guilt and regret. Jorge Carrillo appeared immune to thoughts of this nature, and blithely pursued his *charro* practice under the adoring eye of many of the valley's young ladies. Arriving at the Carrillos' farm with a Mother's Day offering of tamales for Mrs. Carrillo, Lizzy was chagrined to discover both the size of his audience and the partiality he displayed toward one of their number, a redhead named Mary King who had recently come to Lambtown on an extended visit to her uncle and aunt after being expelled from an exclusive private school in New York. From her sunglasses to her pumps she bore all the marks of a rich girl, but neither her wealth nor her city sophistication left her unsusceptible to Jorge's charm of manner. Some of the girls were whispering that he was captivated by her money, but Lizzy was certain her appeal lay only in her novelty.

Kitty, one of the throng arenaside watching Jorge school his horse in the complicated maneuvers of the *charreada*, was inclined to loud expressions of pity for her sister's blighted hopes, but Lizzy discovered that among the emotions excited by her admirer's defection, humiliation predominated. It was impossible not to conclude that her vanity was more severely wounded than her heart. She knew she was disappointing the majority of her acquaintance by failing to be inconsolable, but considering the degree of notice she had lately been attracting in the town, could not regret taking a position of comparative insignificance in the eye of the gossips. Upon reflection, she realized that she thought none the worse of Jorge for his change of focus—a sure sign of indifference, or at least of pride, on her part. He remained in her eyes, whether attached or single, the model of what a young man ought to be; she might regret him, but would not repine.

In fact, her thoughts were much taken up with the next phase of her plans for Lambtown's betterment. Some of the community gardeners—whether intimidated by the town's reception of the project or finding themselves, like Lizzy, less enamored than they had supposed—were failing to perform the routine maintenance on their plots, so Lizzy's workload was considerably increased. As she watered and weeded under the censorious eye of the shopkeepers, she was revolving ideas about the library that had taken root in her mind during the Town Council session.

She could not forget Graciela Albariño or her straightforward portrait of the life she led. It did not take long for Lizzy to realize that for many of the farmworkers' children and wives to be able to benefit from the library, some support beyond what a librarian could offer would have to be provided. It came to her that the garage of her aunt's house could be converted into an informal day care center, and that a woman like Graciela, already an unpaid day care provider for her own children and those of her neighbors, might serve as its staff. Such a person, well known to the children, might reassure nervous friends about the benefits of the library, while earning a small stipend for work already performed for free. Perhaps Graciela or some other might begin to learn to read in such an environment, or at least learn a little English.

When consulted, Melvin Perry was typically cautious but, to Lizzy's secret elation, did not immediately reject the idea. He reminded her of the library foundation's limited income and stressed that licensing day care centers was an onerous under-taking in California. "It would be less complicated if you didn't offer food to the children and limited the hours of operation; but I don't suppose you would be amenable to such compromises." He paused, eyeing his client impassively. "Perhaps your best strategy would be to form a partnership with an existing social services organization that has experience in day care, and let them handle the details."

"As far as hours of operation are concerned, it would be only preschool-age kids during the day, and then older children after school. But I think it's crucial to get women from the farmworker community involved."

"*That* you would have to negotiate with the partnering or-ganization. I imagine you will be able to find some group that will be happy to be flexible in return for the free use of your space. Have you considered what the neighbors will think about noisy children playing in the yard?"

"I suppose that is a good argument for limiting the hours," Lizzy acknowledged. "If the children were there only for a few hours, they could be entertained indoors, and then go elsewhere for more active play."

With all the work this new enterprise required, Lizzy scarcely noticed the passage of May. She did take the time to go in to Santa Barbara to see *Notting Hill* with Mary Gardiner. That lady was inclined to wish Julia Roberts success in any romantic en-deavor, but Lizzy was convinced that Hugh Grant deserved bet-ter than such a nervous, self-absorbed partner. "There is a secretiveness about her character that I can't admire. I think she would have an affair with another actor while on location, and never tell him. Of course, he has only the appearance of merit or sense; like most men, he has fallen for her simply because she is beautiful and acts like a goddess. Perhaps that's why we like him; stupid men are the only ones worth knowing, after all."

"Take care, Lizzy! That speech savors strongly of disappointment. You mustn't allow yourself to become bitter or cynical at your age. We all commit follies in our youth, men and women alike, and the challenge is to learn from them without dwelling on anger or blame. I hope one day you'll attract the notice of a man who's an adult and will draw out all your best qualities. That's the kind of marriage that endures—one that allows both partners to be their better selves."

Lizzy contemplated this picture somewhat wistfully. "I'm not convinced that I've seen many such marriages; it seems that nearly always there is an inequality of intelligence, or character, that requires one party to make the lion's share of effort to sustain the partnership. Most marriages I don't understand at all— which makes me the more determined to make my own way in the world, independent of any man. Look at Charlotte Lucas and Morris Collins: why would a woman like her accept a man who can't even be credited with common sense?"

"Speaking of which, are you going to the wedding?"

"She's invited me to the reception, and really urged me to come, so I suppose I must; but it'll be hard to stand by and watch her make such a disastrous mistake. I hear that Catherine de Bourgh has offered to let them use Rosings Ranch for the reception—can you imagine how Morris will behave in that setting?"

"I expect he'll find his joy difficult to contain," said Mrs. Gardiner. "But I hope you'll enter into Charlotte's feelings on the occasion with goodwill, and not try to show her what you believe her feelings ought to be."

"Oh, I know how to behave myself when I must! And at present I'm such a notorious figure in Lambtown that I mustn't alienate the few friends I have. I promise to say and do all that's proper."

"And if your resolution falters, you can always ask John for his views on the subject."

"Yes, isn't he amazing? Not only does he never speak ill of anybody, he's hurt if *I* do so. He's capable of finding goodness in everyone; but if I mention his own perfections, he denies and disclaims and will have none of it. I only wish he could have the happiness he deserves, but that prospect has never seemed more distant. How can anyone be unkind to someone like him?"

"You're asking others to see people as they are, not as we think they ought to be."

"And you believe I should ask no less of myself first," said Lizzy ruefully. "Well, I'll try—out of respect for the truly good and wise people in my life, like you and John."

This resolve was sorely tested by the Collinses' wedding reception, which was held on Memorial Day, after a private Sunday evening wedding. Lizzy had never before had occasion to visit Rosings Ranch, and her previous experience of its proprietor did not prepare her for what met her eyes. Catherine de Bourgh had struck her as a down-to-earth woman, much addicted to interfering in the lives of others but not to hollow displays of her wealth and importance. In this assessment Lizzy found herself mistaken.

Her first intimation came as she approached the property along one of the usual rural roads, set between pastures turned golden as the rainy season gave way to California's arid summer. Suddenly, expensive green-painted acrylic fencing appeared, a far cry from the post-and-rail fences typical of the area. The verges of the road were lined with rosebushes, which to Lizzy's trained eye were likely to require the water allocations of several families to maintain. Between pastures the dirt tracks were embellished with street signs naming champion racehorses that had surely never been raised within a thousand miles of the spread: Secretariat Street, Man o' War Lane, Affirmed Avenue. The main approach to the house was announced by rows of meticulously clipped topiary curlicues in the French style, and the drive was blocked by elaborate wrought-iron gates manned by a uniformed guard whose primary function appeared to be making visitors feel unworthy of the honor about to be bestowed upon them.

Upon being admitted to the grounds, Lizzy drove past trim pastures, three oval practice tracks of differing lengths, and two massive white barns before reaching the ancestral home of the de Bourghs, built about thirty years previously. The house was constructed in the style known in America as French Château, complete with slate mansard roofs and quantities of wrought iron. Valets ran forward to whisk her dusty pickup truck out of sight, and she mounted the marble steps to the two-stories-tall front door.

The magnificence of the entrance hall appeared to leave some of the arriving guests dumbstruck, but Lizzy found herself quite equal to the scene and was able to observe her surroundings with composure. The hall rose to the full height of the edifice's three stories, with twin stairways spiraling around its walls, and was topped by a small painted dome depicting what could only be presumed to be equine Valhalla. Servants bustled to and fro, issuing forth laden with trays of hors d'oeuvres from a side door and disappearing into the public rooms toward the back. Moving in the same direction, Lizzy discovered that the receiving line was manned not just by the happy couple and Charlotte's parents but also by Fitzwilliam Darcy and Cal Fitzwilliam. According to Charlotte's whispered intelligence, they had flown home after the Preakness to do the family honors in place of their aunt, who, Lizzy could only conclude, had not deemed the occasion of sufficient importance to justify returning from the eastern race season so early. Lizzy was greeted by Cal with enthusiasm and by Darcy with his usual reserve; she wished for but did not possess sufficient brazenness to ask if Charley Bingley had returned with them, and had to content herself with a fruitless search of the crowd for John's absent inamorato.

The assemblage consisted of members of the Enclave set, leading business associates of Morris Collins, and other prominent Lambtown citizens, so Lizzy found few acquaintances whom she would rather not avoid. Having wandered from living room to terrace to library for some time, she heaped a plate with delicacies and retreated to the gardens. There she amused herself briefly in contemplation of the horseshoe-shaped parterres planted with flowers in the de Bourgh racing colors; these were immaculately tended but so boring that she imagined the gardeners condemned to maintain them must suffer the pangs of existential despair. She made her way to the swimming pool and sat under an umbrella to consume her food in solitude, idly watching the fragmented sparkles of sunlight on the water. Nobody came to disturb her reverie for some time, until she was startled to see Mr. Darcy pass through a gap in the hedge and stop at poolside.

He caught sight of her a moment later, and she thought from his demeanor that he intended to retreat; but instead he collected himself and walked over to sit opposite her under the umbrella.

Swallowing her annoyance at the intrusion, Lizzy addressed him politely. "You've been released from the receiving line?"

He nodded but gave no other answer and sat staring, though rather at her plate than at herself. She wondered if he found her selection of appetizers objectionable or wished her to offer him some; emboldened by *his* impertinence, she resolved to indulge her own.

"We were all surprised when Charley Bingley left with you last month," said she. "He seemed so absorbed in the management of The Chocolate Bar. Do you know if he means to return anytime soon?"

"I haven't heard him say so, but it wouldn't be surprising if he spent little time here in the future. Bingley has many interests, and tends to take more pleasure in starting businesses than in running them."

"If he means to be here only rarely, it'd be better for the shop if he sold it to someone for whom it would be a primary focus.

A business is never so well run when the owner is absent and uninvolved in day-to-day operations."

"I wouldn't be surprised if he were to give it up as soon as he receives an eligible purchase offer."

Lizzy could think of nothing in reply, and decided that Darcy would have to assume responsibility for his own entertainment. After a pause, he seemed to take the hint, bestirring himself sufficiently to remark, "I believe Aunt Catherine has taken quite an interest in Mr. Collins's career and welfare. She doesn't often open her house for other people's parties."

"I'm sure she could not have bestowed her kindness on a more grateful object. Mr. Collins won't soon forget the triumph of this day."

"He appears very fortunate in his choice of a wife."

"Yes, indeed; his friends may well rejoice in his having met with one of the very few sensible women who would have accepted him, or have made him happy if they did. Charlotte is a very perceptive woman—though I'm not certain that I consider her marrying Morris Collins the wisest thing she ever did. It is, I guess, a prudent match for her."

Darcy drew his chair a little closer and studied her face intently. "You are dismissive of prudent considerations in a match, then? But surely imprudence can lead to considerable friction in a marriage. You would prefer a marriage based entirely on passion?"

Surprised and defensive, Lizzy thought for a moment before replying. "I can't imagine a lasting relationship that isn't based first and foremost on respect. Where that is lacking, the most rational partnership must in time become a dreary penance. By the same token, it would be difficult for me to conceive of sustaining passion if it didn't have respect at its core."

A variety of emotions that Lizzy could not interpret seemed to pass through the gentleman's mind: he colored, looked away, looked back at her and then at his feet. Silence again reigned, and he appeared relieved a little while later when Charlotte Collins appeared at poolside and approached their table. Rising abruptly to his feet, he muttered his excuses and departed.

"What on earth was that?" asked Charlotte, taking his seat and propping up her feet on another. "How long have you been running off to be private with Fitzwilliam Darcy?"

"It was nothing of the kind," said Lizzy irritably. "I was just sitting here by myself enjoying my food in peace, and suddenly he turned up."

"He must be in love with you to seek you out that way."

"Or perhaps I just happened to be in his favorite patch of shade, for all the effort he put into being civil."

"Perhaps."

"But let's forget about him," said Lizzy. "He always puts me in a bad temper, and this is your happy day! It's a beautiful party, and I've gorged myself on all the delicious food. I enjoyed meeting your cousins from Iowa; how nice that so many of your relations could be here for the wedding."

Charlotte let the subject of Darcy drop, but she could not forbear speculating on what she had seen. Certainly, Lizzy's account of his behavior was not encouraging, but there had been something in his demeanor that implied a degree of interest, if not attachment. Despite her unromantic approach to her own life, Charlotte was perfectly ready to entertain the notion of a romance for her friend, and the incident opened an intriguing path for her imagination to wander. They would make a very handsome couple, and Charlotte was certain that if Lizzy believed herself admired in that quarter, her dislike would vanish. Catherine de Bourgh might not like the match, which could make things awkward for Morris in the short term; but Charlotte was one to take the long view, and the patronage of Fitzwilliam Darcy would undoubtedly prove the greater and more lasting advantage.

Chapter Twenty-two

Oblivious to such speculations, Lizzy continued to work long days throughout June. She discovered that the rhythms of the California gardener's year were very different from what she had been accustomed to in Ohio: this season, with the rains over and the temperatures settling into the steady heat of summer, seemed more like the plants' autumn. After a long and heavy spring bloom, many were dying back and needed to be cut down and thickly mulched to protect them through the long dry season to come.

As she pruned and deadheaded in her aunt's old garden, she gained new respect for Evelyn Bennet's design, where the strong bones of the foundation plants and succulents were interesting to the eye even as the flowers faded. She was standing back to admire the effect of several hours of cleanup when she heard a cheery hail and looked up to see Cal Fitzwilliam waving from his horse, with his cousin riding silently beside.

"We've tracked you down at last," said Cal, dismounting. "You never seem to be where we expect to find you. Darcy said you spent a lot of time at that Chocolate Bar place, but no matter how often we stop in, we're out of luck. I must have gained five pounds waiting in vain for you. I've looked all over the polo grounds for you, and at the community garden—"

Lizzy chuckled. "I confess I do my work at the community garden very early in the morning in the hope of avoiding confrontations with the shopkeepers. As to The Chocolate Bar, I love to spend time with my brother John, who works there, but lately I've had no time to spend! My horticultural dance card is filled.

And the polo grounds? I'm afraid the Enclave is not for working stiffs like me. Nobody in my family is much of a rider—though I would be curious to see a polo match sometime."

"We must find a way to separate you from your work, right, Darcy?" His cousin did not reply.

"Well, I'd be happy to take a break right now," said Lizzy. "I could run inside and get us all some iced tea, if you like."

It seemed the gentlemen did like, for they tied up their horses by the gate and followed her up the path. She had intended that they sit on the porch while she brought out the glasses, but found to her dismay that they followed her inside.

Her plans for the library were still unknown to the neighborhood, so she could only hope that they would be as unobservant as young men often are when in the company of a pretty woman, and not think to question the racks of bookcases in the living room or the newly delivered display case in the hall.

Alas, her charms proved insufficient to the occasion. Darcy stopped short in the doorway to the living room, ignoring her efforts to usher them both down the hall to the kitchen. "I know you for a great reader, " he said, "but are you planning to have unlimited leisure for the pastime in the future?"

The insolence of his tone dispelled Lizzy's embarrassment. "Just because a person completes her formal education, Mr. Darcy, doesn't mean she should cease to expand her knowledge," she replied with spirit. "If you would step this way?"

Cal, caught between two combatants in a war he did not understand, eyed the display case and asked, "Are you a collector, Miss Lizzy?"

"My mother is," she replied, with equal truth and irrelevancy, and ushered them firmly into the kitchen. She sat them down at the counter and thrust the glasses into their hands with less graciousness than dispatch.

"Speaking of the community garden," said Darcy, "I seem to recall mentioning to you at one point the historic value of the bridle path. If you're having difficulties with the townspeople about the project, perhaps it's because you chose not to respect what others value. Greater discretion might have won you greater support."

"I assure you, the location of the community garden was chosen deliberately. I didn't forget or ignore what you, or your aunt, or others said; in fact, your advice helped to guide my choice. I believe there's something seriously wrong when people put sentimentality about traditions ahead of present suffering, and I wanted some of the smug people of Lambtown to be forced to see the reality around them!"

"What you call smug, others might consider no more than realistic."

"'The poor are always with us'? Well, if they have to be with us, at least we shouldn't be allowed to turn away and ignore them. And what you consider 'history' seems to be little more than whatever happened last week, or a year ago. It's as if history began in the late nineteenth century, and there was nothing here for the eons before."

"Our roots may not go as deep as some," said Darcy, "but it's meaningful for us to honor the courage, hard work, and vision that created this community."

"You call it courage and vision—to wrest land from the Californios, who in turn stole it from the Indians, with all the disenfranchisement, and even suffering and death, that sorry history implies? Your definition of 'us' and your notion of history conveniently ignore all those who came before your arbitrary starting point. If I may recast the adage, Mr. Darcy, those who ignore history are condemned to repeat it. Perhaps you could look on my little community garden as compensatory damages for the displaced."

Darcy stood and set down his glass with care. "You appear to have everything figured out. If it pleases you to set us all straight, I would by no means interfere with whatever makes you happy. Thank you for the tea." He turned and stalked off down the hall, and Cal had little choice but to follow, but with a grimace and an apologetic shrug as he departed.

Lizzy waited with dread for word of the peculiar doings at her aunt's house to leak out into the community, but eventually she had to conclude that either the cousins had forgotten what they had seen, or they had chosen not to speak of it. She was soon ashamed of the way she had upbraided Fitzwilliam Darcy, and wondered what Cal must think of her. But hadn't Darcy brought it on himself, with his bad manners and his arrogance? She was not going to be brought to doubt herself simply because he despised her. Consider the source!

As usual, she found a kind of solace in the company of her beloved brother John. His mood was still very unhappy—he was patient and uncomplaining as ever, but not sufficiently in spirits for her to unburden herself to him. He helped her nonetheless, as his sufferings reminded her of how little justification she had for ill humor, and in striving to increase his happiness she restored her own. They had taken to driving west to visit La Purísima Mission when time allowed, simply to walk about the grounds and crumbling buildings together, speaking of their day or remaining silent as the mood took them. The ascetic accommodations of the friars, the remnants of gardens, and the quiet lives of the farm animals still kept there offered an interlude of peace.

Lizzy had once praised the mission to Cal Fitzwilliam and recommended that he visit it, so she was not unduly surprised when, one afternoon as she was walking there alone—John having been detained at the shop—she espied him staring up at the facade of the friars' living quarters. Catching sight of her, Cal abandoned contemplation with alacrity and joined her stroll.

"You were right about this place," said he, "there is something truly serene about it. Perhaps that isn't an acceptably modern view of history—I expect we're supposed to be meditating on the enslavement and genocide of the local tribespeople—but it's hard to stand here and imagine that the impact of the missionaries was anything other than minor or benign."

Lizzy acknowledged the truth of it with a rueful smile. "My mind recognizes the reality of cultural insensitivity and death from exposure to unfamiliar diseases, but my heart tells a different story about this spot. It feels like a happy place, where life's simple rewards were celebrated. Perhaps the friars opened the door to invasion by more rapacious men, but it's hard to believe they were themselves wicked."

"So you'd be disposed to forgive unintentional harm! I'm glad to hear it, or there are few of us who would escape your ill opinion."

"I think the missionaries were probably simple men, raised in a narrow tradition and knowing little beyond it. I'm less tolerant of modern people of sense and education, who've lived in the world, but choose to ignore what's around them."

"This is laid at my cousin Darcy's door, I take it," said Cal. "Perhaps there is more that could be done to improve the welfare of the poor people hereabouts, but I'm not sure Darcy can be expected to be the one to do it. I don't know anyone who has greater responsibilities, or who takes them more seriously. When it comes to his family, his friends, those whose livelihoods depend on him, there's nothing he wouldn't do."

"Oh! yes," said Lizzy dryly, "I've seen the sort of care he takes of friends like Charley Bingley."

"Yes, I really believe Darcy *does* take care of Bingley, in those areas where he most wants care. I have reason to believe Bingley very much indebted to him."

"In what sense?"

"Well, I'm not sure I should give particulars—it's certainly something Darcy would not wish to be generally known, and to be frank, I don't know all the details myself. If it were to get around, things could become pretty unpleasant around here for Bingley."

"I wish Charley Bingley nothing but the best, so you may depend upon my not mentioning it."

"Darcy didn't say much about it, but I gathered that he removed Bingley from Lambtown to save him from taking a step that would have brought scandal down on his head and might have ruined him financially."

"You mean if he came out of the closet?"

"Well, I gather there *was* another man in the picture. But I'm by no means certain that Bingley is actually gay; Darcy seemed to think Charles was unsure, and questioning his sexuality, so he wanted to save his friend from making a rash move that he might later regret."

Lizzy walked on in silence, the tumult of her thoughts rendering her heedless of her surroundings. After watching her for a little, Cal asked her why she was so thoughtful.

"I'm thinking about what you told me," said she. "Why was Darcy to be the judge of the matter?"

"You consider his interference officious?"

"I don't see what right Darcy had to decide on the propriety of his friend's inclination, or why—on his own judgment alone—he was to determine and direct in what way that friend was to be happy!"

"Perhaps he felt there wasn't enough affection in the case to justify Bingley's taking such an irrevocable step," said Cal. "But if that's the case, it detracts sadly from the value of my cousin's achievement."

This seemed so just a portrait of Fitzwilliam Darcy that Lizzy could not trust herself to make any answer; and therefore, abruptly redirecting the conversation, she talked on indifferent matters till they reached the parking lot. She left him there but could not bring herself to go straight home; instead she took the loop road around the Santa Rita Hills, driving at random so she could think without interruption about all she had heard. That Darcy had been concerned in the measures taken to separate Charley and John, she had never doubted; but she had always attributed to Caroline Bingley the principal design and arrangement of them. If Darcy's vanity, however, did not mislead him, *he* was the cause, his own pride and caprice were the cause of all that John had suffered, and continued to suffer! He had ruined, at least for the time being, every hope of happiness for the most affectionate, generous heart in the world; and no one could say how lasting an evil he might have inflicted.

Chapter Twenty-three

With such reflections crowding all other thoughts from her mind, Lizzy was grateful for the solitude afforded by her work. Even the solace of John's companionship was to be eschewed, since the impossibility of telling him what she had learned rendered their habitual candor untenable. Within the family circle she endeavored to conceal her preoccupation, for although her mother, along with Mary, Kitty, Lydon, and Jenny, could be relied upon to be unobservant, she did not wish her father or John to ask any questions she would be unable to answer.

Distraction was provided to all, however, by the arrival of the Fourth of July weekend. Lambtown made a grand show for the holiday, with a carnival and fair all weekend long that culminated in a Mexican-style rodeo on Sunday afternoon. This was the *charreada* for which Jorge Carrillo had been preparing, and the youngest members of the family could scarcely contain their excitement at the prospect of this exotic entertainment. Even Mary, after spending a few hours selling lariat crosses and passing out tracts at her church's table, was able to persuade herself to overlook the ramshackle elements of the carnival, declaring there to be no harm in the rides and other amusements and finding patriotic suitability in the act of shooting a line of tin ducks with a plastic musket for the prize of a plush koala bear. Jenny and Kitty became so rowdy on a hayride that the driver required them to debark from the cart out of consideration for the sensibilities of the children on board, while Lydon managed to talk his way into judging the homemade beer competition and had to be borne home insensate in the bed of Lizzy's truck.

Despite being somewhat the worse for wear, therefore, the Bennets gathered with half the residents on Sunday afternoon for the *charreada*, held at a dusty, privately owned arena on the hot eastern side of town. It could immediately be seen that this was not the sort of event that drew the Enclave set, but Mrs. Bennet's dismay at her surroundings evaporated as soon as the first female precision riding team took the field. She clapped and cheered with the rest as the ladies, riding sidesaddle in starchy tiered skirts and broad-brimmed sombreros, galloped toward the rails, wheeling in unison at the last possible second to charge toward the center again, narrowly avoiding collision as they wove complex patterns of thundering horseflesh. To the blare of mariachis, the precision riders twirled in place, backed and spun, and cantered in interlocking figure eights to the gasps and shouts of the crowd. A team of local teenagers followed them, less polished than the Mexican professionals but demonstrating promise with some original maneuvers, and then it was time for the male competitors. Knowledgeable members of the audience ran for a plate of carnitas and a cold drink while the arena was being marked off into a long lane leading to a small circle in which the competitors were to perform. As the only local entry, Jorge Carrillo was selected to go first.

The sighs of the ladies almost drowned out the trumpets as he appeared on his black horse, in his three-piece black suit richly embroidered with silver. For the locals, nobody could exceed the perfection of his seat or the drama of his performance in the opening event, the *cala de caballo*, an elaborate equine dance that displayed the horse's training and its rider's mastery.

Lizzy was hypnotized by the beauty of the maneuvers, though she dreaded witnessing some of the later roping competitions, which sounded dangerous and possibly cruel, or the culminating *paso de la muerte*, in which the *charro*, riding bareback, would attempt to leap onto the bare back of a wild horse and hang on until it stopped bucking. So she was secretly relieved to observe Rose O'Connor clambering up the risers and beckoning urgently to gain her attention. Curious, she excused herself to her family and followed Rose out of the din.

Rose could scarcely wait until they were clear of the stands to speak, but as she was both more voluble and less coherent than usual, Lizzy had at first some difficulty in taking her meaning. "I was in town after morning Mass, and hoping that even though it's a Sunday and the Fourth of July, perhaps the market might be open to serve the crowds, because I needed some formula for the Villa girl—she's had a baby, you know, though she's only fourteen, and her family don't want to help her because they're ashamed—and that's when I saw it happening! I couldn't believe my eyes at first, and I was just frozen there, staring, because who would believe such a thing? But I assure you it happened, I saw it with my own eyes, and it was *deliberate*. It's hard for me to imagine that anyone, even Catherine de Bourgh, would do such a vicious thing on purpose, but there she was, with her ranch foreman and about five of the hands, all on horseback, and I heard the foreman say, '*That'll* teach 'em!' So it *had* to be intentional. I didn't say anything, I didn't know what to say, and how could I stop them, one person on foot against all of them on horseback? So I ran back to the church to borrow the van and came looking for you, but you weren't at home or at your aunt's house, and I've been hunting high and low till I saw your truck in the parking lot here—"

"What on earth has happened?" demanded Lizzy.

"But I've been telling you! It was Catherine de Bourgh, on her horse—"

"Yes, but what was she doing on her horse?"

"Trampling the garden!" gasped Rose, and Lizzy set off at a run for the parking lot. She easily outpaced her informant in the van on the way back to town and sped onto Main Street, skidding into the first parking spot she could find. Most of the shops were closed but the cafés were open, and a few people had assembled near the intersection of the sidewalk and the old bridle path. Lizzy ran over and stopped dead.

All the strings and stakes and pickets demarking the individual garden plots were torn out and tangled in the crushed remains of squash and bean plants, rows of trampled corn stalks and uprooted fruit tree saplings. Not a single plot had been spared. As people looked on and whispered, Lizzy walked the entire length of the community garden and found nothing salvageable. Already the heat was wilting stalks and turning broken leaves to mush. Returning to her starting point, she kept her face averted so that the townspeople would not see the marks of distress on her cheeks; Rose had arrived, and looked on the scene of destruction. "It was so *violent*," she whispered in distress. "They were jerking their horses to and fro, and striking them and the plants with whips! Miss de Bourgh has always seemed so controlled, but she was almost wild, shouting and waving her arms and bouncing around on her saddle. I've never seen anything like it! I didn't know what to do."

Lizzy couldn't even comfort her friend. She turned away from everyone and walked slowly back to the far end of the path, confirming what she already knew, that the garden had been completely destroyed. Near Jorge's native medicinals plot, she leaned against a wall and inhaled the sharp odor of crushed sage and artemisia, wondering what she was going to do for all the families who had invested their faith and labor in her vision.

It was here that Fitzwilliam Darcy found her, picking his way through the debris to come to a halt some ten feet away. She looked up to acknowledge his presence but could not summon the courtesy to greet him; in that moment the appearance of civility was more than she was capable of. The desire to weep abruptly left her, replaced with a silent rage.

Darcy moved to lean against the opposite wall, but after a moment he pushed away and paced about, glancing at her from time to time. He bent to pull a twig free from his bootlace, then resumed his agitated movements to and fro. Lizzy stood her ground, fiercely imagining him gone.

"My aunt told me what she'd done," said he at length. "I came here immediately."

Lizzy bowed her head but could say nothing.

"I had to know you were all right," he added in an agitated tone.

Lizzy stared at him. "So you could revel in the moment?"

"What? No! You can't think I wanted this to happen!"

"Of course you did. You've made it perfectly clear what you thought about the community garden. Why didn't you join in the fun?"

"I knew nothing about it, or I would've stopped her. It shouldn't have been too hard to do: I'm certainly familiar with all your arguments in its favor. It's true I wished you hadn't torn up the bridle path, but I haven't lifted a finger to interfere. I didn't like it, but it was *your* project, so I wouldn't have done anything to harm it; that would be like harming you."

Lizzy stared at him in astonishment.

Darcy took a few paces away and turned back to face her. "You must know—you must let me tell you—how much I admire you and care about you. I'm in love with you! I've tried to do everything I could to overcome it; it's not as if I don't know what my aunt would say, my friends—you don't exactly make an effort to fit into the culture here, in fact, you're kind of a joke for some people, but I think they don't understand you. Just because you choose to work with your hands doesn't mean that's all you're capable of. Of course, in some ways they have a point: we all owe something to society, and it's a little narcissistic to follow one's own impulses without regard for what others expect of us. If everybody invented the rules to suit themselves, the world would descend into chaos. And you've taken up causes you don't fully understand; people don't want to deal with a crusader who tries to make them feel guilty all the time about problems that are beyond their power to fix. And you don't seem to realize that just because the poor around here don't speak English, you aren't automatically entitled to speak for them. I expect some of my friends will ostracize me for being with you, and with good reason—"

"I can't allow you to suffer such a fate," interrupted Lizzy, unable to keep her tone free of sarcasm. "Let me relieve you right away of the prospective burden of being cast out of the Enclave: I've never aspired to grace the exalted circles you adorn, and never sought your good opinion, which you've bestowed on me so unwillingly. I'm sure I'm supposed to be grateful to you for liking me, and if I could be I would; why would any girl *not* wish to be told that she's stupid and misguided and crude and ill-mannered? It's doubtless one of my failings that I should be unable to feel as I ought in this situation. Let me set your mind at rest: we will never be together."

Darcy took in her meaning with no less resentment than surprise. He struggled for the appearance of composure, and the time required for him to contend with his anger and shock necessitated a delay that was to Lizzy's feelings dreadful. At length, when he believed he had achieved sufficient mastery over his emotions, he spoke:

"And this is all the reply I can expect! I might ask why, with so little attempt at courtesy, I should be rejected. But it doesn't really matter."

"And I might as well ask why," said she, "with the apparent goal of offending and insulting me, you chose to tell me that you liked me against your will, against your reason, and even against your character. Wasn't this some excuse for rudeness, if I *was* rude? But I have other provocations; you know I do. Even if I liked you, which I never did, do you think I could ever be persuaded to care for a man who has destroyed the happiness of my beloved brother?"

Darcy flushed and grew pale again while she spoke, but did not interrupt the flow of her eloquence.

"I have every reason in the world to think ill of you. No motive can excuse the part you played in separating John from Charley Bingley. You can't deny that you were the prime mover in that plot; your cousin told me so! What kind of arrogance allows someone to make two people acutely miserable just to serve his own ideas of social norms?"

With assumed calm he at last replied, "I have no wish to deny that I did everything in my power to separate my friend from your brother, or that I'm pleased with my success. I've been kinder toward *him* than toward myself."

Lizzy disdained the appearance of noticing this civil reflection, but its meaning did not escape, nor was it likely to conciliate her.

"But that's not the only reason I have to dislike you. I'd made up my mind about you long before, when I heard from Jorge the story of your treatment of him and his family. What could you possibly say in justification for your actions there? What imaginary act of friendship can you use to defend stealing his family's land, concealing the documentary evidence of the fact, and throwing him out of work?"

"You take a great interest in George Carrillo's concerns!"

"Who can help feeling an interest in his misfortunes, when they hear what those have been?"

"His misfortunes!" repeated Darcy contemptuously; "yes, his misfortunes have been great indeed."

"And inflicted by you," cried Lizzy with energy. "You've withheld the advantages that are his by right—and yet you treat the mention of his sufferings with contempt and ridicule."

"And this," said Darcy, pacing about in the litter of uprooted plants, "is your opinion of me! I thank you for explaining it so fully. My faults, according to your calculation, are very serious. And yet—" he turned a keen gaze on her—"perhaps my offenses would have been overlooked if I hadn't wounded your pride by acknowledging the issues that kept me from expressing my feelings before now. I might've been spared these shrill attacks if I'd concealed my doubts and flattered you more. But I abhor that kind of pretense. I'm not ashamed of my concerns; they are perfectly reasonable. Could you expect me to rejoice in the inferiority of your situation in life, or to congratulate myself on associating myself with a family that has no idea how to behave in public? Why should I be thrilled about exposing myself to your matchmaking social climber of a mother or your party-animal younger siblings?"

Lizzy felt herself growing angrier every moment, but she tried to speak calmly. "The inferiority of my family and my situation in life rest in the eye of the beholder, but you're welcome to congratulate yourself on *avoiding* exposure to them. You're mistaken in assuming that your manners affected my response in any way other than to spare me the concern I might otherwise have felt about hurting your feelings. If you'd been more of a gentleman, I would've felt sorry for you, but my answer would've been the same."

Darcy still appeared incredulous, so she continued. "Almost from the first moment I met you, your manners impressed me as being arrogant and conceited. You struck me as someone who was filled with false pride and self-importance, as concerned for his own feelings as he was disdainful of the feelings of others. Our first meeting laid the groundwork for my disapproval, which subsequent encounters built into an immovable dislike; and I hadn't known you a month before I became convinced that you were the last man on earth I would ever find attractive."

"You've said enough," replied Darcy with finality. "I completely understand your feelings, and can only regret what my own have been. Forgive me for having taken up so much of your time; clearly you have a lot of cleanup work to do here, and I won't keep you from it any longer."

And with these words he walked hastily away, trampling heedlessly over the plant debris until he rounded a corner and was lost from sight.

The tumult of Lizzy's mind was painfully great, and from actual weakness she sank to the ground and cried for a time. Her astonishment, as she reflected on what had passed, was increased by every review of it. That Fitzwilliam Darcy should have been in love with her, so much so as to wish to overcome the objections to her family and the concerns that had made him separate his friend from her brother, was incredible. It was undeniably gratifying to have inspired such affection. But his abominable pride; his shameless avowal of what he had done to John; his unpardonable assurance in acknowledging, though he could not justify it; and the unfeeling manner in which he had referred to Jorge Carrillo, his cruelty toward whom he had not attempted to deny—all these overwhelmed any pity that the consideration of his attachment might have excited.

She sat in the wreck of the garden till the sound of vehicles on the nearby streets warned her that people were returning to the town center from the rodeo. Feeling herself unequal at present to either undertaking the cleanup job or facing the sympathy or the triumph of onlookers, she beat a hasty retreat to her truck and thence to the privacy of her own bedroom.

Chapter Twenty-four

L izzy awoke the next morning to the same thoughts and meditations which had at length closed her eyes. She could not yet recover from the surprise of what had happened; it was impossible to think of anything else, and feeling unequal to meeting her family or the citizens of Lambtown with the appearance of equanimity, she resolved to catch up on her neglected e-mail. Perhaps one of her friends from Columbus might have written, and in focusing on another's preoccupations she could escape for a time her own.

Having this laudable aim in view, she was dismayed to discover, on viewing her in-box, that the name at the top of the list was none other than that of Fitzwilliam Darcy. With no expectation of pleasure, but with the strongest curiosity, Lizzy opened the message, which was time-stamped at a very early hour of the morning. To her still increasing wonder, she perceived an extremely lengthy missive, composed in Darcy's usual ceremoniously formal style and opening as follows:

Don't be alarmed, on receiving this letter, that it contains any repetition of the declarations that were so disgusting to you yesterday. I am writing without any intention of paining you—or humbling myself—by dwelling on wishes that, for both our sakes, can't be too soon forgotten; and the effort of composing it would have been spared, but my reputation required it to be written and read. You must, therefore, pardon the liberty I take in commanding your attention: your feelings, I know, will grant it most unwillingly, but I demand it of your justice.

Yesterday you charged me with two offenses of very different types: the first was that without regard for the feelings of either, I detached Charley Bingley from your brother; the second, that I somehow blighted George Carrillo's prospects and violated the rights or interests of his family. To have willfully injured a man who was a constant companion in my youth, who was a protégé of my father, who had practically lived on our ranch and had every reason to expect to make his career there, would be an act of depravity out of all proportion to any harm that might come from separating two people who had known each other only a matter of weeks. Your eloquent expressions of blame, however, lead me to suppose that in your mind these crimes are of equal magnitude, and I hope to spare myself further recriminations by giving you the following account of my actions and their motives. If, in laying out the explanation that I believe is due to myself, I cause further offense, I can only say that I am sorry.

Your family had not long been in Lambtown before it became apparent to me that Charley was partial to your brother, but not until the dance hosted by Caroline did I have any idea that he might be seriously attached to John. I have known him a long time, and have observed with compassion his struggles to understand his sexuality. You aren't in a position to know it, but he has never, unlike some men, been certain he was gay. His open heart often leads him to imagine himself in love with some man or woman based on little more than good looks and a sunny temperament. But when he chose to dance openly with John in such a public setting, I realized that he was drawing considerable attention, some of it hostile. My concern was that he avoid labeling himself indelibly in the public mind as gay, should he subsequently find himself mistaken and form an attachment to a woman. This is a small community, where one doesn't enjoy the luxury of privacy as one does in a big city. His actions risked committing him irrevocably to one side of the fence, a choice that could have disastrous consequences for him. So I observed him closely, and I could tell that his feelings for John were more serious than I had ever before seen in him. Your brother I also watched. He seemed as open, cheerful, and charming as ever, but I couldn't determine that he felt any particular affection for Charley. Although he clearly liked Charley, it seemed to me that he didn't have the same depth of feelings toward him, and might even be going along with him only because Charley was his employer. I was even worried that Charley might be exposing himself to a sexual harassment claim! If you are not mistaken in your assessment of the state of John's heart, I must be; your superior knowledge of your brother makes it probable. If I have been misled in the matter, your resentment is not unreasonable. But I have to say that your brother's air of calm was such as might have given the closest observer the impression that, however easygoing his temperament might be, his heart was not to be easily touched. I didn't believe John indifferent to Charley because I wished it to be so—although I did wish it—I think Charley knows that whatever direction his life takes, I will always be his friend. It was my impartial conviction that John was not in love with him.

Of course, my objections were not only on the basis of John being male. I am sorry if it offends you for me to say this, but I was also motivated by the wish to save my friend from becoming too closely entangled with a family that has done little but disturb the peace since arriving in town. Aside from your gardening exploits and John's being gay, I would exempt the two of you from this criticism. But when I saw your mother's naked ambition to curry favor with Enclave members and her matchmaking efforts, and the disorderly behavior of the younger members of the family, which your father never makes the slightest effort to curb, I worried that Charley, who's a bit naive, might end up saddled with burdens far beyond those of his primary relationship.

*His sister Caroline also confided her similar concerns to me;
and between us we decided that the best course of action was to
remove Charley from the neighborhood, and talk to him logically
about it when John was not there before him every day. Charley
has always wanted a behind-the-scenes view of the racing world,
and I was in a position to offer him that distraction. Once we
were away, I was able to detail my objections to him. I don't
suppose my words would have ultimately discouraged him, had
I not also been able to convince him that John was indifferent.
He believed John to be equally attracted to him; but Charley has
great natural modesty, and a tendency to depend more on my
judgment than on his own. To convince him that he had been
mistaken, therefore, was not difficult. From that point his native
commonsense took over, and he decided to put The Chocolate
Bar up for sale. There are enough dot-com millionaires moving
into the valley that it shouldn't be hard to sell. Chocolate lacks
the cachet of wine, but has perhaps a larger customer base.*

*If I have wounded your brother's feelings, it was uncon-
sciously done; and though my motives may seem insufficient to
you, I am not prepared to condemn them. I have no apology to
offer. With respect to the more serious charge, of having injured
George Carrillo, I can only refute it by laying out the whole history of the connection between our families. I don't know what
specific accusations he has made, but I can refer you to witnesses
and documentation that will back up my version of events.*

*The Carrillos were among the first landowners in the Santa
Ynez; their land grant, which came originally from the Mexican
government and was renewed when California became part of
the United States, extended over at least a third of the area. But
by the 1870s, careless ranching and farming practices had left
the land overgrazed and eroded; a drought pushed the family and
their many dependents to the brink of destitution. I have in my
family archives newspapers from that era, as well as the original
land grant papers and deeds of sale. When my Darcy forebears*

and the de Bourgh family came into the valley, the Carrillos were eager to sell all but the most fertile bottomland along the river, some of which they still own. We paid them fairly for the land that has become the Pemberley and Rosings ranches, as well as for the land where Lambtown was established. The de Bourghs became partners in the right-of-way for the narrow-gauge rail that was soon after laid down through the valley, and for a time they prospered from the commerce the railroad made possible. The Darcys found that despite the overgrazing that made raising cattle unprofitable, sheep could still be run here, especially up in the hills—hence the name Lambtown, for the community's first industry. Over time we restored the land and were able to reintroduce cattle and eventually horses.

My father admired and trusted George's father, Frank Carrillo, who worked on the ranch as a young man until he took over responsibility for his own family farm. George was around all the time growing up, and my father liked his intelligence and his charm; he gave George his first summer job and helped support his education. When George left school, my father gave him a full-time job and started training him to eventually fill the post of ranch foreman.

My father was an open-hearted person, not unlike your brother John, and he never looked behind George's facade: he preferred to see the best in people, and engage only with their better selves. But, perhaps because I was closer to George's age, I saw a different side of him. I thought he was unprincipled in taking on the persona of Jorge, playing on Latin-lover stereotypes to seduce girls and cynically using myths of native shamanic traditions to validate substance abuse and drug dealing. I saw him go to any lengths to make money. These things I concealed from my father, because I didn't want him to suffer disillusionment. If any comfort might be derived from the sudden death of my parents, it is that they didn't live to see what happened shortly thereafter.

Here again I'm afraid I must give you pain—to what degree, only you can say. But whatever feelings you may have for George Carrillo, my suspicion of their nature can't prevent me from telling you the truth: in fact, it adds yet another motive. What I must tell you is something I hope you will keep secret; it would only cause Frank and Lupe Carrillo needless pain were it to become public knowledge. I had observed that George was often not where he was supposed to be on the ranch, and that tasks assigned to him were being completed by lower-ranked hands, and without supervision. One day I was riding in a remote area and saw him driving cross-country in a direction he had no reason to go. I followed his path, and discovered, in a hidden canyon at the edge of our property near the border with the National Forest, a large farming operation in the creek bed of sinsemia *marijuana plants, as well as smaller plots of peyote and jimsonweed plants under plastic, all fenced in from natural predators with fencing materials stolen from the ranch supply. He had even used the ranch's skiploader to regrade the hillside and revegetate in the canyon in order to conceal the operation from casual view.*

This put me in a very dangerous situation. Had the federal authorities discovered the plantation, my land could have been confiscated. So instead I called the local sheriff's office, where I am known, and together we managed to arrange that he would be prosecuted outside the area, with no local publicity. In doing this, I was also motivated by a deference to the Carrillos' feelings and their standing in the community, as well as concern for my father's memory. We were able for the most part to keep the matter quiet. He was sent to juvenile detention near Los Angeles, and by the time his trial came up he was able to get off with time served.

I am not sorry to have avoided making his crime public— who would have benefited from it? I certainly didn't want to give any of the local drug dealers ideas about the suitability of the remote canyons on my land for drug cultivation. It's a pity that George has chosen to return to the neighborhood, and if the way he spends money is any indication, he's probably returned to drug dealing, if not production. It is for law enforcement to address that.

This is a complete account of my dealings with George Carrillo. I don't know how he has imposed on your trust, or what lies he has told; but his success in convincing you is not surprising. Ignorant as you were of the circumstances, you could have no reason to suspect him. For corroboration of what I have told you, I can refer you to my cousin Cal, who was here helping me out on the ranch for a while after my parents' death and was therefore privy to the entire affair. Father Austen also helped me with the legal arrangements, though he might consider himself bound to secrecy because I suppose he is George's confessor. Even if your dislike of me should make my word valueless, you can't mistrust either of them on the same basis; and to give you the opportunity to seek out Cal before he leaves, I am sending this message right away, though it might be prudent to let matters lie for a time.

I will only add, God bless you, Fitzwilliam Darcy.

If Lizzy, when she saw Darcy's letter in her in-box, did not expect it to contain a renewal of his declarations, she had formed no clear expectation of its contents. But it may well be supposed how eagerly she went through them, and what a contrariety of emotion they excited. Her feelings as she read were scarcely to be defined. She began her reading steadfastly persuaded that he could have no explanation to give, which she could find credible. With a strong prejudice against everything he might say, she began his account of what had happened with Charles Bingley. She read, with an eagerness that hardly left her power of comprehension, and from impatience of knowing what the next sentence might bring was incapable of attending to the meaning of the one before her eyes. His belief of John's indifference, she instantly resolved to be false, and his account of the real, the worst objections to the affair made her too angry to have any wish of doing him justice. He expressed no regret for what he had done that satisfied her; his style was not penitent, but haughty. It was all pride and insolence.

But when this subject was succeeded by his account of Jorge Carrillo, when she read with somewhat clearer attention a relation of events that, if true, must overthrow every cherished opinion of Jorge's worth, and which bore so alarming an affinity to his own history of himself, her feelings were yet more acutely painful and more difficult to define. Astonishment, apprehension, and even horror oppressed her. She wished to discredit it entirely, repeatedly exclaiming, "This must be false! It's impossible! It can't be true!" And when she had gone through the whole message, though scarcely knowing anything of the last paragraph or two, she closed it hastily, protesting that she would never look at it again.

In this perturbed state of mind, with thoughts that could rest on nothing, she at last got dressed in her work clothes with the intention of going out to clear up the debris of the community garden; but it would not do. In half a minute the message was opened again, and collecting herself as well as she could, she again began the mortifying perusal of all that related to Jorge, and commanded herself so far as to examine the meaning of every sentence. The account of Jorge's connection with the Darcy family was exactly what he had related himself, though a different construction was placed on the original history; and the kindness of the late Mr. Darcy, though she had not before known its extent, agreed equally well with Jorge's own words. So far each recital confirmed the other: but when she came to the denouement, the difference was great. What Jorge had said was fresh in her memory, and as she recalled his very words, it was impossible not to feel that there was gross duplicity on one side or the other. For a few moments she even flattered herself that her wishes did not err. But when she read, and reread with the closest attention, the particulars immediately following the elder Mr. Darcy's death, again she was forced to hesitate. She walked away from the letter, weighed every circumstance with what she meant to be impartiality—deliberated on the probability of each statement—but with little success. On both sides it was only assertion. Again she read on. But every line proved more clearly that the affair, which she had believed it impossible that any contrivance could so represent as to render the younger Darcy's conduct in it less than infamous, was capable of a turn that must make him entirely blameless throughout the whole.

The profligacy that he did not scruple to lay to Jorge's charge, exceedingly shocked her; the more so, as she could bring no proof of its injustice. She had observed the young ladies of Lambtown fawning on Jorge, but had never considered that he might be deliberately assuming a false persona to encourage their attentions. There was no question that he spent more money than his peers: he had the biggest, most expensive truck of anyone she knew, and his horse and *charrería* outfit must have cost him thousands, yet he was never seen to be working and never made reference to any form of employment.

Of his former way of life, nothing had been known to her but what he told himself. As to his real character, had information been in her power, she had never felt a wish of enquiring. His countenance, voice, and manner had established him at once as possessing every virtue. She tried to recollect some instance of goodness, some distinguished trait of integrity or benevolence, that might rescue him from Darcy's accusations; or at least, by the preponderance of virtue, atone for those casual errors, under which she would endeavor to class what Darcy had depicted as the idleness and vice of many years' continuance. But no such recollection befriended her. She could see him instantly before her, in every charm of air and address; but she could remember no more substantial good than the general adulation of the neighborhood, and the regard which his social powers had gained him among his peers.

After pausing on this point a considerable while, she once more continued to read. But, alas! the story that followed of his drug dealings made all too much sense when she recollected the past with this doubt rooted in her mind. He had never spoken to her about narcotics, but she could not forget the tour of the Lompoc winery with his aging hippie friend, and the surprise she had felt about his close acquaintance with a person of such a different generation and way of life. And in what light did the selection of "medicinal" plants for his community garden plot now appear! Most of them had mind-altering or narcotic properties. She experienced a moment of horror at the thought that if he were indeed guilty, she had brought his illicit trade into the center of town, had encouraged him to flaunt his wares in the public eye. It seemed to her wishes that it could not be true, and she almost resolved on applying to Cal Fitzwilliam or Father Austen in the matter. But the idea was checked by the awkwardness of such an application, and at length wholly banished by the conviction that Darcy would never have hazarded such a proposal had he not been well assured of their corroboration. A cousin might support him from motives of loyalty, but Father Austen? The notion was inconceivable.

She perfectly remembered everything that had passed in conversation between Jorge and herself when they met at the Red and White Ball and on their first date in the mountains. Many of his expressions were still fresh in her memory. She was *now* struck with the impropriety of such communications to a stranger, and wondered it had escaped her before. She saw the indelicacy of his putting forward his claims to the Darcy land as he had done, and the inconsistency of his professions with his conduct.

How differently did everything now appear in which he was concerned! His recent attentions to Mary King were now the consequence of views solely and hatefully mercenary; and the mediocrity of Miss King's wealth proved no longer the moderation of his wishes, but his eagerness to grasp at anything. She had probably sought him out as the local dealer! And his behavior toward herself could now have no tolerable motive; he had either been deceived with regard to her economic circumstances, or had been gratifying his vanity by encouraging the preference which she believed she had most incautiously shown. Every lingering struggle in his favor grew fainter and fainter; and in further justification of Darcy's account, she could not but allow that John had reported to her Charley Bingley's assurance that the nineteenth-century land transfer from the Carrillos to the Darcys was legitimate. Of Fitzwilliam Darcy himself, she had to acknowledge that proud and repulsive as were his manners, she had never, in the whole course of their acquaintance, which had given her a sort of intimacy with his ways, seen anything that betrayed him to be unprincipled or unjust. Among his own connections, including those not impressed by his wealth or standing in the community, he was esteemed and valued; even Jorge had allowed him merit as a landowner, and she had often heard Darcy speak so affectionately of Pemberley Ranch as to prove him a responsible steward of the privileges he enjoyed. Had his actions been what Jorge represented them to be, so gross a violation of the principles of fairness could hardly have been concealed from the world; and friendship between a person capable of such evil and an amiable man like Charley Bingley was inconceivable.

Lizzy grew absolutely ashamed of herself. Of neither Darcy nor Jorge—George, as she must henceforth consider him—could she think without feeling that she had been blind, partial, prejudiced, absurd. How despicably had she acted! She, who prided herself on her discernment, who often disdained the generous candor of her brother and gratified her vanity in useless or blameworthy sarcasm. How humiliating was this discovery! Yet how just; *Had I been in love,* she thought to herself, *I could not have been more wretchedly blind.* But vanity, not love, was her true folly. Pleased with the preference of one, and offended by the neglect of the other, from the very beginning she had courted prepossession and ignorance, and driven reason away where both were concerned. *Till this moment,* she thought, *I never knew myself.*

From herself to John, from John to Bingley, her thoughts were in a line that soon brought her to recall that Darcy's explanation *there* had appeared very insufficient; and she read it again. Widely different was the effect of a second perusal. How could she deny that credit to his assertions, in one instance, which she had been obliged to give in the other? He declared himself to have been totally unsuspicious of John's attachment; and she could not help remembering that no gossip had attached to them before Caroline Bingley's party, as would surely have been the case had anyone outside the family circle observed their growing attraction. Neither could she deny the justice of his description of John. John's emotions, though fervent, were little displayed, and there was a constant complacency in his air and manner not often united with deep feeling.

When she came to that part of the message in which her family was mentioned, in terms of such mortifying, yet merited reproach, her sense of shame was severe. The justice of the charge struck her too forcibly for denial, and the circumstances to which he particularly alluded, as confirming all his first disapprobation, could not have made a stronger impression on his mind than on hers. She must believe still that an element of homophobia, and perhaps inappropriate class-consciousness, colored Darcy's opinion, but even had those not been present, he would have had some level of justification for his concern.

The compliment to herself and John, qualified as it was, could not be unfelt. It soothed, but it could not console her for the contempt that had been attracted by the rest of her family; and as she considered that John's disappointment had in fact been as much the work of his nearest relations as of Darcy's or the community's disapproval, and as she reflected how materially the credit of all must be hurt by such impropriety of conduct, she felt depressed beyond anything she had ever known before.

Chapter Twenty-five

With these thoughts preoccupying her, Lizzy was almost insensible of the triumphant expressions on the faces of the Lambtown shopkeepers who found some excuse to linger on the sidewalks and back alleys around the bridle path as she set about cleaning up what once had been the public garden. Righteous indignation was a pose beyond her power to sustain at that moment, and had Catherine de Bourgh appeared just then Lizzy might even have apologized for her arrogance in appropriating the right-of-way in the teeth of all contrary advice—had she not recalled the scenes of poverty she had witnessed in her work with Rose. No; she was still determined to ease the plight of the destitute farmworkers, but how was it to be achieved?

At one point John emerged from The Chocolate Bar and silently handed her an iced mocha latte. She rested her rake against a wall and slumped down beside him on a bench, his quiet support doing more to soothe her than any words of sympathy might have done. After surveying the debris for some while, he remarked, with seeming irrelevance, "One of the things that never ceases to amaze me, working in the restaurant business, is how much perfectly edible food gets wasted all the time. Every day we throw out salads, chicken, baked goods—just because nobody has ordered them."

Absorbed as she was in her own thoughts, Lizzy nodded absentmindedly, but after a minute the purport of his words penetrated her consciousness, and a familiar sensation of excitement began to course through her person. "You and every other café and restaurant in town! That's a lot of food! There ought to be a way to collect and redistribute it to the needy!"

John smiled. "I've heard that such programs exist in New York and Los Angeles—the restaurant owners make arrangements with the food banks and homeless shelters to pick up their excess."

"Perhaps Rose could mobilize some of her volunteers to do the pickup and distribution!" Lizzy leaned over and gave John a quick hug. "Trust you to know just the right thing to do. Why didn't I ask you in the first place, instead of rushing off with my own ill-considered plans?"

"Don't say that! The community garden was a wonderful idea, and I'm sure you'll find a way to revive it—perhaps someplace far enough away from the imprint of Catherine de Bourgh's hooves."

Lizzy giggled. "Her horse's hooves or *hers*?"

They sat for a moment in companionable silence. "How can I be sad when I have you to cajole me out of my ill-humor?" added Lizzy, smiling affectionately at him.

Turning on her an earnest gaze, John said, "Are you sure the destruction of the garden is the only thing on your mind? I would have expected you to be angry, but you seem so—oh, I don't know, deflated. Has something else happened to upset you? Tell me."

Lizzy was cast into a quandary by his familiar command. She longed to tell John about Darcy's declaration: to know that she had the power of revealing what would so exceedingly astonish him, and must, at the same time, gratify whatever of her own vanity she had not yet been able to reason away, was such a temptation to openness as nothing could have conquered. But the state of indecision in which she remained, as to the extent of what she should communicate; and her fear, if she once entered on the subject, of being hurried into repeating something of Bingley, which might only grieve her brother further, stayed her tongue. She hesitated, and turned her gaze aside, until John became suspicious. "Tell me!" he ordered, more forcefully.

Lizzy thought quickly and, resolving to suppress every particular in which her brother was concerned, believed she could safely recount the remainder. Preparing him to be surprised, she related the chief of the scene between Darcy and herself.

John's astonishment was soon lessened by the strong brotherly partiality which made any admiration of Lizzy appear perfectly natural; and all surprise was shortly lost in other feelings. He was sorry that Darcy should have delivered his sentiments in a manner so little suited to recommend them, but still more was he grieved for the unhappiness that her rejection must have given him.

"His being so sure of succeeding was wrong," said he, "and he certainly shouldn't have allowed you to see it; but think how much it must add to his disappointment."

"Well, I'm heartily sorry for him," replied Lizzy, "but he has other feelings that will probably soon drive away his regard for me. You don't blame me, do you, for turning him down?"

"Blame you? Oh, no."

"But you blame me for having spoken so forcefully about Jorge."

"No—I can't think you were wrong in saying what you did."

"But you *will* think it, I'm sure, when I have told you what happened next."

She then spoke of the e-mail message, repeating the whole of its contents as far as they concerned Jorge Carrillo. What a stroke this was for poor John! who would willingly have gone through the world without believing that so much wickedness existed in the whole race of mankind, as was here collected in one individual. Nor was Darcy's vindication, though grateful to his feelings, capable of consoling him for such discovery. Most earnestly did he labor to prove the probability of error, and seek to clear one, without involving the other.

"There's no way you'll ever be able to make both of them good for anything," said Lizzy. "You'll have to make a choice, and be satisfied with only one. There's only enough merit between them to make one good man, and lately it's been shifting around between the two. My inclination is to believe it all Darcy's, but you must draw your own conclusions."

It was some time, however, before a smile could be extracted from John. "I don't know when I've been more shocked—Jorge so wicked! It's almost beyond belief. And poor Darcy! Consider what he must have suffered. Such a disappointment, when he was all alone in the world after his parents' death. And to bear the knowledge of your ill opinion, when he thinks so highly of you! It's really very upsetting. I'm sure you feel it, too."

"Oh! No, my regret and compassion are all wiped away by seeing you so full of both. I know you'll do him such ample justice that I'm becoming every moment more unconcerned and indifferent. If you lament over him much longer, my heart will be as light as a feather."

"Poor Jorge! He's so good-looking, and appears so open and upright."

"There was certainly some great mismanagement in the education of those two young men: one has all the goodness, and the other all the appearance of it."

"I never thought Darcy so deficient in the *appearance* of it as you used to."

"And I was trying to be so clever in taking an adamant dislike to him, without any reason. It's such a spur to wit to have a hatred of that kind. You get to be continually abusive without saying anything fair; but you can't be always laughing at a man without now and then stumbling by accident on something witty."

"Lizzy, when you first read that message, I'm sure you didn't treat the matter so lightly."

"I certainly couldn't. I was uncomfortable enough—even

unhappy. And no John was there to comfort me and say that I hadn't been as vain and idiotic as I knew in my heart I had been!"

"It's certainly unfortunate that you used such strong words in support of Jorge, for now they *do* appear to be completely undeserved."

"Certainly. But the affliction of speaking with bitterness is the natural result of the prejudices I'd been nursing. There is one point, though, on which I want your advice. Do you think I should speak up about Jorge's real character?"

John paused a little and then replied, "I can't see any good reason to expose him like that. What do you think?"

"That I should let sleeping dogs lie. Darcy hasn't authorized me to make the story public. On the contrary, he expressed a concern that other drug dealers might get the idea to use his backcountry for cultivation if they heard about Jorge's activities. And if I try to expose Jorge's follower-of-the-ancient-ways act, who will believe me? Someday he'll be found out, and then we can laugh at everyone else's stupidity in not knowing it before. For now I won't say anything about it."

"You're quite right. To have his errors made public might ruin him forever. Maybe by now he's sorry for what he has done, and eager to turn over a new leaf."

The tumult of Lizzy's mind was much allayed by this conversation. She had got rid of two of the secrets that weighed on her, and was certain of a willing listener in John whenever she might wish to talk again of either. But there was still something lurking behind, of which prudence forbade the disclosure. She dared not relate the other half of Darcy's e-mail, nor explain to her brother how sincerely he had been valued by Charley. Here was knowledge in which no one could partake; and she was aware that nothing less than a perfect understanding between the parties could justify her in throwing off this last encumbrance of mystery.

"And then," said she to herself as she resumed bagging the wilted and crushed remnants of the community garden, "if that very improbable event ever took place, I would merely be able to tell what Charley can explain in a much more agreeable way himself. The luxury of communication is denied to me until it has lost all its value!"

As a distraction from her own uncomfortable feelings, she made an extra effort over the next few days to observe the real state of John's spirits. He was not happy, and still it seemed cherished a very tender affection for Charley. His regard had all the warmth of a first attachment, and from his age and disposition, greater steadiness than first attachments often boast; and so fervently did he value Charley's remembrance, and prefer him to every other man, that all his good sense, and all his attention to the feelings of his friends and family, were requisite to check the indulgence of those regrets which must have been injurious to his own well-being and their tranquillity.

Even her mother saw enough to be concerned. "Well, Lizzy," said Mrs. Bennet one day, "what's your opinion of this sad business of John's? For my part, I'm determined never to speak of it again, as I told Lydon the other day. But I see no sign that they're e-mailing or talking on the phone. Well, Bingley's a very undeserving young man—and I don't suppose there's the least chance of their getting together now. I don't hear any talk of his returning to Lambtown this summer—and I've asked everyone who's likely to know."

Lizzy reflected ruefully on the kind of speculation such inquiries must have generated, but said merely, "I doubt he'll ever return to Lambtown. I understand he may be trying to sell The Chocolate Bar."

"Oh! Well, whatever he pleases. I'm sure nobody wants to see him again. Though I'll always say that he used John very badly; and if I was him, I wouldn't have put up with it. Well, my comfort is, I'm sure John will die of a broken heart, and then Bingley'll be sorry for what he has done."

As Lizzy could derive no comfort from any such expectation, she made no answer. But her mother, once embarked on the path of speculation about her children's romantic blunders, could not rest there.

"So, you've seen Charlotte Collins since her honeymoon, haven't you? They're living very comfortably, I suppose, what with his real estate business and all the favors Catherine de Bourgh does for them. And Charlotte is a clever manager herself; nothing extravagant in *her* housekeeping, I imagine."

"No, nothing at all."

"Yes, they'll be careful never to spend beyond their income. *They'll* never pass up an opportunity to improve their lot in life. Well, much good it may do them! And so, does she gloat over how she got what you might have had, if you weren't so headstrong?"

"It's not a subject she could ever mention to me."

"But I don't doubt they talk about it between themselves. I hope you're happy being the object of their pity. And since you've stolen your aunt's estate away from the rest of the family, you're probably very pleased with yourself and don't care that the whole town is laughing at you. Mark my words, one of these days you're going to get your comeuppance for always thinking only about yourself, and never stopping to care about your loved ones!"

Chapter Twenty-six

It was not a happy time for the young ladies of the neighborhood. The excitement of the rodeo and fair was a thing of the past, and no fresh amusements could be seen on the horizon. Word soon spread that Fitzwilliam Darcy was departed again, presumed to be in Kentucky seeing to the family's horse racing interests. And even Jorge Carrillo was no longer to be seen training his stallion or parading his custom pickup through the center of town; the mysterious tides of young men's affairs appeared to have washed them both away to distant shores.

Faced with such tragedies, all the young ladies were drooping apace. The dejection was almost universal. Lizzy Bennet alone was still able to eat, drink, and pursue the usual course of her employments. And even she felt a certain degree of gloom settle over her spirits, mocked by the bright summer days, whose temperatures climbed relentlessly one after another into the nineties. She had known from the start that California's was a monsoonal climate, but the withering reality of the unvarying summer sunshine was not to be fully appreciated until it was experienced. Plants she had been convinced were drought-tolerant drooped and died in her clients' gardens; she lost money to replacing them and time to the necessity of daily watering.

The work provided occupation for her mind, however, and the continuing absence of the gentlemen afforded her all the relief of tedium. If happiness were not to be had, these lesser satisfactions could be enough for a time. She filled her days and bore all the appearance of contentment.

Very frequently she was reproached for this insensibility by Kitty and Jenny, whose own misery was extreme, and who could not comprehend such hard-heartedness in any of the family. "This place is the pits! Nothing ever happens here!" they would often exclaim in the bitterness of woe. "How can you be smiling all the time, Lizzy?"

Their affectionate mother shared all their grief, and pined for diversion as deeply as they did. "If only we could go on vacation! A week in Vegas would do us all a world of good."

"We've been here nearly six months and haven't even gone to Disneyland!" cried Kitty.

"I hear Venice Beach is happening," said Lydon.

"I'm sure your father takes pleasure in our misery; he certainly has no sympathy for my nerves."

Such were the lamentations resounding perpetually through the house. Lizzy tried to be diverted by them, but all sense of pleasure was lost in shame. She felt anew the justice of Darcy's objections to her family; and never before had she been so nearly disposed to pardon his interference in the life of his friend. Even after a hard day's work outdoors she could find little peace at home, and resorted to spending long evenings shelving books in Aunt Evelyn's new library.

But the gloomy prospect was shortly cleared away at least for Lydon, and his conviction of life's unending sameness belied by a development he had not foreseen. His father-in-law, Brigadier General Hughes, decreed that Lydon and Jenny should pass the remainder of the summer at his new house in Goleta. Lydon entertained a lively fear of his father-in-law, but he reasoned that the general's duties would keep him on base much of the time, and Goleta was a beach town. Even more in its favor was its proximity to Isla Vista, a residential community for students at the University of California at Santa Barbara, renowned far and wide for the festive proclivities of its student body.

The rapture of Lydon and Mrs. Bennet on this occasion, and

the mortification of Kitty, are scarcely to be described. Wholly inattentive to her feelings, Lydon and Jenny flew about the house in restless ecstasy, calling for everyone's congratulations, and laughing and exclaiming with more violence than ever; whilst the luckless Kitty continued in the den repining at her fate in terms as unreasonable as her accent was peevish.

"I can't see why the general shouldn't ask me as well as Lydon," said she, "even though I'm not married to his daughter. I have as much right to be asked as he has, and more, too, because I just lost my job."

"You got fired, you mean, for looking the other way when your friends were shoplifting," said Mary.

"I don't know what you think you know about it—*you* never visited me at work!"

"Hanging around flirting with enlisted men in an Urban Outfitters may be your idea of useful occupation, but I would rather be improving my relationship with God."

"Oh, is *He* a good kisser?" retorted her unrepentant sister, which remark achieved its object, of sending Mary posthaste from the room, allowing Kitty to return to the more appealing subject of her ill-use.

In vain did Lizzy attempt to make Kitty reasonable, and John to make her resigned. As for Lizzy herself, the invitation was so far from exciting in her the same feelings as in her mother and Lydon—regardless of the Brigadier General's reputation for sternness—that she considered it as the death-warrant of all possibility of commonsense for her younger brother; and detestable as such a step must make her were it known, she could not help secretly advising her father not to let him go. She represented to him all the improprieties of Lydon's general behavior, the little advantage he could derive from the company of college-age summer school students, and the probability of his behaving yet more imprudently in a college town, where the temptations must be greater than at home.

Mr. Bennet heard her attentively, and then said, "Lydon will never be satisfied until he's made a fool of himself in some resort or other, and we can never expect him to do it with so little expense or inconvenience to our family as under the current circumstances."

"If you were aware," said Lizzy, "of the disadvantages for us all that arise from Lydon's behavior, I'm sure you'd think differently."

"What, has he frightened away some of your lovers? Poor Lizzy! But such squeamish youths as can't bear to be associated with a little absurdity are not worth your regret. Come, tell me who are these pitiful fellows who have shied off because of Lydon's behavior."

"I have no specific injuries to resent; I'm speaking more generally. We're already shunned by most of the families here in Lambtown because of the attention Lydon, Jenny, and Kitty have drawn. Excuse me for speaking plainly, but if you won't take the trouble to check his wild behavior and teach him that his present activities are not a sustainable way to lead his life, he'll soon be set in his bad habits. He has no more than the lowest form of charm, no good qualities beyond youth and decent looks, and with his ignorance and empty head, in a year or two he won't be able to attract anything but contempt from his peers. And Kitty will follow wherever he leads. They'll be despised wherever they're known, and will involve their family in every sort of humiliation."

Mr. Bennet saw that she was seriously concerned, but he said only, "Don't worry so much, dear. Wherever you and John are known you'll be respected and valued, and your worth won't be tarnished by having a couple of—or, I might say, *three*—very silly siblings. We'll have no peace if Lydon doesn't go to Goleta. Brigadier General Hughes is a sensible man, and will keep him out of any real mischief for Jenny's sake. Being among young people who are a little older and a lot better educated may teach him his own insignificance. At any rate, he can't get much worse without finding himself locked up for the rest of his life."

With this answer Lizzy was forced to be content; but her own opinion continued the same, and she left him disappointed and sorry. Had Lydon and his mother known the substance of Lizzy's conference with her father, their indignation would hardly have found adequate expression in their united volubility. In Lydon's imagination, the visit to Goleta comprised every possibility of earthly happiness. He saw, with the creative eye of fancy, the streets of that gay coastal hamlet filled with scantily clad coeds, a tavern with lax carding policies on every street corner. He envisioned himself the object of attention from scores of young beauties, and being invited to raves on the beach by easygoing surfers. Had he known that his sister sought to tear him from such prospects as these, what would have been his sensations? They could have been understood only by his mother, who might have felt nearly the same. Lydon's going to a seaside resort was all that consoled her for the melancholy conviction of her husband's intending never to take her there himself.

When the day arrived for Lydon and Jenny to depart, the separation between the couple and the Bennet family was rather noisy than pathetic. Kitty was the only one who wept, and her tears were those of vexation and envy. Mrs. Bennet was effusive in her good wishes for the felicity of her son, and impressive in her injunctions that he should not miss any opportunity of enjoying himself as much as possible—advice which there was every reason to believe would be attended to. And in the clamorous happiness of Lydon himself as he bade them farewell, the more gentle adieus of his elder siblings were uttered without being heard.

Mrs. Bennet's nerves were soon to receive a fresh shock, and one that prompted a renewed assault on Mr. Bennet's defenses. Miles away at the eastern extremity of Santa Barbara County, in the most distant reaches of Los Padres National Forest, whose near side approached the edge of Lambtown, a brush fire was ignited. It took hold in the parched summer scrub and roared up into the wildlands of the forest, where soon it could be seen by night flickering on the ridges east of town. Smoke poured down toward the coast, enveloping Lambtown in a brown haze that caught in the lungs and burned the eyes.

"We'll all be burned in our beds!" cried Mrs. Bennet. "We must evacuate! If we hurry, we may escape. Perhaps Los Angeles will be far enough away, but San Diego would be better. If we'd gone to Las Vegas, as I suggested, we'd be safely on the far side of the fire by now."

Mr. Bennet remained unmoved by either the wildfire threat or her travel plans. "Even the easternmost ranchers and vineyard owners in the valley aren't concerned that it'll travel this far west. Here in town, they say, there's nothing to be concerned about. These fires are only difficult to put out where the terrain is rugged and there aren't many roads. Once it gets into developed areas, it's immediately doused."

"Nothing to be concerned about! We can already see it from here! And they don't fly the water-dropping aircraft at night, so it can advance as much as it likes between dusk and dawn. Just yesterday they believed it was contained, but when the sundowner winds came up, it broke through the fire lines and now it's out of control again!"

"I know it looks close to us when we see the flames at night, but it's actually many miles away."

"Do you plan to wait until the fire's licking at our doorstep? Look at how the smoke is billowing over us—that proves the fire's headed our way. And even if it doesn't burn our house down, are we expected to inhale this smoke forever? Poor Kitty—you know how sensitive she is, with her allergies and bronchitis attacks. Have you spared a thought for what she's suffering?"

But Mr. Bennet remained obdurate, even when informed that the Enclave had suspended its summer polo schedule to protect the lungs of the ponies. This intelligence had been obtained by his wife only secondhand, as the Enclave families persisted in snubbing the Bennets.

Lizzy, who worked mostly out-of-doors, might be expected to feel the smoke most keenly, but she did not add her voice to the clamor for precipitate withdrawal. She regretted the loss of habitat in the national forest and hoped the fire line would not reach the beautiful canyons of Figueroa Mountain, which she had come to love; but as none of the longtime residents of the Santa Ynez Valley appeared concerned for their safety, she simply wrapped a damp bandana around her nose and mouth and carried on with her work. And indeed, after little more than a week the fire was contained and eventually extinguished, and everyone forgot about it.

Mrs. Bennet's tenacity was not of an order to be discouraged by the mere removal of imminent threat, however, and she continued to press her spouse for a vacation trip until that beleaguered gentleman took to locking the door of the library, emerging only for a fugitive sandwich long after the rest of the family had lunched.

Lizzy was facing discouragements of her own. Rose was finding that the plan to collect extra food from the local restaurants for distribution to the poor was not embraced with enthusiasm: evidently the *affaire* of the community garden had created sufficient ill-will that few business owners were willing to hear another word about the plight of the immigrant worker. Lizzy had fresh cause to rue her arrogance in pursuing that project with each day she observed the overflowing Dumpsters in the back alleys of Lambtown. Even the strategic deployment of Father Austen dispensing awe and shame did not suffice to soften the hearts of the restaurateurs.

After meeting with several community organizers and nonprofits in the Santa Barbara area, Lizzy was also compelled to admit that some of her plans for the library would have to be curtailed. It seemed that a full-scale day care arrangement for the farmworkers' children would face such regulatory and zoning challenges that the time and expense required to surmount them were prohibitive. She would be able to convert the capacious garage of her aunt's home into the children's section of the library, and even retain the services of one Spanish- and Quechua-speaking mother to supervise youthful visitors; but food, play areas, and other forms of care lay beyond her power to provide. She was heartened to find, on a visit to the Santa Ynez Historical Society, an elderly man of Chumash descent who consented to appear, on a volunteer basis, as a bilingual storyteller on Saturday afternoons. And a community group from San Luis Obispo agreed to send down a literacy teacher to run a class two nights a week.

With these arrangements she had to be content, as in considerable trepidation she prepared her library proposal for submission to the County Planning Commission. The Town Council meeting that had followed the installation of the community garden being still vivid in her memory, she dreaded the fracas that would ensue once her plans became public knowledge. Nevertheless, this challenge had to be faced sooner or later, and as she intended to open the library at New Year's, it had better be sooner. Perhaps Darcy would still be out of town, and she might be able to avoid incurring his further wrath—or, what might perhaps be harder to bear, his disappointment—on the occasion.

She trusted that she would have some support, but did not expect it to come from any in Lambtown's business or ranching establishments. If only Catherine de Bourgh might be persuaded not to burn down the building! Lizzy briefly entertained visions of that lady riding into town at the head of a lynch mob brandishing torches, until her commonsense asserted itself to remind her that the library plan could far more easily be foiled by a few words whispered into the commissioners' ears, and with fewer repercussions for the would-be seditionist.

If her family wondered what was keeping Lizzy so often closeted with her attorney, Melvin Perry, of an evening, they did not trouble themselves to question her, though Mrs. Bennet did mutter darkly once or twice about schemers who plotted to cheat their own flesh and blood out of an inheritance. The female members of the family were more interested in the exploits of young Lydon.

He had promised faithfully to send regular e-mails, but his communications with his mother contained little beyond the occasional tantalizing detail, written in haste. He was learning to surf; he had discovered the music scene in the storage garages on Seville Road, where such luminaries as Ugly Kid Joe and Toad the Wet Sprocket had gotten their start. From his correspondence with Kitty there was still less to be learnt—for these messages, though rather longer, were much too full of exclamation points to be made public. From Jenny (who deprecated the plan) they did discover that Lydon had formed an ambition to travel with a group of new acquaintances to Nevada for the Burning Man Festival at the end of the month. It seemed that Lydon had been concealing this intelligence out of fear that his parents would ban the expedition; but he need not have been concerned.

"At least *one* of us will get to go to Nevada," was his mother's comment; and Mr. Bennet having been barricaded in the library when the secret was revealed, Lydon's father could not be expected to form an opinion about a plan of which he was unaware.

The cat being now at least partly out of the bag, Lydon's communications came increasingly to focus on this prospect. The theme for this year's gathering was "Wheel of Time," they were told; the festivities, the nature of which were left mostly to the imagination but included the burning of a wicker effigy, continued for a week; he would be camping in a minivan owned by a surfing friend; people were traveling from all over the world to attend.

Having failed so signally in persuading her father to forbid Lydon from going to Goleta, Lizzy did not even attempt to remonstrate with Mr. Bennet about this further exploit. John considered doing so, but in the end decided to take the optimistic view that if Lydon's own wife did not wish him to go, the plan would in all probability come to naught.

Mary greeted this fresh evidence of familial depravity with all the horror that might be predicted, but since nobody took seriously her contention that the Burning Man Festival was a neopagan observance and therefore the work of the devil, nobody attended to her homilies on the subject. Kitty, meanwhile, appeared to have grown weary of feeling left behind. Instead of bemoaning the Burning Man expedition as fresh evidence of the unfair treatment that was invariably her lot, she had developed a new coterie of friends, with new interests. They traveled on every possible occasion to the nearest cinema, where they watched the newly released movie *The Sixth Sense* over and over. Soon Kitty's conversational range was distilled into the endless repetition of "I see dead people," until her entry into a room became the signal for everyone else to quit it. Even the term *Y2K* lacked an equal power to annoy.

It is hard to imagine that the family circle could have held less charm for Lizzy than it did at this moment. She accordingly sought companionship elsewhere, in circles where enjoyment was more certain—with Edward and Mary Gardiner. In their company she found cheerfulness to enhance every pleasure, and affection and intelligence to supply it among themselves if there were disappointments abroad.

Lizzy and Mrs. Gardiner were making pesto one afternoon, from the surfeit of basil in the Gardiners' plot, when that lady inquired whether Lizzy had yet obtained a ticket for the hayride.

"What hayride?"

"Haven't you heard about it? Oh, you *must* go; it's not to be missed! It's an annual benefit for the hospital. It takes place on the afternoon and evening of the full moon in September every year. The old Wells Fargo stagecoach road went through this area, you know, and remnants of it are still kept up by local property owners. Everyone dresses in nineteenth-century costume, and we ride in old-fashioned hay wagons from Lake Cachuma through the hills and down into the valley. We end up at Pemberley Ranch, where there's a big barbecue."

"Pemberley Ranch!"

"Yes, the Darcys have always maintained their stretch of the stagecoach road. It's a beautiful drive through the backcountry to the main house: you go for hours without ever crossing a modern road. It really seems like going back in time. You see deer, and wild turkeys, and sometimes a wild pig—and of course the cattle and the magnificent Darcy thoroughbreds."

Lizzy was distressed. She felt that she had no business at Pemberley Ranch, and was obliged to assume a disinclination for the outing. "I don't have a costume to wear, and I'm not sure I should take the time off from work."

"My dear, it's on a Saturday, and you work too hard as it is. I believe you and John between you work more than the rest of your family put together, if you don't mind my saying so. I won't ask John because I know how most men would rather die than dress up in a costume. Mr. Gardiner wouldn't be caught dead! So you'd be rescuing me from loneliness if you came as my guest."

"You're very kind, but it seems like an intrusion on Mr. Darcy's privacy. I can't imagine him tolerating such a mass invasion!"

"His mother always hosted it, and I imagine he continues to do so out of respect for her memory. Not that he often attends; I don't think I've seen him there more than once. No, it's all handled by his staff, and he reaps all the credit without taking any of the trouble."

"So you don't expect him to be there?"

"I'd be very surprised if he were. And you don't have to worry about what to wear; I'll ask around among my friends with grown-up daughters to see if any have left an outfit behind. I'm sure somebody will turn up something that would fit you. *Please* say you'll go with me! The tickets sell out very quickly, so you have to answer quite soon."

The fear of meeting Mr. Darcy while trespassing on his property having thus been removed, Lizzy was at leisure to feel a great deal of curiosity to see the place, and she accepted with alacrity.

To Pemberley Ranch, therefore, they were to go.

Chapter Twenty-seven

It cannot be said that Lizzy anticipated her hayride with as much unalloyed enthusiasm as Lydon did his straw man; her feelings on the occasion, though perhaps more closely examined, were less straightforward. Lydon permitted no shadow of uncertainty to dim the sunlight of his prospects. In vain did Jenny beg that he deny himself a treat the brigadier general would never allow her to share.

"Oh! As far as that goes," said Lydon airily, "it's good for couples to have a little time apart, so they don't become too dependent on each other. I'm sure that by the time I get back I'll have realized how important you are to me, and we'll be closer than ever. And you can spend the time on things *you've* been wanting to do—like going to the butterfly sanctuary you're always talking about, or seeing that chick flick."

Needless to say, this speech had the effect of sending Jenny into paroxysms of weeping so violent as to rival Kitty's best efforts. She even contemplated drawing inspiration from soap operas to claim a false pregnancy, but was deterred by the unwelcome suspicion that such tidings might actually hasten, not prevent, Lydon's departure. Even these reflections, however, were insufficient to impel Jenny to inform her father of Lydon's plans: she did not for a moment doubt that doing so, while putting an end to the Burning Man expedition, would also put an end to her marriage. Lydon would never forgive her such a betrayal.

On the day of his departure, the tail of a hurricane over northern Mexico whipped gale-force winds and heavy rain into Santa Barbara County, giving external expression to Jenny's inner torments and so damaging telephone lines that she could not have reported his scheme even had she chosen to do so; and Lydon was halfway to Fresno before his flight was discovered by the adult to whom his care was entrusted. The brigadier general, confronted with his son-in-law's perfidy, was at first enraged by the disrespect shown for his authority, then disgusted by his daughter's inability to manage her own domestic affairs. And finally, drawing on his extensive experience of youthful airmen, he opined that a few days of R & R would leave Lydon a sadder but wiser man.

"Don't expect me to go rescue him when his so-called friends dump him without a penny on the side of some highway in the middle of the desert," he barked at his cringing daughter.

And so it was small wonder that four nights later, when the call came from a sheriff's station in a Nevada county that Jenny had never heard of, it was to her in-laws that she turned for help.

At first there was some confusion over exactly what had gone awry, because Mrs. Bennet had taken Jenny's call and was so overset that little sense could be made of her utterances. But gradually Mr. Bennet was able to apprehend that their younger son had been arrested on a charge of attempting to buy peyote buttons from an undercover police officer.

By this time Mrs. Bennet was in the throes of an attack of hysterics so severe that John had to help her back to bed and undertake to nurse her, holding her hand, bathing her brow with lavender water, and occasionally sending Kitty scurrying for a tisane or a valium. As Mr. Bennet paced about, muttering, Mary appeared deep in cogitation, from which she eventually emerged to remark, "This is a shocking event, and will bring down all kinds of scandal on the family. We must stem the tide of malice and pour into our wounded bosoms the balm of familial consolation."

Lizzy rolled her eyes but made no reply, and Mary added, "Unfortunate as this experience will be for Lydon, we can draw from it a useful lesson: that our worthiness in God's sight is as precarious as it is precious, and we must be ever vigilant to stay on the right side of the Lord."

"I believe it's the right side of the *law* that should concern us now," Lizzy retorted, but Mary continued to console herself with moral extractions from the evil before them, although no one was paying her any mind.

At last Mr. Bennet broke his silence. "Lydon is of age," said he, "and if he's old enough to go gallivanting about the countryside on his own, he's old enough to extricate himself from whatever difficulties he encounters. It'll do him good to take the consequences of his stupidity! I'll be damned if I drop everything and rush to Nevada to bail him out. Let him sit in jail until he's ready to become a productive member of society."

This attitude, on being conveyed to Mrs. Bennet, brought on such a renewal of wailing that her husband snatched up a pillow and locked himself in the library for the remainder of the night.

Thus it fell to Lizzy to decide on a course of action. She called Jenny to obtain more detailed information about Lydon's whereabouts, and the pitiful quaver in that young lady's voice, as she tried to answer the questions, touched Lizzy's heart. Without further ado she packed a few clothes for herself and Lydon and set out to collect Jenny for the long drive to the Black Rock desert.

The journey was a trying one, as Jenny could do little but cry and ask over and over the same questions, which Lizzy was unable to answer, about how Lydon was to be extricated from his difficulties. No more than her passenger did Lizzy know when Lydon would be arraigned, what his bail might be, how it was to be paid, or whether he would be permitted to leave the state upon settlement of his most immediate obligations. She could not say if he was well-treated in the jail, or what material comforts they might be allowed to supply to him. Her lack of suitable answers did not in any way deter Jenny from pressing her inquiries, and by the third or fourth hour it was with considerable weariness that Lizzy begged her to desist. Just as the prospect of the remainder of the journey became too much to bear, however, Jenny mercifully lapsed into slumber, and Lizzy was left with no more onerous obligation than that of keeping herself awake.

In due course Lizzy located the appropriate sheriff's station, and she and Jenny presented themselves. By this time the day was far advanced and they were not permitted to see Lydon, but a deputy informed them that the following morning was the time appointed for his arraignment. After giving the deputy suitable raiment for Lydon to don for the occasion, they were obliged to settle for possessing themselves of patience and the directions to the courthouse; and they sought shelter for the evening in a motel on the outskirts of the county seat. Lizzy did not find her sister-in-law an enlivening companion, as Jenny was unwilling to be diverted by observations on their surroundings and kept reverting to the subject of her woe. Very soon Lizzy pleaded, with perfect truth, fatigue after the rigors of the drive and sought refuge in sleep.

The next morning they presented themselves at the courthouse at the designated hour. There they discovered a considerable number of Burning Man celebrants assembled to answer for an array of illicit activities. The judge appeared to have extensive prior experience with the festival's annual harvest of malfeasance, and quickly divided the prisoners into groups according to the severity of their offenses. Lydon's, they were pleased to discover, were counted among the least consequential, and in due course he was offered release upon the payment of a fine. Observing his sister and wife in the audience, he smiled and waved, and indicated in pantomime that they were to settle his account forthwith. Little though it suited Lizzy to comply, she could see no reasonable alternative, and so she joined the line of people waiting to purchase the release of their loved ones.

When he eventually emerged from the building, Lizzy and Jenny found that Lydon was Lydon still: untamed, unabashed, wild, noisy, and fearless. As Jenny cast herself, sobbing, upon his chest he pushed her away, saying, "Don't make such a tragedy of it! It's not like I was in mortal danger or anything! The narc was really dumb; he arrested me before I'd actually made the buy, so they really didn't have anything to hold me on. The festival staff has legal advisers who tell you what to say and do. And now you've managed to get away from your dad's house after all—so you can catch some of the festival yourself. At least they let us out in time to get back for the burning of the Man tomorrow night! They say there are these huge fire cannons that'll shoot flames more than a hundred feet in the air before the burning."

Jenny was horrified. "You can't mean to go back there! What if they arrest you again?"

"Oh! Well, I expect I'll be more careful now. How was I to know he was a narc? And I guess I was a little messed up; I have no idea what was in that drink they gave me at Pan's Cornucopia."

Round-eyed, Jenny demanded to know what Pan's Cornucopia was.

"It's a kind of a bar where they mix up cocktails using herbs and juices in some sort of enormous chemistry set. You tell them what ails you and they brew up something to cure you. You get pretty thirsty out there on the dry lake bed in the blazing sun, and most of the other bars were too expensive, plus they saw my ID was fake. I'd basically been living on kava, and was sick of it."

Lizzy, seeing little to be gained from a debate over the wisdom of returning to the scene of his capture and even less likelihood of being repaid the sums she had already been obliged to lay out, merely shepherded them in silence to the truck and started to drive, listening to their artless chatter.

"It was freezing cold the first couple of nights and all the tents kept blowing over, so I was really glad that my friends had brought their VW bus. There was a whole camp of VW buses, and we were much more comfortable than the campers! Because it was so cold until Tuesday, nobody was getting naked other than a few of the real old-timers. The wind was great for the Icarus Camp, though—that's a place with all these different ways to fly, hang gliders and everything. And the U-Hurl was a blast: it was this huge slingshot thing, and you could bring whatever you wanted to and they would throw it across the desert to see how it broke. Once it warmed up there was a place to play water-gun tag, and you could borrow inline skates, and some artist took a gigantic mass nude photo." Glancing over at his sister, he added, "There are all these art installations everywhere, and places you can meditate and worship the Goddess and stuff. And this really cool Tesla coil—hey, Lizzy! You're going the wrong way! You were supposed to turn left back there!"

"Only if I was going to take you back to Burning Man, which I have no intention of doing."

In vain did Lydon plead and threaten; the truck was pointed homeward, and home they would go. Jenny, secretly relieved not to be obliged to experience the delights he enumerated, did her part by leading him on to describe more of his experiences, until he forgot some of his disappointment in the pleasure of instructing others. Once his tattoo and the remnants of his body paint were sufficiently admired and his various bruises petted and cooed over, he was prepared to look back with a measure of satisfaction on a week well spent and settle in to enjoy the journey home.

"It's fun to be crammed into the cab this way! I'm glad you didn't bring the Rabbit, so nobody gets stuck sitting in the back. Now we can talk and laugh all the way home. Did you know Jorge was at Burning Man? He had this whole setup for some Indian out-of-body experience, called Ritual Spirit—billed himself as a shamanic spiritual guide. It was very popular. Mary King wasn't there, though, and I hear it's all over between them—her parents have found another boarding school back East that's willing to take her. She was a big fool to go away, if she really liked him. But I don't think he ever gave a fig about her; he just liked having a rich city girl make a play for him. Well, who wouldn't?"

Lizzy was chagrined to reflect on how she had made excuses for Jorge's attentions to Mary King, when even her heedless brother had seen more clearly where the truth lay.

Lydon beguiled the entire journey with such histories of his exploits and of the pleasures to be found at Burning Man. Lizzy was extremely relieved to deliver them to whatever dubious welcome they would find at Brigadier General Hughes's home; she declined the treat of accompanying them inside to learn what that outraged gentleman might have to say about Lydon's adventure, preferring instead to take herself and her headache back to Lambtown. There she found her father disposed to forgive her for effecting a rescue he had been unwilling to undertake himself, and her brother John, weary from attendance on their mother, grateful for her return and relieved that she brought good news. As for Mrs. Bennet, the intelligence that her favorite child had escaped prison restored her instantly to health and happiness, and her only disappointment lay in Lizzy's refusal to repeat every detail of Lydon's exploits and current condition of health. But Lizzy heartlessly took herself off to bed, and her mother was obliged to telephone her son in order to satisfy her curiosity.

In the aftermath of the Burning Man Festival, Lizzy could not help but reflect on her parents and their marriage. Had her opinion been all drawn from her own family, she could scarcely have formed a very pleasing picture of conjugal felicity or domestic comfort. Her father—captivated by youth and beauty, and that appearance of good humor which youth and beauty generally give—had married a woman whose weak understanding and illiberal mind had very early in their marriage put an end to any real affection for her. Respect, esteem, and confidence had vanished forever, and all his views of domestic happiness were overthrown. But Mr. Bennet was not of a disposition to seek comfort for the disappointment brought on by his own imprudence in any of those pleasures which often console the unfortunate for their folly or their vice. He was fond of his privacy and his books, and from these tastes had arisen his principal enjoyments. To his wife he was very little otherwise indebted than as her ignorance and folly contributed to his amusement. This is not the sort of happiness that a man would in general wish to owe to his wife; but where other powers of entertainment are wanting, the true philosopher will derive benefit from such as are given.

Lizzy, however, had never been blind to the impropriety of her father's behavior as a husband. She had always seen it with pain; but respecting his intelligence, and grateful for his affectionate treatment of herself, she endeavored to forget what she could not overlook, and to banish from her thoughts that continual breach of conjugal obligation and decorum which, in exposing his wife to the contempt of her own children, was so highly reprehensible. But she had never felt as strongly as now the disadvantages that must attend the children of so unsuitable a marriage, nor ever been as fully aware of the evils arising from so ill-judged a direction of talents—talents which, rightly used, might at least have preserved the respectability of his children, even if incapable of enlarging the mind of his wife.

While taking stock of her situation, Lizzy's thoughts could not fail to turn to the gentlemen, now absent, who had so occupied her thoughts in recent months. She rejoiced over Jorge's continued absence from the neighborhood, but found little other cause for satisfaction in her surroundings during the month of September. The entire family was rarely invited to partake in whatever amusements the community might offer, and at home she had a mother and sister whose constant repinings at the dullness of everything around them threw a real gloom over their domestic circle. She had secretly hoped that the end of summer and the absence of the distraction that Jorge represented would bring to her younger siblings a fresh commitment to gainful employment, but no such gratification was to be hers. It was consequently necessary to name some other period for the commencement of actual felicity; to have some other point on which her wishes and hopes might be fixed, and by again enjoying the pleasure of anticipation, console herself for the present and prepare for another disappointment.

The hayride was now the object of her happiest thoughts, it was her best consolation for all the uncomfortable hours that the discontentedness of her mother and Kitty made inevitable; and could she have included John in the scheme, every part of it would have been perfect. But it seemed to her fortunate that there was that single flaw. Were the whole arrangement perfect, her disappointment would have been certain. But by carrying one ceaseless source of regret in her brother's absence, she could reasonably hope to have all her expectations of pleasure realized. A scheme of which every part promises delight can never be successful; and general disappointment is only warded off by the defense of some little peculiar vexation.

The period of expectation seemed endless, but it did at last pass away and, arrayed in a charming gown of cotton lawn with a high neck, fitted bodice, and fishtail hem, she set off for Mrs. Gardiner's house in search of the truth of all her speculations about the famous Pemberley Ranch.

Chapter Twenty-eight

The afternoon was a fine one, the previous day's thundershowers, which had lent an intriguing element of suspense to the prospect of the expedition, having retreated over the mountains to the east. Before they left the house, Mary Gardiner produced a vial of one of her hand-mixed perfumes.

"This was a blend I made especially for Mrs. Darcy, using her favorite scented flowers. It was her signature scent, and I thought we should each wear a little of it in her honor today." Lizzy took a deep breath as she dabbed the tincture here and there, and thought she detected magnolia, lily of the valley, and stephanotis, along with perhaps a hint of heliotrope or lilac.

No fewer than eight wagons, laden with hay and drawn by teams of four horses, had been summoned for the fund-raiser, for who can doubt that the chance to spy upon a rich man's domicile is an irresistible temptation to those with the wherewithal to indulge their inquisitiveness? Before their curiosity could be satisfied, however, several hours of conveyance through some of the most magnificent scenery the county had to offer must be endured. The beauties of Lake Cachuma, the wild hills of golden oat grass scattered with ancient valley oaks, populated by deer and eagles and showy magpies, all were duly exclaimed over. A few of the drovers required their passengers to join them in songs of the Old West, but these drays were mercifully at some remove from the vehicle bearing Lizzy and Mrs. Gardiner, so they were able to converse at their ease. Mary Gardiner, as was her wont, had come prepared with poetry suitable to the occasion, and to the astonishment of the lawyers and doctors riding with them in the wagon, she recited extracts from western poets ranging from Haniel Long to Dana Gioia. Lizzy was unable to equal her mastery of regional literature, but over the sublimity of the scenery itself she was ready to exclaim and admire. "I'm still not accustomed to the scale of the landscape— the long views and the magnificence of the mountains, the big sky. It's such a change from Ohio, though there are many pretty places there. This is truly another world."

As they were borne along, Lizzy watched for the first boundary marker of Pemberley Ranch with some perturbation; and when at length the first cattle gate was opened, her spirits were in a high flutter. The ranch was very large, and contained a great variety of ground. They entered it at one of its lowest points, and drove for some time through a beautiful wood of sycamore and cottonwood, growing along a year-round waterway. Cattle moved slowly through the shady groves, fenced off from the stream banks but drawing sustenance from its waters, which were pumped at intervals into troughs for their use. Birds called out from the trees, and a coyote slipped out of view through the undergrowth.

Lizzy's mind was too full for conversation, but she saw and admired every remarkable spot and point of view. They gradually ascended for more than a mile, and then found themselves at the top of a considerable eminence, where the wood ceased and the eye was instantly caught by the grace and drama of a deep, narrow valley, with the ranch's buildings nestled far below. The main house was an ample wood and stone building, constructed from local materials in a traditional lodge style, with none of the imported European flourishes that added pretension to Rosings, and suited in scale to its surroundings. In front, a stream of some natural importance was swelled into greater, but without any artificial appearance. Its banks were neither formal, nor falsely adorned. Lizzy was delighted. She had never seen a place for which nature had done more, or where natural beauty had been so little counteracted by an awkward taste. Everyone was warm in their admiration; and at that moment she felt that to live at Pemberley Ranch might be something!

They descended the hill, crossed a bridge, and drove to a courtyard surrounded by barns at a short distance from the house. As glossy thoroughbreds poked their heads out of stalls to inspect the new arrivals, all Lizzy's apprehensions of meeting their owner returned. She dreaded lest Mrs. Gardiner had been mistaken. She dared not draw attention to herself by inquiring of an employee into Darcy's whereabouts, and was consequently very grateful when another visitor asked the question of Reynolds, the ranch foreman, who greeted their party. How relieved was she when they were informed that Darcy was away but was expected to return the very next day!

Reynolds offered a short tour of the principal barns and paddocks, and everyone was happy to fall in with this scheme except for a few of the ladies, who wished only to peer through the windows of the house and imagine themselves mistress of such luxuries as they might discover there. Restraining her curiosity—or fancying that she would have the opportunity to satisfy it later—Lizzy opted for the tour. Reynolds was delighted to impress them with the ranch's principal stallions currently standing to stud, the most promising yearlings, and an extraordinary collection of antique tack and show saddles, the pride of the late Mr. Darcy. Many of the pieces were museum-quality artifacts of the *vaquero* era, and the ranchers among the party were clearly much taken with this evidence of respect for the region's heritage.

"And does the current Mr. Darcy take an interest in this collection?" asked Mrs. Gardiner.

"Well, he doesn't add to it, the way his father was always doing, but he orders that it be kept in mint condition. Mr. Darcy is more interested in environmental issues as they relate to ranching."

Lizzy listened with increasing astonishment as Reynolds described the rotational grazing, biological pest control, nitrogen sequestration techniques, composting practices, and biodiversity monitoring that Darcy had instituted on the property. She had supposed him to be a careful landlord, but would never have imagined the degree of responsibility he demonstrated. And when they caught a glimpse of the housing he provided for his employees, she had a fresh source of amazement. Accustomed as she was to seeing rotted mobile homes and tumbledown shacks around the valley, she was not prepared for what met her eye: neat stucco cottages shaded by oaks lined up along the murmuring creek, their porches hung with flowerpots.

There was certainly at this moment, in Lizzy's mind, a more gentle sensation toward Mr. Darcy than she had ever felt at the height of their acquaintance. The commendation bestowed on him by Reynolds was of no trifling nature. What praise is more valuable than the praise of an intelligent employee? She considered how many people's happiness was in his guardianship— how much of pleasure or pain it was in his power to bestow. How much of good or evil must be done by him! And here, on all sides, was irrefutable evidence of his benevolence. Every idea that had been brought forward by the foreman was favorable to his character, and for the first time she thought of his regard with a deeper sentiment of gratitude than it had ever raised before; she remembered its warmth, and softened its impropriety of expression.

And Lizzy was obliged to sustain yet further surprises when she joined the members of the party who were examining the house. Seen at closer quarters, it was even more beautiful than from a distance: gracious without striving for magnificence, it displayed the finest craftsmanship in wood and stone that the early years of the century could offer. On peeping in through the windows, she observed that the rooms were lofty and handsome, and their furniture suitable to the fortune of their proprietor; but Lizzy saw, with admiration of his taste, that it was neither gaudy nor uselessly fine, with less splendor, and more real comfort, than the furnishings at Rosings.

The barbecue was being served on the ample back terrace, surrounded by the gardens that had been Mrs. Darcy's delight. The head gardener was on hand to answer questions, but no other members of the party were at that moment taking notice of her, so Lizzy and Mrs. Gardiner approached her and struck up a conversation. She was a middle-aged lady with the sturdy form and weathered visage of her kind, and Lizzy was delighted by this opportunity to discuss her craft with one who had many years' experience in central California. She exclaimed over unfamiliar plants, inquired about soil amendment mixtures, and admired the meticulous state of maintenance in the borders.

"Have you worked here very long?" inquired Mrs. Gardiner.

"Oh, yes, I started working for Mrs. Darcy just over twenty years ago."

"Twenty years! So this is truly your creation."

"I can't really take that credit. Mrs. Darcy was very skilled, and she created all the designs herself. And since her death, her son has wanted her original plans respected as much as possible. He took the trouble to learn about all the plants, and whenever he can, he comes out to spend a few hours digging in the beds with me."

"So you've known him since he was a boy!"

"Yes, I'm incredibly lucky to have been here so long. In all that time I've never heard a cross word from him. He was always the sweetest-tempered, and most generous-hearted, boy in the world, forever offering to carry heavy things, or bringing me something cold to drink on a hot day. He's never treated me like the help, or put himself above anyone who works on the ranch." She smiled and excused herself to speak with another visitor.

Lizzy almost stared after her. *Can this be Darcy?* She wondered, doubted, and was impatient for more. Although the young ladies of the Enclave flattered and praised him, none had ever cast him in such an amiable light. It was impossible for her to continue to show an interest in trees and flowers; her mind was too full of unfamiliar ideas for rational thought to be entertained.

Mary Gardiner intruded on the turmoil of her speculations. "I'm not a great walker," said she, "and I have to say that the aroma of the food has been enticing me for some time. What do you say to getting some dinner?"

Lizzy wanted only to be alone, to have the luxury of musing on all she had seen and heard. "You go ahead, and I'll join you in a bit. The grounds are so lovely in the evening light, I think I'll wander around just a little longer."

As the light failed and the moon began to rise, she strolled about under the oaks, turning this way and that along meandering pathways, until she found herself near the garage. As she stared absentmindedly at this structure, the owner of it himself suddenly came around the corner of the building.

They were within twenty yards of each other, and so abrupt was his appearance that it was impossible to avoid his sight. Their eyes instantly met, and the cheeks of each were overspread with the deepest blush. He absolutely started, and for a moment seemed immovable from surprise; but shortly recovering himself, advanced toward Lizzy and spoke to her, if not in terms of perfect composure, at least of perfect civility.

She had instinctively turned away; but, stopping on his approach, received his greeting with an embarrassment impossible to overcome. While he was speaking to her, Lizzy, astonished and confused, scarcely dared lift her eyes to his face, and knew not what answer she returned to his civil inquiries after her family. Amazed at the alteration in his manner since they last parted, she found her embarrassment increased by every sentence he uttered. Every idea of the impropriety of her being there recurring to her mind, the few minutes in which they continued together

were some of the most uncomfortable of her life. Nor did he
seem much more at ease: when he spoke, he seemed to be taking
in deep breaths, his accent had none of its usual sedateness, and
he repeated his inquiries as to the state of her health so often,
and in so hurried a way, as plainly spoke the distraction of his
thoughts.

At length, every idea seemed to fail him; and, after standing
a few moments without saying a word, he suddenly recollected
himself and took his leave.

Lizzy scarcely knew where she stood, so wholly engrossed
was she by her feelings. She was overpowered by shame and
vexation. Her coming there was the most unfortunate, the most
ill-judged thing in the world! How strange it must appear to
him! In what disgraceful light might it not strike so vain a man?
It might seem as if she had purposely thrown herself in his way!
Why did she come? or, why did *he* come a day before he was expected? She blushed again and again over the perverseness of
the meeting. And his behavior, so strikingly altered—what could
it mean? That he should even speak to her was amazing. But to
speak with such civility, to inquire after her family—never in
her life had she seen his manners so little dignified, never had
he spoken with such gentleness as on this unexpected meeting.
What a contrast did it offer to the tone of his e-mail message
to her, or the way he had behaved the day the community garden was destroyed! She knew not what to think, nor how to
account for it.

All unconsciously, she had turned her steps toward the house
and the terrace where the food was being served; and now she
was hailed by Mrs. Gardiner, who waved her over to her side.
"You haven't eaten a thing yet, have you? You must, it's all heav-
enly! Maybe it's just spending the day out-of-doors that makes
it all seem so delicious—but I don't care what the reason is, I'm
enjoying it!"

Lizzy listlessly filled a plate and began to eat, but it was some time before she was aware of what she consumed. Her thoughts were all fixed on that one spot on Pemberley Ranch, wherever it might be, where Darcy then was. She longed to know what at that moment was passing in his mind; in what manner he thought of her, and whether, in defiance of everything, she was still dear to him. Perhaps he had been civil only because he felt himself at ease; yet there had been *that* in his voice, in his breathing, which was not like ease. Whether he had felt more of pain or pleasure in seeing her she could not tell, but he certainly had not seen her with composure.

At length, however, the remarks of her companion on her absence of mind roused her, and she felt the necessity of appearing more like herself. She praised the food, the setting, the rising harvest moon, and smiled at Mrs. Gardiner's witty sallies at the expense of their fellow guests, though incapable of summoning wit on her own part.

While attempting thus to take hold of her senses, Lizzy received a fresh shock from the sight of Mr. Darcy making his way through the crowd of visitors. He had taken the time to change into a Victorian costume in order to mingle with his guests in the spirit of the occasion. The greetings and good wishes of those assembled halted his steps every few feet, but his destination was apparent, and was soon achieved. The brief delay allowed Lizzy the time to prepare herself, and she resolved to appear and to speak with calmness, if he really intended to accost her. For a few moments it seemed as if he might turn another way—but he turned back and was immediately before her. With a glance she saw that he had lost none of his recent demeanor of civility; and, to imitate his politeness, she began, as they met, to admire the beauty of the place. But she had not got beyond the words "delightful" and "charming" when some unlucky recollections obtruded, and she fancied that praise of Pemberley Ranch, from her, might be mischievously construed. Would she sound like another Caroline Bingley? Her color changed, and she said no more.

Darcy turned then to Mrs. Gardiner and engaged her in conversation. Lizzy found her nerves to a degree soothed by the consoling reflection that for once he found her in company for whom there was no need to blush. She listened attentively to all that passed between them, and gloried in every expression, every sentence of Mrs. Gardiner's that marked her intelligence, her taste, or her good manners.

For her part, Mrs. Gardiner—unaccustomed to such affability from the remote Mr. Darcy, despite her prior acquaintance with his mother—gave Lizzy a look expressive of her wonder. Lizzy said nothing, but it gratified her exceedingly; she must believe that the compliment was all for herself. As he stayed, and stayed, by their side instead of continuing to mingle with the other guests, Lizzy's astonishment increased. Why was he so different? What could it mean? She could not credit the notion that this softening was for her sake, or that the reproofs she had uttered that day amid the ruins of the community garden could have worked such a change in him.

After several minutes proceeding thus, there chanced to be a little alteration. Mrs. Gardiner, complaining of fatigue from standing, moved a short distance away to perch on a low wall for a few minutes, leaving Darcy and Lizzy tête-à-tête. There was a short silence, which Lizzy broke to say that she had been assured he would be absent before she agreed to come on the hayride, and even his foreman had said that he was not expected home today. Darcy acknowledged the truth of it all, adding that his business had concluded a little sooner than he expected and, his aunt Catherine being eager to consult him about something, he had moved up the day of his arrival without alerting his staff.

"And it's very good of you to support the hospital by coming on the hayride," he added. "This fund-raiser was very important to my mother, and she would have been happy to welcome a fellow horticultural enthusiast into her garden. I wish she were here to meet you; you would've liked each other."

This reference immediately sent Lizzy's mind back to the last time they had met, in the middle of the most disastrous of her horticultural endeavors; and if she might judge from his complexion, *his* mind was not very differently engaged. But the mention of his mother, and of his wish that they might have become acquainted, was most satisfactory; it was gratifying to know that his resentment had not made him think really ill of her. The surprise of it all left her unable to know in what terms she spoke of her sympathy for his loss, or of her admiration for the garden his mother had left behind.

They started unconsciously to walk toward another part of the grounds, each of them deep in thought. Lizzy was not comfortable—that was impossible—but she was flattered and pleased. His seeking her out, despite the manifold awkwardnesses that accompanied such an encounter, was a compliment of the highest order. At such a time, much might have been said, and the continuing silence was very embarrassing. She wanted to talk, but there seemed an embargo on every subject. At last she recollected the hayride, and they spoke of Lake Cachuma and the backcountry with great perseverance. Yet time and Mrs. Gardiner moved very slowly, and Lizzy's patience and her ideas were nearly worn out before that lady appeared again to inform her that the buses were loading to return the guests to town. Darcy then pressed them to come inside for coffee, offering to drive them home afterward; but Mrs. Gardiner was thinking fondly of her bed and would not delay their departure. Lizzy, unable to decide whether she was more relieved or disappointed, meekly followed in her wake.

Once settled in their seats, Mary Gardiner commenced to exclaim over the behavior of their host. "He really rose to the occasion," said she. "He was very unassuming, and so welcoming! His manners are a little stately, but they suit his stature."

"Especially when he's dressed up like Rhett Butler," said Lizzy.

Mrs. Gardiner chuckled. "But he didn't seem at all arrogant—there was nothing superior in his attitude, you have to agree. Why have you always criticized him for being so stuck up around you, Lizzy? He seemed very friendly today. Maybe it was because you were wearing his mother's scent."

Ashamed as she was at the vehemence of her previous expressions, Lizzy had little to offer in her own defense, saying merely that she had never before seen him behave so pleasantly as he had today.

"Oh, well, maybe he feels more comfortable on his home turf. Do you think his stand-offishness might simply be a matter of being shy? He has a good face, and it's hard to believe he could have been such a villain toward the Carrillos as you say. His employees certainly are united in giving him a good character! But I suppose he pays well—there's no expense spared on that ranch—so that would make him a paragon in the eyes of his staff."

Lizzy felt obliged to say, in as guarded a manner as she could, that it was possible to view his history with the Carrillos in a very different light, and that a whole new construction could be placed on his actions when other aspects of the case were known. Mrs. Gardiner was surprised by the change, but as she was really quite exhausted and not entirely disposed to press her young friend about the events of the day without further thinking on them, she let the matter rest.

Chapter Twenty-nine

For Lizzy, the day of the hayride was productive of pleasure and discomfort in equal measure; she could not recall being discovered in the act of inspecting Pemberley Ranch without mortification, but would not have forgone the opportunity to experience Darcy's softened demeanor for any consideration. The question that now preoccupied her thoughts was, how would he behave when next they met? Would he be the new, gentlemanly Darcy, or the old, supercilious one? And when would that meeting take place? She cudgeled her brain for a way to bring it about, but try as she might, could arrive at no satisfactory plan. The recollection of their brief exchanges could not suffice; she must have more, or her confusion would never be resolved. There *must* be another meeting—but how was it to be achieved?

As it chanced, the encounter took place sooner than Lizzy expected, or perhaps was fully prepared for. The very next day he was seen at church, in the Darcy family's customary pew; and after the service was over, she had no sooner gained the Gardiners' side, bent on expressing to Mrs. Gardiner her gratitude for the invitation to the hayride, than he was seeking them out.

Mary Gardiner was all astonishment at the renewal of his notice; and the embarrassment of Lizzy's manner, joined to the circumstance itself, and many of the circumstances of the preceding day, opened to her a new idea on the business. Nothing had ever suggested it before, but she now felt that there was no other way of accounting for such attentions from such a quarter, than by supposing a partiality for her young friend. A glance at her husband revealed that he was entertaining similar ideas.

While these newly born notions were passing in their heads, the perturbation of Lizzy's feelings was every moment increasing. She was quite amazed at her own discomposure; and, more than commonly anxious to please, she naturally suspected that every power of pleasing would fail her. As she endeavored to compose herself, she observed such looks of enquiring surprise from the Gardiners as made everything worse.

When Darcy greeted the Gardiners, it was with renewed astonishment that Lizzy saw him to be at least as much embarrassed as herself. He stumbled his way through the civilities under the earnest, though guarded, scrutiny of his interlocutors; and the older couple soon drew from those observations the full conviction that one at least of the party knew what it was to be in love. Of the young lady's sensations they remained a little in doubt, but that the gentleman was overflowing with admiration was evident enough.

Lizzy, on her side, had much to do. She wanted to ascertain Darcy's feelings, she wanted to compose her own, and to make herself agreeable to all; and in the latter object, where she feared most to fail, she was most sure of success, for those to whom she endeavored to give pleasure were prepossessed in her favor. Mr. Gardiner was ready, Mrs. Gardiner eager, and Mr. Darcy determined, to be pleased.

It was not often that she could turn her eyes toward Darcy himself, but whenever she did catch a glimpse, she saw an expression of general complaisance, and in all that he said, she heard an accent so far removed from hauteur or disdain of his companions, as convinced her that the improvement of manners which she had yesterday witnessed, however temporary its existence might prove, had at least outlived one day. When she saw him thus civil, and recollected their heated exchange in the ruins of the community garden, the alteration was so great, and struck so forcibly on her mind, that she could scarcely contain her astonishment. Never, even in the company of his dear friends at The Chocolate Bar, or of his dignified relations at Rosings Ranch, had she seen him so desirous to please, so free from self-consequence or unbending reserve, as now, when no importance could result from the success of his endeavors.

Mr. Gardiner was recalling to Darcy's mind their meeting at Mattei's Tavern. "Did you succeed in persuading your aunt not to lease her land to the winegrowers?"

Darcy smiled. "She would not be likely to acknowledge it if I had, but I did draw to her attention some articles about an imminent glut of wine grapes and the predicted collapse of market prices, as well as another about the rise of artisanal cheesemaking as a sector of specialty agriculture. Perhaps her interests will take a little turn, to everyone's satisfaction."

"Let's hope she reads them."

"Speaking of reading," said Darcy, with the hesitancy of someone who has reached the true aim of the conversation, "may I say what great pleasure I took in the unique format of your memorial for Evelyn Bennet last winter? I'd heard of your Live Poets Reading Society, of course, but it was my first experience with a collective reading of that kind. I understand that you meet regularly, and am not sure what your membership requirements are, but if there's ever an opening for another reader, I hope you'll consider me."

Mary Gardiner looked at Lizzy, desirous of knowing how *she,* whom this petition plainly concerned, felt disposed as to its acceptance, but Lizzy had turned away her head. Presuming, however, that this studied avoidance spoke rather a momentary embarrassment than any fixed dislike of the scheme, and seeing in her husband, who often felt himself outnumbered by the female portion of the Poets membership, a perfect willingness to accept it, she replied with alacrity that the next meeting was three weeks hence and she would send him a notice via e-mail.

"The theme is 'satisfaction,' and I'm certain you'll have no difficulty in finding something suitable to read. Despite our name, prose is always acceptable for the readings as well as poetry."

Upon securing this invitation he at last took his leave; and Lizzy found herself, when the gentleman had left them, capable of considering the last five minutes with some pleasure, though while it was passing her enjoyment of it had been meager. Desirous of leisure in which to think, and fearful of inquiries or hints from the Gardiners, she stayed with them only long enough for politeness, and then hurried away to seek the comfort of her own reflections.

But she had no reason to fear Mr. and Mrs. Gardiner's curiosity; it was not their wish to force her communication. It was evident that she was much better acquainted with Darcy than they had before any idea of; it was evident that he was very much in love with her. They saw much to interest, but nothing to justify inquiry.

Of Darcy it was now a matter of anxiety to think well, and as far as their own acquaintance reached, there was no fault to find. They could not be untouched by his politeness, and had they drawn his character from their own feelings, and his servants' reports, without any reference to the Bennet family's assessment of him, they would not have recognized him as the same person. And if it came down to that, he had been accused of little more than pride—save perhaps for the claim of injury to the Carrillos, upon which Lizzy had already cast doubt. Pride he probably had, and if not, it would certainly be imputed to him by those who saw little of him socially, even by those who had always regarded him as a good neighbor and a responsible landlord.

As for Lizzy, her thoughts were at Pemberley Ranch even more that evening than the last; and the evening, though as it passed it seemed long, was not long enough to determine her feelings toward *one* there. She lay awake two whole hours, endeavoring to make them out.

She certainly did not hate him. No; hatred had vanished some time ago, and she had long been ashamed of ever feeling a dislike against him, that could be so called. The respect engendered by the conviction of his valuable qualities, though at first reluctantly acknowledged, had for some time ceased to be repugnant to her feelings; and it was now heightened into somewhat of a friendlier nature, by the testimony so highly in his favor, and bringing forward his disposition in so amiable a light, which yesterday had produced. But above all, above respect and esteem, there was a motive within her of good will that could not be overlooked. It was gratitude—gratitude, not merely for having once loved her, but for loving her still well enough to forgive all the petulance and acrimony of her manner in rejecting him, and all the unjust accusations with which she had accompanied her rejection.

He who, she had been persuaded, would avoid her as his greatest enemy, seemed, on their accidental meeting yesterday, most eager to preserve the acquaintance, and without any indelicate display of regard, or any peculiarity of manner, where their two selves only were concerned, was soliciting the good opinion of her friends, and bent on making himself further known to them. For a man who had previously acknowledged his own resentful nature, who had said that his good opinion, once lost, was lost forever, this was a remarkable fact. Such a change, in a person of so much pride, excited not only astonishment but gratitude—for to love, ardent love, it must be attributed; and as such its impression on her was of a sort to be encouraged, as by no means unpleasing, though it could not be exactly defined.

She respected, she esteemed, she was grateful to him, she felt a real interest in his welfare; and she only wanted to know how far she wished that welfare to depend on herself, and how far it would be for the happiness of both that she should employ the power, which her fancy told her she still possessed, of bringing on the renewal of his addresses.

If gratitude and esteem are good foundations of affection, Lizzy's change of sentiment will be regarded as neither improbable nor faulty. But if otherwise, if regard springing from such sources is unreasonable or unnatural, in comparison to what is so often described as arising on a first interview with its object, and even before two words have been exchanged, nothing can be said in her defense, except that she had given somewhat of a trial to the latter method, in her partiality for Jorge, and that its ill-success might perhaps authorize her to seek the other, less interesting, mode of attachment. Regardless of the manner in which that attachment arose, Lizzy had perforce to acknowledge, the resulting feelings could be tolerably powerful, and were not easily to be negotiated away.

But these preoccupations, regardless of their tendency to excite and command her thoughts, must be set aside, and speedily, for Lizzy was now only two days away from the deadline for submitting an account of her arrangements for the library to the County Planning Commission. Melvin Perry had thoughtfully provided a number of sample submissions, and it was now her urgent task to finalize her report. Hours, book collections, readings, special exhibits, resources, staffing, parking, all must be laid out for consideration. Was she doing honor to her aunt's wishes? How would the community react? How would Darcy react?

Her mind returning inexorably to its central object, Lizzy threw a retrospective glance over the whole of their acquaintance, so full of contradictions and varieties; she sighed at the perverseness of those feelings which would now have promoted its continuance, and would formerly have rejoiced in its termination. Would he turn against her when he learned that she had produced yet another radical scheme for Lambtown's betterment? Would the news destroy the newfound goodwill between them?

She wished for answers, but knew that the answers could make no difference in the outcome. Regardless of the consequences, it was for the library that Lizzy had uprooted herself and her family, and moved to Lambtown. More precisely, it was for her aunt Evelyn—to bring her vision to reality, to honor her memory and grant her the measure of immortality to which she was entitled. The attachment of a few days' or weeks' continuance could not be weighed in the balance against her deeper duty to her kin. It was not to be considered.

If Lizzy had assumed that the week between the submittal of her proposal and its public airing would be a quiet one, she was soon to discover her error. She had failed to consider that the mayor would have advance access to the text, and Morris Collins was not the man to keep his feelings on the subject to himself. Nay, his very sense of identity, his sense of duty to the community as he comprehended it, forbade discretion in such a case as this. She learned as much upon encountering Charlotte Collins at The Chocolate Bar on Friday afternoon.

"I hear you're setting the town by the ears again," said Charlotte with a smile as she accepted Lizzy's offer to sit down with her iced tea.

"I'm not sure what you mean," replied Lizzy cautiously.

"Oh, is there *more* up your sleeve than the bilingual library? Your energy never ceases to amaze me."

Lizzy admitted that she had no active plans other than the library. "I didn't realize the proposal was widely known."

If Charlotte was at all conscious that her husband's indiscretion was in any way inappropriate, she gave no sign of it, and responded in her customary tranquil way, "I believe much of the Enclave and the Chamber of Commerce have been made aware of it. You can probably expect the Planning Commission meeting next week to be very well attended. Morris is convinced that Catherine de Bourgh will never give her blessing to the plan, and it can't be denied that the whole business of the community garden hasn't endeared you to the Chamber."

"But it's not even a commercial enterprise! And it isn't located in the center of town, so why would they care?"

"Many of them live in the neighborhood of your aunt's house, and when they see brown faces there, they are apt to think about crime."

"But that's profiling! That's the very problem my aunt wanted to fix by developing her plan for a library that would serve all segments of the community. People here have to stop judging by appearances."

"I'm not sure people are judging *you* by appearances so much as they are judging you by your choices," said Charlotte gently. "You know I'm your friend, and I believe your motives are good. I simply wanted to warn you that you're likely to face resistance, if not hostility. If you hope to succeed, you'll have to calm their fears."

"What are they afraid of?"

"Change. The unfamiliar. They're comfortable with the status quo."

"I suppose we all seek the comfort of our certainties," Lizzy acknowledged ruefully. "I'm sure I've been guilty of that myself. Your advice is well taken, and much appreciated. I'll think about all you've said."

In consequence of this conversation, Lizzy resolved to seek a coalition of her own, and one that might fragment and weaken that of the united Chamber and Enclave. She began with the counselors and principals at the local schools, both public and private. Could she offer off-campus space for tutors to work with struggling students? Indeed, she could. The president of the Historical Society was surprised to hear from her and initially cool, but after learning of Lizzy's efforts to amass a local history collection there was a considerable thaw. And when this worthy heard about the space available for special themed displays, she even thought the Society might be able to provide materials of interest to the community at large. Through these, and other contacts, Lizzy hoped to ensure that voices other than angry ones might be raised at the meeting. She also appealed to Mary Gardiner, who called all the Poets and exhorted them to attend; they were uniform in their praise of the plan to open a new cultural institution that would enrich the lives of Lambtown residents. The words of Mr. and Mrs. Gardiner especially carried weight, in light of the fact that they lived across the street from the library and could be predicted to experience the greatest inconvenience therefrom.

Lizzy emerged from the Commission's assembly exhausted but optimistic. There had been talk of petitions and even legal action in opposition, but opinion was far from unanimous in her disfavor, and the opponents appeared unorganized. Conspicuous by their absence were Fitzwilliam Darcy and Catherine de Bourgh; and many of the Enclave appeared hesitant to take a firm stance on either side, without one of the principal residents on hand to show them the way.

Lizzy did not know what to make of their failure to attend. She hoped that Darcy was seeking to minimize opposition by declining to stand in her way; but she feared that his renewed regard might be too slight and thin a sort of inclination, and that this fresh evidence of her activism had starved it all away. She could think of no way to ask for his thoughts on the subject without appearing self-centered, and with Bingley gone away, she could name no acquaintance who had his ear sufficiently to make inquiries on her behalf. Just when she was most concerned to obtain his good opinion, she feared that her own choices, or the wishes of her aunt, prevented its bestowal. She could only wait, and wonder, and hope.

Chapter Thirty

L izzy's anxiety over Darcy's sentiments was not soon to be allayed, for she learned shortly after the Planning Commission hearing that he was gone again. John conveyed this intelligence to her, on the authority of Reynolds, Darcy's ranch foreman, during a visit to The Chocolate Bar. It appeared that Darcy needed to supervise the finishing of his cattle and conduct other ranch business out of town. For the nonce she would have to content herself with her own quotidian affairs—laying her plans for the fall planting season in her clients' gardens, and fending off criticisms of the library plan.

It came as little surprise that some of the most vociferous of these issued from her mother. "You must have spent tens of thousands of dollars on *books*, though your own parents are struggling to put food on the table! But it was always that way with you, taking care of yourself with no concern for your family."

"Aunt Evelyn put her money in a charitable trust," Lizzy explained again and again. "If I didn't spend it on the library I would be violating the law. The funds have to be used to promote the purposes of the trust."

"You are very remiss in concerning yourself with the legalities," said Mr. Bennet. "What your mother no doubt refers to, when she speaks of struggling to put food on the table, is the impossibility of using an old blender when the latest Cuisinarts sit neglected on store shelves. Why should good money be spent on books, when it could be frittered away on fashion and the latest gadgets?"

"And it's not just the money," said Mrs. Bennet, disregarding him. "You can't go a month without upsetting the whole town about something or other. With the memory of that dratted garden still on everyone's mind, now you're wanting to force everyone to read in Spanish! Is it any wonder we never get invited to dinner?"

"It's like you're really *trying* to become an old maid," said Kitty. "First you're a gardener, and now you want to be a librarian. Could you come up with *anything* more boring? I don't see why everybody gets so excited about you all the time."

"It's true, Lizzy, I fear you do yourself no good in the eyes of the local youth by filling your head with thoughts," said Mr. Bennet. "Spending your time applying makeup and your money on cutoffs full of holes might be more to the purpose. As for you, Kitty, I believe it was Mark Twain who said that the man who *doesn't* read good books has no advantage over the man who *can't*."

"Oh, be satisfied with putting dangerous ideas in Lizzy's head," exclaimed Mrs. Bennet. "Leave Kitty alone; she does well enough with the knowledge she has. At least she knows how to enjoy being young! Everyone else around here is so dreary and serious, I would be miserable all the time if not for her, now that Lydon and Jenny are gone." For indeed, although the summer had ended, the young couple had elected to remain under the dubious supervision of Brigadier General Hughes. An awkward stretch after Lydon's Burning Man escapade having been endured, the young couple had discovered that so long as the general was occupied with his duties on the base, they were free to take full advantage of the activities offered to the students of UC Santa Barbara, without suffering the burdens of matriculation or class attendance. They were little heard from in Lambtown, but since no further calls came from the local constabulary, it could be assumed that whatever trouble they were getting into would produce no lasting consequences.

As the summer heat gave way to chilly nights, windy days, and the occasional rain shower, Lizzy entered on a few weeks of feverish digging and planting. The advent of the rainy season allowed new plants to settle in and develop healthy root systems that would stand them in good stead during the next year's months of drought, so October and November were the time for renewal in the gardens under her stewardship. It was far from the traditional harvest season she was accustomed to; even the wineries in the region had taken in their crops. She found herself missing the turning leaves of an Ohio autumn, and the signs of preparation for Halloween appeared even more than ordinarily artificial. She felt little inclination for the Poets meeting, the only idea lending interest to the prospect being that Darcy had asked if he might attend. His possible presence made the choice of an appropriate reading a matter of vital concern—should she make a traditional selection, perhaps an ode to the harvest from an eighteenth-century English pastoral poet, or one of the Romantics? But rhyme of any kind was anathema to her, and appealing to another's presumed tastes at the cost of misrepresenting her own seemed not only a base stratagem, but also one destined inevitably to misfire. And there were other risks attendant upon choosing a familiar text—for it would never do to have the same reading as another member of the group.

With such ideas did she divert her attention away from her fears that the library plan would come to naught. What then would be her recourse? How would she comply with the mandate of her aunt's foundation? Never in her life had she felt so much uncertainty, nor so much powerlessness to control her destiny.

But even with these doubts to slow the passage of time, the evening of the Poets ultimately arrived. The proper selection and refinement of her dress having delayed her, most of the party was already present when Lizzy put in an appearance, and she instantly discerned the tall figure of Fitzwilliam Darcy upon entering the room. Thus she had a fair opportunity of deciding whether she most feared or wished for his appearance, by the feelings that prevailed upon espying him; and then, though but a moment before she had believed her wishes to predominate, she began to regret that he had come. He was situated at some distance from the door, in conversation with an English teacher from the public school, and as the meeting was almost immediately called to order, Lizzy had perforce to take one of the few remaining seats across the room. While they were all settling themselves she thought she felt his eye upon her, but lacking the courage to look his way, she could not be certain.

The pleasures of verse held little power to beguile her as she waited in suspense to hear what Darcy had brought to read. In due course her impatience was rewarded, and in such as way as to cast her spirits into considerable agitation: he rose when his turn came and announced that he was reading selections from Ralph Waldo Emerson's "Self-Reliance." She only dimly remembered that great essay from high school, and the libertarian tendency of its arguments led her to fear that he would use it as a polemic against her plans for the public betterment. Was he reading it in a minatory spirit, to show her once again the error of her ways?

But at least the recital offered her the occasion to examine his countenance and deportment, so Lizzy endeavored to quiet the clamor of her thoughts and listen:

"It is easy in the world to live after the world's opinion," he began; "it is easy in solitude to live after our own; but the great man is he who in the midst of the crowd keeps with perfect sweetness the independence of solitude. . . . We are afraid of truth, afraid of fortune, afraid of death, and afraid of each other. Our age yields no great and perfect persons. . . . If I can be firm enough today to do right, and scorn eyes, I must have done so much right before as to defend me now."

Was this in defense of his own actions with regard to Bingley and Jorge? Lizzy was not sure; and he was proceeding, so she must continue to listen.

"The prayer of the farmer kneeling in his field to weed it, the prayer of the rower kneeling with the stroke of his oar, are true prayers heard throughout nature. . . . The secret of fortune is joy in our hands. . . . Nothing can bring you peace but yourself. Nothing can bring you peace but the triumph of principles."

His choice of passages gave Lizzy much fodder for anxious speculation, and it was naturally a considerable time before she could collect herself to attend to other readers. Henry Beston, Vita Sackville-West, Robinson Jeffers passed over her head unheard. The words about the farmer in the field could be seen as a reference to her gardening, and if that was his intention, could not the whole be read as a defense of her unconventional activities? Or was she being too self-absorbed, and he had chosen to read these words in pursuit of some internal argument about his own life? He seemed too private a person for such an exercise in self-revelation, but she could not be certain she understood him well enough to guess at his intentions. The questions revolved fruitlessly in her mind, as the time inexorably approached for her to read her own chosen work. She endeavored to collect herself; her entire focus must be on speaking with self-possession when her turn came. When it did, she felt it was yet too soon; but still perforce she rose and announced her selection, once again from her favorite, Pattiann Rogers. "The poem is 'Berry Renaissance,' section 5, 'Gospel and the Circle of Redemption.'"

There are times when I want to be stained,
marked all over by berry wine, baptized,
mouth, fingers, chin and neck, between my toes,
up my legs like the wine-makers of Jerez
who walk round and round in tubs
of berries all day, who return then
to their homes at night wreathed

in berry halos, heady with ripe flower
bouquets dizzy with bees, their bodies
painted, perfumed by purple sun syrup,
their breath elderberry delicious. In the dark
all night, even their sleep is guarded,
lullabied by berry ghosts.

She felt her cheeks flame as she read: never before had she experienced such a degree of concern for the way she would be perceived by her audience. If "Self-Reliance" had been intended as a tribute to her independent spirit, she was failing miserably to live up to it! She forced herself to stand a little taller; if she was to be inspired by Emerson's admonitions, she could not doubt her choice now.

I want to be so immersed, so earth-wined myself
that I'm mistaken for a berry entire.
I want to be plucked, split and gulped whole
by a bacchanal god, swallowed alive by a drunken
savior. I want to rise then from his soul
as his own wild laughter spreading
over the landscape like a berry-colored
evening engulfing blackbirds and cowbirds
and hillside forests and even
every blessing of his own vineyards
and even the way he reclines there,
lordly, generous.

The witty sallies and toasts that greeted her reading at the end went some way toward restoring Lizzy's equanimity, and she became sufficiently easy that she was able to laugh at selections from Dave Barry and Bailey White. After the readings were done and the food was being shared, it was not long before Darcy appeared at her side.

"That poem was almost enough to make me want to turn my land over to vineyard," said he.

"Now that I've seen your land, I would regard that as a great pity. Perhaps you could content yourself with fermenting elderberries from the wild bushes on your hillsides."

"I've long detected in you a pagan streak, and this evening only confirmed my suspicions. Do you think you were a maenad in a previous life?"

"If so, I must be restoring the karmic balance in this lifetime, because I can't imagine actually carrying on in that way. I have to believe the followers of Dionysos must have felt pretty embarrassed when they woke up the day after their ecstasies and had to tramp home naked."

"Much like the Rancheros Visitadores after their revels."

"Being a girl, I can't claim any knowledge of their activities. You must be the authority on such a subject."

"Like you, I'm afraid, I'm in a more repressed incarnation and have never felt the desire to experience the dubious pleasures of the ride."

"And yet you consider yourself a native son of the Santa Ynez!"

"Perhaps I may yet be tempted. There's always my midlife crisis to look forward to."

They were interrupted at this interesting moment by the importunities of a rancher's wife, who wished to pass on to Darcy an inquiry from her husband about damage to a shared fence line, and Lizzy herself was drawn off in another direction. The exchange left her unsatisfied and hungry for further converse with him; its tone, though friendly enough, did not at all enlighten her as to the intentions behind his reading. And the easy flow of his wit implied a mind less turbulent than her own, which suggested perhaps a diminution in his attachment; there was too much nonsense, and too little of emotion, for her to be completely satisfied. No further opportunities for speech presenting themselves, however, Lizzy was obliged to be content with what sustenance her conjectures had received.

The spiritless condition which this event threw her into, however, was relieved the very next day, and her mind opened again to the agitation of hope, by an unexpected event: Mrs. Bennet came home from the market bearing the intelligence that Charley Bingley was returned, and proposed to resume management of The Chocolate Bar the very next day! Here was news that must astonish and please the entire family, and give rise to inevitable speculation.

John had not been able to hear of his coming without blushing. It was many months since he had mentioned Charley's name to Lizzy, but now, as soon as they were alone together, he said, "I saw you look at me today, when we heard the report; and I know I looked a little upset. But don't assume it was from any stupid reason. I was only embarrassed for a moment because I could tell everyone was looking at me. I promise you, I don't feel either pleasure or pain. I am glad of one thing: I believe The Chocolate Bar could be better run than it has been over the past several months, and it deserves to succeed. It's just that I dread people's gossip."

Lizzy did not know what to make of it. Had Charley contacted John in advance she would have believed that his coming betokened a more personal motive than the stated one. But not a word of his plans or intentions had he divulged, so she was at a loss to determine the state of his mind. And she wavered as to the greater probability of his returning to Lambtown *with* his friend's permission, or being bold enough to come *without* it. But it was hard, she thought, that the poor man couldn't come back to conduct business at an establishment that he owned without raising a cloud of speculation; and she resolved not to add to it, but rather to leave him to himself.

In spite of what John declared, and really believed, to be his feelings, Lizzy could easily perceive that his spirits were affected. They were more disturbed, more unequal, than she had often seen them. Mrs. Bennet's continued belaboring of the news provided no opportunity for relief.

"I begin to be sorry that he's returning at all," said John that night. "I could meet him with indifference if only he weren't perpetually talked about. Our mother means well, but she doesn't know how much I suffer from all she says. I'll be happy if his visit is a short one!"

"I wish I could say anything to comfort you," replied Lizzy, "but it's totally out of my power. You must feel it; and the usual satisfaction of preaching patience to a sufferer is denied me, because you always have so much." She would brook no argument, however, about postponing an appointment with one of her regular garden clients in order to accompany John to work the next day.

As they approached The Chocolate Bar, anxious curiosity carried her eyes to the face of her brother. John looked a little paler than usual, but more sedate than Lizzy had expected. Upon entering the shop, Lizzy said as little as civility would allow, and retreated to her customary seat in order to observe the scene. Bingley, when he emerged from the back, appeared both pleased and embarrassed. At first he spoke to John but little, but every five minutes seemed to be giving him more of his attention. John was anxious that no difference should be perceived in him at all, and was really persuaded that he talked as much as ever. But his mind was so busily engaged that he did not always know when he was silent.

When all was in readiness for the lunch rush and sufficient time remained for John to take a short break, Lizzy drew him outside for a walk. His cheerful demeanor showed him well satisfied with the passage of the morning.

"Now that this first meeting is over," said he, "I can relax. I know my own strength, and will never be embarrassed again around him. Everyone will see that we are only indifferent acquaintances, just employer and employee."

"Yes, very indifferent," said Lizzy, laughing. "Oh, John, be careful."

"You *can't* think me so weak as to be in danger now."

"I think you're in great danger of making him as much in love with you as ever."

Chapter Thirty-one

Despite the various uncertainties that continued to beset her, Lizzy rested more easily in the belief that if left wholly to themselves, John and Charley's happiness would rapidly be secured. Though she dared not depend upon the consequence, yet she derived pleasure from observing their behavior, as they speedily recovered much of their previous intimacy. It gave her all the animation that her spirits could boast; for she was in no cheerful humor. Darcy was nowhere to be seen, though it might have been assumed that he would seek the company of his long-absent friend Bingley. She spent all the time she could spare at The Chocolate Bar, but he did not put in an appearance until Halloween night, when the shop was to remain open late to provide a safe venue for the revels of local children.

Charley had outdone himself in setting the scene. The tables and chairs had been removed from the center of the room, with only a few remaining around the walls for exhausted parents to pause and restore themselves. A vat of dry ice concealed behind the counter generated a low, dense fog, spread across the floor by means of a fan; the moving air also gently stirred the elaborate cobwebs in the windows and several wraiths made of georgette and tattered lace that hung from the ceiling. Candles provided fitful illumination, lending a greater air of mystery to the eyeball and skull cookies offered to the guests on black trays. A piñata in the form of a skeletal wolf hung over the center of the room.

John and Charley were in their element, teaching the children how to bob for apples, telling them ghost stories, and twirling blindfolded youths bent on striking down the piñata. The din that echoed off the walls attested to the pleasure they bestowed. Caroline Bingley was present, but confined her attentions to a few of the young mothers with whom she was acquainted. She nodded across the room to Lizzy, but made no effort to converse with her.

Into this scene of bedlam strode Fitzwilliam Darcy. He took one look at the frenzied activity in the center of the room and immediately sought refuge in one of the window embrasures, only to find Lizzy occupying one of two seats there, as she observed the children's games with amusement. He seated himself at her side and accepted the eyeball she offered him from her own plate.

Upon his appearance, Lizzy had wisely resolved to be perfectly easy and unembarrassed—a resolution the more necessary to be made, but perhaps not the more easily kept, because she saw that the suspicions of Caroline Bingley were immediately awakened against them, and Charley's sister had missed nothing of his behavior from the moment he entered the room. Caroline's anxious curiosity did not prevent a smile from overspreading her countenance when Darcy caught her eye and waved; for jealousy had not yet made her desperate, and her attentions to him were by no means over. She interpreted his acknowledgment of her presence as an encouragement, and immediately parted company with her friends to cross to the corner where Lizzy and Darcy sat.

Darcy stood to greet her, and she kissed him on both cheeks, her hand lingering on his coat sleeve for a moment after the embrace. They engaged in a few civilities ranging across the time that had elapsed since their last meeting, and the doings of acquaintances in common, and then Darcy offered her his seat.

Settled thus perforce beside Lizzy, and seeing how Darcy's eyes, rather than dwelling on herself, were returning to her neighbor, Caroline, in the impudence of anger, took the opportunity of saying, with a pretense of concern, "Did I hear correctly that George Carrillo has left town again? That must be a great loss to *your* family."

Lizzy, exerting herself to repel this attack, was able after a breathless moment to reply with tolerable composure that she was not informed of George's whereabouts, having not seen him or his parents for some time. While she spoke, an involuntary glance showed her Darcy with a heightened complexion. Had Caroline known what pain she was giving *him,* she probably would have refrained from making this inquiry; but she had merely intended to discompose Lizzy, by bringing forward the idea of a man to whom she believed her partial, in the hope that Lizzy might betray a sensibility that would injure her in Darcy's opinion. Not a word had reached her of George's perfidies against Darcy; she knew only that he was not approved of.

Lizzy's collected behavior in responding to Caroline's malice soon quieted Darcy's emotion, however, and he contented himself with suggesting that the high volume of noise in the room made conversation undesirable.

At this moment the phone rang. John leaned over the counter to answer it, covering his other ear in an effort to hear his interlocutor at the other end of the line. This was seen to be futile, as he pantomimed to Charley that he would take the call in the back room while Charley should wait to hang up the phone at the counter. John disappeared for a few minutes, then reappeared at the door, waving vigorously to Lizzy to join him. One look at the expression on his face sent her flying across the room to his side.

"What on earth has happened?" she cried as she attained the relative quiet of the kitchen.

Tears had started up in John's eyes, and he struggled to gain mastery of his emotion. Lizzy suffered agonies of suspense while he took deep breaths, attempting to compose himself sufficiently for speech. "The call was from Jenny," he said at last. "It's

Lydon. She needs us to come right away." John paused again, unable to maintain his self-control. "It seems he was at some kind of Native American ritual, led by Jorge—"

"Jorge!"

"—and they were using a native plant—"

"Peyote?"

"No, Jenny said it was—she said—I think—jimsonweed? And Lydon had a bad reaction to it, but nobody realized right away. By the time somebody noticed, Lydon was seriously ill. Do you know anything about jimsonweed?"

"I know it grows locally, along the roadsides. The seeds and leaves were used by some tribes to induce visions, at shamanic ceremonies. But it's very dangerous, and very easy to overdose. People die every year from experimenting with it."

John looked faint. "He could *die?* Jenny said Jorge drove him to the hospital and just left him outside the emergency room door."

"Well, that's probably more than we might have expected from him."

"Perhaps he had a compelling reason to leave," said John hopefully. "He might have been worried that another person at the ritual would become ill, and went back to check on them. In any case, the hospital staff found Lydon, and he had Jenny's phone number in his wallet, and she knew where he had gone, and why, so they were able to identify the cause very quickly. She had been supposed to go with him, but at the last minute she decided not to, for fear her father would be angry if he found out."

"It's a great pity Lydon didn't stand in greater fear of the general's wrath," said Lizzy. "We need to go to the hospital. Do they think they got to him in time? Is he going to survive?"

John's tears started to flow. "Jenny didn't know."

Lizzy turned to go; at that moment the door opened, and Darcy appeared. Her pale face and impetuous manner made him start, but before he could speak, she, in whose mind every idea was superseded by Lydon's situation, hastily exclaimed, "Excuse us, but we have to leave right now!"

"Good God! What's the matter?" cried he, with more feeling than politeness, as she seized John's hand and attempted to move around Darcy to reach the door. Then, recollecting himself, Darcy added, "I won't hold you up, but you seem very upset. Can I help? Are you ill?"

Lizzy hesitated, her knees trembling. "No, we're okay. It's just that we've received some very bad news, and we have to go to Santa Barbara." She too started to cry as she alluded to it, and for a moment her voice was completely suspended.

"But you're too upset to drive," said Darcy. "Let me take you both. Where do you need to go?"

"Oh, thank you, but I think we'll need to have our own car there. Maybe you could give us directions? We're going to Santa Barbara Cottage Hospital."

"A member of your family has taken ill? Who is it? What's wrong?"

"It's Lydon. He's suffered an overdose. He used jimsonweed—given to him by George Carrillo at one of his fake shamanic rituals."

"Carrillo!"

"When I consider," Lizzy continued, in a yet more agitated voice, "that I might've prevented it! I knew what he was. If I'd only explained some part of it—some part of what I learned—to my own family! If they'd known his true character, this couldn't have happened. My father, or General Hughes, would've kept Lydon and Jenny away from him. But it's too late now."

"This is terrible," said Darcy. "But is it certain what happened? What's the prognosis?"

"The doctors don't know yet if he'll survive. We only learned what happened because Lydon's wife was aware of the plans for the ceremony."

Darcy made no answer. He seemed scarcely to hear her, and was pacing up and down the room in earnest meditation, his brow contracted, his air gloomy. Lizzy observed, and instantly understood it. Her power was sinking; all esteem *must* sink under such a proof of family weakness, such an assurance of the deepest disgrace. She could neither wonder nor condemn, but the belief afforded no palliation of her distress. It was, on the contrary, exactly calculated to make her understand her own wishes; and never had she so honestly felt that she loved him as now, when all love must be vain.

But self, though it would intrude, could not engross her. Lydon—his suffering, his very struggle for life—swallowed up every private care; and covering her face with her hands, Lizzy was momentarily lost to everything else. She was only recalled to a sense of the situation by the sound of Darcy's voice, which, though he spoke with compassion, betrayed also restraint, as he said, "I'm afraid you must be wishing me gone. I wish to heaven I could do or say anything that might offer you both consolation. But I can at least let Charley know why you had to leave."

"Please just say it was a family emergency," pleaded Lizzy. "I'd be grateful if you didn't give the specifics. They'll probably come out in the end, but still—"

He readily assured her of his secrecy—again expressed his sorrow for her distress, wished for a happy conclusion, told them where to get off the freeway to reach the hospital, and let them go.

As they drove through the darkness, Lizzy felt how improbable it was that she and Darcy would ever see each other in the future on such terms of cordiality as had marked their last few meetings. He could never lay eyes on her again without being reminded of George Carrillo and his betrayals, or of her family's folly.

But now was not the time for idle speculations; it behooved her to be thinking of Lydon. Would he survive the overdose?

And if he did, what could be done to set his feet on a more productive path? She berated herself again for not having found some way to warn her family about George Carrillo; but would any warnings have served? She had reason to believe that any words linking George and drugs would only have increased his appeal in Lydon and Jenny's eyes. And she had had no cause for particular alarm; all the while she had been seeing George, she had perceived no friendship developing between him and her brother. Perhaps it was simply a matter of propinquity: they had crossed paths, in Lompoc or even at Burning Man, and Lydon had become intrigued by George's line about Native American mind-altering spiritual practices.

The mischief of her father's neglect, her mother's indulgence toward a child of weak intellect and no self-discipline, was now plain in retrospective view. And what of her own responsibility, to guide and instruct her younger siblings? Sweet, gentle John—sitting now beside her, too overcome by emotion even to speak—could have little effect on a wild young man entirely devoted to his own pleasure; his quiet guidance would have been no more listened to than Mary's homilies. Could Lizzy herself have engaged with him better, perhaps entered into some interest of his, with an eye toward steering his course? Should she at least have attempted to supply what her parents were unwilling or unable to do? Instead, she had lived for her own interests and preoccupations, allowing Lydon—and Kitty and Jenny, and even Mary—to pursue aimless lives. Did it require Lydon's possible death to awaken her to her familial duty?

Chapter Thirty-two

Upon their arrival, it was discovered that their mother's sensibilities had rendered her incapable of the exertion of coming to the hospital; Mr. Bennet told them she had taken to her bed with a fit of strong hysterics. He had left her there to the ministrations of Kitty and Mary, and driven in alone. He appeared exhausted, and very grave, but his countenance lightened considerably upon seeing Lizzy and John. The news he had to impart, nonetheless, was not encouraging.

"The doctor says it's a severe case. When he was admitted, he was hallucinating and feverish, and soon started to have convulsions, so they couldn't give him the usual oral medications or induce vomiting. They tried pumping his stomach, but there wasn't much in there." He fetched a breath. "The fear is that he drank a tea made from the leaves, instead of the usual method of eating seeds, so the poison may have already fully metabolized."

"If that's true, what can be done?" asked John.

"There's one medication they can administer through his IV line. It's controversial, and if they use too much, too fast, it can make things worse. So they're trying the very smallest dose at first. And they've wrapped him in cooling blankets and are trying to keep him still, so he doesn't do himself any further harm."

"How long before they expect any improvement?" asked Lizzy.

"They say the symptoms can persist for twenty-four hours, sometimes more."

"Where's Jenny?"

"She was so upset that the general came and took her home."

"Can we sit with him?"

Mr. Bennet began to tremble, and he appeared suddenly old and so enfeebled that John wrapped his arms tightly around him. "I couldn't bear to do it," said Mr. Bennet in a whisper. "He's allowed one family member at a time, if one of you wants to go in."

"I'll go," said Lizzy.

A nurse showed her the way to a cubicle in the Intensive Care Unit. Lydon lay in a disturbed repose, his continual change of posture availing him naught against the restraints that bound his hands and feet. Despite the cooling blankets his skin was red and hot to the touch, and when his eyes opened they appeared unfocused, or perhaps focused on things only he could perceive. Of the nature of his deliriums he could not speak because of the tube in his throat, but from time to time he uttered incomprehensible sounds before sinking back into a heavy stupor for a time. The monitors beeped and flashed. Lizzy took one of his hands in hers, but there was no responding pressure from him.

After sitting for some time in this manner, Lizzy was obliged to conclude that she could not provide any aid to Lydon in his present state. It seemed more likely that her immediate duty lay elsewhere in the family; only the doctors could effect any amelioration in this quarter. She rose and returned to her father and John.

"He's not aware of anything around him," she said as she rejoined them in the waiting room.

Her father sighed with relief. "Yes, that's what I felt as well."

John now proposed that one of them should go home, and impart what was known to Mrs. Bennet. "I'm worried about our mother, waiting there in suspense with only Kitty and Mary to keep her company. I'm sure she'd feel better with a firsthand account of Lydon's prognosis."

This notion found immediate approval with Mr. Bennet,

who, however, was unwilling to depart the scene himself.

"You're very tired, Papa," said John. "Let *us* stay here through the night."

"Don't worry about that," replied Mr. Bennet. "Who should suffer but myself? This has been my own doing, and I ought to feel it."

"You mustn't be too severe on yourself."

"No, Lizzy, let me for once in my life feel how much I've been to blame. I'm not afraid of being overpowered by self-hatred; these feelings will be argued away soon enough."

John reiterated his concern for his mother's state of mind, and it was agreed that he should return to Lambtown in his father's car, leaving Lizzy and their father on the scene.

When he had departed, Mr. Bennet, attempting something of his habitual manner, said, "Lizzy, I bear you no ill-will for being justified in your advice to me last summer. Considering all that has happened, it shows some greatness of mind."

"I can't see that his remaining at home would have made any difference. His natural wildness would've been compounded by the frustration of having his wishes thwarted, and there was nothing to be gained by courting the general's ill-will."

"Very true, and disapproval such as his is not to be risked lightly."

"How did he act when he came to pick Jenny up?"

"It was disappointing to see him in his regular uniform. I felt the full regalia of all his medals and ribbons would've been insufficient to express the outrage of the offense committed against his family."

"*His* family! Well, we must make allowances for a father concerned about the happiness of his only child."

"I would make such allowances if he were more concerned about the *survival* of my child! What *is* wall-to-wall counseling, anyway?"

"He didn't say *that*?" cried Lizzy, incredulous. "I believe it means beating a subordinate to show him the error of his ways."

"Why didn't I think of that?" said Mr. Bennet. "'Excuse me, doctors, while I pummel some sense into my delirious son. You can treat his convulsions after I'm finished.' I warn you, Lizzy, that I will have no more in-laws in this family! We can produce our own edifying displays of unproductive behavior without them. You must none of you try to get married: I'll forbid it."

While grateful for the kind impulse that underlay her father's attempt to summon a smile to her lips, Lizzy could not answer his levity with any wit of her own. Anxiety and hope oppressed her in equal degrees, and left her no moment of tranquillity. The necessity of maintaining the appearance of composure, lest her father lose his own, required every effort of her will. Her inner thoughts, meanwhile, could not be controlled; they darted from one unanswerable question to another, defying her most strenuous efforts to marshal them. What could be done for Lydon if he survived? And—even more impossible to contemplate—what if he did not? She could not begin to imagine what the future might hold for the Bennet family, should it be riven in that terrible, irreparable way. How would her father and mother go on—Kitty—Jenny?

The morning brought a gradual abatement of Lydon's symptoms, and the doctor expressed optimism for an eventual recovery, though he wished to keep Lydon in the ICU a while longer because of the superior monitoring capabilities there. Visiting the patient, Lizzy found him quieter, though listless and unfocused. Her concern now was that her father should get some rest, and John some relief from tending to her mother. She accordingly insisted that they return home for a time, and called Jenny to report that Lydon was better and she should come to sit with him.

Upon their arrival in Lambtown, they all repaired to Mrs. Bennet's apartment, where she received them exactly as might be expected: with tears and lamentations of regret, invectives against the villainous conduct of Jorge, and complaints about her own sufferings and ill-usage, blaming everybody but the person to whose unwise indulgence the errors of her son must be principally owing.

"If I'd been able," said she, "to carry my point of having us all go on vacation together, this would never have happened; but poor Lydon had nobody to look after him. Why did the general ever allow him to go out of his sight? I'm sure there was some neglect there, for he's not the kind of boy to do this sort of thing, if he'd been well looked after. I always thought General Hughes was unfit to take charge of him. What does *he* know about boys that age? But I was overruled, as I always am. Poor child, suffering that way in the hospital! And here I am, suffering just as much! I think I can feel all his symptoms—a mother can, you know. My heart is beating so fast, and I have spasms in my side, and I feel so faint that I can't stand on my own two feet, and my head hurts so much that I got no rest at all last night."

Lizzy offered to bring her some chamomile tea and cookies on a tray.

"By all means," said Mr. Bennet, "and make sure you use a lace doily and a tea cosy. It's so important to observe all the elegancies of misfortune. Perhaps I'll go sit in my library in my dressing gown, and demand to be waited on, and give as much trouble as I can."

It was Monday, and John felt obliged to present himself at work, little though he relished the prospect of spending his day surrounded by the ghoulish decor and delicacies of Halloween; for Bingley, cognizant of the prevalence of Mexican traditions in the neighborhood, was determined to maintain The Chocolate Bar's decorations and specialty treats through All Souls' Day, the Día de los Muertos. Skeletons and ghosts therefore haunted John's sight wherever he turned, and he lacked any will for polite argument when Bingley took one look at him and immediately gave him the day off. For Lizzy's part, there was no question of going to work, as it was beginning to rain. The weather only increased Mrs. Bennet's gloom and Lizzy's duties, and she was kept busy soothing her mother's woe and protecting John's and her father's rest from Mrs. Bennet's demands.

Only a part of her mind could she devote to their needs, however, since she clearly foresaw that Lydon's recovery, now all but certain, would not be a source of unalloyed satisfaction. First, and not inconsiderable, was worry about the cost of his hospital care. His parents' and his own lack of regular employment meant that he was not covered by insurance, and surely the expense of the time spent in Intensive Care alone would run into the tens of thousands. How was half such a sum to be repaid? Where he would go after his release was another vexing subject: should he return, with his wife, to General Hughes's house, his domicile when these disastrous events overtook him? Or perhaps his drug use had risen to the level of addiction, necessitating a stay in a rehabilitation center—at incalculable further expense. Would he instead come home, where the seeds of his misbehavior had been sown? All was uncertain, save for the fact that all these matters would have to be decided in the very near future.

Late in the afternoon John emerged from his chamber, declaring himself very much refreshed and ready to resume the care of his mother. Lizzy was glad to be able to relinquish her fractious charge to his more patient oversight, and returned to the hospital. There she discovered General Hughes, happily engaged in terrifying the nurses and reducing his daughter to tears.

"What a furball!" he exclaimed. "If he was one of my sprogs, I'd have him whipped at the cart's tail and sent off to war. Nothing like combat to make a man out of a spoiled boy. All the pantywaist nonsense the doctor is spewing is just liberal sniveling. I've said it from the start: give him something important to do. Service, sacrifice: that's what the boy needs."

Jenny interpreted these utterances in a whisper. "The doctor thinks Lydon should go to a live-in clinic for a while for addiction therapy."

"Send him to a damned spa! Why not give the no-load a medal while we're at it?"

"I take it the prognosis is good?" inquired Lizzy calmly.

"He's out of danger," Jenny replied, "and they've moved him to a regular room. He can go home tomorrow."

"He can go to hell tomorrow!" roared the general. Jenny started to cry again, and Lizzy excused herself to go visit her brother.

She found Lydon's condition, if not his character, materially improved. He was fast recovering his normal coloring, and despite a certain degree of lethargy, inevitable perhaps after such a crisis, no great revolution in principles had occurred: Lydon was unabashed and unreflecting. He hunched an impatient shoulder when Lizzy said that he had given them all quite a scare.

"Oh! Well, you don't have to make a big deal out of it. I guess I drank too much of the tea. Who knows? Maybe I'm just more sensitive than other people. But I can tell you, it was quite a trip while it lasted. I saw the weirdest things! I hope Jorge comes to see me soon; maybe he can interpret the symbolism of my visions. There was this guy, and he'd removed his head, and it rolled around on the ground following him, except sometimes it didn't follow, it went where it felt like, and it was all covered with black and white fur like a Jack Russell terrier. What do you suppose that means?"

"I doubt Jorge or anybody else possesses the ability to make sense of any of this," replied Lizzy; "and I'm certainly not going to seek him out to ask. Lydon, he nearly killed you!"

"Well, he didn't mean to, and I'm sure he's sorry. Lighten up! I think you're just disappointed that he's not into you anymore—that's why you're so mean about him."

"I hear the doctor thinks you should go into rehab."

"If I do, it'd better be one of those celebrity places where it's really easy to score. Otherwise, forget it!"

"Are you aware of how much all this is costing? How do you expect to pay your bills?"

"I thought if you went to an emergency room, they had to treat you regardless of your ability to pay. What does it matter? If they send me a bill, I'll just declare bankruptcy or something."

It was clear to Lizzy that Lydon would never hear or see anything of which he chose to be insensible, so she ceased to remonstrate with him, and very soon went away again. The interview, however, opened for her a new line of fruitless speculation. What of the instigator of all this misfortune? Would George be arrested, and charged with a crime? She could not even imagine in what quarter to make inquiry, for to set law enforcement on the trail of the dealer could only serve to bring Lydon's own illicit activity under their eye. Would that happen anyway—weren't medical professionals required to report an overdose to the police? She didn't know. And if George were not brought to book, what then? Would she meet him in the streets of Lambtown? How would he behave? How would *she* behave? The very notion was insupportable. There must be a path to justice, but she could not begin to make it out. The entire business was, as the general said, a furball.

Lizzy was now heartily sorry that she and John had, from the distress of the moment, been led to make Fitzwilliam Darcy acquainted with their fears for their brother; for since his recovery was to be so swift, they might hope to conceal his indisposition and its cause from all those who were not immediately involved. She had no fear of its spreading further through Darcy's means, of course. There were few people on whose secrecy she would have more confidently depended; but at the same time, there was no one whose knowledge of a brother's frailty—and George Carrillo's role in it—would have mortified her so much. Not from any disadvantage from it, individually to herself; for at any rate, there seemed a gulf impassable between them. It was not to be supposed that Darcy would wish to associate himself with a family where to every objection would now be added an involvement with the man whom he so justly scorned.

From such a connection she could not wonder that he should shrink. The wish of procuring her regard, which she had almost assured herself of his feeling in the past few weeks, could not in rational expectation survive such a blow as this. She was humbled, she was grieved; she repented, though she hardly knew of what. She became jealous of his esteem, when she could no longer hope to be benefited by it. She wanted to hear of him, when there seemed the least chance of gaining intelligence.

What a triumph for him, as she often thought, could he know that the advances she had proudly spurned only four months ago would now have been gladly and gratefully received! He was as generous, she doubted not, as the most generous of his sex. But while he was mortal, there must be a sense of triumph.

She began now to comprehend that he was exactly the man who, in disposition and talents, would most suit her. His understanding and temper, though unlike her own, would have answered all her wishes. It was a pairing that must have been to the advantage of both; by her ease and liveliness, his mind might have been softened, his manners improved, and from his judgment, information, and knowledge of the world she must have received benefit of greater importance. Yet all this was undone, she was certain, by the recklessness of a brother, and the connivance of Darcy's greatest enemy in that brother's transgressions. At that moment it was difficult for her to care what became of Lydon upon his release from the hospital on the morrow.

Chapter Thirty-three

The gloom of that Monday was succeeded by a morning of brilliant sunshine, however—as so many gloomy Mondays are—and if the smiling weather could not put an end to all Lizzy's troubles, a long day spent digging in her clients' gardens went some way toward restoring her animal spirits. She might not have learned resignation in so brief a span of time, but abject misery was unsustainable with the sun on her back and good loam between her fingers. Had idleness been her lot, she might have fallen into her mother's habit of discontent, but fortunately she had occupation sufficient to direct her thoughts into more practical channels.

She stopped by The Chocolate Bar at the end of her day to collect John, and on the way home aired some of her concerns about the shape of Lydon's future. Of the concerns that lay closer to her heart, and those closest to John's, it was of course impossible to speak.

John, as was his wont, was more inclined than she to take an optimistic view. Perhaps Lydon's brush with death would have taught him to value more highly the important things in life— his wife and family, his health, his freedom. Surely he would be frightened enough by this experience to tread a more acceptable path in the future. John had heard stories of people whose reckless behavior placed their lives in jeopardy, only to find that the experience of hospitalization inspired them to become doctors!

Lizzy eyed him askance. "Really? Lydon?"

"Well, maybe not. But I have to believe he's learned a valuable lesson, and we won't have to worry about him repeating his error."

"I keep wondering what would've happened if we'd revealed something of what we knew about Jorge."

"Perhaps it would've been for the best," replied John. "But to expose the past faults of any person, without knowing what their present feelings are, didn't seem fair. We acted with the best intentions, and without knowledge of the future we couldn't have done better."

"I suppose you're right. But I hate to think of him getting away with this!"

"It's hard not to be angry when we have been so frightened. Still, we have to remember that Jorge probably saved Lydon's life by taking him to the hospital. And Lydon participated in the ceremony of his own free will. Jorge isn't blameless, but he's by no means entirely to blame."

As usual, John's more generous view of things shamed Lizzy into silence, but she doubted that she would be capable of equal liberality of spirit. The sanguine hope of good, which the benevolence of John's heart suggested, had not deserted him even in this circumstance; and Lizzy could only pray that his life would be shielded from any experience that might cause it to harden.

Upon their arrival at home they discovered that Mr. Bennet had been awaiting them, and they hastened into the library, eager to learn what news he might have to impart. Once settled there, however, he seemed loath to satisfy their curiosity. The information he held appeared to oppress his spirits, and clearly he would rather be silent than speak. Yet speak he must, and so in due course all was told.

"General Hughes came to see me this afternoon. It seems he has been very busy over the past twenty-four hours—in fact, he's taken it upon himself to arrange the futures of both Lydon and that Carrillo fellow!—and he kindly paid me a visit to let me know what he has ordained."

"Surely he came to consult with you on the matter," said John. "You're Lydon's father."

"He said events had moved too quickly for consultation to be possible, and he only did what he was certain I would approve of."

"And *do* you approve?" asked Lizzy.

"I daresay it doesn't matter much what I think," said Mr. Bennet. "There was little enough I could do in any case, with Lydon of age."

"But what did he arrange?"

"Well, first of all Jorge, or George, or whatever we're supposed to call him—Carrillo—it seems the general found out somehow about a warehouse he rents in Lompoc. He tipped off the police and they searched the place, and there they discovered a large cache of, shall we say, herbal remedies that have not enjoyed the formality of FDA review. Carrillo himself turned up while they were searching; he fled, but they caught him and arrested him. The general told me the police said he had a felony juvenile record for growing pot, so it's unlikely that he will receive lenient treatment."

"What about the fact that he nearly killed Lydon?"

"I gather the general didn't mention that to the police. We must assume he believes Carrillo will receive a sufficient sentence without the addition of further charges. I'm sure it would do the general's career no good to have his son-in-law mixed up with a major drug bust."

"Perhaps the police might charge Lydon in some way if his overdose was connected to Jorge's business?" suggested John. "We should probably be grateful to General Hughes for keeping Lydon's name out of it. In a community like this, if his drug use became widely known, it would be very hard for him to find a job or make friends."

"Yes, there's no end to what we have to be grateful to the general for. You haven't heard the half of it. I don't know what pressures he brought to bear on Lydon, but he got him to agree to be admitted to a residential rehab facility in Malibu! Lydon was released from the hospital earlier this afternoon, and is on his way there now."

"*Malibu*—but aren't the drug treatment centers there very expensive?"

"I'm sure they are, but the general refused to tell me what it would cost. He said it was all taken care of—along with Lydon's hospital bills."

"But that would be tens of thousands of dollars!" cried Lizzy. "I would never have figured the general for such a generous man—or even that his military salary would stretch to such large outlays."

"Nor would I," Mr. Bennet agreed. "He must have a hitherto undiscovered soft side—or a hitherto undiscovered Swiss bank account—or else his love for his daughter blinds him to common sense."

"We must find some way to repay his generosity," said Lizzy.

"Oh, I doubt that'll be possible. I could offer to do something, but I think the general imagines himself in the role of Providence, and would resist any sharing of the honors."

"And what about Lydon?" asked Lizzy. "If his father-in-law's goodness doesn't make him miserable about what he's done, he doesn't deserve ever to be happy!"

"Well, at least he seems resolved on turning over a new leaf," said John. "We must all try to forget the past and start afresh with him when he's released."

When the news was broken to Mrs. Bennet, her joy was also unalloyed by concern about the debt to their benefactor. Far less than her husband did she pause to question the appropriateness of leaving General Hughes to bear such a heavy burden of expense, or to wonder at his extraordinary exertions on behalf of her adored Lydon. Indeed, she was rather inclined to take offense at the general for placing Lydon in a rehabilitation center so far removed from Lambtown, and one that, as it transpired, did not allow visitors for the first two weeks of his incarceration there. Her mother's love could not find adequate expression in anything short of her immediate removal to a seaside hotel in Malibu, where she could be close to the son she had been unable to visit in the hospital.

Mrs. Bennet was now in an irritation as violent from relief as she had earlier been from alarm and vexation. She was disturbed by no fears about Lydon's future felicity, nor humbled by any remembrance of his misconduct. Her eldest daughter endeavored to give some relief to the excess of her transports by leading her thoughts to the obligations that General Hughes's actions had laid them under.

"Who should do it but his own father-in-law? He's done little enough for all of us, though his daughter lived under our roof for months. And no harm came to Lydon till he was staying at the general's house. He *ought* to pay for the consequences of his neglect!"

This was a bit much for Lizzy to stomach; but, realizing that no persuasions of hers would have any effect on her mother's feelings, she took refuge in her own room, that she might think with freedom.

Poor Lydon's situation must, at best, be bad enough; but that it was no worse, she had need to be thankful. She felt it so; and though, in looking forward, neither rational happiness nor worldly prosperity could justly be expected for her brother, in looking back on what they had feared, only two days ago, she felt all the advantages of what they had gained.

Mr. Bennet, for his part, had very often wished before this period of his life that, instead of spending his whole income, he had laid by an annual sum for the better provision of his children, and of his wife if she survived him. He now wished it more than ever. Had he done his duty in that respect, Lydon need not have been indebted to his father-in-law for whatever of honor or credit could now be purchased for him. The satisfaction of cleaning up his mess might then have rested in its proper place.

When first Mr. Bennet had married, economy was held to be perfectly useless, for the optimism of youth would not be bound to disagreeable notions of restraint. By the time five children had entered the world, it was too late to be saving. Mrs. Bennet had no turn for economy, and only her husband's love of independence had prevented their exceeding their income beyond the level of debt considered a normal part of modern life.

That his son could be rescued with such trifling exertion on his side was a very welcome surprise; for his chief wish was to have as little trouble in the business as possible, and to forget discomforting thoughts as rapidly as he might. When the first shock of the crisis was over, he naturally returned to his native state of indolence.

It fell, therefore, to Lizzy's lot to pursue on her family's behalf any avenues for discovering how and to what extent General Hughes might be repaid. To this end, she paid a visit to him and Jenny on the weekend.

After her conversation with the general at the hospital, she had been more than a little surprised to discover that not twenty-four hours after excoriating the doctor's advice with regard to Lydon's treatment, he had arranged for that advice to be followed. It seemed to her possible that he might now have had another change of heart, and be wishing for release from the obligations he had shouldered. But when she ventured gently to raise the question of repayment, he cut her off with every evidence of determination, and a degree of discomfort that she had even raised the question.

"I don't want to hear any of that nonsense from you, young lady!" cried he, leaping to his feet. "Nobody asked you to stick your nose in. What's between me and Lydon is none of your affair. You leave it be, and go see Jenny. She's in her room, and pretty depressed now that I've grounded her."

To press the issue when it was presented in such terms could only be regarded as uncivil, so Lizzy had little choice but to obey. To her eye, however, Jenny did not seem at all depressed; the immediate crisis being over for Lydon, she seemed to have recovered her usual boisterous spirits. In fact, it was Lizzy's private view that—considering Lydon's confinement in a situation in which he could not make further trouble or pursue amusements distressing to her—Jenny was as happy as not to have a respite from his company. Jenny spoke to him on the phone once a day, but was otherwise free to pursue her own inclinations. In her conversation with Lizzy she was voluble on the subject of her clothes, and her passions for music and celebrities, but of her husband there was a good deal less to say. She did, however, take an eager interest in the news he was able to impart of two movie stars who were sharing space with him in the treatment center, and his words about their addictions and their behavior in group therapy were relayed in detail.

Lizzy paid little heed to most of these disclosures, until a familiar name captured her attention.

"—It's almost as much fun as one of those supermarket newspapers to hear his stories! Who would have thought that boring old Mr. Darcy would have come up with such a great place!"

"Mr. Darcy!" repeated Lizzy, in utter amazement.

"Oh, yes, you know he's the one who got Lydon admitted there, and drove him down as well." Jenny suddenly caught herself short. "Oops! I wasn't supposed to say anything about that. It was all a big secret! You won't tell anyone, will you?"

"I don't know enough about the matter to have much to tell," said Lizzy, burning with curiosity.

"Thank you," said Jenny, "because I'd get in so much trouble if I told you anything more."

Lizzy's ethical standards were just sufficiently high to require her to respond, "Then by all means don't say anything else"; but she so feared the imminent collapse of those standards that it was imperative she end the interview immediately.

To live in ignorance on such a point was impossible, however; or at least it was impossible not to try for information. Darcy had arranged for Lydon to go into rehab, and had delivered him there himself! It was exactly a scene where he had apparently least to do, and least temptation to go. Conjectures as to the meaning of it, rapid and wild, hurried into her brain; but she was satisfied with none. Those that best pleased her, as placing his conduct in the noblest light, seemed the most improbable. She could not bear such suspense—and it seemed that, aside from Darcy himself, only one person could relieve it. She must see the general again. And what if he refused to change his story? What tricks and stratagems might she be reduced to, in her quest to discover the truth of the matter?

After an anxious search, she discovered Brigadier General Hughes in the garden, splitting wood. He noted her presence with a grunt and, she thought, a wary eye.

"General, we need to speak some more about Lydon," said she firmly.

"No, we don't! I told you before, it's none of your business." The ax fell with a violence that caused to Lizzy to flinch, but she pressed on.

"Sir, I've learned that Fitzwilliam Darcy was involved."

The general paused in his labors, bending on her a fulminating look. "Jenny, I suppose," said he; "her tongue runs like a Gatling gun. Well, I can't say I'm sorry; I never wanted to take any credit for the patched-over business. I would've managed it very differently, but the young man was determined, and I had to respect his reasons. I like the cut of the fellow; he would've been better for military training, of course, but at least he has some concept of honor and duty."

"Please, will you tell me the whole story? All Jenny said was that he arranged for Lydon to be admitted to rehab, and drove him there."

"Oh, very well; I suppose you won't stop pestering me unless

I do." To Lizzy's relief, the general laid down his ax. "The night before Lydon was supposed to get out of the hospital, this Darcy turned up on my doorstep. He said he felt responsible for what had happened: apparently, Carrillo had used his land in the past to grow dope, and Darcy had hushed it up, so he blamed himself that Carrillo had been able to go back to drug dealing. Darcy was sure that if he'd publicly exposed Carrillo before, Carrillo wouldn't have been able to use excuses like 'Native American ritual' to peddle his stuff, and Lydon wouldn't have overdosed. I don't know about that; Lydon's the kind of scrag who's going to find trouble, one way or another. But I can't fault Darcy for stepping up to deal with the blowback. He came in high and tight, as we say in a bombing run, with all his strategy in place. And he didn't want to boast about it, either. He insisted that your parents might be upset if they knew a stranger had intervened, and told me I had to take credit for it all. We had a lively debate on that point, believe me! But I saw the logic; and, of course, I was obligated to him as well, so I went along with his plans."

"And what exactly were those plans?"

"Just what I told your father. He'd already scoped out Carrillo's warehouse and tipped off the police, though when he came to see me he didn't yet know that they'd raided the place. He didn't want to associate Lydon's name with Carrillo's if it could be avoided, even if it meant lesser charges for Carrillo. I didn't like that much; young people need to stand up and take the consequences of their actions! But Darcy reminded me that whatever involved Lydon would also involve Jenny; I guess he knew he had me there. He'd also visited Lydon, and convinced him to enter rehab. Who knows if that psychiatry mumbo-jumbo will do any good! I've always thought it was for whiners to learn how to make excuses for themselves. But I'm glad to see Lydon redeployed for a while: it's hard enough keeping Jenny in line now that her mother's gone, and he was always leading her into mischief."

"What arguments did he use to persuade Lydon to go into rehab?" asked Lizzy. "When I saw Lydon that afternoon, he seemed pretty set against it."

"I don't know, but that Darcy seems to carry all before him. He had a pretty shrewd take on Lydon's character, so I expect he tailored his arguments to suit his audience. In that sense he was probably a better person to handle the business than I would've been. When I laid down the law with Lydon, he would always pretend to agree with me, and then go AWOL and do as he pleased!"

"And Mr. Darcy is paying for the rehab?"

"Not just that, but the hospital bills as well."

"We can't be so indebted to someone outside the family! But I have no idea how we can repay him, especially if he doesn't want to be repaid, or even acknowledged."

The general stood for a moment in uncharacteristic reflection. "Sometimes you have to stand aside and let an honorable man be an honorable man," he said at last. "And if that's humiliating, maybe the humiliation is good for your own character."

The revelations of this interview threw Lizzy into a flutter of spirits, in which it was difficult to determine whether pleasure or pain bore the greatest share. She had feared to encourage her vague and unsettled suspicions about what Darcy might have been doing to forward her brother's recovery, as being on the one hand an exertion of goodness too great to be probable. And on the other, she had dreaded that those suspicions might prove true, fearing the pain of being under such a heavy obligation. And now what she had suspected was proved beyond the greatest extent of her imaginings to be true. He had deliberately involved himself in the affairs of the man whom he always most wished to avoid, and whose very name it was punishment to him to pronounce. And he had done so much more for her brother, a boy whom he could neither regard nor esteem.

Her heart did whisper that he had done it for her. But it was a hope shortly checked by other considerations, and she soon felt that her vanity was insufficient, when required to depend on his affection for her to overcome sentiments so natural as abhorrence against involvement with George, or with her miscreant family. Why would he do so much for a woman who had spurned him? That he had gone to extraordinary lengths could not be gainsaid. She was ashamed to think how much. But he had given a reason for his interference that demanded no extraordinary stretch of belief. It was reasonable that he should feel he had been wrong in concealing George's past actions and had seized an opportunity to atone. He had liberality, and he had the means of exercising it. And though she would not place herself as his principal inducement, she could, perhaps, believe that remaining partiality for her might assist his endeavors in a cause where her peace of mind must be materially concerned. It was painful, exceedingly painful, to know that they were under obligations to a person who could never receive a return. They owed the restoration of Lydon, his character, his very likelihood of survival, *everything*, to Darcy.

How heartily did she grieve over every ungracious sensation she had ever encouraged, every saucy speech she had ever directed toward him! For herself she was humbled; but she was proud of him—proud that in a cause of compassion and honor, he had been able to get the better of himself. She repeated to herself the general's words of commendation of him again and again. They were hardly enough, but they pleased her, as having been wrung from a man who rarely spoke in such laudatory terms. These sentiments provided what meager comfort was available to her, under the degrading circumstances in which she and her family had become embroiled.

Chapter Thirty-four

One of Lizzy's greatest fears at this time was the possible effect of scandal on John's hopes for happiness. Were the news to become widespread, she was certain, Caroline Bingley would go to any length to bring about the separation of her brother from John. But as the days passed it became clear that while all of Lambtown was aware of George's disgrace, Lydon's connection to it was not common knowledge.

Not a day went by without word flying about the town of some fresh instance of George's villainy. All Lambtown seemed striving to blacken the man who, but a few months before, had been almost an angel of light. Everybody declared that he was the wickedest young man in the world; and everybody began to find out that they had always distrusted the appearance of his goodness.

Lizzy felt acutely what must be the sentiments of George's parents under this onslaught of ill-will and, upon espying Mr. Carrillo on one occasion in the center of the town, was at pains to address him with especial courtesy, even venturing so far as to give his arm a friendly squeeze. About George she did not feel capable of speaking; but she as well as anyone was alive to the injustice of shunning the family over the errors of one of its members. She asked particularly to be remembered to Mrs. Carrillo, and could see that his heart was touched.

Aside from the prospect of Lydon's prolonged absence from the family circle, life in the Bennet household now appeared ready to resume its normal patterns. Lizzy was kept very busy with the planting season in her clients' gardens, and spent most of her evenings entering data for the library catalog, while John was spending far more time at The Chocolate Bar than his hours of employment required. Mary was studying for her SATs, and Kitty had obtained new employment at a fast-food restaurant along Highway 101, riding to and from that establishment on the bus. She was as resentful of this disagreeable necessity as ever, and when her complaints were partnered with her mother's constantly bemoaning that she was not permitted to go to stay in Malibu, the conversation around the Bennet dinner table took on a tedious sameness.

A change, perhaps for the better, came when Lizzy received a letter from the Planning Department signaling its qualified approval of her proposals for the library. As she had considered likely, the day care element of her scheme was not to be allowed; but so long as she kept all activities within-doors and provided for handicapped access and parking in the driveway, she was suffered to proceed.

To the other demands on her time were now added interviews, conducted with Rose's assistance, with candidates for the position of a bilingual factotum who could serve as emissary to the Spanish-speaking population and guide for any members of that community who wished to take advantage of the library's services. A young woman was eventually located who had risen from migrant worker's daughter to graduate of a local community college; she brought a great deal of energy and enthusiasm to her position, and under the combined tutelage of Lizzy and Virginia Sanchez, the professional librarian whom Lizzy was also able to hire, she rapidly developed plans for the conquest of the farmworkers' children. Together they made arrangements to open the library in January. She also spent some time in an effort very close to her heart, the arrangement of a special bookcase, labeled in memory of Aunt Evelyn, that held all of that lady's favorite books.

Mrs. Bennet could not be expected to let pass without comment this final death knell for her hopes of emolument from Evelyn Bennet's estate, and she expressed her disappointment in her eldest daughter with renewed vigor. Even if the community showed signs of becoming reconciled to the library, *she* would never do so. "Who ever heard of a privately owned library? I never will believe that was what Aunt Evelyn intended. Libraries are run by the town, or the county, where they're located. You should sell the building, and the book collection, to the government, and then divide the proceeds among the family. It's the only fair thing to do." Lizzy soon tired of explaining the infeasibility of this scheme, and simply ignored her mother when she began again to press her cause.

With all these demands on her time, Lizzy was obliged to miss the November meeting of the Poets. She was not entirely sorry. It seemed quite possible that Darcy would have been there; and as he had made no attempt to contact her since Lydon's debacle, she could vividly imagine the sort of awkwardness that would be felt on both sides at such a meeting. It was possible that he had sought for her at The Chocolate Bar, but she had been far too busy to spend time there, and did not wish to excite John's curiosity by making inquiries about him. She also felt that such passive means of seeking her company did not suffice; if he wanted to see her, he could give her a call! That he did not do so told its own tale.

Mary Gardiner, however, duly noted Lizzy's absence from the gathering, and took her to task the next Sunday after church. "Everyone was agog to hear how you would top your last reading, and was very disappointed not to be treated to more dionysian ecstasy!"

Lizzy begged forgiveness and embarked on the enumeration of her various recent activities, until Mrs. Gardiner pled with her to desist. "All right! You're excused. But you must know how disappointed everyone was—particularly our most recent member. Darcy asked after you particularly."

"Oh," said Lizzy.

"May I say how much I like him? You've called him proud, and conceited, in the past, but I've seen nothing of that. He's been an excellent addition to the Poets: a good reader, and an interesting conversationalist. He seems intelligent and well-informed. Perhaps he's not as lively as he might be, but in the right company, that could improve." Mrs. Gardiner waited to see how these observations might be received, but evidently Lizzy could think of nothing rational to say, so she kindly changed the subject. "I hear that John and Charles Bingley are becoming quite the item."

"Oh, dear," said Lizzy, "is it being much talked about?"

"A fair amount, but that was inevitable in a place like this. For many people here, the idea of a gay couple is very exotic, and they don't know what to expect. But John and Charles are both so well liked—John is hugely popular with the kids at The Chocolate Bar, and Charles has earned a lot of respect in the business community—so people seem inclined to take it in stride. It gives them an opportunity to think of themselves as broad-minded, and who doesn't want to do that? Plus, everyone is completely addicted to The Chocolate Bar, so they couldn't shun them even if they did disapprove."

Lizzy smiled. "Chocolate, chocolate, *über alles*?"

"I don't think you need to worry; it's going to be all right."

And so it appeared when, later in the week, Bingley joined the Bennet family for dinner. The lovers cast such a rosy glow around themselves that all within their sphere felt warmed by it. If anything could separate them, Lizzy believed, it could only be her mother's officious attempts to unite them.

"You were away far too long to suit this neighborhood," said Mrs. Bennet, anxiously refilling Charley's wineglass. "I've been wanting to have you over forever, but then you disappeared so suddenly."

Bingley looked a little silly at this reflection, and murmured something disjointed about tending to various business interests.

"No matter, here you are now. And you must consider our house your own; as they say here, 'Mi casa is su casa.' Whenever you miss being part of a real family, you just come right over. No need to call ahead! We can always set another place."

Bingley politely expressed his gratitude for her kindness.

"Tell me," said Mrs. Bennet, "did you see that TV interview on *Oprah* with the editor of *The Advocate* on National Coming Out Day?"

Lizzy was in such a misery of shame at this transparent sally that she could hardly keep her seat. It drew from her, however, the exertion of speaking, which nothing else had so effectually done before; and she hastily intervened to ask Bingley if The Chocolate Bar's Halloween festivities had proved a success.

He seized upon this diversion with every evidence of relief. "Yes, we had a 15 percent increase in our volume of sales over the three-day period. I was especially pleased to see our townie customers take an interest in and embrace the Mexican holiday traditions. I've heard something about your own efforts to bridge the gaps between different populations here, with the public garden idea. Too bad that didn't work out! But maybe you and I can coordinate something. I was thinking about buying a small parcel on the western side of town, and would be happy to let you use a portion of it if you wanted to develop another community garden."

Lizzy was fully alive to the well-meant impulse behind this offer, but she felt obliged to discourage it. "I think I was overreaching a bit with that project," she acknowledged. "Not just because of the business owners' hostility, but also, the enthusiasm among the farmworkers' families was less than I imagined it would be. There was a lot of attrition, as people either didn't have the energy to tend their plots after a long workday or didn't stay in the area long enough to see things through. Maybe some of them weren't comfortable drawing so much attention to themselves in the current climate of hostility toward illegal immigrants. Many of the families I was working with aren't even here anymore; they've gone south to the Imperial Valley for the late harvests there, or north to prune the fruit trees and grapevines in Oregon."

"It's a real challenge, finding the best ways to be helpful. Perhaps you can develop programs at the library that will make local Anglo residents more aware of the lives and cultures of the migrant workers—a sort of 'winning the hearts and minds' campaign, as they say in the military. Make them better aware of the farmworkers as human beings, and let their consciences do the rest."

"That approach is no doubt the wiser course," said Lizzy. "I'm afraid I've been guilty of crusading, and have turned off a lot of people who might've been amenable to a subtler approach, if I'd been more discreet."

"Better crusading than oblivious, any day," Bingley assured her kindly.

"You're too easy on her!" cried Mrs. Bennet. "If it weren't for her, we'd be in the Enclave by now. But she had to go around offending everybody, and spending all that money on a library no one wants. If only she could be more like John: *he* knows how to be discreet, and not confrontational with strangers. You never need to fear being embarrassed by him."

If only the same could be said of my mother! thought Lizzy, in an agony of mortification. At that instant she felt that years of happiness could not make John or herself amends for moments of such painful confusion. Yet her feelings soon received material relief in the observation of how little Mrs. Bennet's words were heeded by either Bingley or John. No inconveniences of familial interference, whether hostile like Caroline Bingley's or supportive like Mrs. Bennet's, could disturb their growing attachment. If Darcy did not again undermine Bingley's confidence, she felt, all must speedily be concluded and a happy outcome attained.

And she found a further source of comfort in her father's behavior on the occasion. There was nothing of presumption or folly in Bingley that could provoke Mr. Bennet's ridicule, or disgust him into silence; and he was accordingly more communicative, and less eccentric, than was his wont. It provided balm to Lizzy's spirits to perceive that there was one at least of her parents of whom she need not be ashamed. She reposed sufficient confidence in Bingley's politeness that she need not fear him snubbing her mother, but it pleased her to think that he might actually derive some degree of pleasure from her father's company. Would that he might also carry the report to Darcy that Mr. Bennet was capable of being a sensible man! And might it, at the very least, inspire Darcy to refrain from trying to separate Bingley and John again, even if it didn't lead him to revise his larger views on the Bennet family? In vain did she strive to banish such speculations from her thoughts; they returned, unbidden, to preoccupy her in every private moment.

Somewhat to Lizzy's surprise, Charley Bingley took Mrs. Bennet at her word, and thereafter made a variety of excuses to invite himself over to the house with increasing frequency. His easy manners and cheerful outlook rendered him a most agreeable addition to their family circle; even Mary relaxed a little in her severities under his kindly demeanor. He bore with the ill-judged officiousness of his hostess, even going so far as to obtain a copy of *The Advocate* and discuss it with her, and heard all her silly remarks with a forbearance and command of countenance particularly grateful to her son.

Mrs. Bennet, however, dissatisfied with his noncommittal responses to her sallies, soon determined to push the affair further by promoting opportunities for John and Charley to be alone. "Mr. B, I'm sure you're eager to get back to your reading," said she, as soon as dinner was over. "And Mary, don't you have to study? Lizzy, you and Kitty can take care of the dishes." She bustled about clearing the room, as John cast Lizzy an agonized glance of entreaty. Faced with a direct command, however, Lizzy felt obliged to obey, though she regretted as much as her brother the appearance of particularity that such blatant scheming presented.

But they need not have feared that Mrs. Bennet's calculations would disgust their visitor; Bingley seemed pleased enough to fall in with her hopes for his future. It was not long before he and John acknowledged that they were discussing plans to move in together.

Lizzy, though alive to the decrease in congenial companionship that she would experience on the domestic front in such an event, was nevertheless most sincerely overjoyed at her brother's happiness. She couldn't help but smile at the rapidity and ease with which an affair was finally settled that had given them so many previous months of suspense and vexation. And this, she thought, was the end of all his friend's anxious circumspection, of all his sister's falsity and contrivance! The happiest, wisest, most reasonable end!

From that point Lizzy had fewer opportunities to be private with John, but on one such occasion, she ventured to inquire into how Charley accounted for his long absence from Lambtown.

"He says he was uncertain of my attachment to him, and felt so strongly himself that he feared what might happen if he betrayed his feelings."

"And why did he have doubts about how you felt?"

"I suppose I was overly cautious myself; I knew he wasn't out, and didn't want to push him. And I believe his sister must have encouraged him to think I was indifferent to him."

"Did he say that?"

"Not in so many words, but what he did say gave me the impression that someone close to him tried to undermine the relationship. But when Caroline sees, as I'm sure she will, that Charley's happy with me, she'll learn to be content, and we can be on good terms again—though it's hard to imagine we'll ever be really close."

Lizzy clapped her hands. "That's the most unforgiving speech I've ever heard you utter. Good boy! As for Charley himself, he made a mistake, but it's a credit to his modesty, and nothing worse."

This naturally introduced a panegyric from John on Bingley's diffidence, and his tendency to undervalue his own good qualities. Lizzy was pleased to find that Charley had not betrayed the interference of his friend, for, though John had the most generous and forgiving heart in the world, she knew it was a circumstance that must prejudice him against Darcy.

"I have to be the luckiest man alive!" said John. "If I could only see *you* equally happy; if only there were another man like Bingley for you!"

"If you were to bring me forty such men, I could never be as happy as you. Till I have your disposition, I can never have your happiness. No, let me shift for myself; and maybe, if I have very good luck, I may meet with another Morris Collins."

Chapter Thirty-five

With her brother's joy to buoy her spirits, Lizzy set about with very good cheer on Thanksgiving morning to prepare the holiday dinner. Not long before she was to put the turkey in the oven, however, her attention was diverted by the sound of a car in the driveway, followed by a loud rapping on the front door. It was impossible to imagine who might be coming to call on a holiday morning, but thinking little of it, she continued stuffing the fowl. Bingley had already arrived, and was leaning against the counter entertaining John with tales of family holidays past. Upon hearing the knock he instantly prevailed on John to walk away with him onto the golf course, seeking thereby to avoid the confinement of such an intrusion. They both set off, leaving Lizzy to the continuance of her conjectures, though with little satisfaction until a breathless Kitty appeared in the kitchen doorway:

"She's here for you!"

"Who is?" asked Lizzy, vexedly wiping the grease off her fingers.

"Catherine de Bourgh! She says she wants to talk to you."

"That's enough, girl! I can tell her myself." The lady swept Kitty aside, more by the influence of her eye than by physical means, and entered the kitchen.

Lizzy was intending to be surprised, but the astonishment of this apparition was beyond her expectation. She could only be grateful that her mother was still upstairs and thus unable to fawn over the exalted guest. She gazed upon her visitor in enquiring silence.

"*That* I suppose is one of your sisters."

"She is," agreed Lizzy. "Her name is Kitty."

Lizzy then asked whether she would like a cup of coffee. This was declined resolutely, and not very politely, and her guest added in abrupt tones, "I can't abide these tract houses, on their tiny lots; but there seems to be some kind of a public common at the end of this street. Walk with me there."

Lizzy covered the turkey with buttered foil, checked on the pies, and removed her apron. As they passed down the hallway to the front door, Catherine peered into the family room and dining room, pronouncing them, after a short survey, to be decent looking chambers.

Once they attained the driving court, Lizzy saw a Cadillac parked near the door with the engine running, chauffeur at the wheel. They proceeded in silence along the sidewalk; Lizzy was determined to make no effort for conversation with a woman who was now more than usually insolent and disagreeable. *How could I ever have thought her like her nephew?* she wondered.

At last Catherine de Bourgh began. "You can be at no loss to understand the reason for my visit. Your conscience must tell you why I've come."

Lizzy looked with unaffected astonishment. "You're mistaken. I've long since given up hoping you'd apologize for destroying the community garden, and I can think of no other unfinished business between us."

"*Apologize?* I'm astounded that you have the nerve to bring up that subject. But however insincere *you* may choose to be, you won't find *me* acting like a hypocrite. I am celebrated for my sincerity and frankness, and in a matter as important as this, I certainly won't change my tune. The most alarming news has come to my attention: not only that your brother was participating in an unnatural liaison, which I had already heard, but that you had sunk your claws into my nephew—my own nephew, Fitzwilliam Darcy!"

"'Sunk my claws' into Fitzwilliam Darcy? What on earth do you mean by that?"

"That you're dating him—sleeping with him—whatever scheming girls do these days to get a ring on their finger. Though I know it must be nothing more than scandalous gossip, though I would never injure him so much as to believe it possible that he could be attracted to you, I came here to let you know exactly what I think of your presumptuousness."

"If you believed it to be impossible," said Lizzy, "I'm surprised you took the trouble of coming to confront me. What were you thinking?"

"To insist that you publicly contradict this rumor!"

"Your coming to visit me and my family," said Lizzy, "would be more likely to confirm it—if there is in fact such a rumor."

"If! Do you pretend to be unaware of it? Haven't you and your family industriously circulated it? I'm sure you're perfectly aware of all the talk."

"I haven't heard a word of it."

"And can you assert that there's no foundation for it?"

"I make no claims of frankness to equal your own. *You* may ask questions that *I* choose not to answer."

"This is outrageous. Miss Bennet, I insist on your answering me. Is my nephew in love with you?"

"You have declared it to be impossible."

"It ought to be so; it must be so, unless he has gone completely insane. But your enticements may have infatuated him to the point of forgetting what he owes to himself and his family. You may have deceived and bewitched him. You may have seduced him."

"If I had, would I be likely to confess it?"

"Miss Bennet, do you know who I am? Do you understand my position in this community? I'm not accustomed to this kind of impertinence. I am his nearest relative, and have a right to know his personal concerns."

"But you're not entitled to know mine; and your behavior isn't likely to induce me to confide in you."

"Let me be clear: the marriage you aspire to will never take place. Darcy is engaged to his cousin Anne. *Now* what do you have to say for yourself?"

"Only that if what you say is true, you have no reason to suppose that he'll propose to me."

Catherine de Bourgh hesitated for a moment, and then replied, "Since they were in their cradles, they've been intended for each other. They've been brought up in the same world, destined for the same way of life. Everyone in the family has always assumed—and now, just when we could all reasonably expect them to launch their careers together, to be thwarted by a young woman of no breeding, inferior to them both in every way! A young woman who has shown herself determined to destroy our way of life here in Lambtown, with her socialist causes. Do you completely disregard the wishes of his friends and family? Because your family are nobodies, do you have no respect for family ties? Are you utterly lost to all sense of propriety? Haven't I told you that he and his cousin are intended for each other?"

"Yes, and I'd heard it before. But what is that to me? If there's no other objection than *that* to my being with Darcy, I certainly don't feel any scruples. You want him to marry Anne Fitzwilliam, and I'm sure you've done all you could to further the match. If Darcy doesn't feel bound by honor or affection to his cousin, why shouldn't he make another choice? And if I am that choice, why shouldn't I accept him?"

"Because honor, prudence, even self-interest forbid it. Yes, Miss Bennet, self-interest: surely you don't expect to be recognized by his family and friends if you willfully act against all our wishes? You'd be despised by everyone if you acted so disgracefully. Nobody will even speak your name."

"You paint a dismal portrait of my misfortunes," replied Lizzy. "But Darcy's partner in life must have such extraordinary sources of happiness that she could have little cause for regret."

"Obstinate, headstrong girl! Aren't you ashamed of yourself? Is this your gratitude for my courtesy to you last spring? I offered to help you join the Enclave! I invited you to dinner! I haven't blocked this stupid library idea of yours! Do you owe me no debt of gratitude? You must understand, Miss Bennet, that I came here determined that you should obey me, and I will *not* be dissuaded. I'm not accustomed to submitting to another person's will. I'm rarely disappointed."

"That will make your present situation more pathetic, but it'll have no effect on me."

"Don't interrupt me! Hear me in silence, since I have to repeat myself. I've told you: my niece and nephew are made for each other. They are equals in fortune, in education, in background. Their families are in the same profession, and have been for generations. They have the same understanding of property. They're destined for each other in the eyes of everyone who matters to them; and what is to separate them? The pretensions of an upstart young woman who lacks any of those qualities? It's intolerable! If you were sensible, if you knew what was good for you, you wouldn't wish to abandon the social sphere you grew up in."

"In dating—or even marrying—your nephew, I wouldn't consider myself to be leaving that sphere. In every sense that matters, I consider us equals."

"*Equals?* What's your education? Who's your family? What about the scandals attaching to the Bennet name? One brother a drug addict, the other a homosexual. Do you imagine I don't know their sordid histories?"

Lizzy replied coldly, "Whatever their histories may be, there's nothing about my brother John that could remotely be considered sordid. And if your nephew doesn't object to my family, it can be nothing to you."

"Tell me once and for all, are you sleeping with him?"

Though Lizzy would not, for the mere purpose of obliging Catherine de Bourgh, have answered this question, she could not but say, after a moment's deliberation, "I am not."

"And will you promise me never to do so?"

"I'll make no such promise."

"Miss Bennet, I'm shocked and astonished. I had hoped to find a more reasonable young woman. But don't deceive yourself: I'll never give up until you've sworn to me that you'll stay away from him."

"And that I will never do. You can't intimidate me into doing something so completely unreasonable. You want Darcy to form an alliance, marriage, business deal, whatever you want to call it, with your niece; but would my giving you my word make that outcome any more likely? Supposing him to be attached to me, would my avoiding him make him turn to his cousin? I have to say that the arguments you've presented in support of your cause are as ridiculous as your confrontational manner is impolitic. You've completely mistaken my character if you think I can be persuaded by these snobbish, classist arguments, or by the mercenary motives underlying them. How far your nephew might tolerate your interference in his affairs I couldn't say; but you certainly have no right to concern yourself with mine. I must ask you to drop the subject."

"Not so fast, girl. I am by no means finished. I know that your brother—and probably you as well, from what I'm told—are mixed up with that drug dealer, George Carrillo, who was just arrested. Are you hoping Darcy will intercede on his behalf? Do you think a Darcy of Pemberley Ranch will entangle himself in that business, just because Carrillo's father worked for his? And what if you get arrested for drug possession? Do you want to destroy Darcy's reputation in the community forever?"

"You can *now* have nothing further to say," Lizzy replied. "You've insulted me in every possible way. I'm going back to the house before my family's Thanksgiving dinner is ruined."

She turned back, and Catherine de Bourgh perforce did also. "You have no regard, then, for the honor and standing of my nephew! Selfish girl! Don't you realize that a connection with you will disgrace him in everybody's eyes?"

"I have nothing further to say to you."

"So you're determined to seduce him?"

"I said no such thing. I'm only determined to act in a manner that will, in my own opinion, give me the best chance at happiness, without reference to you, or anyone else who doesn't matter to me."

"You refuse, then, to oblige me. You refuse to obey the claims of duty, honor, or gratitude. You're determined to ruin him in the eyes of all his friends, and make him a laughingstock."

"We have completely different definitions of duty, honor, and gratitude," cried Lizzy. "As I see them, no principles whatsoever would be violated if Darcy and I were together. And as for the world's indignation and ridicule, people would have to share your values to share your prehistoric beliefs on the subject. Are you so deluded as to believe that everyone thinks exactly as you do, or thinks about the Darcys of Pemberley Ranch at all?"

"And this is your real opinion! You hold family, heritage, reputation so cheap. Very well, I shall know how to act. Don't imagine, Miss Bennet, that your ambitions will ever be gratified. I'd hoped to find you reasonable, but depend upon it that I will get my way."

In this manner Catherine de Bourgh carried on, until they reached her car. The chauffeur leaped out and held a door open for her.

"I won't shake your hand, or wish you and your family a happy holiday," said she. "You deserve no such courtesies. I'm disgusted with you."

Lizzy made no answer, and without attempting to persuade her uninvited guest to return to the house, walked quietly into it herself. She heard the car drive away as she walked back to the kitchen. There she was met by her mother, all impatience. "Catherine de Bourgh came to see you! Why didn't you ask her in? The turkey can wait, and the pies are only a little burnt."

"She wanted to leave," said Lizzy.

"Isn't that just like you! I suppose it didn't occur to you that the rest of us might welcome the opportunity to impress Catherine de Bourgh? But as usual, you kept her all to yourself. Why did she come? Is she going to stop the library?"

Here Lizzy was forced to give a little falsehood, for to acknowledge the substance of her conversation was impossible; and she was grateful for the opportunity of solitude afforded her by her family's general reluctance to help with the cooking, which soon left her alone in the kitchen to think.

The discomposure of spirits that this extraordinary visit threw her into could not be easily overcome; nor could she for many hours learn to think of it less than incessantly. Catherine the Great, it appeared, had actually taken the trouble of journeying from Rosings Ranch for the sole purpose of determining the nature of Lizzy's relationship with Fitzwilliam Darcy. From what source the intimations of an engagement could have originated, she was at a loss to imagine; they had not so much as dined alone together in a local restaurant! It seemed an impossible leap of speculation, even for the fictive capacities of a small-town gossip mill. The only thing she could think of that might connect them in the public mind was his being the intimate friend of Bingley, and her being the sister of John—perhaps that was enough, at a time when the consummation of one romance made them eager for another, to supply the idea. Lizzy herself had not forgotten to imagine that John's alliance might bring her and Darcy more frequently together. Or perhaps the idea had taken root when he had singled her out for his particular attentions at the Pemberley Ranch reception, and begun the inexorable progression from speculation to certainty in the minds of the uninformed. If such suspicions had been conveyed to the

Collinses—for Lizzy believed them to be Catherine de Bourgh's chief source of intelligence about the neighborhood—then it was not to be wondered at. Charlotte Collins would have her own motives for wishing to see Lizzy safely attached.

In reconsidering Catherine de Bourgh's expressions, however, Lizzy could not help feeling some uneasiness as to the possible consequence of the great lady's persisting in this interference. From what she had said of her resolution to prevent a marriage, it occurred to Lizzy that she must meditate an application to her nephew; and how *he* might receive a similar representation of the evils attached to a connection with her, she dared not pronounce. She knew not the exact degree of his affection for his aunt, or his dependence on her judgment in personal matters, but it was natural to suppose that he thought more highly of his aunt than *she* did; and it was certain that in enumerating the miseries of a union with one whose immediate connections and social impulses were so far removed from his own, Catherine would address him on his weakest side. With his notions of dignity, his support for and even embodiment of the Lambtown status quo, he would probably feel that arguments, which to Lizzy had appeared weak and ridiculous, contained much good sense and solid reasoning. And what if his aunt were able to convince him that Lizzy was herself spreading rumors about an attachment between them? Surely he would be disgusted.

If he had been wavering before as to what he should do, which had often seemed likely, the advice and entreaty of so near a relation might settle every doubt, and determine him at once to be as happy as dignity unblemished could make him. In that case he would seek her company no more. If she did not see him by the end of the year, then she would give over every expectation, every wish of his constancy, and focus all her heart on the success of the library. If he proved to be satisfied with only regretting her, Lizzy thought, when he might have obtained her affections or even perhaps her hand, then she would soon cease to regret him at all.

With such reflections filling her mind, Lizzy was unable to take much part in the levity prevailing at the holiday table that evening. Fortunately, the evident joy of Charley and John amply compensated for its absence in other quarters, and by sharing in their happiness even Kitty and Mrs. Bennet forgot to be discontented with their own lives or to rue Lydon's absence. The surprise of the entire family at Catherine de Bourgh's visit was very great; but they obligingly accounted for it with their own suppositions, sparing Lizzy the burden of doing so. The event was not to pass, nonetheless, without making its misery felt; and the wounds were of Mr. Bennet's infliction.

"On this day for giving thanks," said he, "I feel we haven't been sufficiently appreciative of the honor bestowed upon our house. To be visited by Catherine the Great, even if her purpose was only to take one of our number to task for her subversive activities—none of you is properly awed on this occasion! We were noticed—or at least, Lizzy was—by one of the leading lights of Lambtown society. But your jaded palates for notoriety would perhaps only be sated if the king of Lambtown, Fitzwilliam Darcy, came down from on high and condescended to despise us in person. Lizzy, I feel you must cook up a full-scale Mexican insurrection if you wish him to cease ignoring us. Nothing less will do. *His* perfect indifference, *your* pointed dislike; it would be deliciously absurd! We are bored; Lizzy, what will you concoct next to entertain us?"

He paused for a moment, considering his eldest daughter. "But Lizzy, you don't seem amused. Isn't this exactly the kind of attention you most wish to attract?"

Lizzy, acutely conscious of Bingley's bewildered gaze on her, cast about for a suitable response; Charley had yet to fully grasp the peculiar bent of Mr. Bennet's sense of humor, and must feel some hurt at the manner in which his best friend was spoken of.

But John was able to whisper soothingly that his father didn't intend to cast aspersions on the sincerity of Lizzy's motives or to show any disrespect for Darcy, and the moment passed off.

Lizzy had never been more at a loss to make her feelings appear what they were not. It was necessary to laugh, when she would rather have cried. Her father had most cruelly mortified her by what he said of Darcy's indifference, and she could do nothing but wonder at such a want of penetration, or fear that perhaps, instead of his seeing too little, she might have fancied too much.

Chapter Thirty-six

The holiday season now having begun in earnest, there was little enough leisure for the indulgence of idle speculation, however: fears and hopes alike must be set aside amid the press of activity. The merchants of Lambtown had formed the resolve of creating a Victorian Christmas in the center of town; this they attempted rather obscurely to present in contradistinction to the threatened upheavals of the putative millennium turn a week later, though it may have seemed to the dispassionate observer that the effort had more to do with a desire to extend the tourist season beyond the natural terminus imposed by the rhythms of the vineyards. The town center accordingly came alive with the sounds of horse-drawn carriages, roving bands of carolers, and vendors hawking roasted chestnuts, while the designers of shop displays strove valiantly to make the styles of 1999 appear to recall those of an imagined past, little though the imagery might have in common with life in the Santa Ynez Valley, either then or now. Confronted with this anglophile fantasia, Father Austen became enraged and declared that his church, Our Lady of Guadalupe, would stage a full-scale *posada navideña*. Lizzy had rarely seen him so vigorously enjoying himself as when he elaborated the details of his scheme.

"What is a *posada navideña*?" she asked.

"It's a Mexican holiday tradition for children. They dress up as the Holy Family, accompanied by shepherds and the Three Kings, and reenact Mary and Joseph's search for shelter before

Jesus was born. They do candlelight processions for nine nights starting December sixteenth, and they stop at different houses singing a traditional song in which they ask to be admitted. The homeowners turn them away at each house until they reach their designated destination for the night, where they are told they can have a place in the stable. The doors are thrown open to them, and they have a party in that house with a piñata. Each night they are admitted to a different house, and the last night, December twenty-fourth, they end up at the church."

Lizzy was already smiling. "Father Austen, if you weren't a man of God I would say that you are a very wicked person. Do the households that turn the children away know they are playing a role in this drama?"

"In Mexico they do; here, I imagine not."

"Well, sign up the library for one of the parties! I'll set up the piñata in the children's section, and we can whet their appetites for the library opening with a bilingual reading of the Nativity story. You should ask Charley Bingley as well; I'm sure he'll be happy to host a night at The Chocolate Bar."

"There's one other thing. A few days before the *posada* is the feast day of our patron saint, the Virgin of Guadalupe. This is the main holiday celebration for the grown-ups. We'll have a little festival at the church."

"Oh, I know that's a very important saint's day. It honors the Virgin Mary's apparition before an Aztec Indian, right?"

"Yes, in the sixteenth century. When she appeared, she looked like an ancient Aztec fertility goddess, Tonantzin—that's where her icon's attributes come from, why you always see her standing on the crescent moon, wearing a rose-colored robe and a cloak covered with stars. She spoke in Nahuatl to the Indian, who was known as Juan Diego, and told him to build a church on the hill of Tepeyac in Mexico City."

"It's a story that's repeated in one form or another wherever the Catholic Church has been adopted, isn't it? The local goddess gets adapted into a version of the Virgin Mary, where she's safely nondivine but still divinity-adjacent."

"Yes, but in Mexico the Virgin of Guadalupe has taken a central place in the spirituality of the poor people, in particular. She's their intercessor with God, their special protector, their confidante. She gives them courage and hope. The feast day helps renew their strength to face the challenges in their lives. Rose is planning a big free dinner and fiesta on the eve of the Virgin's day at the church, the eleventh, and that will be followed by a midnight Mass."

"Can I help with the cooking?"

"I have a different role in mind for you," replied Father Austen. "Before the fiesta, the parishioners will parade through the town carrying their statues and photos of the Virgin, which they bring to the church for a blessing. A troupe of *conchero* dancers is coming up from L.A. to lead the parade. Usually we carry the church's statue of the Virgin in the parade, on a cart. But I thought this year there should be a live saint. Will you dress as the Virgin of Guadalupe and ride in our parade?"

It was some moments before Lizzy could find speech, so great was her astonishment; her voice was for a time suspended from emotion. "But surely it would be best to select a woman from the congregation," said she at last, "or someone like Rose, who devotes her life to the welfare of the poor?"

"Ha! If she did it, everybody would be thinking of nothing but how the Virgin has aged. I think it should be a less-familiar face. No, my girl, it's you or nobody. The Virgin's message is that it doesn't matter who you are or what you possess, we are all God's children. And for this year, in this place, you are the embodiment of that message."

Lizzy had little choice but to accede humbly to his request. She had small relish for the display, and knew how it would be perceived by the townsfolk; but she believed that Father Austen understood his flock, and if a live Virgin of Guadalupe was what they needed, it was what they should have. So to her many tasks of readying the library for its opening, decorating her clients' patios with pots of poinsettia and cyclamen, and shopping for her family was added fittings for her costume and rehearsing how to remain upright in a jolting cart drawn by four stalwart young men.

The eleventh of December dawned cold and showery, but by midafternoon she was relieved to see the rain moving off into the eastern mountains. The faint, wintry rays of the setting sun shone upon the marchers as they assembled close to the highway at the edge of the downtown area. The *conchero* dancers, dressed in a motley array of garb from various Indian traditions and sporting elaborate feather headdresses, enlivened the scene with the beating of their drums and the stamping of their belled feet. Children with white angel wings pinned to their shoulders ran in and out among the legs of their more somber parents, who wore their Sunday clothes and carried paper lanterns and a variety of images of the Virgin. A few of the young adults bore placards reading *Madre sin fronteras*. Others added to the din by setting off firecrackers.

The cart in which Lizzy was to ride was festooned with flowers. From the center, where she was to stand, radiated out sunrays constructed from cardboard spray-painted gold and strung with Christmas lights. As dusk fell, she mounted to her perch and the procession set off.

Whatever hopes of high drama Father Austen or the participants might have entertained were destined to face disappointment. The greatest outrage at their appearance was felt by the driver of one of the Victorian horse-drawn carriages, whose beast shied at the sound of the drums and the waving headdresses, startling his passengers. Most of the tourists and shoppers, oblivious to political subtext, accepted the parade as a novel form of holiday entertainment laid on by the Chamber of Commerce for their amusement, an attitude toward pastiche that actual Victorian revelers might have seconded. The shopkeepers, finding their clientele blithely undeterred by the disruption, were inclined to ignore that which they had no leisure to abhor. For Lizzy's part, she discovered that once the cart was in motion it became easier to maintain her position. She was able to lean back against the backdrop a little, and this permitted her to maintain stability during occasional lurches of the vehicle. Self-consciousness, too, was soon done away with, as she remembered what the Holy Mother signified to those all around her, and recalled that it was not for Lizzy Bennet that they shouted and waved. Indeed, the drums and the lights induced in her a distracted state of mind in which she did not even notice Charley and John waving vigorously outside The Chocolate Bar, or Fitzwilliam Darcy, standing by their side.

The solemnity of her role in the procession little inclined Lizzy to liveliness, so once the observers had reached the church she excused herself from the celebrations and went to the library. So trammeled were her days that she believed the evening afforded her the best opportunity to advance preparations for the *posada* party, just a few nights hence. There were chairs to be rearranged, rugs to be rolled back, the piñata and paper streamers to be hung. She was thus engaged when there fell a knock on the door. Thinking perhaps to see Mary Gardiner, coming from across the street after seeing lights burning in the building, she went to answer it, and was exceedingly astonished to find Darcy on the doorstep, balancing several cardboard boxes in his arms.

"Oh! Hello," was all she found herself able to say at first; but soon she recollected her duties as hostess, inviting him in and offering to relieve him of a portion of his burden. Together they set down the boxes in the hall.

Darcy declined her offer of a cup of tea, and stood uncertainly for a long moment before gesturing toward the boxes. "I'm glad I found you here," said he; "I've been waiting for a chance to offer you these. I understand you've spoken to the Historical Society about mounting displays of Lambtown history here at the library, and I thought these might make a useful starting point for you."

He bent and opened the first box. Inside were several large, yellowing folders, which he opened to reveal brittle documents, well over a century old. "This one is the original Mexican land grant for the Carrillo rancho, and here is the confirmation of the grant issued by the U.S. government when California became a state," he said, laying them on top of the glass display cabinet in the hall. "These are the bills of sale to the first Darcy to settle here, in the 1870s. The next two folders contain papers relating to the foundation of the narrow-gauge railway in the valley. The other boxes hold newspapers and artifacts from the settlement era, as well as Indian artifacts found on Pemberley Ranch over the years. Would these," he asked diffidently, "be of any interest to you?"

Lizzy instantly apprehended that this offering was intended as an olive branch; there could be no question of spurning such a generous-hearted advance. She was also certain he was trying to prove to her what she already believed, little though he knew it—that he and his ancestors were not tyrants intent on robbing the Carrillos of their heritage, but well-intentioned stewards of land and community. "You've never displayed these documents in public before, have you?" said she.

"No. We heard some of the things that were said over the years, but we knew the truth ourselves and that was enough. Lately, though, I've been thinking that was a mistake. Each generation has its own retelling of history, but whatever form that narrative takes, it should be based on evidence, not conjecture— don't you think?"

"I do indeed," said Lizzy warmly, "and am grateful to you for thinking of the library as a place to present them. I'm sure an exhibit like this will bring us many visitors, and generate a lot of interest." She was thinking rapidly as she spoke, and secretly forming a desperate resolution. "Do you think you might be able to help us write the interpretive materials? The labels for the items, and perhaps a little brochure copy?"

Darcy agreed to this, appearing pleased at the thought. Now was the moment for her resolution to be executed, and, while her courage was high, she immediately said, "I'm a very selfish creature. For the sake of giving relief to my own feelings, I have to risk wounding yours. I want to take this opportunity to thank you for your extraordinary kindness to my brother Lydon. Ever since I learned about it, I've been anxious to express my gratitude. The rest of my family don't know you were responsible, or they would join me in this."

"I'm very sorry," replied Darcy, in a tone of surprise and emotion, "that you were ever told about it. I can imagine that it might've caused you some uneasiness, if seen in the wrong light. I wouldn't have thought Brigadier General Hughes was so little to be trusted."

"You mustn't blame him. His daughter Jenny first gave it away that you were involved, and of course, I wasn't going to give up until I knew all the details. Please let me thank you with all my heart, in the name of my family, for the generosity and compassion that led you to take so much trouble and expense, and endure so much unpleasantness, to give Lydon the chance to turn his life around. I don't know how or when we'll be able to repay you, but please know that we will do so."

"Your family owes me nothing, and I wouldn't let any of you repay me. If you *will* thank me," said he, "it should be for yourself alone. I won't attempt to deny that I was motivated by the wish of making you happy. Much as I respect your family, I thought only of you."

Lizzy was much too embarrassed, and her heart too full, to say a word in reply. After a short pause, her companion added, "You're too generous to lead me on. If your feelings are still what they were last summer, tell me so at once. *Mine* haven't changed, but if you tell me to stop I won't say another word."

Lizzy, feeling all the more than common awkwardness and anxiety of his situation, now forced herself to speak, and immediately, though not very fluently, gave him to understand that her sentiments had undergone so material a change, since the period to which he alluded, as to make her receive with gratitude and pleasure his present assurances. The happiness that this reply produced was such as he had probably never felt before; and he expressed himself on the occasion as sensibly and warmly as a man violently in love can be supposed to do. Concerned lest he be misunderstood, however, he also considered it prudent to articulate his feelings in ways less open to misinterpretation than mere words.

Emerging at length from his embrace, Lizzy found herself unable to encounter his eye directly. Had she done so, she might have seen how well the expression of heartfelt delight, suffused over his face, became him; but though she could not look, she could listen, and he told her of feelings that, in proving of what importance she was to him, made his affection every moment more valuable.

Somehow during the course of the evening they had come to be sitting in the kitchen, though neither could quite say how they had arrived there. There was too much to be thought, and felt, and said for attention to anything else. She soon learned that they were indebted for their present good understanding to the efforts of his aunt, who *did* call him after leaving the Bennets' house, and related the substance of her conversation with Lizzy. Catherine had dwelled emphatically on every expression of the latter that, in her apprehension, peculiarly denoted Lizzy's perverseness and assurance, in the belief that such a relation must assist her endeavors to obtain that promise from her nephew which Lizzy had refused to give. But, unluckily for the grande dame, its effect had been exactly contrariwise.

"It taught me to hope," said he, "as I hadn't allowed myself to hope before. I knew enough of your disposition to be certain that if you'd been absolutely decided to hate me, you would've acknowledged it to my aunt frankly and openly."

Lizzy colored and laughed. "Yes, you know enough of my frankness, as you so politely call it, to believe me capable of *that*. After abusing you so rudely to your face, why would I have any scruples about abusing you to your relations?"

"What did you say to me that I didn't deserve? Even if some of your accusations were based on misinformation, my behavior toward you deserved no better. It was outrageous; I can't think of it without shame."

"We won't argue over who deserves the greater share of blame for that scene," said Lizzy. "Neither one of us behaved well; but since then, I hope, both our manners have improved."

"I can't be so easily reconciled to myself. For many months now the recollection of everything I said and did has been humiliating, and I was surprised every time you were even willing to speak to me. I'll never forget what you said: 'If you'd been more of a gentleman, I would've felt sorry for you.' You can't begin to imagine how that reprimand tortured me—though I have to admit it was some time before I recognized the justice of your words."

"I certainly didn't expect them to make so strong an impression. I had no idea of your taking them so hard."

"I can believe it. You thought me completely lacking in feeling, I'm sure you did. The look on your face I'll never forget, as you said that I was the last man on earth you would ever date."

"Oh! Please don't repeat what I said then. Ever since I got your e-mail, I've been truly ashamed about it."

"Did it really make you think better of me? Did you believe anything I said?"

"Not on first reading; but the more I considered it, the more I realized how wrong I'd been—in my reading of your character, my understanding of events, everything. I felt like a complete idiot."

"I knew what I wrote must give you pain, and part of me was angry enough to *want* to give you pain; but I also felt it was important for you to learn the truth. I believed myself to be calm and cool when I sat down to write it, but I'm afraid I was still very bitter."

"Perhaps at the beginning of the letter; but by the end, you showed great generosity of spirit. But can we forget all that? The feelings of the person who wrote it and the one who received it are now so completely different that they might as well be strangers. I believe we should think of the past only to the extent that remembering it gives us pleasure."

"That may be all well and good for you: what did *you* do that you have to regret? Your reactions were logical and fair, based on what you believed to be true at the time. You weren't in a position to know any different. But for me it's another matter. I grew up learning what was right, what I owed to my position in life and the advantages offered to me, but not how to put myself in other people's shoes. My sense of duty blinded me into thinking I was doing right by others, when really the only person I was serving was myself. I was given good principles, but followed them only from motives of pride and conceit. I didn't really care about anyone outside my own circle, and surrounded myself with people who encouraged me to look down on the rest of the world. And I would've gone on that way, if not for you! You taught me the most valuable lesson of my life—painfully, but only by inflicting that pain could someone get through to me. I actually believed I was honoring you by allowing you into my life; I don't think it occurred to me that you wouldn't be humbly grateful. Instead, I was the one who was humbled! You showed me how unqualified I was to please a woman who deserved to be pleased."

"You believed I was just going to fall into your arms?"

"I did—can you believe it? I assumed you were waiting and hoping for me to take an interest in you."

"I must've done something to give you that impression; my manners must've been at fault in some way. A love of banter is my besetting sin—I get that from my father—and you were so good at verbal fencing, perhaps my enthusiasm for quarreling with you misled you into thinking I was flirting. You must've hated me after that day!"

"*Hated* you? Not possible. At first I thought I was angry at you, but I quickly realized that any anger had to be directed at myself."

"I'm almost afraid to ask: what did you think of me when you ran into me at Pemberley Ranch? I felt like such a snoop going on the hayride, and in fact it was pure curiosity that led me to agree to it. Did you blame me for turning up there, after I'd been so nasty to you?"

"Not at all; I was just surprised. I was sure you'd only want to avoid me."

"Your surprise couldn't be any greater than mine, when you went out of your way to be so nice to me. My conscience told me it was more than I deserved."

"All I wanted," said Darcy, "was to show you that I'd listened to your criticism. I hoped eventually to be forgiven by you, or at least to give you a better impression of me. How long it took for me to start hoping that you might someday begin to care for me, I'm not sure—maybe half an hour. That's why I tried to get acquainted with Mrs. Gardiner. I saw that you admired her, and thought if she liked me, she might soften your attitude toward me."

"She's been very discreet, but I think she sensed something was going on."

"Bingley, too. Every time your name comes up, I feel him watching me, and I can hear the deafening sound of him not saying anything. This evening he caught me staring at you in the procession; I was completely hypnotized. You were the most beautiful thing I'd ever seen."

Distracting though such a sentiment might be, Lizzy was unwilling to let this opportunity pass of raising the question of Bingley and John's reconciliation. Darcy professed himself delighted that they were together; his friend had given him the earliest information of it.

"Were you surprised?" asked Lizzy.

"Not at all. When I went out of town, I believed it was inevitable."

"That is to say, you'd given him your permission. I guessed as much." And though he exclaimed at the term, she found that it had been pretty much the case.

"The night before my last business trip, I made a confession to him that I should've made months ago," said he. "I called him up and told him that I now considered my interference in his personal life to be arrogant and inappropriate. And I said I had reason to believe that I'd been mistaken in my assessment of John's feelings. When it's a case of true love, what other considerations matter?"

"How did he take it?"

"He was astonished, and somewhat angry—at me, for my presumptuousness, and perhaps a little at himself, for having been led by me in such an important matter. But his anger lasted only until he plucked up the courage to talk to John, and knew he was loved. I'm glad to say that he's wholeheartedly forgiven me now."

Lizzy longed to observe that Bingley had been a most delightful friend, so easily guided that his worth was invaluable; but she checked herself. She remembered that Darcy had yet to learn to be laughed at, and it was rather too early to begin. An only child cannot be expected to possess the resilience in this regard that someone from a large family accepts as a matter of course. Instead, she consulted her watch, exclaimed at the lateness of the hour, and suggested it was high time that the evening draw to a close.

Chapter Thirty-seven

In a household as ramshackle as the Bennets', it was not to be expected that Lizzy's return at midnight on a Saturday night would draw much notice; but she fully realized that her family could not remain in ignorance for long. Most painful was her agitation in anticipating what would be felt and said when her relationship became known: she was aware that no one liked Darcy but John, and even feared that with the others it was a dislike that not all his fortune and consequence might do away. Dreading the revelations to come, she rather *knew* that she was happy, than *felt* herself to be so.

Telling John her secret was of the utmost urgency, but it was impossible to do so before church the next day. After the service ended and the congregation was gathered in the forecourt for the usual exchange of gossip, Mrs. Bennet became separated from Lizzy and John as she set out in pursuit of the latest intelligence to be had. So she was mercifully absent when Darcy made his approach, as he wasted no time in doing. Only John, therefore, was present to be astonished by the hearty kiss that he offered, and which was as heartily returned by Lizzy. Darcy remained only long enough to make an appointment for working on the display at the library, and then left Lizzy to John's incredulity.

"What on earth was *that*?" was his immediate demand.

"He lent me some historical documents for the display case at the library, and is helping to write the interpretive materials," replied Lizzy.

"And in gratitude you allow him to manhandle you in front of your big brother?"

"His technique may not be the most polished in the world, but I wouldn't call it *manhandling*. I have to say I quite liked it."

"So it appeared. But what are you playing at? I know how much you dislike him."

"You know nothing of the matter. *That* must all be forgotten. Perhaps I didn't always love him as much as I do now, but in cases like these, a good memory is unpardonable. This is the last time I shall remember it myself."

"I can't believe what I'm hearing."

"Oh dear, I was counting on you; I'm sure nobody else will believe me if you don't."

"Well, if it's really so, I would—I do—congratulate you. But are you certain? Forgive the question, but do you really think you can be happy with him?"

"Slow down, John, it's not like we're engaged or anything."

"But he told you he loves you?"

"Yes, and I've said the same. Aren't you happy for me?"

"Of course! Charley and I have talked about it, how nice it would be, but we gave it up as a hopeless cause. Are you sure about what you feel?"

"Perfectly, dearest. And when I tell you all, you'll probably think I feel more than I ought to."

"What do you mean?"

"Well, I have to confess that I love him more than I love Charley. I'm afraid you'll be angry with me."

"If you keep joking, I don't know *what* to think. *Please* be serious. Tell me, for starters, how long you've been in love with him."

"It's been coming on so gradually, I hardly know when it began. But I believe I must date it from when I toured Pemberley Ranch."

Another entreaty that she would be serious, however, produced the desired effect; and she soon satisfied John by her
solemn assurances of attachment. When convinced on that
article, John had nothing further to wish. "Now I'm happy," said
he. "Because he's Charley's closest friend, I always valued him
more highly than you seemed to, and I liked him, of course, for
singling you out. Anyone who loved my two favorite people in
the world had to have some good qualities—at a minimum, excellent taste! But Lizzy, there's so much you never told me—why
were you so secretive?"

"Before Charley came back, I didn't want to mention him to
you any more than was necessary. My own feelings were so
much in flux, too; and I didn't know what Darcy was thinking,
whether he still liked me or was so offended by all the terrible
things I'd said that he wouldn't look at me again. But you don't
know half of all the wonderful things he's done." And she
rapidly set forth the whole of his share in Lydon's rescue and
George's downfall.

John scarce had time to exclaim his fresh astonishment before
Mrs. Bennet was espied returning to their side, and all further
disclosures were perforce suspended until they could be alone
again. Once the family luncheon was consumed, however, they
spent half the afternoon in conversation. But twice that span
would not suffice to give either of them any notion of how the
other members of the family were to be told of the change in
Lizzy's circumstances. Of the evils that lay before her, Lizzy
could scarcely bear to consider.

She had little enough time to enjoy her dread, for the evening
brought not only Bingley, bent on his accustomed visit, but
Darcy as well. When Mrs. Bennet saw the two men walking up
the drive, she cried, "Good gracious! Our dear Bingley has
brought that nasty Mr. Darcy along with him. What can that tire-

some man be thinking, coming here without an invitation? What will we do with him? Lizzy, I expect you to take responsibility for entertaining him. It's a great pity, but you'll be doing it for John's sake, you know."

Lizzy could hardly help laughing at so convenient a proposal, yet was really vexed that her mother should be always giving him such epithets. This was a sad omen of what her mother's behavior to the gentleman himself might be; and Lizzy found that, though she was in the certain possession of his warmest affection, there was still something to be wished for.

As soon as they entered, Charley looked at her so expressively, and hugged her with such warmth, as left no doubt of his good information; and he immediately gave what explanation he could think of for being joined by his friend for the visit. But either his reasons were inadequate, or the particularity of Darcy's behavior in speaking almost exclusively to Lizzy—and doing so at unaccustomed length—was too obvious, for the suspicions of all the Bennets were awakened against them.

Lizzy could see the wondering looks passing between family members, and was able to enjoy Darcy's company but little from the agitation she felt at the prospect of the inevitable disclosures to come. That she would be distressing her father was a great misery to her; and greater still were her doubts about how her mother would take the news. Whether she were violently set against Darcy, or violently delighted with him for the direction his affections had taken, it was certain that her manner would be equally ill adapted to do credit to her sense; and Lizzy could no more bear that Darcy should hear the first raptures of her joy, than the first vehemence of her disapprobation.

The first part of the evening, nevertheless, passed off much better than she expected. Mrs. Bennet luckily stood in such awe of him that she withheld whatever of disgust or excitement she might be feeling, and ventured to speak to him hardly at all. Mr. Bennet, meanwhile, though visibly startled by the entente he perceived Lizzy and Darcy to have achieved, soon was seen to be exerting himself to get to know the young man better.

But such unwonted decorum could not outlast the visit. No sooner had Bingley and Darcy departed than the anticipated storm broke over Lizzy's head. Mrs. Bennet—never backward in crediting what was for the advantage of her family, or what came in the shape of a lover to any of them—took the first turn.

"Lizzy, you sly thing, what have you been up to? Of all my children, I never imagined you'd be the one to see where her best interests lay, what with your gardening, and your crusades for social justice—and all the time you were at work snaring the richest man in town! So handsome, and tall, and charming, too! I hope you'll apologize to him for my disliking him so much before. It's almost worth losing all of Aunt Evelyn's money! I'm sure he has a lot more than she ever did. You must make sure he asks you to marry him as soon as possible. Can you pretend you're pregnant?"

"That's a terrible idea," said Mary, in a grave tone. "What would happen when he found out you were lying? Deception is not a sound basis for a relationship."

"This from someone who's never had a relationship!" cried Kitty. "What do you think *you* know?"

"Well, I didn't mean it literally," said Mrs. Bennet. "But you must be sure of him as soon as possible. Just think of all the ways the whole family will benefit! They won't turn us away from the Enclave now." Lizzy could only be grateful that her mother had been too afraid of Darcy to speak in front of him.

Of greater moment to Lizzy was what was in her father's mind, and at last he was able to edge in a word around his wife's volubility. "I've always been led to believe," said he, "that you hated this man. It seems I was mistaken."

How earnestly did Lizzy then wish that her former opinions had been more reasonable, her expressions more moderate. It would have spared her from explanations and professions that were exceedingly awkward to give; but they were now necessary, and she assured him, with some confusion, of her attachment to Darcy.

"We all know him to be a proud, unpleasant sort of man, but there's no accounting for attraction. If you like him, there's nothing more to be said."

"No, really, he's not like that," protested Lizzy. "I thought he was conceited at first, but he's actually just shy. He's a good and kind person, in so many ways."

"I know your disposition, Lizzy. Your lively tongue would create all sorts of trouble in a relationship with somebody you don't really admire. I'm sure it's very flattering to be singled out by the greatest catch in the neighborhood—all the other girls will be envying you—but there has to be more than that, or you'll come to grief."

Lizzy attempted to reconcile him by describing the gradual change that her estimation of Darcy had undergone, relating her absolute certainty that his own affection was not the work of a day, but had stood the test of many months' suspense, and enumerating with energy all his good qualities. To complete the favorable impression, she then told him what Darcy had voluntarily done for Lydon. He heard her with astonishment.

"So it wasn't General Hughes after all! I *thought* all that benevolence must be sticking in the general's craw. He took care of everything, did he? Paid the bills, got Lydon admitted to that ritzy rehab center, even saw to it that the Carrillo kid was arrested? So much the better. I'll offer to pay him back; he'll rant and storm about his love for you, and that'll be the end of it."

He then recollected her embarrassment at Thanksgiving, when he had been teasing her about Catherine de Bourgh's visit. "Did she come to forbid the banns?"

"Pretty much, yes. I'm sorry I couldn't tell you anything at the time, but I didn't know how he was going to react to her disapproval."

After laughing at her for some time, Mr. Bennet allowed her at last to go to bed, saying, as she quitted the room, "Kitty, Mary, if you have any lovers up your sleeves, I'll be happy to meet them in the morning."

Lizzy's mind was now relieved from a very heavy weight; and after half an hour's quiet reflection in her room, she was able to retire to bed with tolerable composure. Everything was too recent for gaiety, but there was no longer anything material to be dreaded, and the comfort of ease and familiarity would come in time.

Lizzy's spirits soon rising to playfulness again, on the occasion of their next meeting she wanted Darcy to account for his having ever fallen in love with her. "How did it start?" she asked. "I can understand your attraction growing, once you had begun, but what set you off in the first place?"

"I'm not sure I could name the hour or the day, though I remember being very struck by you when you read that poem about blue jays at your aunt's memorial."

"Ah, poetry—the food of love!"

"So they say. In any case, I was in deep before I fully realized what was happening."

"My looks you'd dissed the first time we met. And as for my manners—my behavior toward you was always bordering on rude, and I never spoke to you without trying to make you uncomfortable. Now, tell me the truth: did you admire me for my impertinence?"

"For the liveliness of your mind, I did. Your intellectual interests are one of the things that made me feel lucky to have met you."

"You may as well call it impertinence. The fact is, you were sick of civility, and of women who were always seeking your approval. I interested you because I was so unlike them. If you weren't a really nice guy, you would've hated me for it; but no matter how hard you tried to hide it, you were always too noble not to be disgusted by all those who courted you. There—I've saved you the trouble of explaining yourself; and really, all things considered, I begin to think the outcome was perfectly reasonable. And it's a good thing, too. After you read from "Self-Reliance," I went back and reread it myself. I noticed that you left out one relevant line: 'If you can love me for what I am, we shall be the happier.' Of course, you don't really know anything good about me—but nobody thinks about that when they fall in love."

"Was there no good in your affection for your brother, or your concern for the poor?"

Tactfully avoiding any discussion of their different approaches to the problems of the poor, Lizzy said merely, "Sweet John! Who could help loving him? But by all means make a virtue of it. My good qualities are under your protection, and you must exaggerate them as much as possible; and in return, it's my responsibility to find ways to tease and quarrel with you as much as possible. And I'll begin right now by asking why you took so long to seek me out, even after your aunt told you about our conversation? You waited two whole weeks, and then only came to see me because you happened to catch sight of me in the procession for the Virgin. If you hadn't happened to be in town that day, would you still be lurking around keeping me guessing?"

"Speaking of keeping people guessing, you didn't exactly give me any encouragement. Haven't you heard? Women are allowed to call men these days, too."

"But I was embarrassed."

"And so was I."

"You might have spoken to me more."

"A man who felt less might've."

"It's very unlucky that you should have a reasonable answer to give, and that I should be so reasonable as to admit it. But I

wonder how long you would've gone on being civil, and infuri-
atingly neutral, if I hadn't had the resolve to thank you for your
kindness to Lydon. And that's problematic in itself, for what useful moral is to be drawn from our reconciliation taking place as
a result of criminal behavior? That's a very troubling sign."

"Don't distress yourself. I'd already decided to approach you
again; that's why I was carrying around those boxes of historical
papers in my truck. I was just looking for the right opportunity."

"Will you ever have the courage to tell your aunt Catherine
that we're seeing each other, or am I to remain your dirty little
secret?"

"I'm too grateful to her for giving me hope to keep her in the
dark. Perhaps I can convince her to be glad that she was so in-
strumental in bringing us together."

"Perhaps—after all, she loves to be of use."

Epilogue

The library's *posada navideña* party, held on the third night of the processions, was well attended and received, many of the Anglo children in the town having begged their parents to be allowed to join in the festivities once they learned that these involved wielding large sticks against hapless piñatas and ensuing scrambles for candy. The occasion afforded the first opportunity for anyone in the neighborhood to explore their new library, which was not officially opening until New Year's Day, and many townspeople seized on any excuse of propinquity to the child of a neighbor or friend to justify their attendance.

Lizzy did not object, though she ran sadly short of refreshments partway through the evening, because the event allowed her to introduce the library's collection and services under circumstances that offered no occasion for a reasonable person to take offense. She left it to her bilingual assistant to introduce the Spanish speakers to the free resources at their disposal, while she and the head librarian devoted themselves to making the English-speaking visitors feel welcome. The goodwill thus expended reaped its reward at the official opening, when it seemed that quite half the valley—all those not too exhausted from Y2K festivities or too enamored of football—found time to pay a visit. The Darcy collection of historical records and artifacts drew extensive interest, particularly because the man himself spent nearly half the day in attendance, answering questions and registering people for their library cards.

By the day of the opening, few people in the valley were left unaware of the change in its most eligible bachelor's status. Young women from across the county came to the library to observe for themselves his demeanor toward its founder; and what they saw did nothing to keep despair at bay. One interested resident, however, did not put in an appearance: Catherine de Bourgh, rendered exceedingly angry by the news, had given way to all the genuine frankness of her character upon its relation, and had spoken to Darcy in language so very intemperate and abusive, especially of Lizzy, that for some time all intercourse between the Darcy and de Bourgh households was at an end.

Mrs. Bennet's objections to the library, meanwhile, were all forgot. For a time the triumph of her eldest son's and daughter's conquests eclipsed her every woe, and Lizzy was reduced to any base stratagem she might devise to shield Darcy from her mother's joy. Mrs. Bennet's elation promised to rob the season of courtship of much of its pleasure, until Mr. Bennet hit upon the happy notion of providing his wife with a fresh source of misery and recrimination. He declared that as the year's lease on the family's ancestral home in Columbus was soon to expire, he had formed the intention of returning there by the end of the month and residing permanently in Ohio. In this he expected to be joined by his wife and his two youngest daughters.

It was not to be hoped that Mrs. Bennet would swiftly be reconciled to such a plan; and in fact her bewailings made their home acutely uncomfortable during the remainder of their occupancy in Lambtown. He was obdurate, however, and his wife found little support among her children. Mary had never approved of California, and was anticipating that her return to Ohio would qualify her for the beneficial rates of a resident when she sought admission to Ohio State University; and Kitty found the rural existence intolerably tedious, now that Lydon and Jenny were not present to keep her company. As for Lizzy and John, though they would miss their father, they appreciated his tact in wishing to put some distance between them and the more objectionable members of the family. It was unquestionably easier to love them all in the contemplation than in the quotidian experience.

What would become of Lydon when his term in rehab came to an end was a topic of much concerned discussion, but here fate intervened to decide the matter for them. In the course of his sojourn, Lydon had developed an intimacy with one of the actors in residence at the facility. The result of this friendship was that Lydon declared himself a convert to Scientology, and communicated to his wife a desire that on his release, they should move to Hollywood and take up residence in the housing provided by that organization, allowing him to pursue his initiation more conveniently.

This proved a step too far for Brigadier General Hughes's tolerance. He roared that no daughter of his would ever join a cult, and if Lydon went to Hollywood, he would go alone. The general had for some time held the private view that in promoting the hasty marriage of Lydon and Jenny he had been acting with the impaired judgment of one facing a crisis, and that the union was proving to be too great a hindrance to Jenny's future. The period of enforced separation while Lydon was incarcerated in rehab had brought Jenny around to her father's way of thinking, so on the day of Lydon's release he was served with divorce papers. He went alone, therefore, to Hollywood, and although it is too much to hope that his character suffered a revolution under the influence of L. Ron Hubbard, he at least found there an existence sufficiently disciplined as to prevent any recurrence of life-threatening episodes or arrest. If it failed to put an end to his calls on his older siblings for loans and other preferments, these sorts of demands were regarded by both Lizzy and John as an improvement over the importunities they might have expected from him.

With the removal of so many barriers to felicity, it could not be long before Lizzy and Darcy attained a deeper and more permanent level of attachment. Although Lizzy was positive that there could be no greater happiness than becoming Mrs. Darcy, she was to learn her error when, on her wedding day, he presented his bride with the gift of a mobile food pantry, to be driven by Rose to any corner of the valley where the pangs of hunger might be felt.

Happy for all Mrs. Bennet's maternal feelings was the day on which she disposed of her eldest daughter in matrimony. The joy of the occasion was dimmed for the entire party only by the reflection that John, serving as Lizzy's maid of honor, and Charley, the best man, could not follow the couple into wedded bliss; a state they both, nevertheless, were resolute in insisting they didn't envy. Even so, it cannot be denied that a few years later, when Canada's laws changed, they were among the first to journey to Vancouver to tie the knot.

I wish I could say, for the sake of Mrs. Bennet's family, that the accomplishment of her ambitions in regard to her eldest children produced so happy an effect as to make her a sensible, amiable, well-informed woman for the rest of her life; though perhaps it was lucky for her husband, who might not have relished domestic felicity in so unusual a form, that she was still occasionally nervous and invariably silly.

For his own part, Mr. Bennet missed his eldest daughter exceedingly, and his affection for her drew him oftener from home than anything else could do. Despite the deep satisfaction of being able to move his library back into the main house from the garage, an amelioration in circumstances made possible by the diminution in the number of children under his roof, he delighted in going to Pemberley Ranch, especially when he was least expected.

Caroline Bingley was deeply mortified by Darcy's marriage, having refused to surrender all hope until the deed was done.

But as she thought it advisable to retain the right of visiting at Pemberley, she dropped all her resentment, was kinder than ever toward John, almost as attentive to Darcy as heretofore, and paid off every arrear of civility to Lizzy.

At length, by Lizzy's persuasion, Darcy was prevailed on to overlook his aunt's offense and seek a reconciliation. Lizzy worked on his resolve by dwelling on the lasting damage that might be done to the de Bourgh acreage by a less scrupulous manager, until he was persuaded to set aside his pride and righteous anger. After a little further resistance on Catherine's part, her resentment gave way, either to her affection for him, or to her curiosity to see how his wife conducted herself; and she condescended to wait on them at Pemberley Ranch. She discovered there that, so far from its woods having been polluted through the acquisition of such a mistress, the grounds were more beautiful than ever for coming under the eye of a knowledgeable and attentive gardener.

With the Gardiners, they were always on the most intimate terms. Darcy, as well as Lizzy, really loved them, and the couple never failed to attend a meeting of the Poets, where the convivial exchanges of good food, better company, and most excellent literature lent considerable satisfaction to their days. They were both ever sensible of the warmest feelings of gratitude toward the gathering that had been the means of uniting them.

FINIS.

ABOOKS

ALIVE Book Publishing and ALIVE Publishing Group
are imprints of Advanced Publishing LLC,
3200 A Danville Blvd., Suite 204, Alamo, California 94507

Telephone: 925.837.7303 Fax: 925.837.6951
www.alivebookpublishing.com

CPSIA information can be obtained at www.ICGtesting.com
Printed in the USA
BVOW07s1905240614

357175BV00001B/15/P